"*Barely Even Friends* delivers the PROMISE OF THE PREMISE of a horny *Beauty & the Beast* retelling . . . There was such a beautiful theme of finding home not only in a place but with another person."
—Alicia Thompson, *USA Today* bestselling author of With Love, from Cold World

"With big-hearted characters you can't help but root for, Bennett's debut is both modern and fresh, yet still hits all the classic notes to perfection."
—Amy Lea, international bestselling author of *Exes and O's*

"Steamy, cozy, and hopeful, this is the perfect modern Beauty and the Beast retelling I've been waiting for!"
—Chloe Liese, author of *Two Wrongs Make a Right*

"A fun, sexy twist on a tale as old as time—filled with loveable, diverse characters and that delicious friction that only grumpy/sunshine can bring."
—Lana Ferguson, author of *The Nanny*

"A delightful tribute to romance . . . A *Beauty & the Beast* retelling that adds the kind of quirkiness to a classic tale that only a romance novel can."
—Anita Kelly, author of *Love & Other Disasters*

"The sexy, bantery contemporary retelling of my dreams. An incredible debut full of heat and heart and delicious enemies-to-lovers energy!"
—Naina Kumar, author of *Say You'll Be Mine*

"*Barely Even Friends* absolutely delights with a steamy debut that ramps up the tension right from the beginning . . . Bennett has taken a classic romance tale and made it her own."

—Ruby Barrett, author of *The Romance Recipe*

"Bennett brings warmth, humor, and joy to this delightful romance. With a debut like this, she is one to watch in the future. I smiled so hard that by the end of the book my face hurt!!"

—Elizabeth Everett, author of the Secret Scientists of London series

"Deliciously spicy, comforting and heartfelt . . . I'm a fan of Mae's for life!"

—Nadia El-Fassi, author of *Best Hex Ever*

"Fresh, creative, and sexy as hell, Mae Bennett spins a classic into a modern bookshelf staple . . . A story like this is why we read Romance."

—Courtney Kae, author of *In the Event of Love*

BARELY EVEN FRIENDS

A Novel

MAE BENNETT

alcove
press

Published in the United States by Alcove Press, an imprint of The Quick Brown Fox & Company LLC.

Alcove Press and its logo are trademarks of The Quick Brown Fox & Company LLC.

Library of Congress Catalog-in-Publication data available upon request.

ISBN (paperback): 978-1-63910-779-7
ISBN (ebook): 978-1-63910-780-3

Cover design by Mallory Heyer

Printed in the United States.

www.alcovepress.com

Alcove Press
34 West 27th St., 10th Floor
New York, NY 10001

First Edition: June 2024

10 9 8 7 6 5 4 3 2 1

For Mums, who always believed I could be anything.
Even an author.

AUTHOR'S NOTE

Barely Even Friends centers on love and what home really means. However, this book mentions the death of parents in a car accident (past, recounted on page), grief, family tensions, familial abandonment (past, briefly mentioned), misogyny, and discussions of fatphobia. Please take care if these are sensitive topics for you.

CHAPTER ONE

It was impossible to take my father seriously when he wore onesie pajamas.

"You must drive Philippe." He made multiple flourishes with his palms, thrusting the keys to his painstakingly restored Mustang into my hand before yanking them back at the last moment. His eyes narrowed. "But please, take care of my darling."

"'My darling' is a bit much." My fingers curled around the key ring, wondering at what point, in the past twenty-six years, I had become the adult in this dynamic.

Dad shifted the pillow behind his back. "Bellamy, my favorite daughter—"

"Your only daughter." Only child, if we were going for total accuracy.

He huffed. "True, but I was referring to the car."

Ouch, that hurt, but, well, the man had insisted on naming his car, so not surprising. Who was I kidding? He loved that car more than anything else. Cars were not my specialty, but no matter its monetary value, it was worth significantly more to my dad.

"I still think we should advise them to hold off a few more days, for when I'm feeling better." His attempt to take a deep breath resulted in a hacking cough, racking through his body and making my heart clench.

"I wheeled you out of the hospital a week ago, Dad. Flu and bronchitis aren't something you walk off. You need rest, not construction dust and mold." It wasn't the first time we'd had this debate. Giving up control had never come easily to him, a biological trait my father had passed on to me. He also happened to be my employer. "I can handle it."

"I trust you. You learned from the best." The attempt to puff out his chest merely gave the cars patterned across his onesie more prominence. "You are the daughter of the great"—more coughing—"Maurice Price. We have a history of excellence to uphold."

But this project wasn't our typical commission. Restoring older homes was losing its popularity as the uber-wealthy coveted modern builds and the latest technology. Most of our recent clients were local governments or nonprofits. That was the risk of working in such a niche market—we were often one contract away from ruin.

"I promise to uphold our family legacy." I raised my palm, swearing fealty to my liege while trying, and failing to not roll my eyes. Mostly, I humored him out of relief. The more demanding he became, the better I knew he was getting. Every moment in the emergency room, which felt longer than only a few days ago, I had sat in fear, while my father lay prone, swallowed by the hospital bed. He was on the mend now, but he still needed to finish recovering.

Dad began to fiddle with the heart rate monitor from his bedside table, a gift from his visiting nurse.

My gaze narrowed as I realized the true reason he was willing to hand over the keys to his beloved car, eager to get rid of me. "Let's not pretend that this isn't about Nurse Betty."

A blush immediately developed on his pale, white skin. "Well, she is most becoming." Dad was a short, portly man, with hair the same deep chestnut as mine. His normally clean-shaven face sported the rough beard he had grown in the hospital.

It was impossible to hold back my groan. "Becoming?" How he had any game at all was beyond me.

"The woman is an angel sent from above."

"An angel sent to keep you alive. Her continued visits now that you're able to feed and bathe yourself might also be a touch of insurance fraud." But what was insurance fraud when it came to love? I, for one, would not criticize the person who was going to be checking up on him. Not when I was about to walk out the door myself. Betty could commit all the scams she wanted if it meant Dad would be taken care of.

"Like you said, I'm still a sickly man." This cough was a bit more forced, his eyes gazing at me in that all-seeing parent way. "You know, this would be a great opportunity to find yourself someone becoming, without your dearest father hanging around. I know how intimidating I can be." He winked.

That was the last thing I needed, a distraction while I dealt with my first solo project, the one that could ruin us or set us up for life. I didn't have time for romance, not with Dan's brush off living rent free in my brain. I eased off the bed, smoothing out the comforter, before pressing a kiss to Dad's forehead. "All right, I'm going to head out."

He caught my hand, keeping me at his bedside. "I'm serious, Bellamy. It's been, what, a year since Dan?"

"Over a year, and I'm fine. This project is too important for me to allow any complications." I did not need my father to lecture me

3

about dating. "Our career doesn't exactly lend itself to relationships. I have other goals right now." Dan was a mistake, a hiccup, one I wouldn't make again. I had learned my lesson and had remained heartbreak-free since we had moved on to our next project.

"Bellamy—"

"Daaa-ad." I stretched the word out into too many unnecessary syllables.

"The Bib would be elated to have you."

I appreciated his shift away from discussing my lack of a love life even as I rolled my eyes the at the reminder of my dream job: curator at my favorite museum. Whenever we were home from a project, I would spend hours, *days*, walking through the exhibits of the Bib, letting my dreams breathe of being the one to plan out the rooms. A position like that would mean no more moving around, from project to project. It would mean staying in one place, putting down roots. "There isn't even an official opening. It's a rumor." One I desperately wanted to be true.

"After this project, they'll create a position for you."

Because world-famous museums did that all the time, sure. All I could do was shake my head. "You need more rest, and I need to get going. It's not exactly a short drive."

With a sigh, he yanked me the rest of the way, wrapping his short arms around my body. "Call and check in every day . . ."

"To get your approval on the plans, go over estimates, and send photos daily with updates," I finished. "We've been through this. Not my first project." Dad was technically my boss, but I couldn't take his authority seriously when, again, the onesie. He gave me a last squeeze, helping to dispel some of my nerves.

"But your first time solo. This is a career maker."

I hoped he didn't notice the way my fingers trembled as I shoved my shoulder-length hair into a messy ponytail. My fuller, curvy frame was all him, though my height and brown hair were from my mother. "Like you said, I've learned from the best." One step at a time: First, the impossible project. Then maybe, just maybe, the impossible job.

"Well, take care." A beat. "I'm referring to the car again, to be clear."

This time I didn't hide my eye roll as I pressed my palm over my heart. "Touching."

"It took me eight years to rebuild it. You merely took nine months to build." He loved that joke.

With a final bittersweet squeeze of his hand, I strode out of our fourth-floor walk-up. Dad preferred to stay on-site for a project rather than oversee from afar, spending his time restoring other people's homes instead of establishing one of our own. His place in Brooklyn was big enough that I had never moved out, since most of the time we were both on assignment outside of New York. We were each other's family; my mother left when I was a few months old, not a fan of Dad's nomadic lifestyle. Her presence was a whisper of a memory; he was the only parent I'd ever needed, the one who'd stayed.

But now, this was my opportunity to prove—to myself, to both of us, to the world—that I was more than Maurice Price's daughter.

Philippe was parked in the underground garage of Dad's building. The Mustang's black lacquer paint job gleamed as if Dad had been down recently for his typical weekly wash and polish. I blew out a breath, resisting the urge to text my annoyance at him when he was supposed to be on bed rest. Not much could keep my dad down.

My life fit perfectly into two suitcases and the backpack slung over my shoulder. My room in Dad's apartment was bare bones. All my effort spent on other people's homes.

I loaded the address into the maps application on my phone, clicked on my favorite playlist, and pulled out of the garage into the cloud-filled day, settling in the driver's seat for my more than six-hour road trip.

The Killington property was located in upstate New York, the portion that meant you were in Amish country, looking to flee to Canada at a moment's notice, or richer than the king. The Killingtons fit into the last category. Their house, a nineteenth-century mansion, hadn't been updated once it received indoor plumbing and electricity. This was going to be one hell of a job—a mix of restoration meets modernization. Our biggest undertaking to date.

Dad had been contracted to restore the property almost ten years prior, but at the last minute, the family canceled the job, forcing my father to scramble to make up the income. This opportunity was a redemption for him and his reputation.

I had joined the family firm, Price Restoration, after college where I double-majored in history and architecture, my dream of working alongside my father coming true. We had talked about me taking the lead on projects, of one day me being the primary, but that was supposed to be years away. With his illness, medical bills, and our bank accounts dwindling, the timetable had been rushed forward, and now here I was, alone and with none of the safety nets I typically leaned on.

No pressure.

When I was forty-five minutes away, having made good time with only two quick stops for snacks and to fill up the tank, the darkening sky that had followed me from the city grew ominous. Nothing but sparse roads needing repair, trees still bare from the winter as far as the eye could see. Houses spaced apart, not by a few feet, but miles.

There was a crash of thunder, and the clouds opened. Raindrops hit the windshield with increasing velocity, until I could barely see, even with the wipers going and the headlights on full beams. Wiry tree limbs closed in on both sides of the car, threatening Philippe's perfect paint job, the road narrowing into a single wide lane. I pressed my teeth to my bottom lip in concentration.

It was too late to turn back, and there were no inns nearby to stop at and wait out the storm, the area too rural. I spotted a few turnoffs, but with such spotty phone service I had no idea where they would lead. Nowhere to go but forward. Slowing my speed as my ETA grew later and later, my sole companions were my playlist and the purr of the engine.

The world shrunk as the rain pounded down on the windshield; my fingers clutched the leather of the steering wheel. The swish-swish of the wipers almost drowned out my music. The ground was covered in dirty snow, left over from a storm a few days ago. At least today it wasn't cold enough to snow . . . yet.

Only the headlights broke the darkness, along with flashes of lightning across the sky, growing more and more frequent. Nope, this in no way appeared ominous for the project I was about to embark on.

I sighed. "Not a sign." I lowered the music as I leaned forward. "Well, that was a street sign." I squinted as water poured out of the sky. "But this is not a sign. The sun is going to come out any moment."

It did not.

There hadn't been a town or house for miles when I turned onto the drive leading to the Killington Estate. I drove another mile until I reached the wrought-iron gate: two posts, each with a gargoyle missing a body part or two. I'd worry later about how expensive the fix would be. First, I just needed it to open—before I had to discover whether Philippe could also act as a boat.

A small, brown, rusted box appeared to be my best option for getting inside.

I scowled as I rolled down the window, wincing at the rain splattering the leather, knowing what my father would say. I pressed the buzzer, desperate for someone to answer quickly. They should be expecting me, even if I was late.

Everything about this project was off: me being in charge, no new blueprints for the estate. By this stage, we'd have sketched out some ideas to present to the owners. But with the Killingtons, they asked, and you said yes. They were a family known for their exacting expectations and old money. This estate was one of many properties they owned located throughout the United States, with more scattered around Europe—and that didn't include the family yacht. At least we had had the old sketches Dad had done ten years back to get us started, since I had been left with almost no time to prep.

The Killington empire had its fingers in multiple industries, investing early and wisely. The family still retained majority shares in the parent company, Killington Holdings, run for decades by Adrian Killington. They were sparse on information but had stated that the only upkeep in the decade since Dad had been unceremoniously dropped was by a caretaker overseeing the acres of property. The Killingtons' approval would lead to more jobs and potentially a contract to work exclusively on their properties, setting me and Dad up for life.

The freezing wind splashed the even colder rain onto my face, leaving every exposed part of me soaked. This wasn't a storm, but pure violence swirling in the air.

"We don't need any," scratched out of the rusted speaker. The caretaker, I had to presume.

"Hello, this is Bellamy, Bellamy Price . . . of Price Restoration." My voice wavered, a combination of nerves and the wind slapping rain in my face, forcing water down my throat. My breath hung in the chilled air, cold enough for me to see it.

Droplets continued to pound into the car through the open window as I waited. The gates opened, and before they could close on me, I rolled up the window and pressed on the gas, the broken gargoyles surveilling.

As I crept forward, poorly maintained hedges lined the entrance, leading to what I assumed was the main house. More bushes waiting for the spring hid the extent of the estate, the world shrinking to this single point, place, and time.

It was another lengthy distance before I arrived, the lane curving a path around the outside of the mansion. The house was imposing: three stories, a sweeping roof. Likely a Georgian influence, from what I could tell through flashes of lightning. The entire estate appeared frozen in time—older, the windows symmetrical, with dead vines crawling up the brick.

I gave up trying to find an overhang to park the car. Grabbing my backpack, I abandoned the rest of my luggage for when the world wasn't ending. Despite my sprint for the front door, I was soaked to the bone. I shivered as another clap of thunder highlighted the weathered door and its brass knocker—nothing to protect me from the elements.

Before I could raise my hand, the door swung open. I leaped inside, skidding as my wet shoes slid against the marble floors. My arms waved wildly in an effort to find my balance and not fall on my ass or smack into the circular hall table.

When I righted myself, the front door banged shut, and my heart palpitated in my chest as I glanced around.

I was alone, standing in darkness, with an overwhelming smell of must.

"Hello?" I called out, my voice echoing.

Silence.

"It's Bellamy Price?" No response. "What in the actual fuck?" I muttered.

I clutched the strap of my backpack as I listened for someone while dripping all over their floor.

I clicked on the flashlight from my phone. A chandelier hung above me, the dirty crystals catching some of the light and bouncing it around the room. A dramatic double staircase wound down from the second floor; the wooden banister needed a few coats of stain.

Must, dust, and age filled the air, making it a struggle to breathe deeply, confirming that the space hadn't received a good cleaning, or been lived in, for a long time. This estate had been in their family for generations—how was there not a staff maintaining the place, even if they weren't in residence?

I swiped away a layer of dust from the table in the middle of the foyer, revealing scratches and dings. If this place weren't in the middle of nowhere, I'd be concerned I was at the wrong residence. There was no way a Killington had lived here recently, if not for decades.

"What have you done?" an angry British accented voice said. "*He* will be very upset."

I spun, searching, but I was still alone. What had I walked into? The floor creaked with every movement I made, maybe even every breath. The place was creepy, though I might have been more anxious it was going to collapse around me than anything else.

I clutched my backpack, as if it could plausibly work as a weapon, and crept toward where the voice had seemed to come from.

"You could not expect me to leave the young woman in the rain? What kind of hospitality is that?" said another voice, enthusiastic with a slight baritone. Adult, but it was impossible to predict an age.

How many people were hiding in this place?

"He will be outraged, and rightfully so." The first bodiless voice filled the space, anger still resonating in its clipped consonants.

"Hello?" My voice carried through the rooms, bounding off the chipped ceilings and the peeling original wallpaper that pained me to even look at. "Is this some kind of hazing? Could someone, uh, come out now?"

"Ms. Price, please sit by the fire, make yourself at home." This tone was welcoming, but a shiver still worked its way down my spine.

Well, at least I'd be warm before the axe murderer killed me. My survival instincts were a mess. "Thank you, but who . . . where are you, exactly?"

"We are the staff of the manor, ma'am. All that matters is that you are comfortable. Concentrate on warming yourself. We will take care of everything. Are you hungry?"

There was a harrumph of opposition; despite that, no one showed their face. What was this? The friendliest haunted house that had ever existed? There was a staff—why had no one shared that information?

The heat from the fire made a small dent in the chill in my bones. I tried to get as close as I could without falling in—there was no grate to protect me from the open flame. "Why can't I see you?"

"That is because I am a—"

A snarl sliced through the muted patter of rain on the lead-mullioned windows. A door upstairs slammed, then footsteps stomped down one of the stairwells into the front foyer. All my organs tried to dive out of my skin at the same moment as my gaze sought for any explanation.

"Fuckity fuck." The axe murderer knew I was here. This was it. I searched for a weapon, but it was fruitless. The furniture and fixtures around me, while dusty, were priceless antiques (well, they would be after they were repaired and restored). Maurice Price's daughter would never risk an antique Tiffany lamp, even if her life depended on it. They were history from long before I was born and would hopefully be here long after me. Which, it seemed as the thumping neared, wasn't likely to be more than the next few minutes.

How can there not at least be a fire poker? I searched for a candlestick to sacrifice, but nothing.

The door to the room I had found myself in crashed open, and I winced at the wood breaking. No wonder this place was crumbling with how it was being treated.

"What are you doing in my house?" Standing behind the chair was the first person I had seen since entering this bonkers place. His body was hidden by the darkness, a hulking outline made larger by the shadow from the fire.

I scrambled farther away, a squeak erupting as I fell against the wainscoting, part of which crumbled at the contact.

"Why are you here?" the axe murderer growled out, contempt dripping from his voice, matching in time with the water droplets I was leaving on the scored wood floor.

"Uh, I was hired . . ." My voice was weak, barely a whisper. I detested conflict of any kind, and this was conflict with a capital C.

"Not by me. Get out."

May we all have the tenacity of a man who is, in fact, wrong. "Um, the Killingtons hired us."

"We don't need any more staff. Leave!" He roared the last word.

Any hint of nerves dissipated. This was a bit much. "Could we have a civilized conversation?" I straightened my spine and crossed my arms over my chest, wishing I didn't look like a drowned rat.

"I don't have civilized conversations with trespassers. Go."

"Listen, asshole, I've been driving for hours, through what seems to be an act-of-god hailstorm, been let into this creepy mansion by disembodied voices, and now there's you. I'm supposed to be here, and I'm not going anywhere."

"I'm the asshole?" He scoffed. "I'm not the one breaking and entering."

My fingers clenched into fists. "Whoever operates your front gate let me in, and yes, *you* are the asshole, skulking in the shadows, trying to be intimidating. Just show me to whoever is in charge, and we can clear all of this up."

He snarled, large hands sliding down the fabric of the armchair.

The fireplace crackled, hail pounding the roof, the water on my eyelashes freezing. Rather than answer my question, he circled the chair, the light dancing across his body, revealing the high-handed stranger.

CHAPTER TWO

Why did the asshole have to be hot? *Why?*

He strolled around the armchair, distracting me from the worn fabric. My gaze caught on black pants hugging the tree trunks he had for thighs, as he ran his hand through jet black hair that was recklessly tied off. A heavy, dark eyebrow rose, slashed above his eye.

"I'm no longer skulking. Now will you leave?" His voice hadn't lost the hoarseness. He defiantly crossed his arms against his barrel chest, a gray V-neck T-shirt tight against his biceps. And he had a beard. I had a weakness for beards, though that was counteracted by the whole asshole banishment thing.

"I'm supposed to be here. If you'd let me explain—" Maybe a calmer tone would ratchet down some of the tension, including my desire to throw a priceless vase at him. I was not a violent person, but he was bringing out something in me.

"Sir—" the friendly voice from earlier hedged.

"Stop calling me that." Another growl. Well, at least he was this gracious with everyone.

But the welcoming voice wasn't put off. "Adrian Killington has hired Price Restoration to renovate the estate."

Silence met the information, and I couldn't hold off the smug smile that spread.

"That's why you're here?" The "sir" leaned against the chair, seeming to regret his decision when it wobbled, his gaze never leaving me. Many of the articles that had come up in my Google search were focused on two of his grandchildren—twin granddaughters. So what did that make this man? A distant cousin? The caretaker? I had spent every moment Dad was sleeping in the hospital trying to research the property, not the family.

"I'm Bellamy Price. Mr. Killington hired my father and me to restore his estate." Attempting to remain professional, I wiped my sweaty palm on my thigh before thrusting it forward.

I shook empty air.

"Well, there's been a misunderstanding. No upgrades needed." Instead of accepting my waiting hand, the man massaged his thigh, shoulders hunched, glaring at me.

It took everything in me to not laugh at his serious expression. The mantel of the fireplace was missing chunks of marble, the fire highlighting the dust that hung in the air. "Is that the judgment of the family of rats in the walls?"

"Sir, we cannot allow her to leave in this weather." Still bodiless, the friendly voice was firm, their point highlighted by another crash of thunder shaking the structure.

The caretaker's T-shirt lessened its death grip on his torso by a smidge. "You can stay . . . for tonight."

"You're too kind, not forcing me to drown," I muttered. I had no patience for his anger or whatever was going on here. He wasn't the only stubborn one in the place. We had established I was supposed to be here. I hadn't missed that he hadn't introduced himself or indicated what authority he had to ask me to leave.

"Would you like to give our guest a tour, sir?"

"No."

With a final growl in farewell, the Douche stalked out of the room. The slam of the door shook the portraits on the wall, and I braced myself, ready to dive if they fell. When they didn't, I inched closer to the fire.

Why had I been nervous? Everything was progressing swimmingly.

"Well, Ms. Price, welcome to the Killington Estate."

It was going to be a long summer: me, mysterious voices, and an asshole.

"I know it's late, so I won't give you a proper tour. There will be plenty of time for that tomorrow. We have had a room readied, and a meal was delivered to your quarters. Please head up the front staircase, and I'll lead from there."

I reached for my backpack, exhaustion hitting me hard enough to no longer be worried about the bodiless voice. It didn't end my curiosity, though.

"Hey, uh, where are you?" *What are you?* was on the tip of my tongue, but I didn't want to get on the wrong side of my sole ally in this place, who had ensured I wouldn't be sleeping in my car tonight.

"Oh yes, I'm sorry. Quite rude of me. I'm an AI wired throughout the house and property. My name is Bl8z3, but everyone pronounces it Blaze. I'm available in most areas, including the garage and the stables. But please don't worry if you are having a private moment. I don't have cameras, merely a helpful speaker system throughout the estate. I will give you the utmost discretion."

Wonderful. While staying in the biggest mansion I had ever seen, I had an omniscient voice who might listen to me take a shit. *Perfect.*

"Is there anyone else, or is it just you, Bl8z3?"

"There are others, ma'am, but they can greet you tomorrow. After readying your room, they left for the evening. They don't live in the main house. You are the first visitor we've had in a long time. But now, it's time for a hot shower, maybe a nightcap, and a good night's rest." The voice had an actual tone and texture, unlike the typical robotic or flat AI voices I was used to.

After I clambered up the stairs, Bl8z3 directed me right, then another right, to the second door. My shoulders sank in relief when I trudged into the room. A queen-sized bed with an iron frame dominated the space. The room was expansive, mostly clean despite the musty odor that permeated the area, containing a wide armoire and a seating area, where a plated sandwich sat on the coffee table, and a maple desk with a chair. The furniture needed to be sanded and stained.

I should research the Killington family, but the storm was affecting my service, my text informing Dad I had arrived taking multiple attempts before sending. My research would have to wait until tomorrow. I was not going to ask Bl8z3 so it could report back to the douche.

Before showering in the en suite, I unpacked, removing a set of underwear, phone charger, my tablet that contained my traveling library, and two framed photos. I tilted the frames to catch the light and smiled at the photo of me and my college best friends, then the other of my dad and me, smiling, in front of the house we'd completed on my thirteenth birthday. Traveling light made my life simpler, but these were my essentials.

Stroking the frame, I whispered to myself I could do this.

The sunlight streaming in through the windows woke me from my fitful sleep. Dreams of being chased by unknown voices had haunted me all night while the house collapsed around me, a hulking shape watching on.

But today was a new day. My luggage was waiting for me outside the bedroom door—the mysterious staff must have collected it from my car. The evening before felt more like something out of a book I'd been reading than reality. I sent another email to Mr. Killington's office to confirm my arrival and schedule a phone call once I'd toured the property.

It was impossible not to wince as the bedroom door screeched on its hinges. Eager to get started, I grabbed my iPad to capture notes and pictures on. My curiosity about this place won out over my hunger for breakfast—I couldn't rely on ten-year-old designs when I was standing in the best source of information. The caretaker, or whoever he was from last night, was the least of my concerns. I had my marching orders from Mr. Killington. If Sir Asshole had a problem with my presence, he could complain to his employer.

Mind made up, I followed the threadbare runner covering the hardwood floors. The sparse lights flickered; many of the bulbs in the sconces were burned out, making the details of the wallpaper difficult to see. My stroll brought me to the final doorway in the hallway, the handles rusted and locked. Mr. Killington had given specific instructions to restore every inch of the property, but for some reason I still checked over my shoulder before bending down.

One of the many perks about growing up with a father who updated old homes: I knew a thing or two about how to enter a locked room. Their mysteries trapped inside, the keys lost long ago. I kept a small tool kit in my pocket for this very purpose.

If this lock wasn't too rusted, I could get in. Picking a lock was easier than trying to break the door or remove it from its frame; my goal was always to preserve something, no matter how damaged it was. A locksmith at the house we were working on when I was ten taught me. It was my passion project, finding the secret rooms, the treasures that were most precious hidden inside.

"It's all about the tumblers," I muttered. I bit my lip, concentrating, closing my eyes as I listened—a little to the left, then to the right. Patience, and a flick of the wrist.

Then, with a soft click: "I'm in." The door creaked as I pushed it open, leaning forward, too excited to stand up.

"What do you think you're doing?" a voice roared.

Losing my balance, I fell flat on my face, jarred for breath.

With as much dignity as I could muster, I clambered up, nose smarting, wiping away the dust that had erupted off my jeans, and glared at the hot caretaker. Couldn't he have announced himself or something?

The poor lighting didn't obscure his roughly maintained beard or the messy hair he'd pulled back, a breath away from escaping the hair tie he used. An eyebrow arched in annoyance—apparently at my existence—he wore yet another pair of black pants and a dark gray T-shirt painted onto his biceps, towering over me.

His gaze dragged across my body, down to my shoes, back up my jeans, tucked in Henley, and my mane that never seemed to stay out of my face, tendrils falling out of my ponytail.

"What are you wearing?"

"What?" I bit my lip, my palms tucking into my suspenders. "Clothes?"

He stepped closer, forcing me to press my back against the closed door while I narrowed my eyes. I might have been tall, but he was taller. The width of his shoulders and the thickness of his arms made me doubt whether I could wrap my hands around his biceps, or his neck—for choking purposes, of course.

He reached forward, and I sucked in a breath. His fingers were long. He could probably palm certain parts of my body—a completely inappropriate thought I immediately banished.

He pointed an index finger at my right suspender, the glare from his gaze almost setting it on fire. "What are these?"

"My suspenders?" My voice trailed off. Suspenders weren't exactly common, but I had never met someone confused by my wardrobe choices. More often it was a comment about how I'd get farther in life if I lost some weight.

"What are you, some sort of eighteenth-century lord?"

"Screw you. I can wear whatever I want." I wasn't a fan of belts. But suspenders were comfortable, and I enjoyed the way they emphasized my breasts. Belts made my round middle seem rounder, showing off the divots. Suspenders were a fashionable and flattering way to keep my pants up.

"I don't understand, why are you still here?" His finger remained suspended between us.

I was ready to petition for his name to officially be "Sir Asshole." The only kindness he was offering was his evergreen scent invading my senses, masking the musty smell of the house.

We were in some sort of "glare-off." My eyes quivered, cheeks hurting from the effort not to smile, to laugh at the juvenileness of it all.

Someone needed to teach him about personal space. "Normally people introduce themselves rather than growling." I cleared my throat, my palms sweating.

A slight rumble emanated from his chest, his gray eyes narrowing.

"Here, I'll go first. Bellamy Price. My father, Maurice Price, is the head of Price Restoration. We restore heritage homes and were hired to restore this estate." Silence. I wanted to kick him. "This is where you introduce yourself."

"Your name is Oliver Killington," Bl8z3 announced, breaking our staring contest, neither of us able to meet the other's eye as he took a large step back away from me.

He was a Killington. Standing before me in a cheap T-shirt you could buy in bulk, scraggly beard, and in need of a haircut. I tried to keep my face blank. He wasn't an unknown quantity, some rude caretaker. He had more money than I would ever see in my lifetime.

Another grunt. "I'm Oliver Killington." He tumbled over his name. "This is *my* estate, and I can assure you, I didn't hire you or your father."

The desire to kick him was only getting stronger.

"Records reflect your grandfather hired Price Restoration."

Grandfather? He wasn't a caretaker but a grandchild, one of the heirs to the fortune. What was he doing here?

"Thank you, Bl8z3." Oliver's voice dropped another octave, not sounding an ounce grateful. Bl8z3 was lucky it did not have a corporeal form at that moment. Unfortunately, I did.

"Well, if you are the owner, we will need your permission." Normally I did not placate people, but there was something burning in my chest with the knowledge he was living here. I had unknowingly invaded his retreat, leaving me conflicted.

"Adrian Killington is the owner of the estate. Oliver Killington will inherit at his demise and is the only Killington on the property."

We were unable to meet each other's gazes at Bl8z3's blunt recitation of the facts. Questions demanded to burst out of me. Why was he staying here in this house, which had seen better days at least a decade ago? And why did my presence seem to offend him so much? You know, light conversational topics. Thins he surely wanted to share with a stranger.

We needed this job but Oliver was the only Killington here. He could make my job miserable. Hold this up. Handling this project alone meant handling him. Lucky me.

I forced myself to speak gently; explaining the parameters of the project was something Dad typically handled. "Houses this old need to be maintained. I'm still walking through and need to consider the blueprints. I plan to ask the staff what will make it more functional for them, and I'd appreciate your input as well. This is your space." I tried to put myself in his shoes as his gaze darted around, snagging on the door behind me, his jaw clenching. I had to assume his aggression was due to the love he had for the property, which created blind spots to what it truly needed.

This time, he sized me up. I attempted what I hoped was a neutral expression, resisting the urge to bounce on the balls of my feet. So much rested on this moment, and I needed to somehow exude confidence and an ability to do this job. Any expressions of sympathy would not benefit me.

"Fine." He stepped back, leaving me colder. "Work on the house. But stay out of the west wing. It's off limits."

I mean, this place was humongous. Were we really going to refer to it as having actual wings? It was a bit much, considering there were areas with crumbled walls, vines intertwining with wires. If it weren't for the age of the estate, the family backing this, the historic value, and the challenge, the discussion would center on tearing it down. It must be nice to have so much money, to have no guilt ordering people to do as you please.

"The west wing?" I wanted to humor him, but there was no way to remodel the rest of the house and ignore an entire section. Not in good conscience, and not in practicality.

He stepped forward again, hand reaching out, grasping the handle of the door I'd just picked open, slamming it shut hard enough that it shook my bones.

"This area is off limits." He clipped each word, his warning clear. "Stay out."

I gaped. "You're really going to be all 'You shall not pass'?" Without a staff in hand, I stomped my foot to emphasize my point. Why wasn't he a reasonable recluse?

"Excuse me?" Oliver's eyebrows twitched. His gaze bore into mine. The darkness in the hallway made the whites of his eyes brighter, the rest of him a blur of shadows.

"You shall not pass." Not an ounce of guilt rose when I stomped my foot again and it landed squarely on his.

"What is . . .?"

Honestly, he struggled with suspenders, and now a basic movie reference? "*Lord of the Rings*, Gandalf?"

There wasn't a spec of recognition on his face.

"Elevenses, 'my precious'—anything?" I'd understand not having seen the director's cut, but never watching *any* of the movies? They're on TV all the time. Modern classics at their finest.

"Has anyone told you you're strange?" His tone implied he thought it was more than a bit.

"Oddly enough, you are not the first." Nor would he be the last. But I liked who I was, suspenders, dorky movie references, and all.

"Stay. Out. Of. The. West. Wing." His voice reverberated through my chest, a growl punctuating each word. From the blueprints I knew that the door led to another section of rooms, but whoever had been supplying Dad with information hadn't given anything on this area before we were unceremoniously fired.

I'd work with this, for now. "Fine." My voice was a squeak compared to the low rumble of his. Maybe I should practice deepening my voice for intimidation or authority.

It wasn't lying. For the time being, I wouldn't go inside the west wing. Eventually I would have to break our agreement. But that was a future Bellamy problem. Right now, I intended to keep my word—let him have his secrets. Whatever he was trying to hide in this mysterious west wing wasn't any of my concern.

He shoved his hands into the pockets of his pants, but he didn't step away. "So where are you planning on staying?"

I couldn't tell if he was intentionally being difficult or hadn't seen my luggage yet. "Here."

"Excuse me?" The growl was back, but all it made me want to do was roll my eyes.

I refused to allow his height, shoulders, and thick thighs to intimidate me. "You want me to repeat myself? I'm living here during the entirety of the project." I spoke each word slowly, ensuring they landed.

My particular brand of snark was failing. His jaw didn't twitch. Though his reaction may have been hidden beneath his wild beard.

"Live here? With me?" Oliver's tone was flat, his eyes narrowing on me, expectant. "Don't you know what they say about me?"

I shook my head. I hadn't even known he existed until yesterday.

He blew out a breath, taking a step away from me, an ominous chill filling the air. "That I killed my family."

CHAPTER THREE

A shudder trembled down my spine, tempting me to sprint down the hallway—until I truly considered him. The vacant look in his eyes as he rubbed at his chest screamed something more akin to broken soul, but I wasn't exactly an expert on emotions. If you needed a consultation on how to restore wallpaper, I was your girl, but if you wanted to have a deep meaningful conversation about your feelings? I would never be your first call.

I recognized the urge to push the world away. Not let anyone new in. *You're never in one place long enough. You don't know how to set down roots. You're not a commitment kind of girl.* The world can hurt you in a million distinct personal ways, and it had hurt Oliver in one of the worst possible.

I leaned against the door as he stared back, stone-faced, the uneven wood poking my spine as I ignored the impulse to reach out, comfort him.

Guilt and pain were coming off him in waves, but none of it screamed killer to me. He felt responsible for whatever had happened, but I had zero belief he had anything to do with it. Or my sense of self-preservation was off.

Instead, I shrugged, refusing to give him what he wanted.

"You're going to stay in this house with a murderer?" Oliver took a step forward, shaking his head.

"You said it's what people say about you, not that it's true." We were playing semantics now, but I refused to be scared off. This didn't change how badly my family needed this project; I would not meekly walk out the door with my tail between my legs. But the eerie hallway, lack of light, the whole crumbly, potentially haunted estate was really working for him.

He didn't appreciate my humor, his shoulders bunching. "Says something about you."

I have a dream and refuse to let you bulldoze over it?

"Well, I don't think murderers warn other people that they're, you know, a murderer. They just kill them." My extensive listening to true crime podcasts had prepared me well. "The murderer doesn't tell you his plan unless it's a Netflix show. Or he's dumb." Oliver didn't appear stupid to me. Controlling, definitely, but there was intelligence behind his gray eyes.

He grunted, leaning against the opposite wall. "Know a lot of murderers?"

"I've worked on quite a few different houses. I'm sure some of those were sites of a murder. Probably haunted too." Sebastian, my best friend, would say, statistically, there was always a chance.

But with him standing here, his broken heart beating from his eyes, I couldn't believe him. It wasn't my place to change his mind about himself. I wasn't here to save him, but his home. "All I care about is the estate."

It was tempting to offer him human solace. The picture of why he was here in this crumbling place was a little less fuzzy, leaving a funny feeling in my stomach. What he had gone through, though, I wasn't naive enough to believe the answers were as black and white as he was presenting them.

But I had a job to do and zero interest in further entanglements with whatever this was. "Listen, I'll stay out of your way."

"Good." His eyes narrowed as he shoved his hands into the pockets of his joggers. With that warm welcome, he turned and disappeared into the estate.

"With all the construction, it's probably best you visit your family's other properties anyway," I called out, but he didn't even acknowledge me.

My stomach sank, his final expression haunting me. I was still tempted to enter the west wing, but I had plenty to consider without tackling that portion of the mansion yet. And even more questions that I needed answered.

Rather than continuing to explore, I almost sprinted back to the room I had been assigned.

Sebastian picked up after the first ring. We had been best friends since freshman year, ending up on the same floor and hating our roommates. The moment we could, we moved off campus, and the rest was history. We couldn't be more different. He was tall, worked out constantly, enjoyed eating eggs raw for the protein, and was madly, undeniably in love with his boyfriend, Finn.

"I'm at the site—" I halted, unsure how to explain my experience so far.

"Good. I was worried about you after the weather last night. Don't worry, we already called your dad to check on him."

Of course he had. My shoulders lowered incrementally. "Thanks, I appreciate it. How is he?"

Sebastian chuckled darkly. "Rushing me off the phone to get ready for someone named Betty to come over. He asked me if I had access to any Viagra."

I shoved my face into my pillow and groaned. Some things a daughter did not need to know. "Betty is his nurse."

"Ah." Sebastian coughed, doing a poor job covering up his laugh.

"I knew Maurice had it in him," Finn called out.

Finn was short, fat, and perpetually happy. And nothing made him happier than sexually dominating Sebastian. I tuned out the details, but they were the happiest, most functional couple I knew, and never complained about my third-wheeling ass following them around.

"You think he could get her to write me a script for—"

I cleared my throat to stop Sebastian from completing his thought.

"Not the time, not the time, understood. But the house—how is it? This is the big one, right?"

"That's actually what I was calling you about." I released a shaky breath. "The mansion has a resident, and I was hoping you could tell me more about him. Oliver Killington?"

There was some mumbling in the background. But no one yelled, *"Get out, he's a murderer!"* so probably a good sign.

"Oh, you may be right there, dumplin'," Finn cooed.

"Don't ruin my persona in front of Bells," Sebastian warned, without any bite.

"She knows all about how I like to ruin you, sweet cheeks."

"If you guys need some alone time, I can hang up." I was all for sexual freedom, but that didn't mean I wanted to imagine the people I loved doing whatever with their sweet cheeks.

"No, we're fine." Sebastian sounded pained, reminding me why phone calls and not video chats were safest with these two. "Finn was advising me of something."

I purposefully held off mentioning the whole "I killed my family" thing. Sebastian was overprotective, and he'd be in his car, on his way here, before I'd even get the sentence out.

"We were thinking maybe he's the missing Killington grandchild?" he offered.

That made me sit up on the bed. "He's not missing—he's right here." What exactly had I wandered into here, some sort of movie of the week?

"Oh, I forgot you don't watch the news." Judgment deepened his tone.

"I avoid it at all costs, yes." There was nothing wrong with steering clear of the constant depression and doomsday on cable news. It was possible to be informed without watching whatever they tried to sensationalize next.

"Well, my ignorant friend, about a decade ago, it was all over the news. The heir to the Killington Empire was in an accident with his wife and eldest child. The parents died, the son was injured too—if I recall correctly, he had a massive football scholarship, a lot of bets on who would draft him. They called him . . . Do you remember, Finn?"

"Beast, I think." The higher pitch of Finn's voice made me miss them even more. He could deliver the worst news and you would smile by the end, thanking him. "He was an animal on the field. Unstoppable."

"Yes, that was it. Beast," Sebastian murmured. "But the accident ended his football career. After he left the hospital, everyone thought he would take over his father's place in the company, but he was never heard from or seen again. There were a lot of rumors."

I placed them on speaker so I could do some sleuthing of my own. "What rumors?" This information was not at all ominous.

"Well, some people believed Oliver planned the whole thing so he would inherit the company." The skepticism was obvious in Sebastian's voice.

I snorted at the ridiculousness of that. "Probably not smart for him to be in the car, then." It seemed especially cruel for people to say he planned to kill his own parents.

"Exactly. The other rumor was about some sort of curse. His family, his football career, the dip in the company stock after that happened—it took a while to rebound. You know how people are when tragedy happens, and no one steps forward to overshare about their experiences. They fill in their own details and make it as gratuitous as possible. Thus . . ."

"A curse," I finished.

"He's technically the heir now, with his dad having died, but his grandfather won't confirm who is next in the line of succession. Articles are written about it every couple of years. How unwise it is, shaking stockholder confidence—that sort of thing. Guesses on who will take over. His sisters both work for the company, but no one believes it'll be them. One of the last few family conglomerates out there—it's a market event naming the successor."

My head hurt with all this information, struggling to figure out what this meant for the restoration. "You know way too much about this."

"Actually, this makes sense. There have been rumors they've been seeking to diversify with the latest stock drop, looking to get into newer technology. I was reading this article yesterday about—"

"Sebastian!"

"Sorry, but information is power." Sebastian was a market analyst, practically a walking stock ticker. Despite our many, many differences, our friendship fit, like him and Finn.

"Back to the issue at hand. You think the heir to a multibillion-dollar conglomerate is living in a crumbling estate like some sort of gothic horror show?" It was impossible to hide my disbelief, even as my internet search confirmed Sebastian's story. Oliver was who he said he was, and more.

"Or he could be the prince in the tower, waiting for someone to save him," Finn said. I could picture him clutching his fists to his chest and fluttering his eyelashes. The day that I finally fell in love was something he had been dreaming about, believing it was only a matter of time, eager for all the double dates we would go on.

"Well, the prince told me to get the fuck out, so I don't think he's searching for a savior."

"He has to want to get saved first." Finn huffed as if it was obvious, and I was being purposefully difficult. While he was a hopeless romantic down to his bones, I didn't have the same optimism for my love life.

"Okay, let's step away from fairy-tale land and return to reality, please. The one where I am trapped in a crumbling home and"—I took the phone off speaker, leaning it on my shoulder, not that it would prevent me from being overheard—"there's some sort of advanced AI system that controls the house."

I was met with silence.

"You realize," Sebastian whispered back, "that makes no sense. You said the place is falling apart. Who puts advanced technology in a shack like that?"

"I know," I hissed, glancing around the still-darkened room. "None of this makes sense. Maybe I was kidnapped."

31

"Oh my gosh," Finn screamed. "Have the aliens taken you? What's the code word?"

"The code word?" Sebastian and I asked at the same time.

"Yes," huffed Finn, "to prove that it's you and not the alien that has invaded your body."

"Wouldn't we need to have established a code word for this to be effective?" I scrubbed my hair, getting my fingers stuck in the tangle of the thick strands.

"Ms. Price?" Bl8z3's sudden question caused every cell in my body to jump. "Breakfast is being served in the kitchen this morning.

"Um, thanks?" Paranoia gripped me. Had it overheard the conversation? "Guys, I have to go."

It took a few minutes longer for me to assure them I would keep them updated and, if I learned any market information, that I would not commit it to writing.

I dramatically collapsed onto the bed, relishing the brief silence. A crumbling house with an AI system. A grumpy, trust-funder with control issues. A multimillion-dollar estate allowed to go into ruin.

I took a single fortifying breath.

Then I got to work.

My newfound information did not deter me from the mission ahead. I needed to finish walking through the mansion, sketch out my plans, and ultimately get them approved. Oliver's presence changed nothing.

Bl8z3 led me on a guided tour, providing tidbits about the history of the estate, when the furniture was bought, the last time the marble counters had been sealed. I did my best to pay attention. My gaze wandered to the few recent family photos, and by recent, I mean the few that were in color, the outfits dated.

In the fresh light of day, without the protective cover of darkness, the decay of the house stood in stark contrast to the pictures Dad had provided. The house had needed updating then, but now there was no choice if it was to remain standing. Most of the furniture was original to the mansion, with a few modern pieces scattered throughout, mostly designed for aesthetics over comfort. The estate had the feel of walking through a museum rather than a family home.

Which made Bl8z3's existence even stranger. Someone had taken the time to wire an AI throughout the mansion, but no other repairs had been done. As I trailed through the house, making my way to the kitchen, everything seemed to be paused: cloths covered some furniture; ladders with layers of dusts stood under portraits; and peeling wallpaper. That may have been deliberate, to begin removal. As if they'd had every intent of going forward with the renovation we'd been hired for years ago. Every room left me with more questions.

But the potential was there: how with only a few changes and lifts—staining the floors, fixing the crown molding, a fresh coat of paint—life could be breathed back into this place. Despite all the cobwebs and the smell—gosh, the smell—this was a place of beauty, each piece chosen with care. The artwork, the faded paint on the walls, the matching threads in the rugs and drapes. Despite the breadth of the project, I had no doubt that I could take this on.

With all my careful consideration, looking at cracks, water damage, and structural issues, I didn't see a single speaker in sight. "Bl8z3, how did you come to be here?" I couldn't hold back the question any longer.

"Well, that is a funny story—"

The door in front of me swung open, and I leaped out of the way. I wasn't normally this jumpy, but this house was doing something to me. It was challenging to predict what was waiting around every corner.

"Good, you found it, Ms. Price."

I struggled not to groan as I recognized the British accent from last night, coming from the man standing before me. Stout, with a mustache and combed-over hair, his suit pressed to perfection. Still displeased with my existence here.

"Bellamy, please." I forced out a laugh before thrusting my hand forward.

The stranger stood rigidly, eyeing my palm as if checking for dirt, which really, what with our surroundings—but eventually his hand met mine in a strong yet brief shake. He stepped aside with a flourish, holding open the swinging door, revealing the kitchen. "I am Ambrose, the butler."

Of course this crumbling mess had a butler. Made complete sense.

"It's a pleasure to meet you—"

Any pretense of being polite fled me as my gaze snagged on the spot in between the marble counters. It was impossible to contain my gasp as I sprinted toward the stove, a Boston Beauty gas oven. It had to be original to the house, something I'd so rarely seen, even in my line of work. Unable to help myself, I glided my fingers along the smooth, aged brass handles. It was entirely impractical in a house this size, but I would do everything in my power to ensure it stayed in some capacity.

"I see you've met my pride and joy," someone spoke behind me.

It took me another moment to pry myself away because I was, well, stroking the oven's smooth lines. Dad was going to be so disappointed to have missed this.

"Rue, pronouns they/them, I'm the chef here." Faded red hair was buzzed on one side of their head, with hair flopping over the side. They were medium height, medium build, glasses with bright red frames, dressed in a polo shirt and jeans.

After another handshake, I was pointed toward a peeling vinyl breakfast nook where a sullen teenager was seated. Based on the red hair alone, she was related to the bubbly chef.

"Nick, be polite and say hello to our new guest," Rue instructed.

"Hey." Nick barely glanced in my direction before returning to her notebook, scribbling what appeared to be a complicated mathematics equation. The kitchen was one of the few rooms not covered in dust, an almost overwhelming lemon cleaning scent making my nostrils tingle. The space would still require work, the hum from the refrigerator promising it was on its last legs of life, but it wasn't in as desperate need for attention as the majority of the mansion. I needed these people on my side—that was my only motivation for holding back my questions about how this place had fallen into such ruin with what appeared to be at least semi-competent staff.

"Nick's also mine. I'm sure she'll be happy to give you a tour of the stables later. That's her realm—we all mostly steer clear. Ambrose shared that you were hired to work on the house, and I can't tell you how excited we all are." Rue clapped their hands while Ambrose slammed the fridge door. He was firmly on Team Banish the New Girl.

"Ms. Price, what can I get you? We were just about to have breakfast." Rue turned toward that beautiful stove, moving with ease around the space, while Ambrose worked in sync with them to pull eggs out of the fridge and begin preparing coffee, as if this was a dance they performed every single day. "Any food allergies or special requests?"

"No food allergies." The vinyl creaked as I leaned back, all the stuffing flattened, my behind planted directly on the wood. "Please, call me Bellamy, she/her. I'm happy to make my own meals. I want to be as small a nuisance as possible."

"Nonsense. It will be a joy to feed someone new. How does an omelet and coffee sound? A serving of fruit?"

"Perfect." My stomach grumbled at the idea of breakfast.

"Did you find the room satisfactory?"

At Bl8z3's voice, I jerked, almost slipping off the bench. "F—"

"He doesn't enjoy being left out." Nick's gaze didn't leave her paper as she spoke. Ambrose set the coffee service down in the middle of the table, eyes narrowing in my direction when I shifted to help him.

"I've moved your vehicle into the garage, ma'am. A car like that shouldn't be left out to the elements. It's in pristine condition," Ambrose lectured. While he didn't seem fond of me, it was clear he would get along well with my father. "The keys were in your jacket. I took the liberty."

I was sure Dad would be appreciative—that was, if he wasn't going to the hospital for exhaustion because of his Viagra use. That conversation with Sebastian would haunt me.

"Uh, thank you. But I wanted to inquire about the—"

Nick coughed, and I paused. I hadn't even gotten to ask my question yet. A smirk lifted the corners of her mouth, and I swiped at my face, wondering if there was something on it. I followed her eye line to the doorway—the hulking shape of the biggest pain in my ass I'd ever met was filling the space.

Wonderful. I couldn't get a moment of peace.

CHAPTER FOUR

"Sir!" Ambrose appeared torn between wanting to bow and salute Oliver in the same movement, while Rue shrieked.

"Please have a seat, sir, I was about to start on your omelet." Rue fiddled with the knobs on the stove. "I'm so glad you are joining us."

Sir Asshole shifted his stance, not moving any farther into the room. "I wasn't planning to—"

"Stay!" All three shouted at once, a mix of amusement and fear across their features. How cushy—a chef, butler, and maybe some child labor at his beck and call.

Ambrose shoved my mug out of the way, almost knocking it over until I rescued it, in order to prepare one for Oliver, who seemed to consider fleeing altogether, before crossing his arms, eyes focused entirely on me as a frown formed on his face.

Yup, I'm still here, asshole.

"This is wonderful timing, sir. We were just getting to know Ms. Price and learn about her plans for the estate." Rue plated some fruit, ignoring his hesitance to sit next to me in a way I respected and admired. I was going to have to ask them for tips on how to handle him.

Despite the activity in the room, we were in our own silent conversation.

"I told you to stay away from me," Oliver's arched eyebrow screamed as he plopped next to Nick.

"I was here first," was my silent response, eyes narrowed, arm extended over the back of the bench as I tried to relax into my seat, which was impossible with the nail digging into my spine. But I would claim my territory. I refused to tiptoe around this place for him.

As I winced—this bench would be one of the first things hauled off—his lips pursed, like he knew the exact reason and enjoyed the idea of me being uncomfortable.

With a final shake of his head, Oliver turned his focus to Nick, who offered him a fist bump, pushing her notebook toward him as he plopped down. He reviewed her work, even nodding along as if he understood, fingers scratching at his beard.

Once Rue finished cooking, all of us sat around the booth, squished in together. I did my best to minimize myself, squeezing my thighs. Rue attempted to keep up a constant chatter, but no one else seemed interested. "We want to hear all about your ideas."

I set my silverware down, smoothing my linen napkin out on my lap. "I'm still completing my plans. I have to examine all the rooms"—Oliver let out a not-at-all subtle cough as I rolled my eyes—"and take some measurements. But if you have any input, any improvements you would like to see that would make your lives easier, please let me know."

"Oh." Rue pressed a steaming chipped mug to their lips. "That would be lovely."

"A laundry room—a *proper* laundry room." Ambrose barely took a moment to ponder my request. I almost did a double take at his willingness to offer me help, let alone be the first to speak. "To iron properly, steam, even sew." His eyes gleamed as his arms waved around, gesturing how the layout would be.

"That's exactly the kind of thing I'm looking for," I said, nodding. "My goal is to bring out the original character of the estate while making the necessary modern improvements. It's still a home people live in, and I want it to be functional and around for generations to come. Not a museum, but a historical atmosphere." I sagged against the bench, almost giddy, my elbow bumping Nick's, thrilled to listen to Rue and Ambrose bicker over whether his new tailoring room should cut into the square footage of the kitchen.

"I am quite modern," Bl8z3 chirped. Could an AI be nervous?

"You have nothing to worry about." My promise tumbled out, unable to stop my head from tilting in the direction the voice came from, still not entirely used to the AI system. I wasn't even sure I had the knowledge to do anything other than try to unplug it. I had to stop falling asleep to movies about robots attempting to take over the world.

There was an electronic chirp that seemed to indicate its relief.

The tough part of the conversation was out of the way, and I was proud of myself for not sticking it to Oliver that the staff was taking things a lot better than he had. I dug into my omelet and almost moaned. "This is so cheesy, it's perfect."

"I usually double the cheese from whatever a recipe calls for."

We grinned at each other. Rue was my kind of cook.

"What do you think, sir?" Ambrose asked, his entire body leaning forward despite the table that separated him from Oliver. All right, maybe I hadn't fully won over everyone yet.

"Stop calling me that." Oliver stabbed his fork into his last bite of food, the room filling with the sound of his chewing as he deftly avoided all eye contact, before rising, finished with the meal and us.

Ambrose almost knocked Oliver over in his attempt to grab the plate. "I have this, sir."

It was entirely ridiculous, but Nick and Rue didn't even blink as Oliver stalked out. I shook my head, eyes briefly closing as he abandoned the room. At least he hadn't banished me again, because I was pretty sure Ambrose would pick me up and boot me himself if Oliver told him to.

Continuing with his efforts, Ambrose cleared the rest of the table as we finished up, refusing all our offers to help, eyeing the knives when Rue wiped down the table. Despite the sorry appearance of the estate, he took pride in his job, as reflected in his crisp outfit and mannerisms. No matter his feelings about me, his support would be essential for me to get this right.

I recognized the kinship there, the fondness. It was something I felt for all the properties I had worked on, lived on for a time, until inevitably moving on to the next, because it was never my place to stay. Ambrose cared about this place. If he could restore this house with his own two hands, he probably would.

Having cleaned up everything, only stopping short of spraying Lysol in my face, Ambrose cleared his throat, perching on the edge of the booth. "Sir, eh, that is, the younger Mr. Killington, he keeps to himself. If you do not disturb him, I am sure we can work something out." Ambrose took a sip of his own coffee, pinky wiggling.

Crap, crap. "This can be difficult to hear about a place that has meaning for you, but my goal is to ensure it's around for decades to come. This house, this estate, has been neglected." I held up my hand as Ambrose opened his mouth. "Not by you. Houses, especially older ones, need certain things for long-term upkeep—new roofs, the pipes to be looked after. I will do my best to ensure this will not disrupt your lives, but I wouldn't be doing my job if I only did half of the things that should be done."

"Amb, admit it: it will take more than a good dusting." Rue raised their eyebrows, finger running along a divot in the counter's marble. "The cracks in the walls—I see the fear in your eyes every time it rains. We're lucky this place is still standing."

"I am insulted by your very insinuation." Ambrose sniffed, lifting his chin in the air. "I am excellent at my job. Bloody hell, I don't even take weekends."

"Stop whining. No one blames you." Rue was unflappable, at ease with the prim and proper butler. "We've only come on as staff a little over two years ago."

And in the space between, the mansion had fallen into disarray. Another puzzle piece was falling into place. I gave Rue a quick nod, appreciating them trying to fight my battle. "Rue is right. If anything, your upkeep has kept the place together longer. The worst homes I've seen are the ones that have been entirely abandoned."

We sat in the silence of Nick's pencil scratching against the paper, none of this ruffling her. Rue had a faint smile on their face, though I knew their ultimate allegiance was to this place and Oliver. Ambrose was as prickly as his employer, just more vocal about it.

"I do not foresee any problems as long as the Young Mr. Killington remains happy."

I would not ask why he continued to speak of Oliver so formally, I would take his acceptance and run with it. "But I thought his grandfather was your employer?" Okay, I couldn't hold the curiosity in fully.

"He may own the estate, but the Younger Mr. Killington is the reason I am here."

"I see." It was not any clearer, but the firm look on his face shut down any of my other questions.

"But—" Ambrose knocked his fist on the table, ensuring all our attention was on him. "This home is special to the few people who also mean something to me." His eyes flashed to Rue and Nick before glancing at the door Oliver had walked out of. "Please treat it with care, as if it was your own. It may not seem like much to you, with all its imperfections, but there are precious memories here, things that deserved to be saved, preserved—" He stopped abruptly, fingers fluttering until he hid them under the table.

"I promise," I breathed out, needing him—them—to believe me. I may not have had a home of my own, but I could bring theirs back to life. Even if their employer was an ass.

I've found him, the love of your life.

The text from Sebastian popped up as I sat in my bedroom's armchair, sketching on my iPad. When I was deep in a project, I hunkered down, barely coming up for air, let alone remembering to eat. Dad had reviewed my drawings and sent some suggestions, potential contacts he'd worked with in the past, but this project wouldn't fully be ours until our proposed plan was approved, and I'd still probably be holding my breath until we started construction.

Bell: *Not interested.*

Sebastian: *Soulmate. Soul. Mate.*

Bell: *New phone. Who is this?*

The screen flashed to show Sebastian was calling.

"Okay, but seriously, I met him last night at a gallery I was touring with Finn. He's a writer, kind of moody but loves animals. Big movie and TV binge-watcher. Could he sound any more perfect for you?"

Sigh. "I told you, I have zero interest in dating right now."

"Are you against dating or is it because you're letting yourself believe those lies that douche told you? You're better off without him."

Was it a lie, though, when Dan had been right? During our project about a year ago, he was the on-site carpenter. He came around daily, even on his days off, the attraction between us undeniable. I enjoyed talking to him, the simplicity of someone else understanding my daily life. He never had a dazed look when I talked about the evolution of chairs throughout history.

Two weeks before the project was scheduled to end, I slept with him. My mind filled with ridiculous fantasies about dating after the project finished. But on my last day on-site, Dan blew those dreams to smithereens, then stomped all over them to ensure they never returned.

"This was a lot of fun, Bellamy, but I never associated you with a relationship. You're the right-now girl, not the forever girl. We had a good time, but you can't expect someone to take you seriously when you're always thinking about the next project, your next destination. You have no roots. Everything about you screams short term, not a commitment."

It hurt because it was the truth. Even with this project, potentially the biggest I'd have in my career, I was already planning the next steps, the job that would hopefully change my life and help me become a person capable of putting down roots. It left me with guilt, wanting something different from what my dad had provided, but it wasn't that he had done anything wrong. I couldn't be prouder to be Maurice Price's daughter—I adored my life, my childhood. He'd taught me everything I knew. But something in me ached, yearned to find a way to take my passion and still relax into something long term. Be able to plan a trip with Sebastian and Finn further out than the weekend before. To have a home, someone waiting for me, who trusted I would come back.

"I told you I'm on a dating hiatus," I reminded Sebastian, shaking my head to return to reality. "I'm concentrating on my career."

"I want you to be happy, and I think you two would get along."

"I don't have time in my schedule to go back and forth to the city, and I definitely can't host guests at a house that isn't mine." My voice came out harsher than I'd intended.

"All right, but—"

"Ms. Price? Dinner is ready." Bl8z3 interrupted Sebastian's protest.

"Okay, you softie, I have to go. But pinky promise I'm happy."

"Fine, B, but please remember that when love smacks you in the face, I'm going to be laughing. Thrilled, overjoyed for you, but still laughing."

"I couldn't ask for a better friend."

I set down my iPad. As much as I adored Sebastian, I was delighted to have an easy exit. "I told you to call me Bellamy, Bell, B, anything except Ms. Price, Bl8z3." Creating some order to all the papers on the desk, I leaned back into the chair, trying to roll my neck.

"It goes against my programming to refer to you colloquially."

I was quickly getting used to the voice that could sound at any moment, full of personality. "Fine, we'll figure out a compromise at some point." A brief dinner break, to clear my head, give my cramped fingers a rest. I had a long night ahead of me.

"How about Young Miss?"

"Not a chance. Though maybe if I can convince you to call Killington Young Grump?"

"Afraid not." Bl8z3 sounded disappointed. Whoever had programmed it deserved a Nobel Prize or whatever you give someone for kicking ass. Still, with its programming, I had my theories.

"Douche Canoe wouldn't be as fun, but also acceptable." Speaking of, I was grateful his rude demeanor stopped him from eating with the lowly staff after that initial breakfast. I had no interest in suffering through another meal with him.

"My algorithm can't tell who would be a bigger fan of that, Ambrose or the Young Sir."

Complete disbelief. "Bl8z3, did you make an AI joke?"

"I have my glitches." Then: "Ba-dah-duh." They not only had jokes, but sound effects.

"You are wasted on this house."

"You are too kind. Dinner will be served in the atrium this evening."

I strolled into the en suite of my room, splashing cold water on my face and tying my hair off in a messy knot. My appearance in the mirror didn't exactly look refreshed, but a little less wired on caffeine and gummy bears.

For the past few evenings, I had been eating in the kitchen with Rue and Ambrose. Nick would sprint in and out but was always desperate to finish her homework or work on some other project. Constant motion, that girl.

I dashed through the hall and down the less squeaky staircase, rotating left toward the atrium.

The momentum took me through the open glass French doors. It was one of my favorite rooms in the mansion; my fingers itched to get my hands on it. Though the room was not too neglected because of how empty it was, Ambrose had told me the plants had all died long ago, with no one ever replacing them. The back exterior wall of the mansion was stone, and the remaining walls of the room were glass, with wooden beams dividing the cloudy panes—which would all need to be restained and refitted with energy efficient panels. But with the sun setting, the splendor of the room couldn't be denied. It was the perfect location for dinner before I went back upstairs and shut myself away.

There was a small table with two chairs down at the other end of the room. And notably, not a single soul around.

"Bl8z3, where is everyone?" I narrowed my eyes, studying my surroundings further. For the first time since I had arrived a few days ago, Bl8z3 was silent. The tile floor was carpeted in rose petals. Candelabras were set around the space, flickering, with a large piece on the table among covered serving dishes.

Alarm bells were going off in my head. I spun around, only to slam into a wall.

"Wha—"

Oliver's warm palms gripped my shoulders, holding me to the solid planes of his chest. He prevented me from collapsing backward; his mouth opened slightly, eyes wide. Probably still expecting me to leave and never return. We stood there for a moment before he gave his head a shake and let me go.

He had kept his promise until now, turning on his heel every time I walked into a room the past few days with my tape measure and camera. Bl8z3 was too useful, taking notes for me as I called out the information. This trap was my reminder that no one, not even Bl8z3, owed me any loyalty.

The frown that seemed to constantly cross Oliver's face was out in full force as he released me, fingers flexing, before he shoved them into the pockets of his pants. His hair was slightly less unruly today, tied back in a neater ponytail. "Price."

"Killington." I acknowledged back.

Everything I had learned about him and his family as I lay in bed Googling, when I should be sleeping, flashed through my mind at his presence. Oliver hadn't been seen by the public since his parents' funeral. There were various theories about why, all stories from not very reputable sources. He had died in the accident with his parents; the accident was all a hoax; he was hiding on some island; aliens had taken him (I forwarded that one to Finn).

I was beginning to wonder if he had been in this house the entire time. Had he been alone until the arrival of Ambrose, Rue, and Nick? I didn't have to like him to be sympathetic, even a little embarrassed by how I'd busted through the doors that first night. It didn't excuse his behavior, but maybe explained it slightly.

The rest of his family wasn't in hiding. Drug overdoses, dating scandals, some insider trading, and a tendency to throw outlandish parties seemed to be a common thread, though I looked at it all with a new sense of skepticism. His twin sisters were paparazzi darlings, in the news more often for the parties they attended rather than their participation in the family business.

"What are *you* doing here?" Oliver's beard-covered jaw clenched.

"Living my life, breathing the air, existing." My pulse raced, his eyes narrowing as I hit his buttons. He made it too easy.

And then it got worse.

The glass door snicked shut, followed by a *click*—the turn of a lock.

CHAPTER FIVE

Oliver's eyes widened. So, the sound hadn't just been in my imagination. I held my breath, stomach sinking, as he attempted to push down the door handle. But a girl could hope, especially if it meant that I wouldn't be trapped in this room, which seemed to be shrinking by the moment, with my least favorite person. His shoulders bulged as he put some more force behind his efforts, but the doors stayed firm.

His right leg pulled back, and I dived forward, grabbing at his T-shirt. "Don't you dare."

"What?" His expression seemed to accuse me—as if any of this was my idea.

"Trust me, this is the last place I want to be, but that frame is solid wood and thicker than the door to your bedroom. All you'll do is ding it, maybe, unless you want to kick through the glass and hope you don't cut anything important before we can get out." More likely, he'd dent his foot. "It was probably just an accident. Let's ask Bl8z3 to get someone to come help."

"An accident, huh?" Oliver nodded to the rest of the room. The rose petals, the candles. Rue and Ambrose were all about ambience, setting the scene, choosing an appropriate wine and place settings for every meal. Yeah, this was looking less and less like an accident by the moment, but I refused to accept it.

"Bl8z3?" Hopefully it would answer me this time.

"Yes, miss?" The reply was prompt. A conspiring AI, wonderful.

"We're stuck in the atrium. Can you or someone else unlock the door?" I was not one to doubt Bl8z3's abilities, including control over the locks.

"I cannot, miss."

I waited, but no explanation was forthcoming. "And why not?"

"We all know how hard you have been working and thought you needed a break."

We, huh? "The doors don't have to be locked for that to happen."

"Let us out," Oliver demanded, still wriggling the handle.

"I have been programmed to ignore your orders for the next two hours, sir."

"Two hours?" I rammed Oliver out of the way, shoving down on the door handle, regretting leaving my lock picking kit up in my bedroom. For my next project, the contract would include a clause that the house be unoccupied. I didn't have time for this; my deadline to provide my sketches was only days away.

"Please enjoy dinner." And with that, Bl8z3 piped soft, romantic instrumental music into the room. I had never felt so betrayed by technology in my life. Maybe those *Terminator* movies had been onto something.

Bl8z3 wasn't exaggerating, I was preparing around the clock for my presentation with Mr. Killington to receive his approval for my plans. I could take a break once everything was confirmed in two days' time. By then, this might even be romantic if I were locked in with anyone else.

Oliver gave the door a solid kick, the glass panels rattling, but nothing else. Not even a divot in the wood. Wonderful, this part of the house was holding up. His soft canvas sneakers couldn't be much help.

The room permeated with the drool-worthy scent coming from the table, at least the part about a meal hadn't been a lie too. "We might as well eat." I sighed, not waiting for him as I ambled over to the table and lifted the dish covers. Two plates were filled with salad and chicken fettuccine alfredo.

I attempted to gracefully slide into the chair. I failed. Should have pulled it farther away from the table instead of trying to be dainty. Now I had to squeeze my way in, almost tipping the chair over. You know, typical, everyday hot girl shit.

The sun set as Oliver continued his assault on the door, fortunately missing me muck up being a human being. When I was at last sitting upright in my chair, he gave up his attempted escape, shoulders hunched as he limped over.

I pressed my lips together. Today's T-shirt was navy, which somehow brought out the color of his eyes. I thrummed my fingers against the lace tablecloth. They had not skimped on a thing—fine china, wineglasses, a roll set on a separate smaller dish with a slab of butter.

Resigning myself to being stuck here for the next two hours, I could at least try to make the best of it. "So, what do you think everyone else is up to?" After planning this wonderful getaway, that I would in no way be plotting my revenge from.

"Let me activate their personal trackers." His tone was as dry as his sense of humor, and his mere existence was a challenge to my patience. Would it be wrong to stab him with my knife? To prove he was in fact human and felt emotion? Maybe he was a robot, an offshoot of Bl8z3.

"None of this appears off to you?" I hissed.

"I've lived here a long time." He studied me as he sipped his wine, his gaze shredding my suspenders. I enjoyed how much they bothered him. Let him squirm a little, for once. I would not change one hair on my head to make him more comfortable. He could join the long list of people who judged me because of my weight.

I couldn't imagine what the staff had been picturing, setting up this "date," thinking we would get along. "Well, it seems they've been watching too many romantic movies." I pressed my fingers to the petals of the fresh flowers in the middle of the table. The bouquet was gorgeous, a vivid mix of pink and white lilies with red roses, the only color in the room.

Grunt.

Anger licked across my veins. Did he think I wanted this, to be set up with someone who detested me? I was here to do a job, nothing else.

"I can assure you I want to be here even less." His words snapped my head up, and I slapped my hands over my mouth, realizing I had spoken aloud rather than kept my thoughts to myself. Oliver did not bring out the best in me. I'd barely gotten a few hours of sleep the last few nights, desperate to give Mr. Killington options in the restoration, to prove myself.

The lack of decor and the darkening sky meant there really wasn't anywhere to look but at the person sitting across from me. The way his lips enveloped his fork with every bite, slowly chewing with determination. My presence probably made his food taste worse.

"Do you normally eat in here?" I cringed as my words broke the silence, heat crawling up my neck, but I couldn't sit here feeling this uncomfortable. I wasn't programmed that way.

"In my room." Oliver's fork stabbed into a tomato before he bit down, having no problem avoiding my gaze.

"Oh." The wood of the chair creaked as I continued to shift. The crunch of each piece of lettuce echoed off the windows, frosted with age. I couldn't help but cringe at every movement of my jaw, never more aware of how much noise I made chewing. I wished I could hide under the table. I didn't do uncomfortable silences, didn't do uncomfortable at all.

"How come you're not eating there, then?" Even shoving food into my mouth could not stop the compulsion to ease this tension, at least temporarily.

Oliver rolled his shoulders, and I winced, realizing how rude my words had sounded.

"Nick asked," he muttered.

"Ah."

We had both been tricked. But they clearly cared about him, so I wasn't sure why they'd thought it would be a good idea to lock us in a room together.

"Maybe when we finish eating, they'll let us out?" I hypothesized.

They didn't.

Bl8z3 ignored us, continuing to play what I could only assume was some sort of romantic music playlist. Any dream I'd ever have of being seduced via acoustic piano was dead, buried, forever ruined.

I ended up on the freezing tile floor, sitting cross-legged, as Oliver paced back and forth, checking on every pass to see if the door would magically open this time. The temperature had dropped significantly without the sun to warm the room. I did my best not to tremble, but I hadn't exactly planned to be trapped in a cold room this evening.

I spun one lily between my fingers, the colors of the bouquet echoing the way I wanted to incorporate a few brighter choices into this room; they'd reflect off the light from the windows. The current design scheme was mostly drab, faded from age and sunlight.

Needing to be productive, I closed my eyes and imagined the sketch of the kitchen I had been working on, placing the appliances in a better configuration, a kitchen island, a breakfast nook with plush seating. The flooring needed to be ripped out and replaced with a nice maple, though oak could work too. Kitchens were always a struggle to modernize—it was hard to restore older kitchens to their original state without asking the owners to cook their food over an open flame.

Something—really some*one*—nudged my foot, and I exhaled before I slowly slid open my eyes. Oliver towered over me.

"Y-yes?" I tilted my head.

"You're shivering."

This was actual torture. "We're tr-trapped in a not very well insulated room with no heat source, and it's nighttime. Anything else you would like to point out?"

He pressed his palm to his brow, and I waited for him to start pacing again. I still needed to decide whether the kitchen island should have an additional sink. Instead, he sprawled next to me, back against the stone, which felt warmer than the glass, pressing his body to mine. I jerked, almost whacking him in the eye with my elbow.

He was touching me.

Intentionally.

Oliver didn't have a sweater or anything else to offer me, but he had body heat. Body heat aplenty, apparently, with the warmth that was seeping into my skin.

And I hated it. Hated that I needed him for something as essential as not freezing to death. I was the person people relied on by my friends and Dad, especially right now. Worse, I was tempted to snuggle even closer, but I held back.

"Th-thank you."

He grunted, his body stiff as a board, arm rigid as it pressed against mine. Every single moment I spent with him, he seemed to broadcast his distaste for me in any way he could.

"Do I smell or something?"

Oliver was silent for a minute before he snorted. "Or something, Price." But then he lifted his arm, wrapping it around my shoulders, stuttering over the strap of my suspenders, pulling me against his chest. His palm rubbed up and down my upper arm, creating friction. He wasn't exactly relaxed, but the tension thrumming through him had lessened fractionally. Then after a moment, he muttered, "It's been a while."

It was difficult not to react to his confession, my breath catching. "You have experience being locked in a room with someone you hate?" I eased a little bit more into him; the warmth was intoxicating.

The bark of a laugh he let out rumbled his body into mine, the sound vibrating throughout my chest.

I slid my legs out in front of me, our pants the only thing separating our skin from touching. The candle tapers were noticeably burned down, wax dripping on the floor, the rose petals. My palms were trapped in between my thighs, fingers twitchy. We were *cuddling*. For survival reasons solely, but it was happening.

"It's strange seeing you without your tape measure." His voice was gruff, and I was tempted to peek up at his expression, but I kept my gaze on the door, waiting for something to happen. They couldn't keep us trapped in here forever. "No pencil here." His finger didn't touch my ear, but rather traced the air around it. Were goose bumps possible on ears?

Despite all his running away, I guess he'd noticed me. Well, not me but my tape measure and pencil. The man had a fascination with my accessories; I wasn't sure what to think about that. "You know I'm not here to make you hide in your own home, right?"

His shoulders lifted, taking my head along for the ride. "I'm staying away, Price, like we agreed."

It was probably for the best. I didn't need any distractions, especially not ones that came in the form of the bicep under my cheek right now.

"We could plan our revenge." I nudged his side with my elbow, squishing slightly.

He huffed, his breath warm against my cheek. "I'll make dinner."

I rolled my eyes. Still a privileged asshole. "You're really cruel, Killington."

"They didn't tell you?" His eyebrows shot up.

A giggle erupted out of me. "Okay, explain."

"Do I have to?" He gave my arm another squeeze, his fingertips soft, the motion causing my head to lean against his shoulder. His scent flooded my senses, a mix of clean and evergreen and something else I couldn't name but was probably an expensive cologne designed to mess with my pheromones.

Neither of us said a word or shifted away. The room was only growing colder in the evening air, especially since we were sitting on the tile floor, but it was tolerable being with Oliver.

This was it: an olive branch.

But then his grip loosened, still close enough for warmth, but somehow creating a level of separation between us. "I don't want to bore you."

"Tell me." I pulled a knee up, wrapping my arms around my leg.

He shook his head. "Trust me, I'm under no impressions that a gorgeous, smart woman like you would voluntarily eat a meal with me, let alone want to listen to me talk about all the things I've failed at."

What now? I pressed my face into my knee, releasing a few shaky breaths. The situation was getting to both of us. We needed a reminder of why we were here.

"I've, uh, been working on my plans. I didn't know if you wanted any input." My voice was halting, awkward even to my ears.

"I gave my input." His gruff tone had returned.

Lovely. *Stay out of the west wing.* We were back to this, were we? "I thought you might want some say about the changes being made."

"I don't have any money, if that's why you're being nice to me." His fingers flexed, now only touching me along my clothes.

I shrugged out of his hold, the chill returning, but I'd rather freeze than let him touch me. "Notice I didn't ask about money." My initial impression of him had been spot on; it was silly to think otherwise.

The cords of his neck stood out as he glared at me. "Fine then, consider this to be a job interview." Disdain dripped from his voice, his arms crossed, biceps bulging. "What made you pick this as a career?"

Fuck you. There was an alarm bell going off in my head, but I ignored it. We were trapped, and he was angry, but what else was new.

"Tell me, what makes you want to work on other people's homes? Don't you have one of your own?"

It was as if he was gazing directly into my heart, pressing along the fault line, the very thing that would shake me.

"Why do you have to be such a beast?" I scrambled to stand up, lips pressed together, fists clenched at my side. Turning away from him, I stomped straight for the door, not caring if it was fruitless. I needed to do something with this energy that had suddenly filled me. Our time had to be more than up.

Click.

Without so much as a goodbye, I stalked out. But I wasn't headed for my room. Despite its size, it was too small for the feelings caged inside me. I began picking up speed as I escaped until I was full-on sprinting.

I ended up in front of a set of double doors on the opposite end of the house. The space was so different from when I had seen it earlier in the week, in the middle of the day, filled with sunlight. My lungs burst from the exertion.

Of course the Killington Estate had a ballroom. It was two stories, with a vaulted ceiling decorated with an Italian fresco. The paint was cracked and faded like everything else in the house. The back wall was lined with windows, observing the outside world, but not a part of it.

The full moon didn't provide quite enough illumination, and I missed my step, slipped, and landed on my ass, groaning at the ache in my muscles. I lay there, half propped up against a marble pillar, legs sprawled on the dull and scratched floor.

Oliver was right—I didn't have a home. You couldn't grow up the way I had and not burn for one. All the hotels, the temporary rooms, surfaces that weren't mine to decorate or paint. But a home was more than walls. It was the memories those walls contained, the stories they soaked up and remembered long after its people were gone. I could picture the people who'd danced in this very room, but I could never imagine myself being one of them.

This week I'd searched for those spots in the house that made it unique. The markings on doorways showing how the children had grown, a name carved into a baseboard, and paintings on the walls. One room had a burn mark on the ceiling from a magic trick gone wrong.

The moon crept higher in the sky. I was not in any rush to get back despite my nerves over my upcoming meeting.

It took another hour for me to dust myself off, battle down the emotion that wanted to erupt, my eyes no longer filling with tears. This had been a home. It wasn't lost to the past; it had a future.

Not for him, but for me.

CHAPTER SIX

Today was "P Day"—Plans Day. All my sleepless nights, avoidance of a certain nameless, entitled asshole, and all the mascara I had put on had led me to this moment.

The evening before, I had presented to Mr. Killington's team under Dad's watchful eye. I was interrogated by men who had never even watched an HGTV show before. I answered questions I would bet money on they'd gotten off Google: *what to say when you want to sound like you know what you're talking about.* They'd have been better off actually reviewing the materials I had sent in advance.

I received the endorsement of Mr. Killington's assistant and financial advisor. Now either Mr. Killington would give his approval of my plan, or we'd be fired, face bankruptcy, lose any prestige my father had garnered after almost forty years, and squander any chance at my dream job.

No freaking pressure.

"Aren't you spruced up, Dad."

He straightened his tie, primping a bit for the camera. We had been texting all morning. Last-minute suggestions about the presentation, outfit ideas. The best tie for him (one that didn't have Philippe replicas on it), the sweater that would imbue me with authority. Everything had to be absolutely perfect.

My lucky suspenders were hidden underneath my favorite blue cardigan, holding in my beating heart, ensuring it didn't fly out of my chest.

"Still on the mend?" I slid my chair into place, adjusting the tilt of my iPad to get the angle just right.

"Practically back to normal."

"That's great." It was a relief to see him healthy, wearing actual clothes and not onesie pajamas, the glow back in his cheeks.

This job may have fallen into my lap, but I wanted it. It was mine. My training wheels had to be taken off at some point. Even if I fell flat on my face, it was time to learn and prove myself. "When do you think you'll be making it to the site, then?" I drummed my fingers on the table, not sure what I preferred his answer to be.

"Oh, I—" Dad's gaze drifted away from the camera to some spot I couldn't see. "Not soon. Some more recovering to do."

"Dad!" If he was still sick, maybe I shouldn't have left him. Why hadn't Betty called me? Maybe I—

"I'm fine, I'm fine—promise." He held his palms up as if to stop all my thoughts from running rampant. "But you are more than fine. I've seen all your drawings, your extensive lists"—he chuckled—"your contingency plans. You are beyond prepared. This is your baby." It may have been me being hopeful, but there seemed to be a hint of pride in his voice.

I scrubbed my hand across my heart, crashing into a dose of reality. "I appreciate that, but Mr. Killington hired you, not me. We're not the Price and Daughter firm."

"We'll go with Price and Price instead. If you do a good enough job, I'll even let you be the first Price." There was a flash of mischief on his face that warmed my chest.

"Not funny." A smile broke itself free. He always knew what to say when I was nervous.

"I'm sorry." He wiped the grin away—or tried to. The only person who thought Maurice Price was a comedian was Maurice Price. "But you truly have this. There's nothing left for me to do—other than admire your beautiful sketches and pat myself on the back for how well I trained you."

"Hopefully, I'm as humble as you in my old age." A flush crept up my skin. He'd always been effusive with praise, but that he wasn't coming spoke volumes of his trust in me.

"We can only hope, Bells, we can only hope. You don't need me there, taking credit for your brilliance."

I sucked in a breath, letting his words wash over me as they clashed with every doubt I had ever experienced. "And if I fail, we end up in debt, disgraced, never to work on another home again?"

"No idea where you get this tendency to exaggerate." He winked at me. "If that happens, you can blame me entirely. It'd be like the time when we lived in that impossibly small cabin. Think of all the father-and-daughter bonding we could do."

There were a lot of great memories from that year we had moved into a glorified log cabin, but I had also been seven. I groaned as the tightness in my nerves eased. I knew what we were waiting on, what he was distracting me from. The clock taunted me.

But I'd already allowed myself my moment of doubt a few nights ago.

The staff had been appropriately chagrined when they saw me for breakfast the next morning. Since then, there'd been no more mentions of the "sir" joining us or any new complaints about me overworking myself.

"*All* the blame?" I attempted to get comfortable, crossing and uncrossing my ankles, smoothing my hair, refusing to take another sip of water so I wouldn't need to suddenly go to the bathroom. There's nothing worse than being in a high-stress situation and needing to pee. Nothing.

"All of it. Make a doll with my face and stab it repeatedly." He emphasized his point by punching his hand.

Which made me picture another face I wanted to punch. "You've got yourself a deal."

"And how's Philippe?" The casual air of his voice gave away how he had been holding himself back.

"Wow, you waited five whole minutes before asking about your favorite child."

"Good—you realize your place."

I heaved a sigh, more for him than anything. "He's being well kept in a garage."

"And are you . . .?"

"Driving him around every few days, even though I don't go anywhere other than this decrepit estate, yes." The eye roll was genuine this time.

"I earn that father-of-the-year mug you made me every day." He raised it up, and I had to snort. I had painted it when I was six, and he still acted like it was the best gift anyone had ever given him, bringing it with us to every job.

The clock struck noon.

One of the grandfather clocks in the hallway clanged, my heart right along with it, just in case I wasn't aware, giving the moment an ominous feel.

Right on time, Mr. Killington filled the screen, seated in his boardroom. A few employees sat next to him on either side, all dressed in suits. Their stooped postures deferred to him in every way. Even their chairs seemed to be lower.

"Price," Mr. Killington barked, giving a perfect impression of his grandson. My primary goal was getting his approval, but a bonus would be for Mr. Killington to see the benefit of having Oliver vacate the premises. Immediately would be best.

"Good morning, sir," I began. "I'll start with our plans for the front foyer." I clicked to share my screen.

"Why is a woman talking? I didn't hire you—I hired Maurice Price. Price, talk."

And now I knew where his grandson got his charm. "Sir, I'm Bellamy Price, his daughter. I am on-site."

"And why isn't Maurice?" He inquired as if the people there would provide the answers, or my father would magically pop up in the boardroom. We were already failing to meet his exacting expectations. A fine sheet of sweat broke out on my forehead.

"We contacted your office multiple times, Mr. Killington. I'm getting over a hospital stay, but Bellamy has kept me appraised and gone through the designs with me. She has done an excellent job of bringing out the original highlights from the home. She has more experience than I did at her age, or that most do in this industry." Dad spoke in his quiet but firm tone. It usually worked, but this wasn't a typical client. "An exceptional eye to detail," he added.

"I'm paying a lot of money for this." Mr. Killington's gaze glanced away from the screen again. His features shifted as he seemed to receive confirmation. "And I'm paying for Maurice Price, not the unknown one."

I wish I could say that was the first time I'd heard something like that. My youth, weight and gender they all worked against me in these types of situations, no matter how dressed up I was or that I'd spent an hour trying to subdue my hair. I'd stand in front of a group of old white men, and they would always prefer another man. They'd never consider that a woman might be in charge, especially one that looked like me.

It had nothing to do with the quality of my work. All Mr. Killington cared about was the name behind it. Being able to brag to his friends as they sat on their yachts, headed to their private islands, that *the* Maurice Price had worked on his home.

"We shouldn't be paying Price prices then."

His threat was delivered with a bit of glee; clearly he thought he was the first one to make the joke.

Dad refused to back down. "There is no one better. She is who you want on your project. And you'll have the benefit of saying Bellamy Price restored your estate, which will only increase its value, I can promise you."

Silence spread. Mr. Killington appeared to weigh my father's words while I subtly wiped at the dust that had drifted into my eyes. The inside of this house required a power washing.

In view of the camera, Mr. Killington unlocked his arms and folded his hands on the table. "Fine, but I don't have time for this presentation. I have one question, Miss Price."

Sitting on my shaking hands, I gave a stiff nod.

Mr. Killington knocked once. "I'd like to see the plans for the west wing, which you have conveniently left out."

Crap, double crap. I had tried to use the blueprints to flesh out what Dad had worked on years ago, but there was no way to fake it. Not with the level of detail I had gone into with the rest of the mansion. Despite my frustration with the jerk formerly known as

"Beast," I couldn't force myself to invade his privacy and enter the west wing. The grief on his face as we'd stood outside the doors haunted me every time I considered it. This was what being a good person got me: screwed—and not in the fun way.

Before I could reply, Mr. Killington demanded for someone to "Get my grandson." The people in the surrounding room burst into action; a cell phone was pulled out, the rest murmuring in a rising panic while my hands shook all over again.

I'm embarrassed to admit I assumed they were contacting some other grandson whom I had never met and who had never tried to banish me from his home. I lived in that fantasy world for only a moment, but it was glorious. Then another box popped up, and there was Oliver, sitting in the study downstairs, glaring at the camera.

"Ollie—good—you are at the estate?"

"Yes."

It was touching to see he was as sociable with his family as he was with me.

"Excellent. This is what we are going to do. Ollie, you will oversee this restoration. To ensure that this project is going as planned and because of her"—his hand waved in what I had to assume was my direction—"inexperience, someone must command things."

No one spoke a word as my dream became hitched to the person who despised me most in this world. This was a nightmare, and I couldn't figure out how to wake up. We were going to be trapped together for the foreseeable future. There would be no getting rid of him.

"Ollie will provide my assistant with weekly—if, necessary, daily—updates."

I stared at the box containing Oliver's face, hoping to communicate he should back out, that surely his oversight was unnecessary. But nothing. As his grandfather shackled us together, he remained as stoic as ever.

"I'm not sure that is necessary." My voice cracked as I tried to be authoritative, but I also understood that Mr. Killington could cancel the project or, at minimum, my part in it.

"I very much think it is." His eyes narrowed at me. If the resemblance to Oliver hadn't been obvious before, it was too pronounced now. "You have a strict deadline—I will be hosting an event at the estate to celebrate the end of the summer."

The end of the summer? "That's only six months from now." My presentations had all included a projected timeline of one year. "I'm not sure—"

"I will not throw millions of dollars to an unknown without some guarantees."

It was difficult not to gulp. These types of jobs with extensive structural issues were expensive. If more damage was found once we began, which was almost guaranteed with the state of disrepair, it would easily extend any timetable by another six months to a year. There were few professionals who had the required experience with these heritage homes. Panic was rising in me at the idea of completing this project within six months.

"This also aligns with our discussions, Ollie. It's time you stopped hiding away and accepted your role in this company and this family."

Every person on this call who didn't have the last name Killington shifted uncomfortably in their seat.

Mr. Killington cleared his throat. When nothing happened, he cleared it again, tossing a pencil and hitting a man two seats down on his left.

The man shuddered before shuffling the pile of papers in front of him. "Mr. Oliver Killington, your grandfather, as you are aware, is in charge of your trust." He coughed, and a bead of sweat ran down his forehead. "You are required to do the following by your thirtieth birthday, September third of this year."

Good, in case Oliver had forgotten his own birthday. What *was* this family?

"You are required to accept an executive position in Killington Holdings and begin shadowing your grandfather, as well as establish a residence in the city. A timeline will be set to announce you as CEO.

"If you do not comply with these terms, you will only be eligible to receive a tenth of your remaining trust, in dividends, at the discretion of your grandfather." With a swipe of his sweaty forehead, the lackey glanced at Mr. Killington.

"I am throwing an end-of-summer dinner party the last week of August. The restoration will be completed, coinciding with the announcement of your role within the company, Oliver."

The pronouncement was met with silence. The panic wasn't rising—it was fully enveloping my body. But Oliver hadn't even twitched, as if he had been expecting this.

"I won't fix the stock value," Oliver finally responded.

Mr. Killington steamrolled forward, as if his grandson had never spoken. "Does that timeline present a problem for anyone?" His tone made it clear that no was not an option.

"We will have to pay a premium on materials in order to ensure that timeline," I hedged. It was the truth. I needed the cheap billionaire to help me out with this impossible deadline in order to complete everything in less than half the time that I needed.

"Forward all receipts to my office. They will be paid promptly. I will also add a bonus incentive if everything is finished on time, if not early, and to my standards."

I made one last attempt. "These projects are delicate, sir. It's often not until you dive in that the structural and underlying issues are revealed."

My father's eyebrows raised, and it wasn't at the thought of the money. I was committing to an almost impossible promise, setting myself and our business up for failure. That nightmare of ending up homeless and never working again felt like a real possibility.

But also, fuck Adrian Killington.

Mr. Killington rose to his full height, teaching me a thing or two about intimidation through a computer screen.

I held in my frustration. "Price Restoration is the best."

"Good. The details about the party will be forwarded once I receive the plans for the west wing." And with that, he was gone. A moment later, so was Oliver.

My dad and I were the only ones left. "Bells—" The concern was evident in his tone.

"It's fine, Dad. Money talks, and I won't be stingy with my estimates."

"I believe you can walk on water and are the most brilliant person in the world, the single best thing I've ever done in my life." I could hear it in his voice. There was a *but* coming. "But not even you can make the impossible happen."

My emotions were sliding back and forth from *What the heck did I do?* to *Fuck yeah, I can do this.* "I got us into this mess, it's on me to solve it."

"All for one, and one for all," Bl8z3 chimed in. It was still on my shit list, but I couldn't deny the advantage it would be to this project, and I needed every advantage I could get.

This would either be the greatest accomplishment of my life or blow everything up.

The only way forward was to break into the west wing and ignore Oliver's very specific instructions. Changing his mind seemed as impossible as the deadline I had been given.

The moment Dad signed off, I allowed one emotion to override the others. Anger. I was fucking furious at the audacity of Oliver to let himself become my unofficial boss for this project. Who did he think he was? After that disastrous almost-date, why would he even want to stay here?

The stakes had exponentially increased. Now he wasn't merely being difficult; he was impeding on my livelihood. Unacceptable. I was going to be the Bib's newest curator, and Oliver Killington would not stop me.

CHAPTER SEVEN

165 Days Until the Deadline

Storming out of my room, I made it to the study in record time. I twisted open the knob, without knocking, to find him still sitting there, glaring at his computer screen. "Oh joy, it's you."

"Could you be any more of an ass?"

"Please, Price, tell me how I've wronged you."

I tried to think calming thoughts, but the sight of him reclining in his leather chair, arms up, palms behind his head, flashing his forearms at me . . . I had never wanted to commit violence more.

"What are you doing? Why did you agree to oversee the restoration? You don't want me here, and you hate everything about this project. You're only going to hold things up."

"Just because I have zero interest in your HGTV show—"

"Do you see cameras anywhere?" I gestured around, even though a crew of camera people and producers would be impossible to miss, even for him.

"Fine." Oliver pushed out of the chair, letting it slam against the wall, and stalked over to me. "My grandfather owns this place and is fully aware of how desperately I want it. I have no choice."

We stood face-to-face, both of us breathing hard, my hair falling out of the barrette I had used to clip the straightening ironed strands back. Oliver's cheeks were ruddy, fists balled at his side. All I could see was red when it came to him; I had never been this irrationally angry in my life.

"Fine. Then tell me, why is this place so important to you?" The wisps of hair around my face fluttered in my exasperation.

"It doesn't matter." Oliver gave nothing away in that stoic manner of his. "If I don't do what he says, he'll kick me out. If I follow his rules and begin a miserable life as upper management, I'll be able to have this place but never see it with how busy I'll be."

"Sounds like a very warm family."

He brought his hands down to rest on the curved edge of the desk, knuckles turning white. "Sure."

"How would you describe him, then?" I worried my lip, unable to imagine his grandfather ever offering someone a hug.

"Stubborn. Driven." Oliver's voice reverted to that flat tone I associated with him, his hand tugging at the scruff of his beard.

"Even after your parents died?"

His shoulders stiffened, making me regret my words. "He gave the twins a home, something I'm not capable of. He's"—another breath—"he's done his best." His eyes narrowed on me, warning me from challenging him further. Clearly his sisters were a touchy subject.

What he hadn't learned about me yet was that I never backed down from a challenge. "There are a lot of ways to show you care."

Oliver scoffed, tilting his head to meet my gaze. "Like what?"

"Like apologizing when you snap at a person who has suffered through the world's most awkward dinner."

He rubbed at the back of his neck, avoiding my gaze. "I have to imagine there have been more unpleasant dinners than that."

"You want to keep doing this for six months?" I gestured between us.

Oliver squeezed the desk again before returning to his full height, head ducked to ensure our eyes caught. "We don't have a choice."

In the gray of his eyes, closer to the iris, I could almost see flecks of blue. "Fine."

He took a step toward me, his lips pressed together, slightly hidden by that stupid beard of his. Those gray eyes were inescapable as they bored into mine, examining all my layers in a way no one had before. It was unnerving.

My skin broke out in angry, fury-filled goose bumps.

"Then I guess we're stuck with each other."

164 Days Until the Deadline

I spent the evening spiraling through all my feelings. Mostly, a single sensation: rage.

Experienced it, let it flow through me and motivate me, but I refused to let it overwhelm me. Instead, I reread one of my favorite romance novels, curled up on the bed, returning to the safety of a story I adored, as two beloved characters fell in love, squeezing my heart in the best way. I was a romantic solely when it came to fictional relationships.

But tomorrow was a new day. Oliver did not get to ruin this opportunity for me.

The next morning, armed with my stack of stickies, I stalked around the mansion, marking pieces that would go directly to storage, for trash, and those that would need to be restored. It was tedious. Every vase, lamp, picture frame, and knickknack needed a tag. Which gave my brain space to stretch, breathe.

And yet it was still empty of any idea of how to convince Oliver to let me into the west wing.

A sparkle of laughter, a foreign sound in this house, made me glance around. Another laugh. I pressed my nose to the window facing the backyard, the sitting room already half covered in my stickies. The glass had been distorted by age, but I could just make out Nick outside. Her smile wide, she wore her standard outfit of overalls and a T-shirt.

I slid the pane open, needing to confirm what I was seeing. Oliver was with her, tossing a football, taking a step back after each arc of the ball through the air. He wasn't smiling, but there was an ease to his shoulders. It was off-putting, watching him out in the sunshine rather than sulking around the halls. I was too far away to hear what he and Nick were yelling back and forth, but it was nice to know not being mean to children was his asshole line.

There was a satisfaction to his movements—he was skilled; those articles had not lied. Watching him in his prime must have truly been something. He easily tossed the ball to Nick, each throw a perfect spiral whizzing through the air before it landed in her arms.

Oliver was still mostly a stranger to me. A stranger who, even I saw, could use a friend. I wrapped my arms around my middle; it was impossible not to recognize he had insulated himself from the world in this crumbling estate. His words were a defense mechanism to make sure I stayed far, far outside his walls, away from the west wing.

Nick caught the ball with a resounding smack as it made contact with her skin, before she sprinted past Oliver, spiking it on the ground, and throwing her arms up in triumph.

Inspiration had struck.

Ultimately, it took a lot less convincing than I had been expecting, which likely spoke to how badly they felt. But this was for all our benefit. I needed to get into the west wing, and I wasn't above guilting Rue, Ambrose, and Nick into conspiring with me. They all wanted the mansion restored too—the kitchen updated, a sewing room—and this was the only way for us all to get what we wanted.

Oliver strolled into the dining room, blinking rapidly as I sat at the table set for two. At my instruction, Nick had asked him to help with her homework over dinner. He peeked over his shoulder, and I couldn't blame his paranoia. I struggled to shut any more doors after our recent incident.

"I thought we should talk." My foot jiggled under the table as I waited for him to decide.

After a roll of his shoulders, Oliver took the seat next to me and glanced down at his mushroom risotto. "This is my favorite."

I silently gave thanks to Rue, tilting my head down, the full force of my smile aimed at my own plate. "Oh?" My voice broke. I was not one for subtlety.

"Price."

"Hmm?"

"What's this about?" He pointed his spoon at me, accusing me of wrongdoing like some sort of made-for-TV detective.

I smiled. "If we're going to be stuck here together, I thought there should be a peace offering."

"Meaning you asked Rue what my favorite meal was?"

"Hmm?" I shoved a bite of food in my mouth. I mean I had, but solely to butter him up, not because I actually cared if he enjoyed his dinner.

Oliver smirked, an eyebrow arching, before diving into his own plate.

The door to the butler's pantry swung open, wood cracking as it slammed against the wall, my coconspirators appearing. Both dressed in suits, Rue carrying a tray stacked high with cupcakes, and Ambrose playing the bagpipes. I didn't have many options at my disposal, so I'd work with what was available. The assignment had been to show Oliver the benefits of restoring the estate, and I had allowed them to decide, wrongly assuming it was the best course since they knew Oliver better than I ever could.

"May I present dessert?" Rue slid the tray in between us, pride brightening their face. "Red velvet with cream cheese topping. Though if I had the tools . . ." Rue let out an exaggerated sigh, eyes lifting to the ceiling as Bl8z3 played backup music to Ambrose's bagpipes. "I wanted to pipe them with liquor filling, but with my oven, I—" They let out a wail in time with the sound of the bagpipes.

I pressed my napkin to my lips, sneaking a horrified glance at Oliver for his reaction. There was a crinkle around his eyes I couldn't read, and his hands were hidden underneath the table. What had seemed like the perfect idea a half hour ago was quickly blowing up in my face.

"If only I had the precise tools to truly feed those I care about— oh!" Rue cried, and with the bagpipes, I had to stop myself from covering my ears, my shoulders rising. "Even these clothes, practically threadbare compared to what we could have with a proper tailoring room."

Rue stepped back, and my posture relaxed against the back of my chair.

But it still wasn't over. "If there is ceiling plaster in the food, my apologies."

Oliver started coughing, mid-bite, my palm rising to smack his back as Rue's jaw dropped, looking between me and their employer, raising their eyebrows as if to ask if that was too much. *You think?*

Once his risk of death was over and he took a sip of water, Oliver nodded to Rue, offering proof of life.

"Well, we'll leave you to it." Ambrose sucked in a deep breath before resuming his blaring tune as he and Rue exited the dining room, and none too soon. Maybe Oliver would understand their passion? Maybe he'd experienced a blackout?

"They're kidding about the ceiling plaster," Oliver said as he used his fork to dig through his meal.

I couldn't help myself. "If it makes you feel better, it presumably has been in your food for a while, what with the state of this place. You've probably built an immunity or something."

It was time for Act Two: Nick shuffled in, wearing what looked like a version of Rue's and Ambrose's suits, except that a pair of scissors had been taken to hers, poorly shortening the length, threads hanging at her ankles.

"I am but a young, pathetic child." Nick's voice was monotonous, almost robotic. What in the hell was she doing?

"This was not what your card said," I hissed. I had provided some suggested language, things for them to highlight. How was this supposed to convince Oliver of anything?

"Have you ever heard of method acting?" Nick whipped out a handheld fan with expertise, fluttering it, but it didn't improve her performance. "Without the restoration, I will be forced to join the circus, with my horse, and live the life of a nomad without a home.

And hope I never come across a witch"—she started waving a shaker of salt in the air with her other hand—"who would curse me to an eternity of—"

"Okay." I clapped. "I think the point was made. Thank you, Nick."

Oliver had his fist pressed to his jaw as the resident thespian gave a deep bow to every angle of the room before leaving with a final flourish.

He bent his head, but when his shoulders shuddered with laughter, I knew it was safe. This was going to work.

"All right, 'fess up." Oliver tilted his head to meet my gaze, lips parted.

"Funny you should ask." My iPad was hidden under the cloth placemat. Things hadn't gone exactly to plan, but I could adapt. "I'm almost ready to get started on the restoration. All that's left is—"

"No."

The rage would not win, nor would this stubborn man. "Listen, it doesn't matter how rich you are: magic and wishes can't hold this place together. This isn't about appearance; the structural integrity is at stake."

Oliver raked his fingers through his hair, yanking it out of the ponytail, leaving it to fall around his shoulders. "We've been through this."

"Yesterday changed that."

"Why can't you leave it alone?" The gravel in his voice caused my stomach to flip over.

It wasn't so simple as "I'm wrong and he's right." This was something I had to do. Otherwise, I'd be replaced by another firm, someone less competent, who would never even consider his feelings or how special this place was.

I felt for him, but not in place of my self-preservation. This was my life, my career on the line. I was sick of tiptoeing around him, catering to each and every whim of the Young Asshole.

"You heard your grandfather—this is my business." My fingers splayed on the screen of my iPad protectively as I hardened my voice. Frustration was filling me. He'd made us enemies—it had never had to be this way.

"Price."

I stood up, the feet of the chair squeaking, catching on all the grooves worn in the floor, the opposite of the smooth movement I'd intended. "It's not fair of you to set me up for failure. My life, my family, my future depends on this." My fists clenched at my sides. I was frustrated with him, and angry at his grandfather for putting me in this situation, but walking away would solve nothing.

"It's not fair? *This* is not fair?" Oliver gripped the arms of his chair, all of him wild—his poorly maintained beard, the hair he'd finally let loose, the way his gaze met mine. "Go, then. If the wing is so important, don't let me stop you."

Snatching up my iPad, I marched out of the room before he could change his mind. Forward was the only direction I ever lived my life in.

The music cut off the moment I left, silence following me as I made my way through the front foyer, my footsteps echoing off the hardwood. Momentum propelled me to the west wing. With only a nudge on the handle, the doors swung open.

This section had clearly been sealed off longer than the rest of the estate. The musty smell was overwhelming; my eyes watered as I flickered the light switch. Nothing, not even the buzz of electricity. Reaching into my back pocket, I pulled out my cell phone, the flashlight offering some light in the bleakness.

The wing continued along another hallway with multiple doors on either side. The few windows were more than dirty—they were filthy, blocking the sunshine from coming in.

The first door on the left opened with a twist of a knob, and then I knew—*I* was the asshole.

It was a child's playroom: dust covering the collection of toys, the older television in the corner—it was obvious. There was none of the fancy furniture found in the rest of the estate.

This was the family area, in contrast to the museum atmosphere in the majority of the mansion. Whoever had lived here last, this was where they had raised their family. Family photos hung on the wall, souvenirs from trips—all the personal items that make up a life. I might as well have walked into a different home altogether.

And I had a not-so-sneaking suspicion I knew who had lived here.

My heart sank when everything was confirmed by the photographs in the next rooms: Oliver's sisters' bedrooms. Their contrasting personalities had never been more obvious—the different posters on the walls; one room painted in a yellow that had now dulled, the other in a navy blue. Both rooms overflowing with family photos, snapshots with friends, movie stubs, and concert tickets. I swiped at my eyes, forcing myself to keep going.

Dust layered every piece of furniture and knickknack as I took shallow breaths. Things weren't preserved here, like in the rest of the house. This place had been locked up tight, meant to never be seen again. Mr. Killington must have known this was the reason Oliver had blocked me from entering.

I dug my fingernails into my palms.

The next door I chose led to Oliver's room, and my heart sank further. A full bed that his feet would hang off of now was pushed against the wall, football trophies lining the bookcases, books dispersed over every available surface. But what really made my chest hurt were the snapshots. Oliver as a child with his parents and his sisters, Oliver with his arms around his teammates. Signed jerseys hung on the walls. A book with a piece of paper sticking out of it was waiting for him to pick it up and finish it.

The home he'd criticized me for never having, he'd had. I was standing in it. This was his safe place. And it had been ripped from him. Every suspicion I'd had about why he'd stayed here at the estate was confirmed tenfold over.

"Still seem unfair?" The quiet way he spoke was worse than him yelling; his fists were shoved into his front pockets, shoulders hunched. I hated that I had brought him this pain.

My voice caught in my throat. An apology wasn't enough, but it was all I had. "I'm sorry. I am. This is none of my business." I shifted, plucking at my left suspender, desperate to be anywhere else, wishing I had just tried to make something up in my sketches.

"It's not." He stepped closer. "Leave."

This time, the banishment was different—there was no temptation to smile and push back at him. All I wanted was to disappear through the floor.

He tilted his head down and pointed at my chest, where I still hugged the frame.

"Oh." I wiped the glass with a corner of my T-shirt before setting it on the desk.

He ventured farther into the room, picking up the frame. A ring of dust marked where it had sat undisturbed until I had barged in.

I watched him as he studied the room he couldn't have been in for close to a decade. It seemed wrong to leave him alone, something compelling me to stay.

"I had to move into another suite during my recovery, and I never came back." His voice was thick with emotion. His recovery after the car accident that had killed his parents and ended his sports career. He'd been here the entire time, hiding from the world.

The light from my phone was barely sufficient in the large space, thick dust hanging in the air from our movements. He was mostly a hulking shadow, reminiscent of how he appeared on my first night.

"In the city, we'd be in school, my parents working, most of my free time taken up by football, but here we were all together. Life seemed to slow down, frozen in these perfect moments, even if we were only visited for a couple weeks or a random weekend."

"It felt like home," I said, but I wasn't sure he'd heard me as he scanned the space, soaking it all in.

"It seems irrational to preserve this place when they won't come back. I've accepted that they died and my part in that. I've gone to therapy, all kinds of therapy. But I'm—"

"Stuck?" I offered.

The blot that was his head nodded. "Cursed people don't deserve happiness. And they don't get to move forward."

CHAPTER EIGHT

I stepped closer to Oliver. "What do you mean, you're cursed?"

He shifted, hands skimming a bookcase, and I let him have this moment, to make it easier in whatever way I could.

When I pictured a home, I envisioned memories that were filled with joy. I had always believed I restored people's happiness, their past, while giving them a place for their future.

But not every memory was happy. There were deep aches. In the same way, it hurt every time I packed and unpacked my belongings, meager as they were. This was my life. My legacy would be other people's homes and their restored memories.

"It doesn't matter." His voice lacked the firmness of his words. My palm reached out but didn't close the distance between us.

"You don't have to talk about it, but you can. I'm a random person who trespassed into your home. No judgment, no consequences." I held my hands up as if to say I was unarmed. "And one day, I'm going to leave. You're never going to have to see me again."

He swallowed. "Thanks." Even stranger, it sounded like he meant it. He sat on the edge of the bed. "Can we sit here for a while?"

No one was more surprised than me. Maybe it was my guilt, but I collapsed on the floor, my back pressed against the bed, next to his legs, which he had spread out. I didn't have to like him to feel empathy for him.

I reached for my iPad, drawing out the layout of the west wing, making notes about my observations, priority lists, relaxing into the familiarity of it.

We sat surrounded by his memories as I roughed out an outline, marking different places I hadn't been sure of based on the blueprints, noting measurements I'd need to take. I wouldn't be able to complete it until I saw everything with the thick curtains opened to the sunlight, but it was a start.

"What are you're doing?"

I glanced up. His focus was on the screen. He shifted to the floor to sit next to me. His voice was soft, the anger gone. He wasn't apologetic, but an apology was unnecessary. The person who should apologize was his grandfather, for putting us in this situation.

I walked Oliver through my process, explaining how I designated doors, windows, support beams. How I made notes of things I would have to confirm with the contractor.

He asked a few questions, but mostly he nodded along. "You're good at this."

"Oh, um . . ." I had no idea what to do with a compliment from him, as my cheeks heated.

"Are you this good at drawing other things?"

I let out a small laugh, relieved to be on solid ground. "Not at all. This is concrete lines, drawing what I can see. One of my best friends is a professional. His art is all about imagination, soft lines. I might as well be drawing stick figures compared to him."

"Ah." The screen of my iPad illuminated Oliver's face, but it offered little. I was desperate to see anything, though he never revealed much, still in hiding.

"You must be excellent at playing poker." I blurted out.

His gaze met mine for the first time since he'd entered the room. "Not random at all."

Fine, but he was always so circumspect. "It made complete sense to me."

He snorted. "I'm not going to ask."

"You're smart, Killington. I'll give you that."

"You didn't even wince when you said that." His shoulder nudged mine, knocking my pencil off course for a moment.

"Duh, because I'd be an amazing poker player, too."

"Don't test that theory." His thumb brushed along his lip. "So, do people typically stay at the house when you're working on it?"

"Nope, most properties are already vacant, or the owners use the project as an opportunity for an extended vacation. Lifestyles of the rich and famous."

"Ah."

While lightly sketching, I waited for him to tell me he was going to leave. The door was open, figuratively and in reality. There were a million reasons for him to cut his losses, including the wormhole of grief I had forced him to open. It would only get worse as the project went on.

"But they miss out on all the fun parts, like knocking down walls, smashing things." I had no idea why I was still talking; it would be best for both of us if he left.

"Great." There wasn't an ounce of malice in his voice this time. His head tilted back, leaning against the mattress, gaze burning through me.

I wouldn't exactly call it comfortable between us, but I wasn't experiencing an inclination to commit violence against him or scream, so it was something akin to progress.

"I wouldn't mind smashing some things," he offered.

The corners of my mouth twitched. "I think I can make that happen."

157 Days Until the Deadline

It was here. The first day of the restoration.

In the week since I'd first explored Oliver's secrets, I had submitted my plans for the west wing, received the final approvals I needed, and moved forward with hiring. It had been a whirlwind, and I was only getting started. But the mood in the estate had shifted as everyone prepared for the oncoming storm.

Rue seemed to derive the most pleasure from the excitement, leaving me a rose on my breakfast tray. Rue, Ambrose, and I had reached a settlement of sorts, where I protested but let them take care of my essentials, as if I were a guest at a hotel when they gave me no other choice. It was the strangest bed-and-breakfast I'd ever stayed at. I refused to get used to it, but it was lovely being taken care of.

Standing in front of my mirror, I stuck the stem of the rose through my ponytail, straightening my suspenders, ready for what the day would bring. I could do this—knock it out of the park even.

"Bellamy!"

The moment I stepped out the front door, Jeff, the sole contractor I'd considered, pulled me into a hug.

"You weren't joking when you said this place was a mess. I kind of hoped you were sending me pictures you found on Google, but this is . . . wow." He snatched the baseball cap off his head, curling the brim, before shoving it on backward.

Jeff was ten years older than me and had been a staple for many of Dad's projects for almost that long. He enjoyed the messier structures and leaped in without fear. Dressed in his typical vintage comic-book shirt and jeans, he was an inconspicuous expert in nineteenth-century architecture.

"You are such a weirdo. You're happy this place is a mess." I laughed, pleased he wasn't scared off yet.

I'd met Jeff the summer before college. It was his first time being hired as the contractor rather than merely a member of the crew, and he'd always appreciated that Dad took a chance on him. That was his "it" project, his Killington Estate. All his baseball caps had ended up bent out of shape, curved to extremes, broken pencils surrounding him wherever he stood, but the Queen Anne–style mansion sitting at the end of the bay ended up better than any of us had imagined.

"The bigger the mess, the better the reveal at the end. This is going to be fun." He rubbed his palms together, muscles flexing, his arms dusted with sandy-brown hair. "Come on—walk me through before the rest of the crew gets here. Knowing you, a million to-do lists are already prepared."

He had seen much of it because of the drawings and photos I'd previously sent him, but like me, he had to experience the space to truly form his plan. Being in a place, breathing it, was always different. It was part of the reason Dad always preferred to live on-site.

"What are you thinking—a week to empty, and then jump immediately into gutting?"

The wiring, ancient copper plumbing, and lead paint all required removal and replacing. "Exactly." I nodded.

"And the deadline?"

Oh, that little insignificant thing? I coughed as we wandered back outside to wait for the rest of the crew to arrive. "I told you—the last week of August."

He whistled. "Even with the budget we have, that's going to be tight."

"Do what you can, but this is a make-it-or-break-it project for me." I tugged on my suspenders as my heartbeat increased.

"So those rumors about you leaving the restoration world to take that cozy museum job are true?" His shoulder shoved mine as we started unloading rolls of tape and his toolbox from his truck.

I shook my head. "There's no job."

"*Yet.* Your phone will never stop ringing if this goes to plan. Most people would be scared off by a project like this."

I rolled my eyes as he stalked off to welcome the crew as they arrived. Many were people we had worked with before, or locals hired based on recommendations. It was almost double the number of our typical crew, but because of the size of the house and the deadline, we had no other option.

As I greeted familiar faces and introduced myself to the newbies, the chatter died down to whispers, everyone turning in the same direction.

I glanced around, trying to figure out what the cause was, when the breath left my body.

Oliver jogged down the paver driveway, sweat dripping down his face, hair clinging to his scalp, his gray T-shirt soaked to the roundness of his stomach. Black jogging pants clung to those thighs. Mouth suddenly dry, I licked my lips.

Then the whispers reached me.

"It's him, the lost Killington heir."

"I heard he was disfigured. That's why he never goes out in public."

"Heard he sits around counting his money, enjoys going swimming in it."

"My sister told me about a family curse."

"All right." I clapped my hands as loudly as I could. "You're here for this house. No one's 'lost' here, nor should anything or anyone else be your concern. This project is going to be tough, especially with the time frame we have. Get your assignments from Jeff. Let's get going on emptying this place out so the real fun can begin."

It took another moment, a few stragglers still staring as Oliver made his way to me, blatantly ignoring the looks, his face flushed. He favored his right leg, not exactly limping, but as he got closer, I could see his forehead was wrinkled in discomfort.

"Price." He was breathing heavily, his chest expanding with every inhale. Fingers massaging his left thigh muscle, he glanced around as the crew shifted nearby. They had returned to work, but many were still openly gawking at Oliver, the whispering more subdued but still there.

I needed to get his mind off it. "Killington."

He blinked rapidly, his gaze meeting mine again, gray eyes focused. "So, where are the cameras?"

I bit my lip hard to hold back a smile. "Still not an HGTV show."

"Probably for the best. This is a lot of people."

"It is. How was your run?"

Oliver grabbed his collar, scrubbing away some of the sweat from his face, leaving behind a ruddy complexion. My gaze tracked the skin he exposed.

"It was more of a power walk. Been a while." It was impossible to miss the way some of the sadness in his eyes, a constant, seemed lighter. "I wanted to stretch my legs, get out of the house."

"That's, uh . . . good."

"How many pairs of suspenders do you own?" His gaze carved up from my waist to my shoulders, skimming as if his hands were on me.

I shivered in the breeze, regretting not bringing a sweater with me. "Enough."

"Mm."

"Well, this has been riveting, but I should . . ." I jerked my head to the house in a chill manner, the sounds from the crew flooding back to my ears. For a moment, it had felt like we were the only two people here, the only two people in the world.

"Yeah, I should—" Oliver reached for my shoulder, and goose bumps broke out across my skin. His hand brushed the fabric of my T-shirt before pulling away, holding a "petal." He whispered the word, cupping the red petal in his palm before flicking it onto the grass.

"Oh, thanks." I drew the rose tighter into my ponytail, spinning away before the flush and embarrassment overtook my body.

I ended up not needing the sweater, sweat building under my shirt, arms aching as I carried boxes, hauling away items meant for the large dumpster. The March New York air had a chill to it, but all of us were too busy to notice. Rue and Ambrose had set up a hydration station, which Nick was in charge of.

Rue directed the boxing up of the kitchen, taking one worry off my shoulders. The fine china alone would take a day to properly wrap up and another to store.

Ambrose had been running around demanding everyone be gentle with the antiques. When I suggested he ensure everything was properly packed in the truck for storage, he leaped at the chance.

I stood off to the side, watching my dream happening. My project, my plans. This would work—it was working.

"Hello?"

A car door slammed, and a tall, gangly man stood at the threshold of the estate. His suit was ill-fitting, hair needing a trim or something for that cowlick. He jumped quickly out of the way when Jeff treaded by lifting an end table I was eager to get my hands on to sand and stain.

"Hi, can I help you?" It was wrong to judge. I wasn't exactly dressed to impress, wearing a pair of jeans and an oversized T-shirt with paint splotches from more than one project, underneath my lucky suspenders.

"You've got to be kidding me." Oliver perched behind my shoulder.

I glanced back. "You know him?"

"My cousin," Oliver growled out, prickling my skin. "Carter, what are you doing here?"

I shifted out of the way, just in time, as Cousin Carter barreled toward Oliver, yanking him into a hug that Oliver didn't return, arms limp at his sides. "Can't I visit my favorite cousin?"

"I haven't seen you in eight years, which means Adrian sent you."

I was glued to the spot, fascinated, observing Oliver interact with someone who didn't call him sir.

"He might have suggested a visit, but it's been a long time. Too long—I mean, the last time I saw you was . . ." Cousin Carter had a frenetic energy: bouncing on the balls of his feet and trying to brush back his hair, which had too much gel in it. "When was it? I'm trying to place it. Was it that Christmas party?"

"No."

"The—" Cousin Carter snapped his fingers. "There was Sally's party. I mean, I wasn't invited, but I heard all about it and, um, I felt like I was there and—"

"No. Obviously not."

"Wait, it was the funeral." Cousin Carter sighed in satisfaction until the realization of what he'd just said broke across his face. I took a step forward, but Oliver stopped me, finger looped around the back of my suspender, holding me in place.

Oliver slicked back his sweat-soaked hair. "Did you come to help with the construction?"

"Oh, I'm not dressed for that, not at all. But I can't tell you how surprised I am to find you with a girlfriend. Hiding away in your love palace, I see. Smart, very smart. Keeping out of the eyes of the paparazzi, while you two . . ." He made an obscene gesture with his hands that was somehow less insulting because of how completely awkward he was.

It wasn't until Carter's eyes landed on me that I realized who he was talking about. A snort erupted from my mouth at the thought of Oliver and me getting along enough to date, or to two-hand gesture. "Oh no, no, no." I shook my head, giggling uncontrollably. "No, no, no."

"Maybe say 'no' one more time," Oliver grumbled.

I didn't peek at him, aware of his annoyance at the very idea of dating me. Could two people be less compatible?

"Oh, sorry." Carter glanced between Oliver and me, brows knitting together as his gaze shifted between us. "But it seems like things are going well, so I'll get out of your hair."

Oliver grabbed a box from a crew member who was relieved to have the weight lifted, before thrusting it at Carter. "You're not going anywhere until after you've helped. Don't want to give the appearance that you came here to spy on me."

Carter's face flushed with guilt. "Me? No, I could never, would never—"

"Save it, Carter."

The initial intrigue of watching Oliver interact with his family was crushed. He'd been all alone in this house, his family abandoning him to it. I didn't blame him for the way he stood tall, using the inches he had over his already tall cousin to show who was in charge here, calling Carter and his impure intentions out.

The way Carter's knees were shaking, it wouldn't take much for him to say "sir." "I lack upper-body strength. My mom says . . ."

Oliver didn't even blink.

"Too much, too much—understood. Maybe we can talk about what's going on with the stock. Do you know anything about the new investment? Because if things aren't going to turn around, do you think maybe I should cash out or, you know, buy in more, or should I—"

Oliver crossed his arms, committing to a stare down that appeared to be effective on everyone else but me.

"At least introduce me to Price, the man in charge?" Carter's eyes drifted to the crew working around us.

Oliver lunged toward his cousin, fists clenched, my arm blocking him from—well, whatever he had planned.

"Easy there." I thrust out my free hand toward the mess of limbs in a suit. "I'm Bellamy Price. It's, er, pleasant to meet you, Cousin Carter."

"Oh." Carter fumbled with the box he was still holding as he attempted to offer me his hand and failed. "I'm Carter. Are you related to the person running this show?"

I held the snark back. "I'm in charge. Was there something you wanted?" His jaw dropped, staring at the curve of my stomach, in the familiar way that screamed I didn't fit the idea he had in his mind of the person who should run this project—too female and too fat. After so many minor slights, each new one hurt a little less.

But I didn't have time to humor Cousin Carter, who staggered under the weight of the box and Oliver's scowl.

It was time to return to my task list, check in with Jeff, and see if we were on track for the day.

"Don't you want to hear the story of how Oliver and I are related?"

Not really, no. "Uh . . ."

"My grandfather is his grandmother's brother," Oliver said flatly. "They despise each other. See? Story done."

This time, I didn't hold back my smile as I faced Oliver, his gaze smoldering; I needed to locate where that hydration station was.

"Well." Carter coughed as neither of us made a move to take the box that was too heavy for him. "In its simplest form, yes."

"Great. Well, thanks for stopping by. I have about fifty places I need to be right now." I swiped the sweat off my brow; my muscles had been glad for the break, but the day wasn't even half over yet.

"Right, of course. Very important. I have had similar experiences. I don't have an official title, but I've done many favors for Uncle Adrian, and any day now he's . . ." Carter trailed off, distracted by all the surrounding chaos, still standing in the middle of it all.

"Carter." I clapped my hands in an effort to bring him around. Oliver grabbed my shoulders, nudging me out of the way as one of the couches was removed.

"Yes, uh, Uncle Adrian wanted me to thank you for sending over the drawings of the west wing."

I was tempted to drop that heavy box on Cousin Carter's head. Oliver's fingers pulled away like he had been burned.

"This has been enlightening, Carter, but I should get this place emptied so the construction can begin."

Carter aggressively nodded, the bravado of a man who had no idea what he was talking about but was going to fake it until he made it. "Oh, of course. I'm sure there's much to do."

"There is, so go drop the box off or give it to someone who will."

Carter was all too willing to shove the box at Oliver, and I was so close to making my escape. But it seemed our gathering had attracted the Oliver Shits Pure Gold Gang.

CHAPTER NINE

"Sir, what are you doing?" Ambrose asked, grabbing the box from Oliver, almost yanking it away.

"Helping." Oliver's brows knit together.

I laughed as I watched two grown men fight over who would carry the box. Dad always said the first day speaks to how well the project goes. The chaotic energy confirmed I was going to be on my toes.

Oliver's biceps bulged as he relented. "I want to help."

"Of course, sir, but you shouldn't have to." Ambrose swept past us, heading to the truck.

"I backed up my servers in case there were any electrical hiccups, and did some checks of the estate's systems I am connected to. I will email you the results, Ms. Price." Bl8z3 sounded proud. It wasn't worth mentioning that I hadn't shared my email address.

I bit my lip while Carter spun in a circle, eyes wide as he hunted for that bodiless voice that seemed to come from everywhere and nowhere all at once.

"The kitchen is coming along, about halfway packed, I'd say. This crew is efficient," Rue offered while easing Carter out of the way.

"I'm happy to offer some advice. I recently moved into my first apartment." Carter's proposal was ignored.

"Ms. Price is allowing me to pick all the new appliances. Anything I want." Glee brightened Rue's face as they bragged to Ambrose. His idea of casual wear appeared to be an untucked dress shirt and khakis, all ironed to perfection.

"I'm getting my tailoring room," Ambrose boasted right back.

"Sorry, sewing machines do nothing for me. But an industrial fridge? It is going to be wonderful. And a new stand mixer that won't have wires poking out of the bottom!"

"This place might no longer be a fire hazard." Bl8z3 brought us back to reality.

"Well, it's a long drive to the city. You might want to get going," Oliver reminded Carter, then hoisted another box from the pile in the foyer.

Ambrose yanked it out of his hands, marching off with a glare, daring Oliver to try it again.

"I thought you wanted Carter to help," I tried to whisper as a giggle circled my chest.

"Then I realized he'd have to stay the night," he hissed back, his eyes daring me to contradict him. Which was tempting, but I didn't want Cousin Carter to stay any longer either.

Teeth pressed to my lips, hard, I faced Carter. "Appreciate the offer, but I think we have it handled."

Carter puffed out his chest. "Always happy to provide my expertise."

"I'm sure you are," Oliver grumbled.

"Drive safe." I waved at Carter as Rue and Ambrose started another debate over who had more power concerning the reconstruction, ambling back toward the kitchen.

Oliver cleared his throat. "I still reserve the right to banish you."

I nodded sagely. "Of course."

"Glad we have that settled." He stalked off.

I stood there for another moment. "Asshole," I muttered despite my smile.

148 Days Until the Deadline

"Are you sure I shouldn't stay?"

Jeff sighed. "There's no reason. This is the most dangerous period, as your extensive list pointed out, while we figure out what this beauty is hiding under all that fancy wallpaper." He was much too eager, palms rubbing together.

I opened my mouth.

"Which I will protect as if it were my child. I've heard all your lectures about the importance of preserving the original wallpaper. You go do your job—find some fabulous period furniture—and let me do mine." Jeff knocked on his hard hat.

With so many bodies inside the house, he was right, I would only get in their way. But this was *my* project. What if something went wrong? What if there was an emergency?

"Fine, but I'm a phone call away. If anything major comes up—"

Jeff raised his palm. "I promise."

"All right." I opened Philippe's door. "If you're sure."

"Oh, one more thing."

With my body halfway in the car, I hopped back out. Ready for whatever.

"There's someone else that needs to go with you. The estate staff are doing other things today, but there's one other liability I can't have in the house."

"Jeff, no." I knew what was coming even before Oliver strolled into the garage, shoulders clenched almost to his ears, clearly as thrilled as I was about this turn of events.

"Well, I guess this wasn't your idea." Oliver's eyes rolled over me as I clutched the doorframe, unable to decide if I wanted to get out of the car or back into it. "Nice suspenders."

"You have nothing else to do today?" It would be truly pushing my professional abilities to spend a day alone with him.

"I thought I was supposed to be observing you." Oliver leaned over the roof of the car, as if daring me.

"I didn't realize you wanted to be your grandfather's lackey."

Jeff coughed, reminding us we weren't alone. "Well, on that friendly note, I'm off to go break some shit."

Oliver opened his mouth.

I rolled my eyes. Every occasion when we had been alone together had been a disaster. All I craved was to listen to Taylor Swift and pretend I had the day off, not think about what was going on at the house without me. "He's just saying that. We talked about this—ripping it down to the studs in a few places so we can figure out what we're working with." I climbed into the car fully. "It's part of the process."

Oliver stiffly nodded, opening the passenger door. After one final glance back at the estate, he removed the messenger bag he had slung across his chest, sliding into the passenger seat. "So where are we going?"

I pressed my forehead to the steering wheel. "How were you convinced to do this?"

"Someone might have told me it was a good idea to get out of the house, especially if I'm considering a job in the city."

"Ah, Rue, huh?" I was going to refer to the chef as "the meddler" soon. Though I did agree with their logic, Oliver slowly venturing in the world would probably be an easier adjustment than being dropped, cold turkey, into a job at his family's empire. "Very persuasive when they want to be."

"Yeah." Oliver rubbed his hands on his thighs.

While shoving him out of a moving car was tempting, I took pity on him. Something about him felt a little less defensive today. "I'm going to a warehouse about two hours away. They have historic furniture and replicas. The George II armchairs alone are worth the drive."

"Will there be many people there?"

A chuckle escaped as I pushed the key into the ignition, listening to the hum of the engine as it flipped over. I was too used to boring people with my love of antiques. "I'd be surprised to see anyone else except us and the owner. Trust me, this is a niche place. They mostly do online sales."

Oliver clutched at his beard, fingers fluttering.

"Big open space," I continued. "No one else. And you can wander by yourself or stay outside. The road it's on isn't even paved—very off the beaten path—but the owner makes decent coffee."

Oliver still wouldn't glance at me.

"Or you don't have to come at all. I could drop you off somewhere."

We remained in the garage, car running, the driveway leading to the world beyond in front of us. The sounds of the house were muffled, but there. And we were in between; in between all the action, in between a choice. For once, I didn't flick on the radio to fill the silence.

Oliver's hand lifted, hanging in the air, maybe to open the door again. Instead, he stretched, clicking his seat belt in place before reaching over and somehow gripping my entire thigh, the heat from his large palm searing me through my jeans.

"I haven't been to many places in the past few years. And when I have, I tend to get a reaction like the first day the crew showed up—plus cameras. I prefer to prepare myself for what to expect."

He started to remove his hand, but I clasped his fingers with mine. "If you change your mind and want to leave, say the word."

His skin was soft, and goose bumps broke out across my own as our hands hovered midair between us. His eyes widened and his palm shook slightly when his fingers enveloped mine. It wasn't a handshake, but it was something. Something was happening here, but I couldn't name it and didn't know how to read his expression as his gaze drifted from our hands back to meet mine.

And then we untangled. I shifted my hands to the steering wheel, clutching it for a moment until my knuckles went white, before putting Philippe in drive and pulling out.

"No petals in your hair today?"

I smoothed out my ponytail; already a couple of strands had gotten loose. "Didn't think it would stay in with all the driving."

It sounded like he said, "A shame," but he faced toward the window.

"So, you're considering the job with your grandfather?"

He shrugged. "Someone reminded me it's time to stop living in the past."

"Rue again?"

"No." He shuffled his legs, nervous energy filling the car. "You."

That was the last answer I'd been expecting. I glanced at him, to find him staring right back.

"Eyes on the road," he ordered without any bite.

"Yeah, yeah."

There was a future for him in a management position.

"Any thoughts on the reconstruction so far?" I was partially hunting for a compliment, but I was also honestly curious.

"Can we not talk about the house?" He rubbed at his thigh, legs jiggling.

"Okay, let's play a game."

"Can't we drive in silence?" His arm brushed mine, maybe by accident or on purpose, and every part of my body lit up. Even my appendix began doing a strange thing. Stupid, unnecessary organ.

"You're the one who wanted to come along. It'll be fun. I know that's a foreign concept." His elbow bumped into mine again. "We'll have a rule. Any question you ask, I have to answer. Same goes for you too."

"Why would I care what your response is?" His retort was all aloof and chill.

And he was back to making me want to hit him. "Because we still have over an hour in this car, and I can't stand silence."

"Would never have guessed."

I huffed out a breath. I was going to count down the seconds until we arrived.

"Fine. But I go first," Sir Stubborn announced.

"Ask away." I gestured for him to continue.

"What got you into house restorations?"

"You mean how did I, a sad, homeless girl, get involved in restoring homes?" Okay, so maybe I was still feeling defensive. But could you blame me?

He let out a huff. "Are you passing on the question?"

"It's how I grew up. I enjoy imagining all the happy memories, the people who lived there, the people who will live there in the future. I like to think I'm helping give them a place to build more memories."

"You never wanted to do anything else?" His voice rose an octave, as if I'd surprised him. Why had I started this when I couldn't see his face?

"My dad tried to get me to take internships in high school and college, but I hated sitting at a desk. I had options, a choice, and I made it."

His fingers flexed, fluttering on his thighs. "What's that like?"

My heart gave a squeeze, knowing how lucky I was to have Dad, even if our life wasn't perfect. I couldn't imagine love being this conditional thing, like it seemed for the Killingtons. "Nope, that was your question—no cheating."

"Wait, don't I have to answer too?" It meant something that he was willing.

"I'm not that cruel. You have time to make your decision, you have a choice, take it." I was interested in what his plans were with his grandfather's ultimatum, but not to torture him. His family did that all on their own.

Oliver hummed under his breath.

I racked my brain, blurting out the first question that came to my mind. "Are you dating anyone?" I asked with complete nonchalance and lack of interest. This was a game, after all. I wanted to stump him. Instead, now I was desperate to jump out of the moving automobile I was driving, wishing I could take the words back.

"Yes, I kidnap them. Haven't you discovered the dungeon yet?"

"Excuse me?" Somehow, I didn't jerk the car into the next lane.

"What does this have to do with anything?" Apparently Mr. Gruff Hostility had never left.

"Just making conversation." Think. Think. "Forget it—then I don't have to answer either." Which was for the best.

I fiddled with the stereo; my innocent curiosity had pushed things too far.

"I told you: no one comes to visit me. Living as a recluse isn't exactly something that encourages dating. I'm not exactly a catch."

"No one?" I squeaked.

"Yes, it's pathetic. You don't have to tell me." He shifted to lean his shoulder against the passenger door.

"Hey." My hand hung in the air, hovering, before I returned it to the steering wheel. "I don't think you're pathetic. It's just surprising because, you know, you look like you, and if you wanted to be with someone . . . It just makes me sad you've been alone." Word vomit all over the car. My entire body cringed.

"Bigfoot, that's what I resemble."

I had the world's biggest mouth, and I'd had to learn not to shout at Finn every time he asked how things were progressing with my roommate when I called to check in with him and Sebastian. "Listening in on my phone calls?"

He sniffed. "The house isn't that big."

Liar. "It's a mansion."

"All right," Oliver interrupted. "So, there are Bigfoot aficionados I should attract?"

"Bigfoot wasn't fair." I wracked my brain for a better comparison that wouldn't show my hand or the feeling in my stomach. I could, objectively, find him handsome while still not being able to stand him.

"Are you calling me attractive?" His tone was flat.

"Your word choice." Probably mine too, but subtlety was my middle name.

He hummed, my body vibrating to the same tune as I shifted in my seat. "You have to answer too," he reminded me.

"I'm single." A rush twirled within me before plummeting, leaving my palms sweaty and my stomach a mess. Why had I agreed to any of this? "All right, next question."

"That's it?"

I flicked at his thigh. My fingers went tingly at the contact.

"It's your fault for answering more than was asked." He didn't need to hear about my ex.

"Thank you, *Law and Order*."

"Oh, so *that* show you watch?" Of course. Can't check out one of the best film trilogies ever made, but *Law and Order* he's seen.

"I had to. The lawyers required it when they did an episode based on me." His dry reply made my stomach sink.

Crap, I had heard about that. I was always saying the wrong thing around him—mostly unintentionally. The few times it had been intentional, he'd deserved it.

"Nothing sends you to therapy faster than having a popular show accuse you of murdering your parents." Resentment filled the car.

"But wasn't the guy on the show found not guilty?" I had seen the episode years ago, never connecting it with the man next to me until now.

"Yeah, after paying off the jury. Screams innocence."

"Oh." I was doing great with this game.

"It's fine." Something about his voice said it wasn't, his body pressed against the door.

"It's okay if it's not."

"What's the point of complaining?" he toyed with the neck of his black T-shirt.

"Sharing your emotions isn't complaining, it's . . ." I was desperate to say the perfect thing here. "It's sharing the load."

"No one wishes to hear about my feelings."

"I do." I tried not to cringe as we sat in silence, the low buzz of the radio not doing enough to distract from the lack of filter between my brain and mouth.

"Because you're leaving?"

I leaned my elbow against the doorframe, fisting my hair. "Yeah, of course."

Oliver didn't speak another word until I flicked the turn signal, the car rumbling over the gravel of the parking lot of the diner on the side of the road. It was partially filled, but I'd bet good money that most of the cars belonged to people who worked there. The diner had been a suggestion from Dani, the owner of the antique furniture place we were headed to.

"Bathroom break?" Oliver asked. "I might have a cup you can pee into."

I huffed out a sigh, leaning into the backseat to rummage. I had an idea where he could put that cup. "This is an all-day outing. Might as well be well caffeinated."

I set a baseball cap on his head, offering him my sunglasses, brushing a few wisps of hair out of his face.

"What do you think you're doing?" His gray eyes dilated, roaming over my features.

"Giving you a disguise." I blew out a breath, pressing the brim of his cap down, as a slight blush crept over his cheeks. I stepped out of the car. A moment later, he was next to me, reaching forward, holding the door open, sunglasses covering up those eyes that I knew were watching me.

"Booth or table?" the hostess asked, popping a hip out.

"A booth would be swell." I dropped my voice a couple of octaves. *Perfect.*

"What in the absolute hell are you doing?" Oliver hissed at me, placing his large palm gently against my lower back.

"Helping you stay undercover."

"I think whatever accent you're doing is making us more noticeable."

"Don't worry about it, buttercup." I nudged him toward the last booth so he sat with his back to the rest of the restaurant as I plopped down across from him. "See? No one's noticed you."

He seemed conflicted, torn between scowling and smirking, and it was doing funny things to my appendix again. Maybe I was carsick.

"Nothing is ever simple with you, huh?" he asked.

"Nope." My gaze roamed the diner, the laminate, the mini jukeboxes at each table, the smell of burgers and grease in the air. "I love this place. Let's never leave."

He chuckled while browsing his menu. "Careful, Petal, you're going soft on me."

Our mugs of coffee were set down, giving my heart a moment to recover, as I concentrated on putting the right amount of milk in mine. "Petal?" The warmth from the coffee spread over my cheeks. "I remind you of a wilting flower? Or maybe the thorns?"

"Not even close."

I leaned forward on my elbows, hating how curious I was to understand him. "Have I told you how annoying I find you?"

"Constantly." His sip of coffee did nothing to hide the smirk. Smug bastard.

"Good."

We ordered food, then I browsed the jukebox.

He slid me a few quarters. "You can't stand silence, can you?"

"I spent my childhood having to entertain myself while my dad was working. It was less lonely to have music or TV playing in the background. I got used to it, I guess." I grinned, finding the perfect song: "Black Balloon" by the Goo Goo Dolls.

"It was like that after the funeral."

My eyes bounced across the table, landing on him as he nudged his mug around.

"Just me. After a while, Ambrose, Nick, and Rue were there during the day. But at night, it was . . ."

"Quiet," I finished.

"Yeah." He met my gaze. "So, I attempted to find a hobby or something since I couldn't play football anymore."

My head tilted. "Like what?" He was probably perfect at everything.

"Well, at first, I couldn't walk much. So, I tried knitting, then pottery."

I imagined some strange version of *Ghost*, with Oliver bent over a pottery wheel, fingers fluttering against my chest.

"Later I tried horseback riding and writing fan fiction."

"You wrote fan fiction?" I had to find this. "What was your fandom?"

"I will take it to my grave."

"There's a plot of land where I can make that happen. Tell me." That he didn't sit back on the privilege of his family, but wanted to contribute something to society, was surprising.

"Next was restoring cars, but my hands weren't able to fit into all the tiny spaces. Apparently, you shouldn't be scared of heights if you want to learn to be a pilot. Who knew?"

"Who knew?" I echoed.

"Needless to say, I've tried to find my next thing, job, hobby—anything—for a while now."

"You haven't found one?" I had to doubt that.

"It has become clear that I was only ever good at one thing in my life and . . . well." He waved at his legs under the table.

The jukebox had gone silent, but I didn't select the next song. We just sat there, all the things he had lost in the accident taking up the space between us: his parents, his future.

But I couldn't let him give up, not with the memory of how he and Nick had looked tossing that football back and forth. Of the empty rooms of the west wing, waiting for his parents, his family, to fill it again with memories. "Well, this renovation might as well be a career fair. There are lots of specialties you may have never thought about."

"Actually, since you bring it up . . ." He cleared his throat. "I think we should, uh . . . call a truce."

CHAPTER TEN

"What was that?" I licked my lips, intrigued.

He rolled his eyes. "Don't make me repeat it."

"Don't think I haven't noticed you waited until we were alone."

Oliver shifted in his seat, leg knocking into mine. "Do you want to hear this or not?"

"The table is yours."

He grunted. "I was thinking that there's a way for us both to get something out of this."

"Which is?" I kicked him, aiming for his right leg, just in case he was thinking about stopping there.

"I may have overheard someone saying that this project was going to lead to your dream position."

What a gossip Jeff was; he wouldn't be able to hide from me. "Jeff is such a big mouth."

"Listen, I'll stop fighting the restoration." He let out a deep breath, shoulders falling as he clutched at his mug. "I might have been a bit hostile in the beginning because I assumed Grandfather sent you as some sort of spy."

"So much to unpack there. 'A bit hostile' or that I was a spy?" If I was a spy, I was a terrible one. He'd caught me the sole time I'd tried to sneak around the mansion.

"No one's purposefully come to the house in years; then with his demand, the timing seemed suspect."

It made some sense until you met me. "I don't think I'm even capable of being covert."

"Trust me, I know. Your face gives everything away. Especially when you blush." His voice almost made it sound like he was teasing me.

"It seems rude for you to say that." I pressed my hands to my cheeks, hoping I wasn't blushing right now.

"Why? Because it's the truth?" Oliver leaned back, the bench creaking, his legs stretching out beneath the table, ankle pressed to mine.

"I thought this was a ceasefire."

"It is. I like talking to you."

Oh. Everything was too warm. I fiddled with my coffee cup. "You're not so bad, I guess."

"Careful—that compliment was overwhelming." He was almost laughing at me . . . maybe with me.

Everything in me was concentrating on our single spot of contact. Ankles had never been a thing for me before, but after today, even with our clothing separating us, they were officially an erogenous zone. "Don't think I will ever forget you admitted you like it when I talk."

"Well, you do it so rarely."

"You are so rude." My words weren't helped by the fact that I was giggling.

"Mmm," he hummed.

Something was doing loop-de-loops in my stomach—it was a pleasure I had not experienced in a long time, and not something I should experience with the person I was sitting next to.

"But what do you get out of it?" I hadn't missed his failure to explain his end of our truce.

Some of the grief that had been missing from his eyes returned as he dug through the messenger bag I had forgotten he'd brought along. A canvas notebook emerged. Oliver set it on the table, palm pressed tenderly to the surface.

"The estate was supposed to be restored years ago. Designs— everything was decided."

I gave a quick nod, unsure if I should mention I was already aware of that.

"My mom was involved. She was consulted on all the plans and had some ideas." His fingers curled around the notebook before opening to the first page, a reverence in his touch. "She wrote them in here."

"Oliver—"

He barreled on. "It was canceled when they died. The house, me—all at a standstill until you came."

Tears filled my eyes. I swiped furiously.

"This notebook has everything she wanted. You asked for my input on what I want to see. Well, I know it's been almost ten years, but I was hoping you could use some of it." His voice cracked, as he shoved the notebook the rest of the way toward me.

"Of course."

"Thank you." Our fingers brushed on the top page, neither of us letting go until the waitress returned with our food.

I offered him a soft smile, sliding a quarter toward him and nodding at the jukebox.

He picked out a song I had jumped on the bed to as a kid, in that log cabin I'd shared with Dad, screaming at the top of my lungs.

"I meant it when I said my money's gone."

I almost choked on my milkshake. "What do you mean?" Was this some sort of scam where I would not get paid for my work?

"My trust fund. My family still has money, but mine is pretty much gone."

Another puzzle piece was falling into place. "It's why you can't buy the estate from your grandfather?"

Oliver nodded.

"What did you do with the money?"

"Donated it." He bit into his burger, unaware he had rendered me speechless. "Mental health nonprofits, organizations that help with grief, LGBTQ groups, not-for-profit coding schools, that kind of stuff," he mumbled.

"Helping people is admirable." His emphasis on people experiencing grief did not pass by me. Few would consider doing that with their resources, but would instead buy boats or a house they would only stay at once a week. I knew because I had watched Dad restore a few.

"Yeah, but it's not a job."

It could be, I almost said. A few acts of kindness weren't enough to make me like him. I knew that; my brain knew that. But another part of me, probably my appendix (definitely not my heart), that unnecessary organ that should have been removed years ago was misbehaving, seeing him in a new light.

And for a moment, I let my appendix take over.

Barely Even Friends

Oliver's mom's notebook contained more than Dad's files did. Swatches of cloth, idea boards, and new layouts for the rooms. It didn't take much reorganizing to integrate some of her ideas. It felt like unlocking some missing piece, the true heart of the estate.

The excitement of what was to come was overshadowing all the nerves that had weighed on me since I'd walked out of Dad's apartment.

But we still had to finish emptying the last few rooms, except for the two Oliver and I would be staying in. It was all part of my detailed, multipage, bulleted plan. We both would shift to restored rooms before the end of the project, and nothing would be missed. Every hour, every moment, down to every bed, was accounted for.

There was a knock on the door. "What are you doing in here?"

"Packing." I didn't even lift my head to acknowledge Oliver.

"It's lunchtime."

"Would you believe I already ate?"

"Not a chance." He didn't seem to pick up on the hint my back was giving him.

Though his presence reminded me of something. "Oh, I found something earlier I wanted to show you. Come with me." I finished wrapping the clock, gently placing it in the box marked "Fragile."

Our truce was in effect, and we were both honoring it—not picking fights, offering polite nods when we ran into each other. The problem was me, unable to stop thinking about the way he'd looked as he entrusted me with his mom's notebook. How soft his fingers felt against my callous-covered palm.

"Food first." He was too used to getting his way, and clearly unaffected. This was becoming a habit for him, ensuring I ate, which I had a tendency to forget when I was stressed.

I liked to think I'd made him realize he couldn't always get what he wanted. "Why are you like this?"

"Because I enjoy riling you up."

"Fine. Fine. Whatever *sir* says."

That earned me a snort. And a small—minuscule, barely there—bit of joy that I'd made him laugh.

I allowed a quick detour to the kitchen. Rue passed me a sandwich, and I refilled my stainless-steel water bottle, eating as I walked.

"Is it a dead body?" Oliver asked, taking a bite of his own sandwich once he confirmed I was nourishing myself.

"Excuse me?"

"Trying to think of things you would want to show me in particular."

Honestly, I was tempted to show him something horrifying now. "Listen, if you don't want to see it . . ."

"Show me."

"Really, I don't have to." Truce didn't mean I couldn't enjoy riling him up too.

"Show me," he growled out.

"Always so grumbly."

"I may not have been, uh . . ." Oliver's nose wrinkled as his shoulders climbed somehow even higher.

"Kind? Welcoming? Offering basic human decency?" I filled in the blanks, as I led him to our destination.

"Well, I'm—"

"An emotionally constipated man confused by the thing thumping in your chest?" I took another bite of my sandwich, hiding my smile.

"Rude."

"True," announced Bl8z3, and I snorted. If Bl8z3 agreed, it must be accurate.

Dust clung to every inch of Oliver—his beard, a smudge across his cheek, and those thighs. Every day since the crew had first arrived, Oliver had bolted immediately into helping with the furniture removal and emptying the house. When Ambrose wasn't nearby to lecture him, of course.

Oliver's eyes narrowed, but his shoulders had lowered.

I put my hands on the door handles to what had immediately become my favorite room in the estate once I had discovered it, and glanced over my shoulder. "You aren't appropriately excited about this," I said, unable to stop myself from bouncing on my toes. "Is this not killing you? The anticipation?"

"Nope."

"I am withering away in front of you. Take pity on my soul. Fake it if you must." My toes were wiggling, hidden in my shoes. I needed him to appreciate this.

"Or what?" He met my gaze. He was no longer glaring, but I couldn't call what was going on with his face a smile either. Neutrality. I could work with it that.

"Or Bl8z3 will ensure you hear my voice everywhere. I'll haunt you."

"I am capable of that, Ms. Price, if you would like me to set that up for you," Bl8z3 offered.

"What happened to loyalty?" Oliver groaned.

The smartest being in the estate, Bl8z3, remained quiet.

"You want to guess?"

"No. I need you to step aside and let me in." When I didn't move, he kept going. "Oh, the anticipation is killing me." He pressed his palm to his forehead as if he were overwhelmed, rolling his eyes at the same time. This mansion was home to the worst the-ater troupe I had ever seen.

"I will pretend you said that with actual enthusiasm." I spun on my heel toward the doors.

"I'll do whatever you want." Oliver's breath was warm against my ear.

A shiver built up my spine, picturing Oliver leaning in the rest of the way, pressing my body against the door. The anticipation get-ting to me. "Now I'm scared I'm going to disappoint you."

"You could never disappoint me."

Everything in me clenched for a minute, my knuckles squeez-ing. I pushed open the double doors in a sweeping gesture, because how could I not? I loved the effect.

Despite not owning a single physical book, I was a sucker for a library—and this estate had the most glorious home for tomes I'd ever seen. And this was before I'd gotten my hands on it.

More than wall-to-wall books, it was floor-to-ceiling, with bookcases wrapped around the curved walls. A spiral staircase led up to the second floor, where there were—ready for it?—more books.

Boxes covered the hardwood. It was taking a while to pack them all up—I was taking great care with each book, using tissue paper and housing them in a controlled climate. Construction had begun in other areas of the house, but I refused to allow the most beautiful collection of first editions I'd ever seen to be tossed into boxes. They deserved special care.

Even the shelves had me weak in the knees. Handcrafted built-ins with intricate detailing. Large, overstuffed chairs had been placed in small reading pockets and were the first to be carried out to the trucks. The Tiffany lamps, for when the overhead chandelier was too much, went after that.

It was a room built for knowledge, thought, quiet contemplation, and a care for the preservation of all these ideas.

"This is a book paradise. Do you smell that?" I took a big whiff.

"Dust?" He took a huff of his own, face screwing up as he let out a hacking cough.

"Yes, but also the pages, history, stories, escape, a world of adventure. And an epic romance section." It was a joy to see so many of the books I only owned digitally. The crisp pages, the stepbacks—the touch of a physical book was a unique sensation an e-reader could never recreate.

I was giddy and couldn't hide it.

"To be clear, you wanted to show me *my* library. You don't think I've seen it before?"

"You are impossible." I lightly punched his arm before yanking on it, ensuring he followed me; his short-sleeved T-shirt meant I was touching his skin. "No, I came across something when I was packing."

I had discovered books on the history of the estate throughout the years—they were going to be endlessly informative on how to restore it accurately. Even with the black and white photos, I could figure out the colors somewhat, based on the shading. There was info on the art, the placement of various pieces. But that wasn't what I wanted to show him.

I sat on the floor by the box I hadn't yet finished loading, grabbing the book that was on top. Leather bound. They didn't make notebooks like this anymore.

I waited another breath before handing it to him.

His brows knit together as I buried my face in my hands.

He slowly opened the book, staring at each page, fingers caressing, tracing the letters.

The longer it took for him to say something, the more I struggled to sit still. Maybe I'd been wrong. Maybe this wouldn't be a happy memento for him, but another piece of his broken heart I was reminding him of. Just because books were something that brought me comfort, that didn't mean the memories associated with this book were good for him.

Every moment of silence became excruciatingly worse, my palms sweating, fingers wiggling. Until I couldn't take it any longer.

I threw myself at him, grabbing for the book. "Well, I should get back to it. Thanks for the lunch break."

His focus had been on the softcover, not me, and down we went, me falling on top of him, flat on the wooden floors. The notebook landed somewhere next to us, and Oliver's hands clasped my hips as he huffed out a breath. We were much closer than I had calculated.

Every move I made to escape just made things worse, as I was unable to get my feet firmly on the ground. I was starfishing the man. My face heated in embarrassment.

"Just"—Oliver grunted as I elbowed him in the gut—"stay still for a minute. What are you doing?"

"Examining the floors," I leveled. "You got in my way."

Then he—*wow*—he chuckled, and it might have been my new favorite sound. I mean, it was pleasant and fine, a thing people did. But his laugh reverberated from his body to mine, and I wanted it to happen again. To be the one to make it happen again.

Oliver's lips were at my ear, voice low, as if sharing a secret meant solely for me. "My mom loved that thing, insisted we fill it out every time we grabbed a book off the shelves."

The moment he mentioned his mother, I stopped squirming, my face buried in his neck, realizing the rapid beat of his pulse was for a different reason. The notebook was a ledger keeping track of all the books loaned out of the library. Over a hundred years of entries. I'd flipped through the pages until I landed on Oliver's childish handwriting tracking books for him and his sisters.

"If you couldn't find her, she was here, lost in a book. My dad used to joke she married him for his library."

I couldn't blame her. This place was magnificent—if the ceiling didn't cave in on you while you were reading. But the risk was worth it.

"Thank you, Petal. That was something I never wanted to lose."

His hands glided from my hips to my lower back until I realized what he was doing. Hugging me.

He started to pull away, but I pushed my arms through his, tugging on his biceps, giving a form of a hug in our position, holding on. "You're welcome." *Don't let go.* His arms wrapped around me, strong, comforting, holding me in a way I knew meant he wouldn't let anything hurt me.

We lay there for a moment. My eyes closed, pressed to the space where his neck met the beginnings of his messy beard, and it made me smile, the hair brushing my forehead. I didn't even mind the sweaty scent we both had from another long day of work, as the days had begun to grow warmer.

"You want to go ride on those ladders, don't you?" he asked, releasing me slowly. I was reluctant to let him go but wouldn't push whatever this strange moment was.

With his help, we made it off the ground, neither of us able to meet the other's gaze. I left him to his book because I did, in fact, want to take a ride on the ladders. Every dream I'd ever had of a home always involved a library that required ladders to access all the books. It was easy to dream of impossible things when you wouldn't ever have them.

Pulling myself up, I shoved off with my foot, trying to read the spines as I slid by, enjoying the atmosphere more than anything. This was better than a bookstore; I could make my home in this very room.

I savored the ride, the way my hair lifted off my neck, not even attempting to hold the giggle in. It was a rush. I could sense his eyes on me, but I waited until the ladder stopped, before I glanced back at Oliver.

Because of the beard, the book, and his normal stoicism, I couldn't judge his mood. But I was learning. "So, what's the verdict?"

His gaze drifted down to the book in his hands. "I hadn't let myself think of the positive memories for a long time. Mostly it was work not to think of the bad ones. I couldn't let anything else in. But this—" He hugged the ledger to his chest, over his heart. "This is an excellent memory. Thank you." His eyes glowed with emotion.

It was overwhelming to have his focus on me like this. The weight of it, the intensity, was too much. I stared at my feet. "You're welcome."

Every time I thought about the preceding eight years, him alone in this house, it hurt my soul. A man haunted by the past, stuck in it. And maybe furious with the world for moving on without him.

"This is my favorite room in the house," I said.

His focus was still on me. "Mine too."

"I'm glad."

"Why?" Suspicion and interest mixed on his face.

"Because no matter how angry you pretend I make you, it's more proof that we like and value the same things."

He growled at the back of his throat as he sprung, the weight of his body propelling us until my spine pressed against the closest bookcase, his hands on either side of my shoulders, holding onto the wooden shelf.

"I am angry—you're right."

His chest was heaving as he ducked, bringing us almost to the same height. It was thrilling being this close to him, feeling the heat from his body, the temptation to touch him.

"My grandfather and his strong-arming us makes me angry."

I couldn't say a word, fascinated by this burst of emotion as he gazed at my lips. Conflicted, frustrated, and burning with something that my body felt too, I rubbed my thighs together in an effort to relieve whatever was building low in my stomach.

"But that's not what's driving me to distraction. I'm angry that you wear these stupid suspenders. I'm angry that you're in every room, invading this house. And I'm furious at how much I think about kissing you."

I was a bone-melting, knee-wobbling jumble of *He said what now?* with so much relief that it wasn't only me experiencing these feelings. "Would it help if I told you your beard makes me angry?"

I scratched against the edge of his jaw. Despite its wild appearance, the hair itself was soft, as if to encourage my fingers to make their new home there.

"No." His voice was strained. "I don't think that helps at all."

"Then maybe you should, uh"—I licked my lips, my gaze stuck on his—"kiss me." A shiver broke out across my skin, and I couldn't pretend it was from a breeze. Everything I was experiencing was due to my proximity to this man.

"That will make it better?"

This was a dangerous game. The project was in its early days, and he could return to being an ass tomorrow. Maybe his grandfather would even fire me if he found out? Kissing Oliver could ruin everything I had been working for. I never wanted anyone to say that I had gotten this job and succeeded at it because I was screwing the owner's grandson. But it was getting harder and harder to remember the reasons not to as every deep rumble of his voice struck something in my chest, my breasts heaving as if I had run a mile instead of being frozen in his gaze. "Can't make it worse, can it?" I asked. Just one kiss wouldn't hurt anyone, right?

He leaned close enough that we were breathing each other in, the scruff of his beard brushing against my face. "Fucking suspenders," he muttered before closing the distance.

If this was him angry, I'd encourage it with everything I had. Because he didn't just kiss me, he owned me.

Sucking on my lower lip, he bit down for a moment, and I moaned. When he released, my tongue smoothed across my tender skin. But he took that as an opportunity to suck on my tongue, drawing it into his mouth. Kissing him felt like an illicit activity.

His hands remained on the wood, which groaned under the pressure of his fists. I had no such control. I scratched my fingernails against his chest, moving down to his stomach to grab his belt and draw his hips closer to mine, our fronts almost touching. If this was my one chance, I was going to take advantage. Let every single inhibition go. He had dug himself under my skin; his attempts to keep the world at more than arm's length only made me desire to get closer. No one had ever been consistently worried if I was eating enough, getting enough rest, staying hydrated while working on a project.

He brushed his lips against my jaw, down my neck, licking along the V of my shirt. Only his mouth touched me, but it was more than enough to light me on fire, my hips seeking his. It all made me dizzy with something that I could finally admit to myself was desire.

He allowed the single point of contact, as we learned each other, until his lips slowed, the creaking sound by my ears getting worse.

He breathed against me for a moment before pulling back, his gaze raking over me. I didn't need a mirror to know I had been wrecked by his mouth, teeth, and that tongue.

Not that he had fared any better, hair tie long gone, hair down to his shoulders, lips puffy. What were he and this house doing to me?

"We have to stop." Jaw clenched, his focus lowered to where my fingers were buried in his T-shirt. "I'm not a good man." Slowly I released my grip, palm pressed to my lips, as if to preserve what had just happened. "You should run in the opposite direction."

I was desperate to touch him again, for our bodies to be pressed together. "Shouldn't I be the judge of that?"

"Trust me." His voice was a rasp. "You deserve so much better."

My eyes closed as he brushed a last kiss against my forehead. A goodbye before we'd barely even started.

The moment had woken me up, offered me a bite of the apple, and then it had been plucked away. I had never felt more like Charlie Brown in my life, and I wanted that football.

Before I could respond, he snatched up the notebook and left the room, leaving me a quivering mess against the bookshelf. Kissing Oliver had not been on today's to-do list and would never be on the agenda in the future—not with how easily he was able to walk away.

For the first time I was left wondering if it was really worth it to restore this crumbling wreck or if it wouldn't be better to tear it all down.

CHAPTER ELEVEN

123 Days Until the Deadline

"I want to talk to you about the roof. Can you come outside with me?" Jeff asked with a face that promised it would not be a cheerful conversation. But maybe he wanted to tell me it was in better shape than it appeared. A girl could dream.

The project had been going smoothly, too good to be true. We'd emptied the house of every belonging except in the rooms where Oliver and I were sleeping. But with houses this old, it was impossible to predict everything. We were on deadline, meticulously checking off my list on schedule, but only just. The ridiculous budget helped, as did our continued dropping of the Killington name.

We stood at the west side of the mansion, the stables in our line of sight, as Jeff pointed out the obvious structural issues. Spoiler alert: old roofs warped and changed with age and weather, which was why they had to be replaced periodically. But in this case, I'd allowed myself to hope appearances were deceiving.

"It's bad." Jeff crossed his arms, still staring up as if the roof would give us divine answers, maybe magically repair itself. The biggest problem wasn't the roof; replacing it would be relatively simple, and I had built it into the schedule. It was the rotten boards and black mold that had resulted from the water damage.

"Tell me there's some sort of good news?" My tone was more hopeful than I felt, but I allowed myself one more moment of false belief. There had to be a but at the end of that sentence. Structural issues, mold—neither would help my timeline.

"No. It is that bad." Jeff shook his head, meeting my gaze. *Fuck.* "It's the worst roof I've seen that's on a building not made of wood shingles."

Double fuck. "No kinder way to break that news to me?" I was struggling to do the math on how to handle this without going beyond my deadline.

"That *was* the nice way. We haven't gotten to the structural and water damage the roof caused. When do you think it was last updated? I mean, it can't be the original roof, but it's at least fifty years old. Honestly, I'm amazed this place is still standing." This phrase was repeated daily—a few of the crew members had made a drinking game out of it.

My response was a long moan as I patted my iPad against my forehead. This was the "other shoe," the thing that would delay everything. Oliver wasn't cursed, but his house was. I gritted my teeth, annoyed with myself for even thinking about him. We had switched roles: ever since the library, over two weeks ago, I was the one running in the opposite direction every time we crossed paths. Mostly I was pissed he could act like nothing had happened, while my heart raced at the very sight of him.

Trying to puzzle through it, I had confessed the mishap to Sebastian and then made the mature decision to avoid my best friend too. This project was all I had room for in my brain.

The kiss hadn't meant a single thing to Oliver. I refused to be that girl who saw something more. Not again.

"Tell me we can carry on and move up the timeline based on when the roof crew is arriving." I opened my email.

"They should be here within the hour. Somehow the bones of this place don't want to fall, and the structural engineer gave us the okay, but I'd still like to hear it from the roof guys too."

"Thank you." One less thing to worry about.

"We've had this conversation before, but it'd be cheaper and less time-consuming to wreck this money pit and build something in its place, right?" Jeff leaned back on his heels.

"Do I even have to respond?" Not that it wasn't tempting.

"We do what the client wants. Just had to say it." He squeezed the brim of his cap.

"Think of the pride you'll feel that you overcame this mansion that wanted to get the better of both of us." I was one step from pumping my fist.

"I need to walk away now. You're too cheerful," he grumbled.

"One of us has to be. Don't worry—inside I'm crying." This project was doing its best to beat me down, but I refused to let it. "It's our Everest."

He rolled his eyes at me. "Everest kills."

A loud honking came from the driveway.

Jeff looked as confused as I felt. "I thought everyone was on-site?"

My meticulous to-do lists accounted for every single member of the crew for each day of the restoration. We had no room to deviate or have someone show up late. Not today of all days.

Jeff shrugged as we headed to the front of the house, the honking getting more aggressive. With my luck, Cousin Carter had stopped by for another visit.

A small crowd of workers gathered around the vehicle making all the noise. Wonderful: more delays. I needed to put the world on pause so I could go upstairs, scream, then sit and make a plan. After I called the roofers and moved up their arrival.

Tonight, I would dig into my secret emergency stash of candy and dive into a historical romance novel: a brush of a wrist and a fainting chaise would make everything better.

Oliver was one of the last to venture outside, hovering at the front stoop as if he couldn't decide if he should care enough. His hair pulled back in that ponytail, and his T-shirt with a deep V exposing the breadth of his chest, made my fingers itch.

The car doors popped open, finally putting an end to the horn.

"Where is she?"

My head snapped forward, stomach sinking. I recognized that voice. It was not supposed to be here. It was supposed to be very, very far from here.

"No, no, no . . ." I stepped backward, violently waving my hands as if I could shoo him away, but Jeff remained behind me, halting my progress as he peered around me.

"Where is she?" he demanded again.

I was rooted to the spot.

"Bell, darling, where are you?"

Of course he wouldn't come alone. This was not happening. Not another distraction I didn't have time for.

"Belly, Bell, Bells. We are ringing for you!" Now he was singing. Once, for my birthday, he'd enjoyed doing this, accompanied with actual bells and a tambourine, in the apartment we'd moved into right off campus. It was normally a happy memory, but not in this setting.

"No, no, no . . ." I shook my head vigorously, desperate to wake up, *please.*

"What's wrong?" Oliver had made his way over to me, reaching out, as if he was going to touch me—hold my hand?—before the hand dove back into his pants pocket. That familiar clench was back, my chest echoing with it. "Do you know them?"

"I wish I didn't."

"Bells! There you are."

The crowd parted, leaving a direct route for Sebastian and Finn. A surprise visit from Dad, even Adrian Killington, would have been better than this.

I adored my friends. We'd experienced a million adventures together. Late nights writing papers, waiting in line for midnight showings of movies, some terrible double dates they swore never to discuss again (they'd lied). Sebastian and me standing around Finn's art shows trying to sound intelligent about brush strokes, lines, and interpretation. Mostly, we drank wine and talked about how Finn possessed more talent than everyone in the room combined.

On any other day, I would have been thrilled to see them. We had a slumber party tradition whenever I got back from a project. I'd visit Dad, then trap myself with these wackadoos for a few days, getting caught up on life, new movie releases, and the stocks Sebastian thought I should invest in. These were my people. I didn't have to overthink what I said or keep up my self-confidence shield when I was with them.

But they had never once visited me on-site before. For good reason.

Chaos reigned whenever they were around.

A prime example was the way Finn rushed toward me while Sebastian peered on with a half grin that betrayed a flash of guilt because he knew. The asshole *knew* this wasn't okay. But he'd come anyway—curiosity was going to kill Sebastian. Well, *I* was, but because of his curiosity. I'd make time for the body cleanup—it would be worth it.

But before Finn could tackle me, which he had every intent to do, based on the eagerness in his eyes—and also because I knew him, Oliver stepped in between us. Finn stopped short with a small yelp.

"Oh, hello." He ducked around Oliver. "Is this him, the guy making your life miserable?" Finn's eyebrows wiggled lasciviously, and I waited for the ground to open up and eat me whole.

Except that would be an expensive fix, and I was dealing with enough of those.

"When the other person doesn't come rushing at you, it's a sign to back off." Growly Oliver was back in full force, fists clenched at his sides.

"And you growl. I didn't believe that part. This is going to be so much fun." Finn rubbed his palms together as he glanced back at Sebastian.

"Hey, don't speak to him like that." Sebastian made his way to us, glaring at Oliver, lips pressed firm.

This continued to get better and better. Oliver had a couple inches on Sebastian, but where Oliver had gone softer in the middle, Sebastian was built like a brick wall. One that wanted to slam into my housemate. Two stubborn idiots facing off against each other.

"Yes, I'm the one making a spectacle here." Oliver spun to glare at me. "Should I have them escorted off the property?" His expression made it clear who would do the escorting, and gleefully.

"So, you're a bully to everyone, not just Bells," Sebastian fired back, pulling Finn behind him, fingers curling into a fist.

"Stop!" I yelled. Sebastian and Oliver weren't the only ones surprised at my outburst. We had earned ourselves an audience. "Back to work—nothing to see here." I forced a smile onto my face.

There were some grumbles, but everyone else left; even Jeff slowly walked away, backward.

"Sebastian and Finn, this is, uh . . . Oliver. Oliver Killington. And Oliver"—Oliver blinked at me, rubbing at his chest—"these are my *former* best friends, Finn and Sebastian."

Shockingly, no one offered a hand in greeting. One problem at a time.

I turned toward Oliver. "The property and the rebuild are fine. Nothing for you to worry about. You can go back to whatever you were doing."

Something shifted on his face, his mouth opening for a moment, gaze tracing my features, before he snapped his lips shut, his head giving a slight shake, enough to ruffle the soft hairs framing his face. And then he did what he does best: he marched off, proving that all he cared about was the estate.

"And you two—"

The grins on Sebastian and Finn's faces immediately dropped.

"What are you doing here?" I sighed, trying not to be rude, but they hadn't given me any notice. Not even a text saying: *Hey, we're in a neighborhood that isn't close to anything else. Thought we'd stop by and see you.*

"Rules. We have rules for a reason." Sebastian shook his cell phone at me. "Seven days and absolutely nothing. The rule is three, and Finn had to talk me down daily that you weren't being dismembered in some secret dungeon. Everything you said gave me bad vibes about that guy. Then the last text you sent?"

Right, after a week of nothing from Oliver, I had finally confessed to my best friends how I had made out with my housemate in some sort of fever dream of library fetishness, and then he had stormed away. Then in in my embarrassment I had ignored all their responses.

Whoops.

Finn nodded, focusing his glare on me.

"I've been busy, guys. I'm sorry." And avoiding thinking about the kiss that never should have been.

"Tell her all of it." Finn pushed Sebastian in my direction.

"Fine." He sighed, reaching for my hand, giving it a squeeze. "I also needed to ensure that he didn't think he could jerk you around."

My annoyance lessened, warmth flooding me. "You're very sweet."

"I am no such thing." Sebastian crossed his arms.

"Don't worry—I'm still beyond exasperated with the two of you. Unless you brought an air mattress, there isn't room. The crew is renting houses a few miles away, and they're full up too."

"We can stay with you. It'll be like one of our slumber parties. Stay up all night eating candy and gossiping." Finn kept his arm wrapped around Sebastian as he glanced around the grounds.

"There is no gossip other than the stress of the schedule. Trust me, it will be boring." Having them here for any length of time would mean talking through everything I had been pushing away the past two weeks.

"Give us a tour, and if you still want us to leave afterward, we will." Not waiting for my answer, Finn yanked me into the house, Sebastian following us.

It was easier, and faster, to comply. So, we went room by room, showing the progress we had made stripping the place down, pointing out my ideas for the space. My favorite features, the wainscotting, the paneling, and of course the wallpaper. They were the perfect captive audience, the perfect ego boost.

We were about to stroll into the kitchen via the dining room when Finn placed his palm on my bicep. "This would be perfect." His eyes spanned the blank wall in front of us, the room empty. Even the chandelier had been removed for cleaning and repair.

"Perfect for what?"

Sebastian laughed, shoulder bumping mine. "You didn't think we came here just to see you, did you?"

Finn strolled closer to the wall, hands up as if to measure. "I know you always refuse our help, but if you want, I should be able to do it in two or three days, depending."

It took a moment for it to click. He was offering to paint a mural. I clapped my hands against my mouth. "Are you serious?" These two were devious, restored to elite best friend status.

Finn grinned at me. "Your first solo project, of course. This house will be your calling card; you have to make a statement. I'd be honored to help my very best friend."

"Hey," Sebastian protested.

"My very best friend I don't have sex with. If you want me to, of course. Not the sex, but the art. No hurt feelings if it doesn't mesh with your design. I'll need to see your boards to make sure what I've been sketching will fit in."

My mind rushed through all the possibilities that this blank wall now held.

"You're the best." This time I was leaping at Finn, trying to pretend there weren't tears brimming at the corners of my eyes. This was beyond anything I had ever thought to ask for.

"And I brought my assistant with me." Finn nodded toward Sebastian, who was too busy making heart eyes to even listen to the joke. Oh, these two—I had missed them.

"So hard to find good muscle nowadays," I teased as Finn nodded.

"He's not bad, but if you have any new suggestions?"

I elbowed him hard, bringing them into the kitchen. They still hadn't earned the right to be told where the secret stash of Rue's chocolate chip cookies was, but I figured once Finn started painting, they would fully redeem themselves.

A Finn original. Or I should say a Finnister original. The name his youngest brother had called him as a child had stuck. By now, he could sign a blank canvas and make money from it.

"Wait, I think I have the perfect inspiration." I left them there as I sprinted to my bedroom, grabbing the notebook Oliver had given me.

The moment I revealed the page, Finn bobbed his head. "Oh yes, this is perfect."

"While he's getting set up, don't think you are getting out of talking about what's going on in this house, and specifically that kiss." Sebastian wrapped his arm around me, pulling me against his body.

"I'm a very busy person. I don't have a lot of time to . . ."

His flicked at the rose I had looped around my suspenders today. "Make time."

"I—"

"I can ask the other half of the party responsible." He knew what he was doing with that threat. Watching Sebastian and Oliver butt heads would be entertaining, but I had no desire to create more damage to the estate.

Seeing my friends was a comfort. Worse, it might have been exactly what I needed.

121 Days Until the Deadline

Slumber parties are fun when you're a child. Squished into a bed, giggling all night, desperate to stay awake. I didn't have many growing up, but the few I did had left a memorable impression.

As an adult, they were different, primarily because no one is child-sized anymore.

Try to shove three full-sized adults in a bed not built for three people, and—well, there's a lot less giggling and a lot more grinding, and not the good kind, but the kind when your best friend's knee is in your back as you hug the edge of the bed, attempting to sleep.

I had missed my friends and truly appreciated their initiative, despite all my protests that I didn't need their help. They'd dropped their regularly scheduled lives to check on me, which was a very them thing to do.

But I wished they'd had the foresight to bring an air mattress. I should have left a spare room furnished, but that's hindsight for you: the past kicking my ass for not predicting the future.

Which meant that in the morning, coffee attempted to be a replacement for two nights spent with very little sleeping involved.

Finn had his art, Sebastian his spreadsheets, and me—I had a normal and typical soft spot for restoring vintage wallpaper to its former glory. These were my favorite parts of a remodel. The quiet, small moments that can make the biggest changes. My childhood was littered with memories of learning the secret to paint edging, tricks to restuff furniture, and the times I offered a suggestion to Dad over dinner, and he went with it.

I had my bucket of filtered water, clean towels, my AirPods. Everyone else had their assignments, in any room but this one. This I was in control over and could ensure it was completed on time.

Before I could slip the headphones into my ears and drown out the world with Taylor Swift's powerful lyricism that spoke to my soul, the door clicked open.

CHAPTER TWELVE

The sunlight backlit Oliver, his gaze mapping the room before he rested it on me. "Hello." It was the same gruff voice that had greeted me when I'd first arrived, leaving me to wonder if I had made up that brief flash of a truce between us.

I had zero interest in providing him with entertainment or whatever I was to him today. He had been through something, but that didn't give him carte blanche to jerk me around.

"Goodbye." I bent over the bucket, squeezing out the cloth.

He stepped into the room, closing the door behind him, refusing to accept the hint. "Does that make it easier to take the wallpaper down?" He gave his chin a nod in the bucket's direction.

"Shh, don't say that." I smoothed a palm over the delicate silk, appreciating each bump and thread. "Don't listen to the mean man. I would never remove you. All you require is a little tender love."

He shook his head. "You realize you're talking to an inanimate object? It can't talk back."

"I resent that," Bl8z3 chimed in. "Everything has a voice, but not everything communicates in a way you would expect."

"Nice job, asshole." It came out crueler than I meant, but that was safest. I was a bright, shiny, new thing to him; I could have been anyone that walked through that door. "I'm pretty busy in here, so if you don't mind . . ."

He heaved a sigh, shifting to lean against the frame, crossing his arms. "I can't figure out what to say to you."

"Then say nothing." It should be easy; it was his default setting.

His posture was stiff, muscles rigid. "I'm not a good guy."

"You won't get any argument from me." Giving the cloth an extra squeeze, I gently pressed it to the antique silk.

"I don't know how to do this."

I closed my eyes. No one was asking him to do anything, least of all me. "Do what?"

"*You* confuse me."

"Yeah, I make you angry, blah, blah." Been there, done that, not looking for a repeat.

"No, it's not—" His voice cracked with emotion, but it wasn't anger. "You force me to feel . . . feel things I haven't in a long time. It's a lot to process."

He truly enjoyed stunning me into silence.

"I'm sorry. I'm an ass." His arms lifted for a moment before coming to rest at his sides, as if that was all he had to offer. Himself.

Embarrassment flushed my body at the memory of how I'd thrown myself into that kiss, held nothing back. The way my lips still tingled at the memory. But I couldn't put myself out on another limb. Not when he'd so easily walked away.

I concentrated on the wallpaper. Something I was confident about, that didn't leave me wondering if I was nauseous.

"The wallpaper isn't ruined; it's just seen better days. I'm restoring it." Something uncurled in my stomach as his eyes widened in interest, nodding for me to keep talking. "You make the cloth damp, and carefully clean the fabric. It's tedious and time-consuming, but worth it." Dad had shown me the technique as a child. It kept me occupied in a place that had a million things a kid shouldn't touch or could hurt themselves with. "I don't just give up on things because they're hard."

His beard shifted incrementally, maybe his jaw clenching. "Can you teach me?" He didn't move away from the door. Left the choice in my hands for what happened next.

"It's slow, delicate work," I hedged. I had zero interest in messing up my hard work just so he could feel better. I was here for a job and nothing else.

"Does that mean you don't want me to help you?" A hint of a challenge lay in his eyes.

"I didn't say that."

"So, you want me to help?" He gently bit his lip, my body clenching in memory of the way his teeth felt on my skin, betraying me.

"I didn't say that either." Confused was an understatement for the feelings knotted up inside of me. But finding some sort of peace would ensure Sebastian wouldn't try to pick a fight for the remainder of their visit.

"How about this? I'd like to help you." Oliver lumbered over, hesitating, still giving me the out, reaching for another towel hanging off the side of the bucket, wringing it out before coming to stand by me.

Everything in my chest fluttered.

"This is my house. I should contribute."

"Of course." I had spent too much time listening to Finn wax poetic about love. My brain had been sucked into his world viewed with rose-colored glasses. My glasses were vintage and clear as day. This was better, be on the same team, reach the same goal. It was about the estate, it was always about the estate.

"You must be glad to have your friends here."

I gasped, my fingers involuntarily releasing the cloth, which landed with a plop on the hardwood, my mouth gaping.

"What?" His eyebrows drew tightly together.

"Did you just willingly speak to me?" My wet fingers clutched at my chest.

"I have before." He sounded offended, a breath huffing out, nose scrunching up in a way that was not adorable at all.

"Voluntarily ask me a personal question?"

"You make me sound like a—"

"Inquire how I'm doing?"

"All right, now you're being—" He focused on his task, his shoulders hunched.

"Bl8z3, have you recorded this? It deserves to go down in the history books." I couldn't be stopped.

"I'm reaching out to the Library of Congress as we speak," Bl8z3 promised.

I had zero interest in addressing what had happened in the library. Self-respect refused to allow me to ask what made him walk away. The point was, he had. I didn't need more details about his rejection. Did he frustrate me, his ability to brush past it as if it hadn't happened? Did the moment keep me up at night, a sweaty mess, tossing and turning in my bed sheets? Not at all.

"Hilarious." He cringed. "Am I that bad?" The hunch in his shoulders had gotten worse, his back tensing.

"Bad?" I feigned ignorance, not inclined to make this easy on him.

"Rude?"

"I wouldn't say you've been the friendliest person to me since I arrived." *Other than that time you took me into the library and kissed the heck out of me. But we don't talk about that because of an unspoken agreement that I'm sure your attorneys will forward me any day now.*

"Yeah. I guess I'm not used to people anymore." He gestured to the room, the estate, the grounds. "Not that I was ever social."

"You, the football stud?" I refused to glance in his direction.

"Being successful on the field does not mean you're successful off it." He gently, almost tenderly pressed his cloth to the wallpaper. "That's the second time you've mentioned you find me attractive."

"Third, but who's counting?"

"I am," I thought I heard him mutter, but I was hearing what I wanted to.

He cleared his throat. "I've been difficult. You came here with a job to do."

The sentiment was nice, but I would not leave him alone on the ledge. It had been a lot. Me showing up, the renovations, now the crew, all the changes. I couldn't hold him to that charged moment. Offering his mother's notebook, finding her ledger, I couldn't pretend that was nothing. Even as I continued to think about it, let it sing through my veins. Our kiss had made me feel alive in a way I hadn't in years.

"Truce," I spoke up. "We agreed to a truce, and I will honor that. A parlay, if you will."

"Parlay?" The tension in his features eased and so did part of the knot in my chest.

"Not into pirates either?" I had secondhand embarrassment for his lack of knowledge about films.

"Are you?"

"Can't go wrong when a film involves a childhood crush pining for years, saying nothing because they think they're not good enough."

"I can understand that." His gaze raked over me in what appeared to be a statement, a silent communication I was desperate to interpret but too scared to ask.

He stepped closer. "So, we're . . ."

"Friends." The word tasted wrong in my mouth, but it was the first one my brain supplied, so it would have to do.

His hand dragged down his scraggily beard, drawing my gaze to his lips. Those lips that had kissed me and made me moan. He could call me whatever with those lips. I could dislike him and still want to haul him to the library and do very inappropriate things to him, right? That was the type of friendship I wanted.

The idea of those lips made me rub my thighs together, fingers clutched to the hem of my shorts as I had to fight the temptation to see if he remembered.

I stayed up at night thinking, dreaming, wondering what would have happened if we hadn't stopped. I was being haunted in this crumbling estate. But not by any ghosts, by this real-life man and his lips. Ass. Hole.

"It's been a long time since I've had a friend."

My heart squeezed at his words. If I wasn't already on board, I was now. Who could say no to being his friend? Well, unless you couldn't discount the grumpiness, tendency to speak in orders, and general lack of knowledge of social formalities.

"I'm wounded, sir." Bl8z3 was pushing the bounds for what an AI was capable of outside of the movies. Sarcasm was part of its programming, apparently.

"Stop calling me sir." He released that growl I knew, and, uh, thought absolutely nothing about, especially at night.

"It's against my programming," Oliver mouthed along with Bl8z3.

"Friend." I twisted the word over in my mouth. "It's nice to have a friend."

He nodded, dipping his cloth in the water again. "I could still banish you if I wanted to."

"Empty threat." A smile broke out. "But as a friend I have to tell you"—I tried to cover my chuckle—"you are terrible at this."

Oliver blew out a breath, rolling his eyes. "I'm dreadful at everything."

Shaking my head, I shifted closer. "You're being too gentle." Placing my cloth next to his, I attempted to show him what I was talking about.

"Like this?"

I nibbled on my lip. "No, no." Leaving my cloth at the edge of the bucket, I laid my fingers on top of his hand. Pressing down slightly, showing him how to move the cloth so as not to soak the silk.

Oliver's thumb brushed mine, goose bumps breaking out in its wake.

We stood, shoulder to shoulder, slowly cleaning, mostly allowing our fingers to dance together, his skin brushing against my pulse point. I had to wonder if he could feel it.

When the cloth was too dry to clean any further, Oliver released my fingers long enough to turn his palm around and hold my hand for real. Tossing the cloth back into the bucket, he cupped my chin.

I waited another breath before I lifted my gaze to meet his. He gulped, gray eyes bright.

"Thank you." His fingers squeezed mine, thumb pressed to my rapidly beating pulse point.

"For what?"

"Not giving up on me."

CHAPTER THIRTEEN

Partway through the day, Finn popped his head into the study, inviting Oliver to join us for dinner. I could tell by Finn's expression, his intentions were more meddlesome than polite.

Still, I almost fell over when Oliver accepted the invitation.

This was going to be awkward.

Rue whipped something together with only a hot plate—better than most could with a stove. The small card table that typically sat in the kitchen was set up on the patio, with place settings for four, the sun setting behind us. Elegant, despite the plastic utensils and paper plates.

"I am salivating. How in the world did you hire a Michelin chef? What kind of wine are we having?" Finn stopped, staring as Oliver lumbered out onto the patio.

"I think it's a rosé." I swooped in, uncorking the bottle, and pouring four generous plastic cups, taking a sip of mine while plopping into my chair.

"Have a seat, Oliver. It's time we have a talk." Sebastian was never subtle.

I had to give Oliver credit—he didn't even blink, just sat as we passed around the food.

Plates piled high, Sebastian held off as the rest of us dived in. "So, I'm curious. You have an actual person made of sunshine and joy living in your house, and you somehow were compelled to be cruel to her. Care to explain yourself?"

"Sebastian," I begged, sliding down in my chair.

"Oh no, I think it deserves an answer, don't you?" His glare was set entirely on Oliver.

All Finn and I could do was blink at this showdown.

"You're right." Oliver's fingers curled around the edge of the table.

"Come again?" I blurted out at Oliver's admission.

"I told you earlier, you didn't deserve my behavior." Knees bouncing, Oliver stared at his plate.

It was the closest I was going to get to an apology. "I thought you were huffing fumes from the wallpaper."

Finn giggled, which Sebastian didn't appreciate. "I'm curious why you would even stay here. You've done enough damage. Let Bell work in peace."

"Sebastian." I bristled. "He's overseeing the project, and this is his house. You can't . . ." My mind blanked on any other word. "Banish him."

"Yeah, that would be a terrible thing to do," Oliver deadpanned.

It was the worst possible moment for him to crack a joke. My gaze caught his, a single eyebrow raising, and to Sebastian's horror, we broke into laughter.

"I mean, really, what kind of jerk banishes a person?" I giggled.

Oliver's thighs spread close enough to touch his knee to mine. My breath shifted from a laugh to something else stirring in my chest. Friendship had never brought electricity to my veins.

"Well, if you are going to stay here with our Bell, it's time we learn about you." Finn's grin had an edge to it.

"What do you want to know?"

"Favorite movie?"

There was no holding back my snort as Oliver pretended to glare at me.

"I don't watch much TV."

Finn gasped. "What do you two even talk about? TV and films fill all the lonely parts of her."

"Darling, I don't think you meant to say that last part," Sebastian gritted out as I sank further into my chair. Any lower, and I'd be hiding under the table.

"Watching TV isn't a sign of loneliness." Oliver's pinky brushed mine, causing me to take another gulp of wine with my other hand.

"No, but a beard like that might be." Sebastian smirked.

"I don't think he's had anyone to tell him that. For the past few years, he's only lived with people who call him 'sir.'" I pressed my glass to my lips. Despite its wildness, the beard was growing on me.

"Kinky," Finn quipped.

"My programming requires me to refer to Oliver Killington as 'sir,'" Bl8z3 offered.

Sebastian and Finn jumped in their seats.

"Is that the . . .?" Sebastian whispered, eyes wild, drifting across every surface. I nodded as Sebastian pointed to the ceiling. "How do you get used to it?"

All I could do was shrug. Somewhere along the way, it had become normal for Bl8z3 to speak up.

Sebastian's eyes kept shooting up to the ceiling before resting on Oliver. "Stop making her doubt herself. Bells deserves to see herself the way the world does, and to accept how absolutely spectacular she is, a source of blinding sunshine."

My eyes filled with tears as I considered my best friend. "That doesn't sound pleasant."

His foot kicked at mine under the table. "You get what I'm saying."

"Yeah." I sniffled. "Can we eat now? I'm hungry."

"Fine, but Oliver, tell me who your team is."

I held my breath, wondering if this was too far. If Oliver had pushed away all the happy memories of his family, thinking about football had to hurt in its own way.

"College or NFL?" Oliver's palms moved to his thighs, sliding back and forth, slowly, my heart pounding in time with his movements.

"Either." Sebastian shrugged, voice conveying that this mattered.

"I'll be honest: it's been a while since I've watched." Oliver sipped from his cup.

I held my breath. Would anyone notice if I got up and went to find some gummy bears? Maybe hide out in the kitchen for a while?

"But I was always a fan of LSU," Oliver confessed.

Sebastian popped a fry into his mouth. "Well, decent people can still make bad choices." His eyes filled with mirth, as a weight lifted from my chest. "All right." Sebastian leaned forward. "Do you know anything about the new technology your family's company is planning on investing in? Because I have some theories, and if you maybe blink when I say something that sounds correct—"

I coughed loudly. "Insider trading."

Oliver's foot nudged mine.

And with that, my accidental roommate became a tentative accidental friend with mine.

Long after we finished eating and opened a second bottle of wine, I watched Oliver interact with my favorite people. Sebastian laughed, full-throated *laughed*, at something Oliver said while Finn ensured our Solo cups remained full. I rubbed my knuckle at the emotion building in my chest.

It seemed impossible, the intersection of these two worlds, but here it was, seamless, easy. Not that it mattered when I'd be leaving in a matter of months.

120 Days Until the Deadline

I returned from the kitchen with a glass of water and some of Rue's cookies, to discover an argyle sock hanging off my bedroom door handle. A sock. Like we were still in college.

I should have realized something was up when Sebastian asked me to grab him a snack from downstairs. The way he shoved me out the door as Finn nodded aggressively.

We were adults now, with our own bedrooms and doors. I was more than delighted to give them alone time. Finn's mural was a beautiful burst of colors, abstract, a variety of flowers practically exploding from the wall. It was going to be a statement when it was finished—he had outdone himself, making me even more appreciative they were here. Except when they were in *my* bedroom.

I smacked my palm on the wood, hoping I was interrupting a particularly intimate moment.

"Ten minutes," Sebastian called out.

"Thirty," corrected Finn.

I gave the door another smack before plodding down the stairs, grumbling to myself. "You're up at least, Bl8z3?"

I was met with silence, only proving the point that it was time for me to be in bed.

I dug around the barebones kitchen, brewing myself a cup of chamomile tea. Setting the kettle on the table, I dipped my tea bag, relaxing into the routine.

Sebastian and Finn's relationship was something that made me happy to witness. But it was also a glaring spotlight on what my life was missing. What Dan had pointed out I would always be lacking.

And maybe, just maybe, I was horny. I wouldn't mind having a reason to put a sock on the door. I knew they wouldn't lock me out the entire night, at least not on purpose, but—

"Couldn't sleep either?" Oliver stood at the entrance to the kitchen, fists stuffed into his pajama bottoms.

His hair was loose, landing at his shoulders in disarray, as if he had just run his fingers through it.

But what had me staring, struggling to swallow, was his beard. Oliver was still the bearded hulking man I had become used to, but it was no longer unruly—now it was trimmed close to his face, the edges straightened. The cheekbones I had only seen hints of before were prominent. The mystery of where Sebastian had disappeared to today suddenly revealed itself.

"Your beard . . ." I was gawking, but unable to stop.

He shifted his stance, hand moving to stroke it, but coming up empty. "Is it okay?"

"I'm surprised you didn't shave it off." It was a fresh start, another change, like the house around us, though he had been frozen even deeper in the past.

"Not a beard fan?" An eyebrow quirked up.

"I didn't say that." My response was too quick, too telling. My heart, on red alert, beat rapidly in my chest.

I couldn't stop staring. There were those lips I had kissed, no longer hidden. His nose seemed straighter now. My eyes feasted, having never fully gotten a view of his neck, thick and leading toward those broad shoulders I remembered gripping.

He shifted, shoving his hands into his pockets. "Good." A slight nod.

He looked almost touchable, not so separate from the world. It took me another moment to put my finger on it. His eyes were lacking the tension lines, the grief he carried with him, and the realization opened something in my chest. My palm pressed against my sternum, as if I could grab it, touch it, preserve it, whatever it was.

Gazing at him caused me to clutch my teacup harder. The past few days had been a mess of highs and lows, hot and cold. The strumming in my veins was a reminder. But now, it was as if I was truly seeing the real him for the first time. The man who had held my hand and thanked me for not giving up on him.

The silence had to cease, to get me to stop staring, put an end to these wild thoughts running through my mind. "I was sex-blocked from entering my room." It sounded ridiculous even as I blurted it out.

Oliver's eyebrows popped up.

"Sebastian and Finn never gave up the honeymoon phase. They like to treat every new place like it's a vacation."

"So, they're having vacation sex in your room?" A single eyebrow arched up, drawing me along with it.

It sounded worse when he said it. I stood up, reaching on the shelf for the bottle of bourbon, pouring a generous shot into my cup. "Yup."

"Where are you sleeping?" Oliver didn't even sound surprised, which was fair after what he had witnessed during dinner. Sebastian and Finn had no problem with PDA. It wasn't too much, but they seemed unable to not be touching the other for an extended amount of time. I had never felt that way about another human, my skin hungry, desperate for contact.

"Hadn't gotten that far." The garage? The lawn? My only options were terrible.

"There still water in there?" His head nodded toward the kettle.

I moved to grab him a cup, but his hand at my elbow stopped me. Instead, he made it himself, refreshing mine in the process, before sitting down across from me in the breakfast nook. His gaze skimmed my body, making me remember I had taken my bra off when I changed. I glanced down discreetly. *Crap.*

Oliver cleared his throat, gaze firmly above my neck. "They don't seem like an obvious match."

"The artist and the financier? Sebastian is much more straight-laced; he likes his routines and sticks with them. Finn's life is almost chaotic." My feet rested on the edge of the bench across from me, close but not touching his leg as my fingers clutched my elbow.

I required sleep, or at least heavy drugs, to stop whatever this was.

"But they make it work," he said, a statement, not a question.

"Through sheer force of will and love, yeah. It gets messy and they adore complaining to me. But even the things they enjoy nagging each other about are things they truly cherish." The little sigh

I released was accidental. Not everyone got some great love. Sometimes your career was your passion, the thing you connected with and sat alone with for hours.

"Do you think that can last when two people don't have a lot in common?" His head tilted, focus on me, as if invested in my answer, like it mattered.

"Yeah, I do. On paper they make no sense, but when you meet them, you can't imagine them with anyone else."

"I had friends like that."

"Had?" The word tumbled out. It bothered me more and more every day. Him here, lonely. Even if the house had been full of people, something told me he still would have felt alone with his guilt and shame.

"My social life is a reflection of this house." Oliver glanced around the room. "Well, before you got here." A finger traced around the rim of his cup, a finger I wanted tracing me. "You do any work for individuals in social Siberia?"

"You know me. I love a good fixer-upper." I hid my smile behind my teacup, the steam wafting to my cheeks, warming them.

Oliver tried again to tug at the beard that was no longer there, the curve at the edge of his lips revealed.

I ached to touch him, help him complete the smile. Feel what he was feeling.

"How long have they been together?" His knee brushed my ankle, staying there, acting as an electricity conduit. At dinner we had been in an enclosed space, a table meant for children, but now there was no reason for him to do this other than for the pleasure of it.

My breath hitched. "Sebastian and Finn?"

Oliver nodded.

"Since our final year of college. Though it's more like forever, they're such a unit." They weren't codependent, but I couldn't imagine one without the other.

"Are they the marrying sort?"

"Sebastian thinks it's outdated, more about a person's tax status than anything else. Finn's a romantic, and he's not so subtly leaving pictures from wedding magazines around their apartment."

"I bet Sebastian has a ring." Oliver stretched, the bench creaking.

I released a bark of laughter. *Got it in one.* "For a year, sitting in his drawer, awaiting the moment Finn least expects it."

"Do you think you'll ever get married?" Oliver peered at me over his cup.

I appreciated that he didn't assume it was an automatic yes. Marriage was not for everyone. "I guess I haven't thought about it. I'm such a nomad." One of the biggest symbols of commitment, it seemed far out of my reach.

"Because of your job?"

The lonely sensation that had been overtaking me until he had made his presence known returned with a vengeance. "Yeah, but also, I'm not even sure how to be settled. College was the longest I was in one place. Every vacation and break, I met Dad at whatever project he was at. I'm just a short-timer." I was never in a place long enough to set down roots, I didn't exactly scream "stable relationship material."

"Your partner could travel with you, if that's something you wanted." Oliver's voice was quiet.

"That's a delightful dream." I didn't wish to keep talking about this. Not with him. He knew I wasn't a girl with a home; he recognized it in me. "What about you?"

He quirked an eyebrow. "Ah, the game again?"

"Fair's fair."

"I told you, I'm beating them off with sticks. Who wouldn't wish to live in a crumbling estate with a recluse?" I could have mopped the floor with the sarcasm dripping from his voice, then knocked him on the head with it for his nonsense.

"You went through a trauma, and that was not what I asked."

"Fine." He grunted, shifting in his seat. "I wouldn't be opposed to marrying the right person. To consider it. One day." The halting way he spoke made me want to reach my palm across the table and touch him.

Instead, I tucked my foot underneath his thigh. A compromise.

"Well, be grateful you have a bed. I'm not traveling back upstairs to check if they're done yet." I'd make Sebastian snake the toilets before he left. That would teach him. Especially since they were all getting replaced.

"I'm not leaving you to sleep down here." Oliver glared at me as if I were the person in the wrong here.

"I'm a big girl. I'll survive." Worst-case scenario, I'd crash on the bench—you're never too young to have a back spasm.

"I have a perfectly good bed upstairs."

What now? My palms broke out in a sweat. Sleep in the same room as Oliver? That sounded like pure torture. What were we going to do, share the bed? My fantasies had gone well beyond thinking about his lips, that kiss. My knees wobbled at the memory, and I was still sitting down.

"Uh." My mind was blank. Parts of my body were yelling out, *Hell yes.* Other parts were admitting that this was a terrible idea and would lead to a night of sleeplessness and torture by sexual desire. The goal was to get some sleep, not lie awake panting.

Did I mention how much the beard was working for me?

He lifted his palms in surrender. "Just sleeping, I promise."

My stomach sank. Because of course this meant something different to him. One of us had walked out of that room without a glance back. This was a peace offering. A kindness, pity. "I'll be fine."

He leaned back, arm running along the top of the bench as if he was settling in. "You stay, I stay."

"Do you have to be so difficult?" I attempted to wiggle my foot, but the weight of his thigh kept me firmly in place.

Realizing he'd won, he stood, gathering our things from the table. He deposited the cups and kettle in the sink before rotating toward me, a softness in his gaze. "Don't overcomplicate this. Tomorrow is going to be another long day where you work yourself to the bone harder than anyone else. You need sleep."

I took a breath and stood up, hoping my legs could keep me steady. "Sleep, yes, sleep, it's a thing we do. Uh, let's . . ." Redesigning a house, I was competent. Stand me in front of what was the most gorgeous, complicated man I had ever met? Have him care about my well-being? A romantic disaster.

"Come on." He gestured for me to lead the way, behind me the entire time in those sweatpants clinging to his thighs, and another T-shirt that he seemed to have an endless supply of.

Walking temptation.

CHAPTER FOURTEEN

I had seen a glimpse of Oliver's room before, but now I was inside the inner sanctum.

A queen-sized bed with white sheets and a dark gray bedspread sat in the middle of the room. A sofa that wasn't quite big enough for him to stretch out on was set in front of a bureau. There were no pictures, no football trophies. Bare and lacking a personal touch, it reminded me of a sparsely decorated hotel room. Or my room in Dad's apartment.

"I moved in here after the accident." He rubbed his left thigh.

"You forgot to decorate." Here I was, the pot calling the kettle black.

"Not all of us are as talented as you."

Heat filled my cheeks as I concentrated on the bed. "Okay, but these pillows are criminal."

His lips pursed in a way that hinted he was trying not to smile. "Having pillows is criminal?"

"These two lifeless, flat objects lying on your bed? Yes. Where is the neck support, the fluffy softness you are desperate to fall into every night?" I held up the offensive pillow, watching it limp over. My neck hurt at the very sight.

"That's what you look forward to at the end of the day?" He scrubbed down his face, square jaw grinding.

"You don't? A weighted blanket wouldn't hurt either." I could picture it, how to make this space his, or at least comfortable.

"Probably not my first thought when I think of beds."

A flush crawled over my skin as I tossed the pillow. "What do you think about, then?" And now I was word vomiting statements that could be considered flirting. I guess I should be thankful it was a full sentence.

Oliver moved to sit at the end of the bed, rolling his neck. "I'm thinking you might be right about that neck support."

"Never be in charge of redecorating." I perched next to him, shoving my hands between my thighs.

"Isn't this what they call monochrome?"

He was trying, and it was adorable. "This is more, uh, bachelor pad." I glanced at the mismatched couch. "There isn't a scheme, more a collection of things. Aren't you supposed to be a *rich* recluse?"

"Ouch." His hands came up as if I had wounded him. But we both knew it took more than that.

I nudged his shoulder with mine. "We all have our strengths."

"It feels like throwing a dart at a board while blindfolded." He leaned forward, elbows on his knees, head ducked, his shoulders scrunched, tension rolling off him. "Maybe everyone only gets one thing, and I've already had mine."

My heart squeezed. "You'll find something else—you probably already have." My heart sank; I was the one who had made him feel this way. "Can I?" I wiggled my fingers at him, needing to do something to bring him some sort of relief.

"Said with the confidence of someone who has found their thing." His shoulders rolled, easing back toward me. My fingers immediately met with the knots in his back, the weight he carried, the physical manifestation of it. I couldn't change his past, but I could relieve some of it in this moment, taking some of his pain from him.

"I fell into it. Got lucky. I loved the work Dad did." He released a soft moan as I dug into the muscles along his spine. I wanted to press my forehead there, acknowledge the trust that he was giving to me for a moment, this silent beating thing. The world had tossed him around, and still he was able to be here with me, the heat from his body drawing me closer. I couldn't not be touching him. I never wanted to stop.

"I understand family legacy. It's constantly breathing down your neck." He tilted his head to consider me, cheeks flushed. "You're good at this."

"Should I become a masseuse?"

"Wait until you finish with the house."

I squeezed his shoulders. "You're only saying that so you don't have to share me."

"Guilty."

My fingers stopped moving as his gaze captured mine. Those gray orbs had been haunting me. My thumb brushed against the juncture of his shoulder and neck, watching his pulse point beat rapidly in time with my own.

I was leaving in a matter of months, and he'd be off inheriting the family business. We were running parallel for the briefest moment before our lives diverged in different directions.

But my palm remained against his neck, curling as I leaned in, propelled by some hidden force that had nothing to do with my brain. All the reasons not to were growing quieter and quieter as everything in my body tingled, gathering low in my belly.

"You going to kiss me, Petal?" he asked as our noses brushed.

"Do you want me to?" Part of me was still hesitant, remembering how he'd run out the last time.

He surged forward, wrapping his arms around me, lifting me until I straddled him. "We shouldn't."

"Oh." I leaned back, pulling my hands away from his shoulders, but he caught them, pressing them to his chest. His heart was racing, maybe more than mine.

"We shouldn't, but I want to."

His lips captured mine, and fuck, it was worse, so much worse than I had prepared myself for. Because it was better than the last time—impossibly, earth-shatteringly better. Fireworks went off in my brain, an "Out of Office" sign, away messages. I released a moan, desperate for more.

My fingers delved into his hair, his beard brushing against my cheek as the soft press of his lips became more confident. His sweatpants failed to hide the bulge pressed between us, hitting my center.

All of him was designed to wreck me. Then the curve of his lips lifted. Oliver smiled as our lips continued their dance.

"Fuck." His voice echoed my experience—insides burning, gasping for breath.

He bit his lip, and I couldn't help myself—I chased after it, bringing him back. I ran my tongue along his bottom lip as he opened, angling my head, shifting my hips, pressing him where I was aching. Separated by our pajamas, it wasn't close enough.

I scratched my fingernails down his biceps, my hand unable to circle him, holding on. He was soft and hard in all the best places.

I had never been so knocked off center, and I wanted more. My greedy hands pulled at his T-shirt, lifting.

"Tell me it's as good for you as it is for me," he demanded in a low voice as I sat back to admire the breadth of his shoulders. I wasn't attracted to the overly slim runner types. I enjoyed bulkier builds, a bear of a man, as Sebastian would say. Oliver was every daydream I'd ever had, but *better*.

I wanted to taste him. My tongue crept down his shoulders to his pecs, biting. I had a very specific goal in mind, desperate to stay in control of this moment.

"What are you doing?" His voice was hoarse as I shifted to the floor, in between his thighs, my lips still on him, licking along the trail of black hair.

"Blowing your mind." I grinned as I reached for his pajama bottoms.

Before I could touch him, he halted me, his other palm clenched on his left thigh, rubbing the muscle there. "It's not that I don't want it. All I crave is you." He pressed my hand to his erection. He was huge everywhere, and my pussy clenched, already imagining it. "But I haven't done this in a while and . . ." He played with a tendril of my hair that had fallen.

"There's no pressure." I shifted my hand to twine my fingers with his. "I want what you want."

"Can we"—he ducked his head down, fingers picking at the hem of my shirt—"can the pants stay on?"

"Of course." It was better this way, one of us keeping our wits about us, going slow, not baring it all. He had mentioned he hadn't dated anyone in a while; sex was likely part of that too. Lonely in a million different ways, and here he was letting me in. I didn't know what to do with that but understood it for the gift it was.

"Okay." He took a breath, then said with more confidence, "Okay."

He kissed me softly this time, cupping my cheek, gliding his lips across mine in a tender caress while I clutched at his shoulders. My veins were on fire, liquid burning through my body, my smile stretching across my face.

His palms gripped my hips, shifting me to straddle him again, as I landed directly over his erection, both of us hissing out a moan as our mouths connected, tongues licking the fire that danced between us. My nipples were practically poking a hole through my shirt to get to him, my thighs aching at the spread.

"I'm not sure I'm going to last very long." The hunger returned to his eyes as he released a nervous laugh, our stomachs pressed together.

"I got this," I promised, knees digging into his mattress, as my fingers gripped his shoulders, dragging his erection against my throbbing clit. It was delicious and all our clothes were on. This was safer, in my control, but that control was quickly slipping away from me. My gaze drifted up to his face to check in.

He leaned back, eyes heavy lidded, watching me, my breasts bouncing as my hips rolled.

"You're too good at this." He moaned, falling further, landing on his elbows, pulling me down with him, nipping along my neck, fingers clutching at my hips. "Don't hold back." He growled, shifting his hips, his erection pressing along the front of my pajama pants, hitting all the spots that made my toes curl.

Every part of me was turned on watching him enjoy this, as my body clenched on nothing. He brushed his fingers against my nipples, my palms landing on either side of his head, squeezing the comforter.

He overwhelmed me, his clean scent surrounding us, the taste of his skin, every growl from the back of his throat, the flush

covering his body. Kissing him in the library hadn't been a blip—
it was a taste, and now I was getting another course, hungry for
more.

I rocked into him, stars flashing behind my eyes, building, and
building. And burst.

"Petal," he breathed against my lips.

We ignited together from nothing more than grinding in our
pajamas. I liked it way too much. The gentle way he kissed me,
thumb brushing against my cheek, smiling again, like for tonight,
we had a secret.

We cleaned ourselves up and ended up back on the bed.

"You'll stay?" His hand grabbed at the thick part of my waist,
holding me to him. Every single part of him was telling me he
wanted this, wanted me, at least for tonight.

I avoided glancing toward the couch. "Yeah, I can stick
around."

"Good." His eyes were at half mast, and it was hard not to be
smug. "In a minute, I'm going to get my hands on you."

"Sure you are." My fingers scratched along his scalp.

"I have," he yawned, "to keep feeling you."

"I know, stud." My limbs were heavy, sated.

I should have moved, gotten under the covers, lain on one of
those flat pillows. But I couldn't, mesmerized by the peace on his
face, no scowls or frown lines. Relaxed. His enormous palm gripped
my hip, keeping me partially on top of him as he slept.

My eyes tracked the darkened room, seeming larger with so few
possessions in it. In his space, his heartbeat under my ear, it was too
easy to fall asleep.

Barely Even Friends

119 Days Until the Deadline

A pocket of sunshine forced my eyes open, one curtain pulled back, head resting on a too flat pillow in the middle of a mattress. I was in Oliver's room, in his bed.

My palm swiped out, but I was only met with cool, soft cotton that Ambrose had probably ironed before he had made the bed.

I was alone.

It was for the best. Made things simple. I could slip out, avoid any awkwardness.

I hurried, fixing my clothes, throwing my hair back in a pony-tail, hoping my room was empty now so I could shower and change.

As I reached for my cell phone, the en suite bathroom door opened, and my heart leaped in my chest, ending any chance of a simple escape.

"Morning." Oliver stood in front of me, water glistening on his shoulders as he toweled his hair. Another towel was swung across his hips, leaving his delectable chest bare.

My cheeks were still flushed from his beard as I watched a drop dip down his skin, my body lighting up for a moment, tin-gling from the memories of the night before, how he'd gripped my hips, the grunts he made, the intimate way his gaze held mine as he came.

"Morning." I bit my lip hard.

"Did you sleep okay?" He took another step into the room.

"Yeah, uh . . . did you slumber restfully?" I was focused on the newly exposed freckles on his shoulders, which I had been too dis-tracted to discover the night before. I wanted to count them, mem-orize them, trace their pattern.

"Yes." His face contorted, almost confused. "I did."

"I should . . ." I gestured toward the door, inarticulate. But what do you say? *"Hope the make-out and grind session was as good for you as it was for me?"* I was a walking disaster and had to leave before I said something embarrassing. Like, can we do it again sometime?

He took another step, but he seemed miles away from this room. Probably figuring out the best way to let me down gently. "Petal, I—"

"It's okay—I understand. We don't have to do the morning-after thing." It was safer. He had mentioned he hadn't done this in a while. No need to make it worse with my awkward tumble of morning-after feelings as messy as my hair.

"The morning-after thing?" He genuinely seemed confused.

Why couldn't he let this be easy? Give me one of his stiff nods and let me overthink all of this in peace.

"Where you ensure I'm not in love with you and am not going to expect sleepover privileges from now on. We're good, I promise." I held my hands up as if I could convince him, or at least clarify I wasn't trying to act out every romantic comedy I had ever watched.

His hand fell to his side, face unreadable. I was baring my heart as I shifted my stance, fingers curled around the hem of my sleep shirt. My body screamed, *Defenseless soul! Try not to break her, please.*

"Are those the only options?" he asked.

"What else is there?" It was tempting to tell him he was relying on an expertise I'd never had that didn't fit into my escape-as-soon-as-feasible plan. He was vulnerable, lonely in a way I understood. He didn't want a fuck buddy; this had been a one-time-only thing.

When he said nothing, I accepted it as my cue to leave. I gave him a small salute, which was guaranteed to ensure I was never getting laid again, especially by him.

My room was blessedly empty as I stood in the shower, hoping to release some of the tension that had wrecked my body moments after I'd awoken.

Worse, I was still keyed up from the night before. I circled my clit in smaller and smaller circles, desperate for relief. But it wasn't enough, my fingers were too small, it wasn't enough pressure, and I was still aching.

Unable to stop myself, I imagined the roll of his hips, the weight of his erection as he thrust against me. Touching myself, I fantasized it was him, wondering if anything could ever compare.

The shower didn't get rid of my embarrassment, but helped it melt into my skin, releasing the tension so I could face the day. The grumble of my stomach reminded me I couldn't avoid going downstairs forever. One hookup didn't have to change everything. One night to knock it out of our systems, that was all it was. Now things would be less . . . tense between Oliver and me.

I passed Finn, pausing briefly, even though he was absorbed too deeply to give me more than a nod before bringing his brush to the wall in that deliberate manner of his. Every time I saw him paint, I was struck by his talent. He'd taken the inspiration Oliver's mom's notebook provided, putting his own spin on it. His work inspired me on how to reupholster the dining room chairs, helped me decide between my carpet options.

Hopefully, Oliver would feel the same way.

Sebastian's eyebrows lifted in surprise as I strolled into the kitchen. Traitor. Even with my shame, the deadline didn't allow for horny breaks.

"And where have you been?" Sebastian's voice was filled with laughter.

"Oh, now you care?" I not so accidentally stomped on Sebastian's foot as I grabbed a bagel, placing it in the toaster.

"I may have deserved that. But you are suspiciously well rested for someone who didn't sleep in her bed last night in a house with a shortage of beds."

The desire to pick up a bagel and smack the smugness out of him with carbohydrates filled me. "I don't wish to talk about it."

He squirmed, slightly contrite. "I'm sorry. We didn't exactly plan it, and trust me, you didn't want to come in when you knocked."

"Yes, thank you for the favor you did me." I reached for the cream cheese and a plate. The aroma of the coffee carafe was calling my name as I prepared my breakfast, sitting across from the man formerly known as my best friend. "Don't make me stab you with this knife."

"Did you get stabbed with something else last night?"

"You are the absolute worst." I avoided all eye contact as I took a bite out of my bagel. Given what had happened with most of our clothes on, I wasn't sure I could handle a naked Oliver. "Besides, I thought you didn't like him."

"It's hard not to empathize with someone who's survived something horrific and got a bit stuck." His foot nudged mine under the table. "I can't be mad at the person who put that flush on your cheeks, or is that beard burn?"

"Anger. It's an angry flush." I defended my body's betrayal.

"Hate sex is great too. Finn and I role-play sometimes, and I'm the—"

I covered my ears in desperation. "I beg of you, what do I have to do to stop this conversation from happening?"

A not-very-subtle smirk erupted on Sebastian's face, but he didn't continue pressing. "Come on. You can tell me anything." Switching tactics, he pulled out the puppy eyes, blinking a few times. No matter how cold the soul, those eyes had a seventy-six

and a half percent rate of success, though it was one hundred percent with Finn. "I'm filled with guilt."

"Yeah, I'm sure we're the reason you didn't get any sleep last
night." I was going to have to make sure the sheets were washed
before I went to bed, not that Ambrose would allow me to use the
washing machine.

"It's possible."

I took a vicious bite out of my bagel. "Live in mystery. Your
betrayal does not earn you information."

"Think of the story you can tell your grandchildren."

"Grandchildren?" I snorted. "How my best friend sexed me out
of my room? A heartwarming tale."

"Fine, we'll decide on something better. But come on, did you
spend the evening with the grumpy owner of the castle?" Since
Finn, Sebastian believed every good love story was a fairy tale
brought to life. Preferably a queer one that was not rated G. His
cynicism that had bonded us initially had been forever wrecked
once he found love.

"Trust me, he's not Prince Charming." It went without saying
that I wasn't a damsel in search of someone to order me around for
the rest of my life. "He and I, we're . . . barely even friends."

Work was what I knew: how to reconstruct a house. Recon-
structing my heart was not something I was equipped for.

CHAPTER FIFTEEN

99 Days Until the Deadline

What's worse than someone avoiding you for weeks, even though you live together?

Them *not* avoiding you, like that bump and grind brought you closer together as *friends* and not a single thing more.

I was fine, things were fine, everything was fine. Fine. Fine. Fine.

It didn't help matters that Cousin Carter had stopped by for another surprise check-in. But even he wasn't enough of a distraction. Every time I ran into Oliver, my heart gave an extra beat, palms sweaty with expectation, as if this would be the moment he would want to discuss the way I could not stop staring at his thighs or noticing how he kept shoving his fists into his pants pockets. Which only tightened the fit of his pants, and I was not staring at his dick. I wasn't.

It was nothing. Not a thing. Just walking around with the slightest breeze turning me on. The brush of my suspenders against my breasts made me . . . okay, there might be some residual tension.

During the day, I survived, mostly. When I was absorbed in the work, I was able to ignore him. Except for every time he walked into a room I was in, his gaze catching mine as he put all his effort on whatever task I had assigned him for that day—sanding the tables or removing the hardware from the walls—no matter how menial. Or all the times he checked in with me, making sure I ate.

But at night, I stood under my showerhead. The hot water beat on my back as I tried to relieve the tension that had built up. Tonight was like every other, me putting the pipes to the test. Fingers buried deep in my pussy, trying to make that ache that haunted me go away. My forehead pressed to the tile, thumb brushing my clit, having long given up the pretense I bore during the day that I wasn't fantasizing about Oliver storming into my room, glaring, heated, searching for something to complain about, chest heaving. Which would only lead to me shoving him into a closet, my shorts ending up on the ground, his mouth, fingers—*any* of him—on me, in me, scratching that itch because my delving fingers were not doing it despite all my attempts.

Oliver would make that growling noise in the back of his throat as he—

The pipes clanged, and I screamed—*not* in pleasure. The water sputtered as it sprayed freezing cold. I hastened to twist the knob all the way, but the hot water didn't return, as the banging sound continued, the icy deluge breaking up in spurts, smacking me in the face.

I switched the water off; the banging immediately ceased. The water heater was probably busted, a common thing in older homes.

I'd call Jeff, get another here in a day or two. Nothing to be concerned about.

Then the thumping started up again, louder than before. My eyes pressed closed as I made a wish. With a final clang, a pipe burst through the wall directly outside of the shower, chunks of plaster dropping, water gushing on the floor, spraying wildly, soaking everything in its path.

Chaos erupted around me as I stood buck naked, water dripping down my body, trying not to shiver, my brain struggling to comprehend how I had gotten here.

"You have got to be fucking kidding me," I screamed as I ran to my bedroom. Bellamy disaster mode activated. My suitcase contained an emergency kit—a necessity after so many builds. I was no contractor, but I could handle basic things. The after-hours repair person always ended up being me, with Dad's oversight.

"Turn off the water, turn off the water," I chanted to myself. There was no room to worry about anything else, like the cause or the damage, as gallons of water poured out of the rusty pipe.

The door slammed open as I continued my search, but I didn't have time for distractions.

"Bell, are you okay?" Oliver called out before sprinting into the bathroom, feet slogging through water.

"I have to find the water shut-off valve," I yelled from under the sink, over the sound of damage happening in real time.

"Uh, I . . ."

"Success," I muttered mostly to myself, using the wrench to twist the pipe. Most people figured I was pretty weak because of my weight. That I was out of shape, not capable. With a final yank, everything ceased, the water still dripping for a few moments. I plopped on the toilet hard, surveying the devastation, my stomach sinking to my toes.

The water was an inch deep by the time the chaos had—well, "calmed" wasn't the right word, but the situation was less urgent. The carpet in the bedroom had soaked up a lot, to its sopping detriment. But it was the spraying that had caused the bigger mess. From where I was sitting, I could see the damage done to my clothes hanging in the open armoire, leaving them soggy and unwearable.

"Bell, Petal, you are—"

"I'm fucked is what I am. This means there's a problem with the pipes." Now that the immediate issue had been addressed, I absorbed how royally screwed I was. This was not a simple fix. My deadline, three months away, beat against my brain. Between the damage the leaky roof had caused and now this, I'd be lucky if the estate was still standing by the time Mr. Killington's party rolled around.

It would be countless hours of work, replacing all of the pipes, and if it had to be done for the entire house? The damage to the walls, leaks, searching for water damage, mold. My mind ran worst-case scenarios as I folded my legs underneath my body, my sock floating by Oliver, who stood with murky water to his ankles, feet bare.

"What? What did you want to tell me?" I buried my face in my hands, every inch of me damp too, still dripping from the shower. "How everything that could go wrong has? The roof, water damage—if there wasn't mold before, there probably will be now. I just—"

It hit me then, and I gasped with the pressure of it. It wouldn't be possible to make the deadline. This dream job I had been holding deep inside, that I tried to pretend I wasn't thinking about constantly, it was floating away with my sock, drowned with the rest of my belongings.

I glanced up, catching sight of the framed photo of Dad and me, arm in arm, floating by. My favorite photo of us, the one I took everywhere with me, the first one I always set up to help me settle in. I didn't know how to feel at home, but at least I had that. Sprinting, I snatched it up, but it was already too late. The water had seeped in, warping the memory.

And everything in me crumpled, my body turning into itself. I hugged myself, shivering, as I clutched the picture frame. Now my face was wet for a different reason. There was no coming back from this. All I could do was—

"Well, I was going to point out that you are, uh, naked." Oliver's voice broke through my panicked thoughts as I hiccupped.

"I'm what?" I glanced down, and yes, things could in fact get worse. I was absolutely boobs-swinging-in-the-wind naked. Perfect. This was absolutely perfect and exactly how I'd pictured Oliver seeing me nude for the first time. Dripping wet from the shower, standing in a puddle of stale water as we stared at each other.

I sniffled, trying to get my emotions under control and failing at that impossible endeavor. Here I was, rock bottom, with the last person who cared.

I reached for the towel I could never wrap around my full-figured body, wishing I had somehow had the forethought to grab it in all the chaos before he had come racing in, trying to be a water cowboy.

As I struggled to drape the too small fabric around my not-one-size-fits-all figure, I was tugged in the opposite direction. Oliver lifted me with ease, setting my body against his.

"I'm going to get you all wet. Put me down." I sniffled, too pathetic for this moment, my hands trying to clutch the edges of the towel together and pretty much failing.

"Uh, Petal, look around."

Everything was soaked. Nothing had escaped the rage of the pipes, not even Oliver. As he softly chuckled, another sob escaped from my chest. My normal glass-half-full philosophy broken, the glass had spilled everywhere.

Rather than be repulsed, he drew my body into his warmth, his chest softly meeting my skin. "Hey, it's going to be all right." He patted my arm, the angle making it awkward, but I still relaxed into it. "When I heard you scream, all I could think about was getting to you. I thought something bad had happened."

"Something bad *did* happen," I wailed before I pressed my face into his soft, if wet, T-shirt, hiding.

"You're going to handle it like you've handled every other bump and mishap. All while dealing with the largest crew I've ever seen, and me."

I snorted. "I don't deal with you." Crap, did I just admit that out loud?

"Right, I'm very easygoing."

There was no holding back my cackle this time as my body shifted with his as he began to walk. "Where are we going?" I was exhausted, wrung out, needing another shower to clean myself off from this mess, and too tired to figure out solutions tonight.

"You need a place to sleep and something to sleep in."

How was he not stressed about this? "And where exactly will I find this holy grail? There aren't a lot of options." Déjà vu again.

"My room."

A very, very dangerous idea. My protest was halfhearted as Oliver's thumb brushed against the skin of my inner arm. I glanced up, but his gaze was focused straight ahead. The room where it had happened, where it had gone down.

"I don't think you have any other options."

"It's not that, I . . ." I trailed off. He was right. The bench had been ripped out of the kitchen. The only comfortable surfaces left that weren't waterlogged were all in his room. I typically planned for every eventuality. Why hadn't I planned for this one?

"Petal." He lowered his head, even as I did my level best to avoid his gaze. "It's been another long day. You're exhausted, working yourself ragged on this deadline. Let me take care of you?"

The "no" was bursting out of me on an initial impulse. I even formed the word. But the baritone of his voice, the soft rumble of it under my ear that only made me nuzzle in closer, the part of me that was beaten down and tired, that part won. Because I was exhausted. Exhausted from fighting so hard and being so impossibly strong every moment of every day to prove I didn't need a single person.

I refused to overthink it as he carried me through the doorway of his bedroom. Normally closed shut, it was hanging open after what I could only imagine was his rush to get to me.

The room was just as I remembered it: the bed, the sheets that smelled like him, the uncomfortably flat pillows. The creak of the mattress as we moved together, the gentle way his fingers cupped my face, how he'd held me as we slept. It had been on a constant loop in my mind.

"I'll take the couch." The *this time* was implied as he sat me on the edge of the bed, legs dangling.

"It's your room—I should have it."

He grunted, ignoring my offer as he grabbed me something to wear from his dresser. I had given up on the towel, mostly using it as a blanket to cover my front bits, star fishing on the bed in the most dramatic fashion I could because I was a quivering wreck, shaking from nerves, attraction, and the cold that had seeped into

my skin. He moved around the room, calm, collected, nothing ruffling him.

He stalked out of his bathroom with a towel and a T-shirt. I
stood, barely keeping the edges of the towel from exposing what
he'd already seen.

"Let me."

I had forgotten I was clutching it, not letting the frame go,
until he gave it another tug. Our fingers brushed, both of us frozen,
caught in the electricity of each other's gaze, until I shivered.

"It's silly." I murmured.

"That's your dad?"

"Yeah." We were in matching Mordor Fun Run shirts, the
words too blurry from the water to read any longer.

"I—"

"It's fine." I snatched the proffered clothing, softly closing his
bathroom door behind me.

When I emerged, his T-shirt stretched across my breasts and
stomach, covering me in his scent, hanging to mid-thigh. Oliver
had changed out of his sopping clothes too, dressed in gray sweats
and another T-shirt that clung to him in a way I was tempted to. He
had gifted me a pair of boxers which I slid up my legs, glad to not
be so exposed.

I wrapped my hair up in a dry towel as he continued to shift
around his space. Oliver grabbed one of the flat pillows and the
knitted blanket that was folded at the end of his bed, laying them
on the too small couch.

I flopped back onto the mattress, scrubbing the towel through
my hair. I had no experience with this. My nomadic lifestyle
ensured I never ran into exes or, more likely, the romantic partners
who had rejected me after we'd slept together.

"Can I?" Oliver stood in front of me, hand reaching.

"I can do it. Leave me here to drown in my patheticness."

His fingers cupped my chin, and I hated myself for the little sigh that escaped. "I know you can. The point is you don't have to. Let me." His voice broke as if I was the one doing him a favor.

"Oh, I'm the stubborn one?" I crossed my arms but set my feet on the floor, hedging my bets.

"You took care of me."

My eyes widened. Well, it had been a mutual taking care of each other, if we were going to be honest.

"Not what I meant." He read me too easily, and I didn't know what to do with that.

I sucked on my bottom lip before nodding. The bed dipped further as he settled next to me. Our fingers brushed as he grasped the towel, and then he began to methodically dry my hair. I closed my eyes, holding myself back from leaning into him.

I was too aware I was naked under his shirt; could he see the way my nipples tightened, my stomach quivered? Without intending to, I relaxed against his chest, his fingers massaging my scalp, easing my concerns, as if he was taking it on himself. Helping me escape in the same way romance novels typically did. Except romance novels couldn't actually reach out and touch you, their breath warm against your neck, fingertips brushing against your ears, making everything tingle.

Then, to my libido's immense joy and disappointment, it was over. Torture by towel. I was no longer a drowned rat—now I was drowning in sexual tension.

CHAPTER SIXTEEN

His chin dropped to the top of my head, neither of us moving, living in the silence, the breath in between, the almost.

And then it broke. Oliver shifted me to sit up as he eased out from behind me, attempting to fluff up the remaining pillow that seemed only flattened further.

We both settled, him on the couch, legs hanging over the edge, me alone in his bed.

"Well, goodnight," I called out, unable to not say anything.

Oliver grunted, the couch's cushions creaking. I wasn't in much better shape, flopping around, searching for the perfect pocket to fall asleep in, his body a burning flame too close and yet too far away.

All I wanted was to make the ache disappear, finish what I had started in the shower before I was so rudely interrupted. Bury my face into his pillow, hump his mattress—wild and electric and impossible with him only inches away, able to hear me. Why was that appealing?

"Stressing about the pipes?" His voice was low, testing if I was awake.

"Yes, uh, yes, can't stop thinking about it." I closed my eyes, trying not to groan.

"I slept . . . that night."

"What?" My legs were restless against his cool sheets, the dark space making it seem like he was lying next to me.

"That's why I was up so early. It was the first night of rest I've had in . . . a long time." His voice tipped up at the end as if it still surprised him.

If I had to guess, he hadn't been sleeping well since his parents' death. "It was?"

"Yeah, I should have told you instead of standing there ogling you."

"You weren't—"

"I've avoided people for so long." His words escaped in a rush. "Rue, Bl8z3, Ambrose, and Nick kind of forced themselves on me. But it's different, having someone who—" He hesitated.

"Isn't obligated to stay?"

"You want to be here, I recognize that, but it's not for me. It's for the house." His voice ached with something that made me wish I could see him, or at least reach out and hold his hand, close the distance.

I scrunched my nose. The memory of that night, the drag of his dick, his voice in my ear as I came, it was all twisted up in the cold sheets of waking up alone.

"I should send Jeff an email. Figure out how extensive the damage to the pipes is. Gut my room so mold doesn't set in. Bring fans in. And we should—"

"Tomorrow." He interrupted my list, my mind racing. "There's nothing you can do about it now."

"Yes, but—"

"But nothing." There was that firm voice again, the one that haunted my dreams.

I was scared. The pipes, the damage to the rooms. But right now, I was petrified about what I was doing in this bed, tempted to ask this man to sleep next to me, let his body curl around mine, but it couldn't only be for tonight. We were going to be stuck like this for the foreseeable future.

"They're not going to be able to fix it tomorrow," I pressed, my stomach sinking with the realization.

"If this is about the picture, Petal, I can—"

"No, they're not going to be able to fix my room. All the mattresses have been tossed. The furniture delivery isn't for months. I don't have a room to stay in." The words were rushing out faster and faster as my mouth was catching up with my brain. "My bedroom will have to have the carpet torn out, and the floors are being redone in all the other rooms too. I guess I can get an air mattress, but then I need to figure out—"

"Bell." Oliver's voice sounded like this wasn't the first time he had said my name. "You're not sleeping on an air mattress."

"Been hiding another wing from me?" At this point I wouldn't put it past him. He had seemed almost chipper lately—well, chipper for him—and it was disconcerting.

"Cute, Petal."

"Explain yourself, Killington."

"You'll stay here." It took a lot to stun me into silence, but here we were. "I'll take that as your agreement."

"Oh, that's a great idea. What will you be proposing next—bunkbeds?"

"If that's something you'd be into."

My mouth suddenly went dry. "You're going to get sick of me. Besides it's just a bad idea."

"Why?" Was he really going to make me be the one to say it? "You're fixing up my favorite place in the entire world, and I was . . . not great in the beginning. I can give up my bed for a while."

"You don't owe me." I licked my lips, searching for the words, trying to understand him, this thing between us, taking its own shape, delving into my chest and taking up residence there.

"If I can take this one thing off your shoulders, can you promise to let me?"

I twisted to lay on my back, staring into the darkness, unable to answer because I wasn't sure if that was something I was capable of.

88 Days Until the Deadline

"Okay, all I need is a time machine, an understanding of string theory, and a way to make the day thirty hours long," I announced to the room. We were seated at the folding card table in the skeleton of a kitchen that Rue could still operate like a Michelin-starred restaurant. What they could do with a hot plate alone was mind-boggling.

"Time is merely a social construct, but I'd be happy to explain string theory to you." Nick smiled at me before taking a bite of her omelet.

"Well, this social construct is ruining my life." Maybe Mr. Killington would accept "time is a social construct" as my explanation for why the restoration couldn't be completed on time. Yeah, probably not.

"Here, have a muffin, baked fresh this morning." Rue set the corn muffin on my plate, fresh from the oven of the cabin they lived in on the property with Nick and Ambrose as I offered them a grateful smile. I was well fed in my desperation.

Despite the varying levels of construction the kitchen was undergoing, it remained our gathering place in the mornings before the crew returned each day. Somehow, I had become part of the routine: Nick sharing what she was learning in school, her excitement for summer vacation; Ambrose occasionally allowed me to brew the coffee when he was otherwise occupied, only grumbling a few times about how I was almost as bad as Oliver; Rue had begun teaching me the secrets of their cooking—well, tried to in the few moments it took me to scarf down breakfast. The three of them listened raptly as I puzzled out whatever hiccup had popped up.

"Morning."

My gaze shot up, egg falling out of Nick's mouth as she stared over my shoulder.

Ambrose jumped out of his chair so rapidly he fell out of it, sprawling on the ground as he stared at the doorway. "Sir, you're here. What can I do? What do you require? Have I forgotten something?" Distressed was an understatement.

Oliver was standing in the doorway, dressed in khaki pants, a black T-shirt from his collection, arms crossed protectively over his chest; and now that his beard was trimmed back, a slight blush highlighted his cheeks. In the months I'd spent at the estate, he'd never joined us once since that first morning for breakfast, always choosing to have it alone. With the destruction of my bedroom, we spent time together every evening before we fell asleep. Talking until we couldn't keep our eyes open anymore.

"I thought I might, uh, join you for breakfast?" He stood ramrod straight, fists shoved into his pockets, his muscles shifting, eyes switching between our faces. As if he assumed we would send him away.

"Nonsense." Ambrose had never moved so quickly, almost throwing his half-eaten meal at the wall to get rid of it. "Please sit. I can make you a plate. What would you like, sir?"

Nick resumed chewing, cautiously, as if a bomb were about to go off.

"I have some muffins, an omelet, toast?" While not leaping out of their chair, Rue shifted back into action too, snatching a fresh mug to pour Oliver a cup of coffee.

"Whatever is easiest." Oliver eyed the open door, shuffling his feet.

Ambrose jostled my cup and paperwork into a pile. "Please, leave some room for others at the table, Ms. Price." I had to cover my mouth to stop myself from laughing.

I gathered my papers while Ambrose practically shoved Oliver into the seat beside me, his body colliding with mine from the momentum. My skin hummed from the slight contact, then Oliver's palm gripped my thigh. "Don't leave on my account."

"No, I . . ." I could sense his effort to step out of his routine, to stop hiding away, even from the people who cared for him. I knew what this meant, though I was unsure how to vocalize it. I reached down and squeezed back.

Rue set toast and a muffin in front of Oliver. "I'm so glad you joined us. So many changes happening, all due to our new friend."

I ignored the pointed look they sent in my direction, instead continuing to stare at the hand that remained on my leg, how right it looked, my fingers intertwined with his. He let go to tackle his breakfast, and I flexed my suddenly cold fingers.

"Sit." Oliver gestured to the empty chair and Ambrose.

"I much prefer standing, sir."

Nick raised her eyebrows at me. All I could do was shake my head and drink my required caffeine fix.

"I haven't seen these suspenders yet," Oliver observed aloud.

I jerked back, knocking my shoulder into his, jostling my cup. The moment Oliver spoke, everyone froze, staring at us as if we were a museum exhibit. I wanted to be absorbed into the ground and never be heard from again.

"Yup." I needed the attention off me immediately, off us and the hearts Rue had in their eyes.

"They have little construction tools on them." Oliver's finger hovered over the curve of my shoulder, and I choked out a breath.

"Yup."

"Should I be scared you're not talking?" He gazed down at me, eye contact steady, pupils slightly blown. I wanted to stab him. And also lick his exposed collarbone. I was a woman of many mixed emotions.

"They were a present from my father. Anything else?"

The jerk chuckled, which made everyone else's eyes go wide, like they'd never heard the sound before. Which only motivated me to have it happen more. He kept it up, his body bumping, leg staying pressed against mine, eyes shining. My heart clenched.

"Have another muffin. I'm making a fresh pot of coffee." Rue rushed toward me. "Anything you want, anything you need."

Ambrose met Rue's gaze with a single raised eyebrow, an almost smile before refiling my cup of coffee himself.

"Oh my gosh." Nick's jaw was practically on the floor. "I never thought I'd see the day. He should have hired you years ago to *restore* this place." Her eyebrows wriggled.

A sinkhole would be a blessing right now.

We survived the day, but breakfast haunted me. Ambrose had *smiled* at me; it was eerie.

I could still remember the whispers about me and Dan, the assumptions the crew had made. The hope it filled me with, that there was truly something there—there had to be if everyone else saw it. And how wrong I'd been.

Everything about Oliver was a weapon designed to wreck me, and my heart wouldn't survive. How I'd caught him Googling his sisters, checking up on them in the middle of the night. Sometimes even looking up wallpaper restoration. No one cared more than him, no matter how much he tried to hide it.

"Ready for bed?" The ass was preening, running his fingers through his hair as he left his bathroom, gray sweatpants clinging to his body, making me sweat.

"Firm, eh, firmly ready." The man's thick thighs were distracting. I wondered for the millionth time what they would feel like, pressed to mine, with no clothes separating us. "Don't you want to put a shirt on?"

His smirk put an indent in his cheek. "Nope." Instead, he scratched at his left pec, my eyes following along for the ride.

I refused to let him distract me. "It goes without saying, but please don't mention our sleeping arrangements to anyone." Each night he slept on the couch, relaxed, falling asleep while I lay awake in a puddle of sexual frustration.

"Really, because I wanted to sit for a cup of tea with Ambrose and pour my heart and soul out to him." The smirk grew wider, his eyes lighting up.

"I hate you."

"Say it again. Maybe it'll stick." He stood there, all smug.

"Absolutely the worst."

"Mmm."

He was giving me a peek at those freckles on his shoulders again while he checked out my skin exposed by his oversized T-shirt. Every night we were playing a dangerous game, and I didn't know how to stop it. Not with the fire building in my lower belly and the memory of the way his skin tasted on my tongue.

I couldn't think, not while my skin was on fire, pure electricity, fingers clutching the sheets so I wouldn't get up and do something stupid, like kiss him.

"Let's get some sleep." With his gaze on me, it was impossible not to notice how his tone softened more and more often, especially when we were alone. He looked at me as if he could see right through each defensive layer I had put up.

I exhaled, sliding fully underneath the covers, shoving at the flat pillow I hadn't replaced yet.

He flicked off the light. Only a few feet separated us. The distance seemed to shrink every night, not that he'd made any indication he wanted to sleep anywhere else. I had considered establishing rules to ensure nothing further happened between us, but he didn't seem to be suffering the way I was. The words caught in my throat any time I was inclined to bring it up.

"Can't sleep?"

My foot twitched, kicking the empty space beside me. "You startled me."

Why was he awake?

"You weren't exactly subtle with all the rustling around."

I was the worst platonic roommate of all time. "I'm sorry. I can go."

"That's not what I meant." He huffed as the couch squeaked. "What's keeping you up, Petal?"

The way I can't tell if it means something whenever you call me Petal. "Nothing. The impossible project, the impossible timeline, how my career depends on something I am almost guaranteed to fail. So, planning out alternative careers." The weight of the world pressed on my shoulders, and an ache throbbed between my legs.

"Come up with any viable ones yet?" His laugh was soft, curling around us. Like he understood.

"Nope. *'I have a very particular set of skills.'*" I held my breath, waiting.

"That's from a movie, isn't it?" It surprised me that he could at least distinguish that, because I had zero belief he'd actually seen the film.

"Recognizing that is half the battle."

"Would watching it help you fall asleep?"

"A movie about a woman being kidnapped? Unless you're looking for me to sleep on top of you, nope, don't think so." More, I was curious what he would be interested in. *Taken*, maybe a fantasy or a documentary? There had to be something.

He cleared his throat. "So, what will help?"

"Being hit in the head." That seemed like a much better idea than continuing to fantasize about him and his sweatpants.

"That's how you get a concussion, not sleep," he deadpanned. I could picture the flicker of amusement across his features.

"Fine. Uh, talk to me?" I wanted to bite back the words the moment I uttered them, but somehow he didn't make it weird. Didn't mock my honesty.

"My voice puts you to sleep?"

"No, I like your voice." The truth poured out of me, something I hadn't even admitted to myself. I needed to fall asleep immediately before something worse popped out.

"I like your voice too."

I yanked the sheet up to cover my mouth, hide the smile that lit my entire being. "Fine. Uh . . . What about you? Any progress on making your decision?"

His growl held no bite.

"It looked like things were going well with the carpenters?" Or the 'floor nerd crew,' as I enjoyed referring to them. It had been his latest attempt at finding a new skill the past few days, leaving his hands red and raw and his whole body covered in wood shavings and stain.

"I think we found the one thing that not even you can overcome."

That was becoming the general consensus of the crew after Oliver almost demolished a load-bearing wall, while his painting and staining skills were such that someone else would have to redo his work. He put his heart into everything he tried, but somehow, he failed each and every time, and I was determined to help, if only to avoid having to see that look of devastation flash across his face ever again. It was a stab to my chest every time.

"All right, pretend you aren't a Killington—what would you do if you could be anything? No responsibilities, entirely selfish." CEO of a massive corporation didn't seem to be on his employment wish list. From what I could surmise from his grandfather, that involved a lot of travel and a holier-than-thou attitude.

"That's a pretty out-there fantasy," he said.

"You asked what would make me fall asleep. If you don't want to help . . ." I was being manipulative, and I didn't care. I wasn't sure I had ever met anyone more in need of someone to talk to.

"Fine." With his grunt, I knew I was forgiven. "I went to school for computer science and graphic design."

I bit my lip hard, holding back the question I was desperate to ask. Almost since I had entered this place, I'd wondered how Bl8z3 came to be in this crumbling mess of an estate. My current theory was that the reclusive Killington was the architect of the beyond advanced AI. But I wanted him to admit it to me when he was ready.

"Like coding?" I would fail at any test of subtlety, but I was also dying to know. To peel back another layer.

"Somewhat. I enjoyed designing websites the most, and sometimes I do freelance work. Something to fill my days with."

"Hey." I hated the defeated tone of his voice. "Lean into the joy. If you have something you love, do it. I personally am aware of a website that could use some help."

I was only half kidding. Price Restoration's website was a mess. We mostly relied on word of mouth.

"Yeah?" His excitement sent a thrill down my spine, curling my toes. I clenched everything I could, including my self-control. "Sounds like a great idea."

The drawl in his voice made me wonder if we were talking about something else.

CHAPTER SEVENTEEN

"You don't have to," I rushed out.

"I would be honored." His voice was low.

"Honored, huh? Did that hurt coming out?" This was having the opposite of the intended effect. I was wide awake, wanting him to keep talking, continue sharing that grumpy snark that was becoming a vital part of my day.

"I'm trying out this compliment thing. Figured I'd practice on you."

"You must enjoy practicing on me." I instantly winced at the memory of us in this bed. Practice for his future relationship with someone who wasn't me.

"Hmm."

His noncommitment was worse when I couldn't see his face, check if he was being sincere.

"Well, not that it matters, but I think you'd make a great website designer. Maybe you can show me some of your work."

"Really?"

I wanted to get rid of his surprise. But I also couldn't stop being me. "Yeah, you have excellent people skills."

He snorted. "I like to believe I'm getting better, Petal."

"Maybe." I was glad my smile was hidden. It meant a lot, him opening up to me, admitting this truth, this selfish thing. "You could use your new skills to reach out to your sisters?"

"They don't want to hear from me." His clipped tone declared the topic was closed.

"You read minds now?" I sat on my hands so I wouldn't go wrap my arms around him.

"I abandoned them when our parents died. Instead, our grand-father took custody of them. My parents would have been so disap-pointed." Emotion punctuated his words. The guilt he carried swelled in the room.

"You were, what, twenty-two-years old, recovering, and a trauma survivor?" My question was rhetorical. "Sounds like you did what was best for everyone."

He grunted.

"Have you talked about it with them?" I wasn't sure why it mat-tered to me, but it did. I wanted some sort of insurance he wouldn't go back to his reclusive ways when the project was over.

"They don't want to hear from me—it's been eight years. There have been birthday cards, small things, but . . ." The couch creaked. "Maybe it's time." A kernel of hope grew. "It's your turn, Petal."

"Turn for what?" I smashed my fist into the pillow, folding it in half, but nothing worked to make it less flat.

"I want to hear about this dream job of yours."

"Oh, you're not sick of hearing me talk about my job?"

He let out a growl of frustration. "Why do I have a feeling I need to kick someone's ass?"

I clutched his pillow to my chest, tempted to tell him. Sharing was easier in the dark.

"Tell me about the book you're reading, then."

About the library sex that was to erupt onto the page. That was a hard nope.

"Petal." His voice sounded closer, but it was impossible to tell in the dark. "I want to hear about the job, I promise."

"If you start snoring . . ."

"I won't."

"Fine." I smoothed the sheets. "You know the Bib?"

"The museum?" he asked.

"Yeah. They specialize in antiques, lifestyle. Showing how people in the past lived. Rooms that resemble a thirteenth-century African hut, an igloo from Greenland. The first floor rotates every six months: a cabin from the Titanic, the bedroom of Louis XIV's mistress."

He gave a sound almost as if he was interested. "You'd design historical rooms?"

"Yeah." The Bib was my favorite spot in the city. It was a combination of all the things I loved about my work, all in one place.

"It sounds perfect for you."

My face flushed. "It's prestigious. They never advertise openings because they know who they want to hire. It's all about networking and having your name out there."

"There's no way you aren't on their radar."

I wished I had something to throw at him. "Whatever. Dad's theory is that me taking on this project myself will be big enough to get me noticed."

"And you want it?" Oliver asked.

"Yeah . . ." Something made me complete the thought. "It would mean not having to move around with every job. Settle down, have roots, stability."

"That's what you want?" he repeated.

"It doesn't matter. It's a pipe dream."

"Humor me. If you were offered, would you accept the position?"

"Yeah. I'd also love a pot of gold from the end of a rainbow, a few wishes from a genie, and eternal youth."

"Smart-ass."

I yawned, snuggling in.

"You deserve the world, Petal," he whispered.

69 Days Until the Deadline

If this deadline doesn't kill me, the horniness will.

47 Days Until the Deadline

"Good morning."

I choked on my coffee as Oliver strolled by, straight onto the patio that led to the backyard. Each and every shade of his black hair somehow highlighted despite the cloudy sky. He'd seemed to adapt more and more to having his home invaded by workers. Every day he jumped onto a new assignment, trying.

Me? Oh, I was getting more sexually frustrated by the day. One of these days I'd wake up humping his mattress, and it would be all his fault. He hadn't put a hand on me, tried to touch me, or done anything since that fateful night. Instead, we lay there, me on his sheets that never lost his scent despite how often Ambrose washed them, and him on the couch. Talking about what he missed about his sisters, dumb things I'd done with Sebastian in college before he started dating Finn, what movies he had seen, and how he hadn't watched a football game since his accident.

Talking, always just talking.

At least I had work to distract me. "Hey, Jeff." I waved as I stepped outside.

"Bellamy, another beautiful day, huh?"

Was everyone being dosed with something? "I guess. I wanted to talk to you about—"

"Yeah, give me a minute."

Jeff strode with purpose, heading straight for Oliver, who was sanding a bedroom door before it was repainted. At some point over the past few weeks, Jeff had developed a not-so-subtle crush on Oliver.

Today's list had me headed toward the furniture tent, which meant I had to go in the general direction of Jeff and his flirty eyes.

"I was impressed yesterday. I saw you lifting those wood planks." Jeff flexed his bicep to emphasize his point, and I held in my scoff.

"Oh." Oliver's gaze dropped. "Just doing my part."

"We rarely have homeowners willing to help. Your support of the project is appreciated. Though, here, let me—you want to go with the grain." Jeff placed his palm next to Oliver's, gliding it over the wood. How very helpful of him.

Oliver wiggled away, running his fingers through his hair, seeming to forget it was tied up. "Oh, it's nothing." His gaze jumped from Jeff to me.

"It's not." Jeff's smile grew, and he winked at me. "The owners aren't usually so attractive either."

It was for the best that there were no sharp power tools in my possession.

"We're working pretty long days," he began, "but I was wondering if you would want to—"

I didn't need to hear the rest. The lean of Jeff's head implied what was about to happen. They were two consenting adults.

Jeff's laughter trailed me, and I power walked, trying to nonchalantly wave at the gardening team. It may have come off as aggressive, but they knew what I meant.

I liked him. That stupid man, with his stupid beard, his stupid hair that he tied up during the day and released at night to hang over his shoulders. How like clockwork at lunchtime he'd appear to make sure I ate. I hated that I liked him, because nothing could come of it, primarily because he didn't feel the same way. Which was for the best. I wanted to leave here with no entanglements, only a recommendation and a step toward my future.

But it didn't mean I needed to watch him fall for someone else.

A single crash of thunder shook the earth, and the sky opened up. The irony was not lost on me. A storm hadn't been in the forecast, but who could trust a weatherman?

"Come on." Oliver grabbed my hand, pulling me toward the stables, and we took off at a run, my heart caught in my throat.

We breathed heavily as we sprinted through the stable doors, soaked to the bone. My hair was plastered to my head, and Oliver's was the same, both of us sopping wet.

I tracked the water droplets that dripped over his body, his neck, and down the bridge of his nose, falling off his eyelashes as he wiped his face with his enormous hand. He was beautiful. His determination, his strength, every single thing down to the stubborn set of his shoulders and the T-shirt plastered to his skin making my heart race more than the run had.

"It's just a quick summer rainstorm," I said, hoping aloud as I glanced at the sky, covered in storm clouds. Being stuck in close proximity to him was the last thing I needed; every night was torturous enough. The daytime was my reprieve.

"Well, we're stuck here until it's over."

"Splendid." Exactly what I wanted, to be trapped here with him. If only I had been closer to the furniture tent, I could be productive instead of trembling, dripping water everywhere.

The horses stamped in their stalls as I paced, my body needing something to get this energy out.

"A bit testy today?"

I whipped around. The wet pieces of hair that had fallen out of my ponytail smacked me in my face as I glared at him.

"Something bothering you?" The arch of his eyebrow screamed he had his suspicions.

I shoved my hair back into a messy knot and resumed my pacing, ignoring him. The storm would be over soon, and then I could get back to work and away from him.

"It wouldn't have anything to do with my conversation with Jeff?"

My voice rose about twelve octaves. "Zero idea what you're talking about."

"You were staring." There was a hint of a laugh in his voice, making me want to scream. He was so smug. "We're friends, right?"

I spun and crossed my arms, hating the way my shirt and suspenders were pasted to my body, revealing every curve. "What else would we be?"

"Good, because I need advice." Probably for his upcoming date with Jeff.

"About what?" I stepped farther into the stables. Maybe there was a task in here that required renovation—something that wouldn't get me in trouble with Nick for botching it.

"So, I have this friend . . ." His eyes twinkled.

I called bullshit. "You suddenly have quite a few new friends."

His eyebrow raised. "Can I go back to my issue?"

I leaned against the far wall, the panels of wood catching against my suspenders as I gestured for him to continue.

"Thank you. So, I have this friend. Let's call her Nettle."

"Mr. Popularity, you have two new friends, Petal and Nettle." Honestly. "Ambrose is going to be jealous."

"Nettle is a bit prickly. Likes to be all friendly and bright on the outside, but deep down they are—"

"Watch yourself." I narrowed my eyes at him, rain pounding the roof, the storm not giving any sign of letting up anytime soon.

"Complicated."

I crossed my arms, feigning patience, not like I had anything else to do. The air had that clean scent that only comes with rain, which overpowered, somewhat, the stench of horse.

"As I said before I was so rudely interrupted, I have this problem." Oliver stepped closer. "I have an . . . attraction. Hmm. That's not a strong enough word." He closed his eyes for a minute, thumb brushing against his lip. "I hunger for them."

"Oh?" My thighs rubbed together, and I pressed my arms to my chest. "That must be inconvenient," I squeaked. I could not let this get away from me. "Probably not something you should mention to Jeff on your date."

"Jeff did, in fact, ask me out." His eyes dilated, reminding me what a jealous thing I was.

"Ah." Banging my head against the wall right now wouldn't be a good idea.

"Want to know what I said?"

Yes. "That's between you and Jeff."

"Do you think Nettle would care?"

"Maybe you should ask her."

He smirked, and I hated how much I liked it. How I wanted to trace my fingers along his soft lips, push them all the way up into the smile that shone in his gaze.

"Well, if I was talking to Nettle, I would tell her I said no thanks to Jeff."

"Oh." My heart gave a flutter of relief.

"Yeah, oh." His voice dropped an octave.

"Nettle might enjoy being told. You know, depending on who Nettle is and their feelings about you." My fingers curled into fists to stop the impulse to touch him, to feel the heat of skin beneath my palms, to press my thighs to his and kiss along his collarbone—anything.

Another step. "So, my problem is, when I'm with Nettle, all I can think about is kissing her. Every inch of her perfect skin." His voice dripped with the same desire currently choking me. "Suck, nibble, hear the moans she lets out, feel her fingers scratching along my back."

I trembled as the temperature in the barn seemed to rise. "That sounds, uh, difficult."

"So, what should I do?" Another step, his eyes searing my skin with delicious heat.

I pressed my palm to my pounding heart. "Sounds like a real conundrum."

With every step he took, I pushed myself further against the barn wall, but it refused to yield. There was no escape, and all the reasons I should run were being washed away with the storm.

"I dream about how she tastes." He growled out the words, sending a thrill down to my toes.

"Oh." My voice betrayed the excitement in my chest, buzzing down, down . . .

"Her lips. They were—" He flexed his fingers, and my thighs parted in anticipation. "All of her is so soft. I wonder what sounds she'd make if I touched the rest of her." His voice was dripping with the same hunger coursing through my veins. "It keeps me up at night."

Maybe I wasn't the only one struggling. "The dream might be better than real life." My shaking voice betrayed my nerves.

"Impossible." He placed his palms against the wood on either side of me, face tilted toward mine. His eyes traced along my features, leaving me tingling. I licked my lips, my gaze exploring the small wrinkles at the corner of his eyes, the drops of water that clung to his eyelashes.

A breath separated us. All I'd have to do was lift on my tiptoes, and his mouth would meet mine.

"Tell me what you're thinking, Petal." His jaw clenched.

"I kind of hate Nettle." The words were out before I could stop them. Because it was there, the nagging, illogical worry that he *was* thinking about someone else, even as his eyes burned into mine, teeth biting his lower lip in the way I was desperate to.

"Petal, it's you. Only you." His tongue dipped out, licking his lower lip. Any reason not to kiss him fled me.

Our mouths met, and I was lost. My arms wrapped around his shoulders, and I stood on my tiptoes to bring him closer. He was right. It was better than every memory and dream I'd had since that night in his bed.

His tongue brushed my lip before he took me in another bruising kiss. I almost climbed him like a tree, fingers tracing down his spine, to grab at his ass.

We both let out a combined moan, a rush of relief, as his erection pressed against my center.

"Fucking suspenders." His hand slid down the elastic, separating it from my body for a moment before releasing it to lightly snap back against my nipple. My moan this time was louder as he did it again on the other side, his eyes lighting in excitement at my reaction.

We were all groping, teeth nipping, as he continued to play with my suspenders, play with me, our wet clothes making it difficult, but I didn't care. It was a relief to let go, to admit that this was what I had been craving—him.

"Can I take this off?" His hands rested at the edge of my T-shirt, and I yanked it off to get it out of his way.

It took a couple tries for the clasp of my bra to release for him, leaving me in only my shorts and my suspenders. Oliver sucked in a breath, that made me clench. "Is it possible to have a suspenders kink?"

He didn't give me a moment to respond before kissing me again, sucking on my tongue, smooth palms molded over my breasts, thumbs brushing across my nipples. It had been one thing to hear him talk about touching me, but the way he caressed me, everything inside me screamed, *More, more, more.*

There was a slight shake to his fingers as he popped open the button of my shorts, taking his time sliding the zipper down until his hand was in my underwear. I gasped against his mouth, somehow shifting the restlessness that had been burning into something new, something demanding, hungry.

"Better than my dream," he said against my lips as his fingers slid, trailed against the crease of my thigh before dipping in, discovering how wet and aching I was for him. I sank my face into his shoulder, not even embarrassed with how badly I wanted this, wanted him.

"Do you know how many times I've touched myself, thinking of this exact moment, while you're in the shower every night?" One finger, then two. He started to finger fuck me, growling out the words as I clenched around him.

"Why do you think I take such long showers?" I mumbled against his skin, gripping at his T-shirt. Every part of my body was alive, as if he were touching me everywhere at once.

And then he said: "Should I fuck you like this?"

CHAPTER EIGHTEEN

I nodded, desperate for him not to stop as his thumb increased pressure against my clit, my palm sliding on top of his to show him how I needed it, stoking the horny fire that raged through my veins.

"No, I don't think I will."

His fingers slid out of me before I was ready, shoving my suspenders down my shoulders, before taking them, my shorts, and underwear in one swoop, leaving me naked while he stood fully dressed in front of me. His gaze was hungry as it swept over me, and I let him look his fill over every curve and dimple.

But then he got down on his knees, my breath leaving my body as he gave me a rakish glance, a single warning before his tongue swept against me.

I wasn't cool, calm, collected. No, my knees chose that moment to buckle, as I collapsed into him.

But he rolled with it, taking me with him as he lay on his back on top of a blanket. "Even better," he growled, pulling my pelvis toward his face. Before I could squeak a protest, his tongue returned, making itself at home in my pussy, my knees on either side of his face as his tongue traced my wetness.

It was too good, he was too good, as he showed me each and every thing he'd dreamed of doing. I pitched forward onto my palms, fingers curled into the edges of the blanket.

The push of his cheeks against every sensitive spot was an additional unexpected thrill, his nose brushing against my clit, because somehow this man was smiling while going down on me.

"I'm going to smother you." My words didn't match the way I shifted to get his mouth exactly where I wanted him, craved him, pelvis grinding along his beard.

"Then smother me," was his response before sucking on my clit, his fingers returning, three this time, curling, encouraging me to ride his face. Every moan and grumble he made against me caused a full body tremble. Stars formed behind my eyes. Everything concentrated on the places where he was touching me, toe-curling pleasure I never wanted to end.

Fire raged inside of me. Wild and alive.

There was no point pretending anymore, at least to myself, that I barely tolerated Oliver. He was burying himself under my skin, the same way his fingers were buried in me, and I couldn't protest. All I wanted was more. More of his snark, more of that tongue, more of the way he talked to me until I fell asleep. I was a greedy mess.

"Stop holding back," Oliver grumbled underneath me.

I didn't want to tip over that dangerous precipice. I needed this moment to never end. The after was unknown, but right here in this bubble we had created, we were infinite.

But nothing, no matter how perfect, can last forever, especially when the person between your thighs is doing everything they can to bring you as much pleasure as possible.

My moan came out as a grunt and I fell to my forearms as my pelvis squirmed against his face, the scratch of his beard only heightening the experience, the world blurring at the edges, heart thumping and throbbing, in my chest, unable to stop myself from the free fall.

He didn't release me, his mouth licking a softer path now, tongue tracing, teasing me as my body quaked, carrying me through.

Without planning it, my right arm slid until it met his palm, and our fingers intertwined as he stroked me to a second orgasm, intense in a different way. My body could barely hold my weight, not that he seemed to mind, fondling my thighs, running up my ass to touch the skin of my lower back. His hand still clutching mine, squeezing in time with the beat of my heart.

I was lost to the sensation as he shifted me to sprawl on top of him. My face pressed to his neck, my new home, his hands caressing my naked body, as electricity continued to buzz, his pulse my new favorite song.

I tried to shift away—well, ease to the side at least. "I'm a mess," I protested weakly, the comfort of his embrace not enticing me to leave.

"You don't see me complaining." He brushed his thumb down my body; the slight tickle and warmth spread, making me hiccup in pleasure.

His erection pressed against my thigh. Any moment now, when I could move, no longer in some sort of blissed-out coma, I would get my hands on him.

In a minute.

"I'm sure you'll think of something." I snuggled in further, lips brushing against the edge of his beard. My thighs were probably covered in beard burn, and I was not so secretly gleeful.

"Do you have something to complain about?" His words came out halted, muffled by my hair. The calming movements of his hands froze. The pulse at his neck beat rapidly, in time with the rain.

"Merely that I'm not sure when I'll be able to walk again." The ache between my legs was pleasant, a reminder of where he had been. This had happened. It was real.

He squeezed my ass cheeks. "Yeah?"

"Try not to sound so smug." He deserved to be—I was a ruined gooey mess of a human all because of him.

"I make no promises." His palm smoothed along my spine, and I let out a sigh, fingers delving under the sleeve of his T-shirt, craving to touch more of him.

"Such an ass."

He squeezed again. "I like your ass."

I like all of you. The words bubbled in my chest, wanting to erupt, but I held them back. Hookup—this was a hookup. I refused to read more into this than what it was. I refused to see something that was not there again. I refused to overinterpret, believe there were feelings. I had learned my lesson painfully. The only one I could blame if my heart got broken this time was myself.

I slid my palm further up his bicep to trace the freckles I knew lay on his shoulder, while I shifted to straddle him, pulling on the buckle of his pants. Oliver's palm immediately lay on top of mine, halting me from going any further. "I didn't come here for that. You don't have to."

"I didn't plan to ride your face today, but it doesn't mean I didn't want to."

He gave a low chuckle. "I want to, trust me. It's just . . ." His eyes were pleading with me to understand something.

"Was it, uh, okay for you?" I asked, and bit my lip, hard.

I tried to shift away, but his arms wrapped around my back, holding me to him as he sat both of us up, so I remained straddling his waist. I was reminded I was the only one naked, my arms crossing to hide my breasts at least, which mostly shoved them together.

"Hey." His fingers tilted my chin up, waiting until I met his gaze. "Better than I imagined, better than anything I could have fantasized. Now I'll just dream about the next time we can do that again. You're amazing, you know that?"

He was laying it on thick. My skin flushed, betraying me, making me wish I had some clothes on. "I'm not—"

"Amazing. Spectacular." His lips pressed to my forehead.

"You already said amazing." I slid my fingers underneath the back of his T-shirt, feeling better touching his skin. Casual anything was not something I was used to, but what else could this be? We were destined for different things, different futures.

With another kiss, he pulled his shirt off. "Lift your arms."

In a moment I was wearing his shirt while he was topless now. Broad chest, a fine shimmering of hair. He was my favorite thing to look at in the entire estate, especially those freckles across his shoulders.

"Sick of my breasts already?" I hadn't been lucky enough for the rain to have let up during our time-out from reality. Now that we had finished, surely, he would want me to leave.

"Never." He lay down, making sure I came along for the ride. "Thought you might be more comfortable this way." And incredibly sweet, because he was right, it felt a bit fairer, that I wasn't the only one lying here in her naked truth. He needed to stop it before I fell even further in like. "This is what I want more than anything right now."

Oliver's hand reached down to the part of my thigh his shirt didn't cover, drawing unknown symbols. "You would have liked me before. I was, uh, more in shape." Oliver's legs shifted under mine.

"I like you now."

Somehow, this was the most romantic moment of my life. Me, laid out on top of him on the ground of this stable, the rain still pouring down around us. My cheek cushioned against his chest, better than any pillow.

"Do you ever think about the house you would build for yourself?" He cleared his throat. "If that was a thing, you, uh, wanted." He curled a piece of hair around my ear.

I took full advantage of this opportunity to touch him with free rein since we weren't going anywhere. He didn't seem to mind the callouses on my palms as I slid against the hair on his chest. There's a simple joy in touching another person and knowing they gain pleasure from it. I wanted to store it in my cells. Remember this moment forever.

"I don't spend a lot of time thinking about it." It seemed safer that way. I spent my days dreaming about other people's homes, the memories other people would make. One day, maybe, I'd have a home of my own, but until then it was cruel to think about what I didn't have.

"Let's pretend you did. Not that you ever plan anything, obviously." That earned him a pinch. "I definitely do not find your lists randomly taped around the house."

"They help guide everyone on their projects."

"I know, Petal. It's nice seeing your handwriting, you, everywhere I look. I don't think anyone else could have turned this into such coordinated chaos. We're all very lucky you came into our lives."

"Oh." My breath let out in a rush, a flush worming its way down my body, as I scratched his beard.

He lifted his knee, slightly knocking it into mine. "Tell me. Tell me all of it."

Well, maybe I had thought about it a bit. "Definitely not a new build." My childhood had made me run the opposite way from modern construction. I was a purist. "I prefer to feel like the house has been there for years, decades, even centuries."

"Who wants a new build? Amateurs."

I giggled. "Have powerful feelings about architecture, do you?"

"Keep telling me what you need . . . in a home. Does it have a library?" His lips brushed against my forehead, nuzzling me.

"Of course. Built-ins galore. An unnecessary, obnoxious amount of built-ins."

"Of course. Where else are you going to put all your books?" So smug. "What else?" His fingers pressed into my hips.

"A gallery wall of family photos." He was getting all my secrets from me.

"Why?"

"I have a few snapshots and an album at Dad's, but nothing permanent. Nothing that screams 'This is my life.'" I swallowed thickly, the memory of my favorite picture damaged beyond repair too fresh.

"I like that."

"A home theater or a fancy TV, at least."

"Goes without saying—how else are you going to watch all your movies?"

I smiled, picturing it while pulling his arm tighter against my body. "A massive bed, with heaps of pillows and blankets."

"And where would this perfect house be? In the city, close to the Bib?"

When I pictured my forever place, it involved a lot of land, far away from everything else. A workshop where I could mess around with furniture or draw up ideas of my own. A place with infinite possibilities, somewhere I could always come back to and feel at home the moment I walked through the doors.

When I was little and Dad was working somewhere else on-site, I'd spend my day making my own houses with whatever was lying around. Small pieces of wood, bits of paint, plaster. Built my own little folk who lived there, their own lives. My very own imaginary worlds. I told everyone Dad made fairy-tale palaces filled with magic because I believed it myself for a long time. An embarrassingly long time.

I opened my mouth to explain all of that. Oliver played with the ends of my hair, waiting patiently to hear what I had to say. But I couldn't. His questions reminded me why this would never work. I couldn't set myself up for heartbreak when I left. Not again.

"How come I'm the one doing all the talking?" I nipped at the skin underneath my cheek before smoothing it with a kiss.

He gave a low chuckle. "Because it's a day that ends in 'y.'"

"Well, I guess intermission is over now."

"*No,*" he almost yelled, arms tightening around me. "No, I'll talk." I could almost hear the wheels of his brain working. "Fine. I told you how I can't cook?"

"Yeah. You might have mentioned you struggled with certain things." I found it cute how bad he was at some stuff despite how hard he tried. Made me want to wrap him up in a hug. I was invested now. It was only a matter of time until we discovered something he was good at.

"When I was first rehabbing, they wanted me to keep the weight off my leg, and I figured I could learn from some YouTube videos. How hard can it be to boil water or make scrambled eggs?" His body heat seeped into mine.

"You're going to tell me how hard, aren't you?"

"Whose story is this?"

I pressed my lips together, eager for more of this, more of him, my heart pounding in an entirely different way now.

"I might have also had a bit of confidence. My sisters and I would sneak out of our rooms in the middle of the night and I . . . wait, I think I want to tell you another story now."

Oh, we were getting to the good stuff. "Nope, no backsies."

"What if I go down on you again?"

Tempting. "Stop stalling."

"Fine. I made us some excellent bowls of cereal."

I waited a moment for him to continue, and when he didn't, I couldn't help it. I burst out laughing. "You thought you were a chef because you could pour a mean bowl of cereal? Did you do something wild with the milk?" Rue had guaranteed job security.

"We ate them dry."

"You live life on the edge."

He laughed with me, my favorite sound. "I learned that cereal was what I should stick to. I can try my best to hold to a recipe, follow it exactly, but somehow it always comes out wrong. It gets burned, tastes funny. I tend to create small fires."

"Fires!"

"Did you notice we don't have a microwave? I'd been through five before they insisted I stop buying new ones."

I was a giggling mess. I could picture it, him incredibly stubborn, swearing the next meal would be the one he'd get right. How the estate was still standing was truly a wonder. "Keep going."

"My sisters would rope me into their plays."

Now I was a goner. He was nice to his sisters. My heart would never survive. Sibling relationships fascinated me. Someone always there to play with, to share secrets.

"They gave me the roles they refused to play. And with only three of us, I had to be multiple characters, which involved a lot of wigs."

I let out a snort. "I hope there's photographic evidence."

"It has been burned."

"I demand to hear more about these wigs."

"What if I promise to give you something you want more?" Oliver's voice was low, palm cupping my cheek. Everything out of his mouth sounded sexual.

"What could I possibly want more?"

"*Smallville.*"

"A show you've actually seen?" I was impressed.

"Yes, but that was my fandom."

Another piece of the Oliver puzzle fell into place. But each little nugget made me ache to know more. Which was dangerous because I had to slow down whatever was happening here (and also hunt his fanfic down immediately).

Nothing had changed between us other than the two orgasms. Two amazing, back-bowing, knee-crumbling orgasms.

I was in so much trouble.

"I'm still not telling you my pen name."

There were a few tricks up my sleeve to get him to change his mind. I nuzzled my nose against his throat.

"I'm sorry." We both jumped as Bl8z3's voice filled the stables. I had forgotten for a moment it was wired even in here. "But Jeff is searching for you, Ms. Price. It seems urgent."

"Crap. Crap." There it was, reality setting in. Because this bubble wasn't real, and here I was on the floor, having hooked up with the grandson of the man who had hired me. It was all anyone would talk about if it ever got out, not my work at the estate. I would be boiled down to an accessory. Oliver Killington, pictured, and his plus one. "I'm coming. Don't tell him where I am. I'm on my way."

"Of course, Ms. Price." Bl8z3's voice was soft, as if it was reluctant to have broken this up. "Take your time and be careful. It's still raining out there. Should I send someone with an umbrella for you?"

"Unnecessary." The last thing I needed was anyone discovering us, wondering what we'd been doing this whole time.

Oliver helped me up from the pile we had become, patiently removing his T-shirt so I could put my own clothes on quickly, soaked from the rain and wrinkled from the haphazard way they had been thrown on the ground.

He clipped my suspenders on, handing me my hair tie, which had somehow made it around his wrist. His thumbs wiped away at what I could only imagine was dirt on my face. His face was an unreadable mask, eyes searching mine for something, maybe the same thing I sought from his. But I had nothing to offer in this moment except a to-do list and a flood of reminders of how close I was to losing everything.

"We got caught out in the rain—nothing to worry about. If they say anything to you, send them my way."

"That'll help. You pummeling everyone who mentions it won't be suspicious at all." Heritage home restoration was a small community. When Dan rejected me, everybody had known what he had said and the circumstances, and made their own assumptions. This would be devastatingly worse.

"Who cares what they think?" He pulled my hair into a messy bun, the same way I wore it at the end of a long day. His fingers drifted down the back of my neck, massaging.

But I couldn't relax into it, not this time. "My professional reputation cares what they think."

"Petal . . ."

I shook my head and sent my wet hair flying. My life had been filled with too many fantasies, dreams of what other people's lives were like, what my life could be like. It was time to live in reality. "Don't worry—I know what this is." I stepped away, shivering in my wet clothing. This was as good as it was going to get.

"This again." The annoyance in his voice made my head snap up.

"Yes, this again." Clearly, he had no desire to talk about it, which was fine with me.

"Should I be insulted that my tongue is not enough to make you want to stalk me?"

I narrowed my eyes as my body begged for a repeat. "It's not a bad tongue."

He clutched at his chest. "Oomph. What happened to not being able to walk?"

"You didn't ask about your fingers."

His eyebrows drove into his hairline. "Oh, these fingers?" He wiggled his digits at me, causing my insides to clench.

"So humble."

"Maybe I just like the pretty flush on your cheeks?"

The gray of his eyes drew me in, bottomless pools of emotion, while his messy beard was evidence of what an effective seat he was. He cupped my face, and for a single breath I let him pull me into his depths as if this was a normal thing we did. No consequences, nothing to worry about, a moment filled with possibility.

But everything that happened between us was of consequence. We lived together, worked together. I had been burned too many times by leading with my heart. I wouldn't give him the power to wreck me.

CHAPTER NINETEEN

I stepped back, turning away from him. "Well, I'm glad we got that out of our systems. Things can return to normal. No more tension. Banged. That. Out." I clapped my hands in beat with my words, because if I could make something more awkward, I always would.

"What?" His eyes narrowed as he attempted to close the distance between us.

"I should go, lots to do, but, um, thanks."

"Thanks?" Now he sounded pissed. But I wasn't here to keep growing his ego.

"Yeah, for the uh . . ." I waved vaguely at the ground where I had sat on his face.

"Oh no, you're not—" He reached for me, but I was gone, fleeing into the rain, trying to pretend it could wash away any desire I had to repeat what we'd just done.

I was screwed. In more ways than one.

But the moment I stepped into the house, Oliver was there behind me, chest heaving. His hand wrapped around my wrist, guiding me into a corner, away from prying eyes.

"Petal, please, talk to me," he begged.

"What else is there to talk about?" I was about as good an actress as Nick. Why couldn't he let me—I mean this—go?

"This isn't a hookup, Bellamy. This is—"

"It's madness. I'm thrilled for you—truly I am. Getting back out into the world, finding your passion. But you shouldn't settle for the first person who falls into your house." I refused to be his practice for his forever person.

Oliver jumped away as if I'd slapped him, mouth gaping open. "I'm not settling. That's not—"

"Sir, I'm so happy I found you." Ambrose raced around the corner, towels in his hand that he thrust at me before beginning to wipe off Oliver. "You have visitors, and I wasn't sure what to do."

"Visitors?" Oliver acted as if Ambrose was speaking a foreign language. He gently but firmly pushed the butler away. It must be something important for Ambrose to not lecture us about the mess we were creating.

"Your sisters, sir, are—"

"We decided it was time for a visit with our big brother. Hey, Ollie."

I would have recognized them anywhere, both from the media saturation, their faces gracing tabloid covers weekly, and by their resemblance to Oliver. The same sharp nose and heavy eyebrows. Remy shared her brother's coloring, while Grace's hair was almost a shocking shade of red. Both women were curvy, and Grace's engagement ring was almost blindingly obscene.

"I—" Oliver stood frozen, jaw halfway to the floor. Ambrose backed out of the room with a bow, but I was trapped next to Oliver.

"Thought it might make sense to have the family reunion before the shindig Granddad is throwing." Grace crossed her arms. Apparently the ability to be inscrutable was another shared trait.

My muscles tightened. It felt a bit like a gotcha moment, but I also knew if they had given Oliver a heads-up, he probably would have begged off from seeing them. Not that I would have blamed him, what with tarps everywhere and the strong scent of paint permeating the air. I should leave them to their reunion, but with a backward glance at Oliver, the desperation in his eyes screaming *"Help me,"* I had to stop myself from reaching out to hold his hand.

Which left only one other option. "Hi, I'm Bellamy Price. I was hired for the restoration. It's a pleasure to meet you both." I thrust out my palm, towel swung around my neck, wishing I looked a bit more presentable.

Grace didn't even blink. "A pleasure. This place needed the refresh."

They both had firm handshakes and blank expressions, lacking the emotion the small space was fraught with.

"Bellamy, maybe you could give us a tour rather than all of us staring at each other uncomfortably while we ignore the elephant in the room." Remy was blunt, but I appreciated it. Oliver hadn't been in the same room as his siblings since their parents' funeral, and I wasn't sure how best to ease that gap between them.

I shook out my arms as I led a winding tour through the atrium, the library, and front hall, walking them through the process. This was the stage of the renovation where it was difficult to visualize the end result—the entire house was a construction zone—but at least it had lost the stale smell and was brightened up with the fresh coats of paint and refreshed wallpaper. The bones of it were there, the potential, and I could see it, close my eyes and picture the placement of a lounge chair, a restored art piece hanging on the wall, a fire warming the space.

We ambled into the dining room. Before I could explain the vision, Oliver's sisters stalked toward Finn's mural, hands hovering above the surface of the flower petals caught in the snow. It was his best piece yet: warm, with hope somehow blooming in an impossible moment. I wanted to live in it.

"This looks like something our mom would draw." Grace darted a glance at Oliver before returning to the piece.

"Yes, we were lucky enough to find a sketch of your mother's. An artist friend of mine was able to use it as an inspiration." I rocked on my heels, unsure if this was a success or disaster.

"It's perfect." Remy breathed out, gaze glued to the various flowers that made up the piece.

"Oliver gave me the sketch." There was no denying that the guy needed to win some points with his sisters, required a jumping-off point. They had made the effort to come and deserved to know how much he cared too.

The four of us stood in silence as I tucked myself into the corner to allow them some semblance of privacy, wishing I was closer to the door that led to the butler's pantry.

"Eight years is a long time." Remy turned toward her brother. "Barely a text, phone call, message by pigeon, or edible arrangement."

I clenched my fingers, torn between wanting to defend him and the knowledge that this was between the siblings to solve.

"There's no excuse," Oliver said, his voice raw. "I thought about it, thought about you both more times than I can count. But the accident, the recovery for my leg, dealing with it all, it was—"

Oliver's hands gestured to the house that was still being repaired. The back of my palm brushed against his before I pulled away.

"The phone works both ways." Grace bumped her fraternal twin's shoulder. "But every time I thought to pick it up, I remembered the last thing you said."

Oliver hung his head.

"You told us you killed our parents, Ollie. And then we never saw you again."

I rubbed at my breastbone, my gaze drifting back to Oliver.

"Is that what you really think?" Remy scraped a hand through her hair.

Oliver's silence spoke volumes, his shoulders slumped, as he scrubbed at the back of his neck, unable to meet anyone's eyes. A lonely island cast in the middle of the ocean.

"We don't blame you—we were just angry with you for taking our only brother, away too," Grace confessed, voice wavering, fingers picking at the silver bracelet on her wrist.

Oliver's head popped up, and I watched as more of the pain that had been so familiar when I had first arrived at the estate eased. It wasn't magically better, but it was a start. As much as I was tempted to stay for Oliver, he deserved this moment to reconnect with his family.

Mending his relationship with his sisters was important. He wanted a connection with his family, whether he wanted to admit it out loud or not, which meant returning to being heir to the Killington fortune at the end of the summer. Hopefully, I would have my future in front of me too. This was reality smacking us in the face.

And it hurt.

41 Days Until the Deadline

It had been a week.

A week since Oliver's sisters visited. They'd spent the rest of the day with him but had their driver bring them back to the city after they had shared dinner, promising to return for the banquet that was barely a month away.

A week since the barn, when every feeling I'd had about him had washed over me. It hadn't made things easier or gotten him out of my system.

Now, Oliver curled inward and kept to himself. Even when he helped with renovations, he was silent. I'd known reuniting with his sisters would bring back the ghosts of his past, but I hadn't accounted for how much I would miss him. I missed talking to him about whatever romance book I was reading, him offering to help me put on my suspenders, laughing whenever I stroked wallpaper. He'd become the person I went to for the little things, without me even realizing it—every victory, every misstep.

How lonely it was, even with him sleeping a few feet away; he was back to keeping every thought to himself, and I was too cowardly to bridge that gap, to find out what he had chased after me to say. It was pointless. With my deadline approaching, so was the date of my departure.

But as I left Ambrose's updated and fully furnished tailoring room, one of the first rooms to be finished, and after Ambrose pinned me for the dress he had insisted on designing for me, I discovered Oliver leaning against the half-painted wall, waiting.

"Hi." He clutched a few flattened boxes, bouncing them against his right leg.

"Hi." I wished I had something to fiddle with as I snapped my suspenders.

His eyes widened, gaze drawn to the movement. "There's, uh, this thing I realized I needed to do ever since I saw my sisters. I've been building up my courage, but I thought that maybe . . ." He gnawed on his lip.

"What?" I had to stop myself from reaching out and tugging on his mouth to stop his hurt.

He raised the boxes toward me. "The west wing."

We'd been stalling the west wing for as long as possible—it hadn't been the most practical system, and as Jeff liked to remind me constantly, it in no way helped our impossible deadline. But it had been the plan designed to cause Oliver the least amount of heartache. But there was no more delaying, not if we wanted to finish on time.

"That's a great idea." I couldn't help the slow smile that erupted as he quirked an eyebrow at me.

"Thanks."

"I'll tell everyone to stay away—take your time. There are plenty of other things." I had a list a mile long, detailed down to the minute. Was I lying awake at night scared we wouldn't finish? Of course, but while I was awake, I might as well make more lists.

"I was wondering . . ." Oliver's gaze shifted to the space between our feet. "If you would help me?"

My answer was an immediate "Yes." I relieved him of two boxes, fingers brushing with his. Warmth filled my chest. He'd taken another step toward healing, and he'd taken it on his own— well, with the help of the weekly therapy appointments he maintained.

We lumbered up the stairs and down the hallway, the new runners pristine, wall sconces lit. Oliver pushed the door open. The bleakness and chipping paint were a stark contrast to the finished rooms, and the smell was almost overwhelming.

"Where do you want to start?" I asked, placing my palm on his arm, a reminder he wasn't alone.

"You should send someone in for my sisters' rooms. It doesn't seem right for me to dig through them." His voice was quiet, cutting through the must, gaze roving down the hallway, each door leading to more memories.

"I can do that."

We lived in the silence and stale air, his muscles flexing as if he were working up the nerve to begin. He picked the playroom to handle first. After I wiped clean the windows to let in some air, we packed up old VHS tapes and DVDs, childhood classics I recognized, and others I didn't, along with home videos that he reverently placed in a box of their own.

The act of walking through the doors opened something up in him too. It came pouring out of him: the time his sisters were supposed to be playing pretend and instead cut each other's hair two days before the first day of school. How the siblings would take turns waking up their parents by jumping on their beds. The song his mom sang them awake with, even when they were teenagers and slept until noon.

The stern set of his shoulders lightened; we weren't storing these treasures away for them never to return. We were walking through the memories he had packed away to protect himself all those years ago. Allowing them to breathe, return to the spaces, just as we would hang the family pictures back up.

We made our way to his parents' bedroom, the walls and surfaces covered in photos of Oliver and his twin sisters. Photos of the family laughing at a beach and playing football together. Their wedding photo sat on the bedside table.

"We were dysfunctional." Oliver's voice cracked as his eyes traveled over every inch of the dusty space. "But we loved each other."

Maybe this had been too much to do in one day, too much to ask of him. "I can pack up this room when I do your sisters'."

"No, it should be me. I owe that to them." His voice cracked. "I failed them."

Oh, darling. "You were in a terrible accident. You didn't fail them. You're lucky to be alive."

"It's my fault."

When I tried to reach for him, he stepped away, plucking up their wedding photo. It was a candid—their infectious grins were the first thing anyone would notice.

"This isn't some sort of misplaced guilt. I know what my sisters said, but they weren't there. I killed them." He was full of conviction; this was his truth.

He sat on the edge of the bed, palm scrubbing at his left thigh. "There were only a few weeks until graduation. My dream NFL career was within reach. All I wanted was their approval before the draft. But Dad was vehemently against it.

"We were arguing in the car, headed to the city, some sort of family dinner, the twins were waiting for us. Mom and Dad insisted they wanted to pick me up. Really, it was to talk about my future, convince me football wasn't the right path." He was rushing through the words. Maybe he thought the faster he rid himself of them, the less they would hurt. All I could do was close my eyes and go along on the ride with him.

"Dad swore I would be failing the family. Said it was time to buckle down and get serious." His eyes were distant, fingers scrubbing his beard, his breathing harsh, reliving the worst moment of his life while I clutched his other hand. The photo lay on the moth-eaten bedspread.

"I wanted to be drafted, then decide. Football was easy, natural for me. All I had to think about was the game, the next play.

Not investors, stocks, or the family's reputation. It was separate, and mine.

"Mom sided with him too, which hurt more. She said it was because she didn't want me to get injured. But it was more than that. She'd married into this family, accepting what it entailed. I was letting her down by not wanting it too."

Oliver stared at our intertwined palms, thumb rhythmically running over the back of my hand, as if I were the one that needed comfort in this moment.

"Dad wasn't watching the road. The driver in the other car was drunk and swerved. Mom screamed. Then I woke up in the hospital. Grandfather was in the chair next to my bed. They'd had to sedate me for two days.

"My leg." Tears streamed down his face as I pulled his hands against my chest, crying with him. "My femur had been shattered. It's all rods and pins now. A giant scar." He waved at his thigh.

"It is not your fault."

"But it is. If I hadn't been fighting with him, if he had been paying attention . . . if I had agreed . . . I let them down. Abandoned my sisters. Abandoned it all." He spat in disgust. "After my accident, I let myself get stuck, as if the world weren't still moving around me if I stayed here.

"I'm cursed. I ruined my family by being selfish. There is no choice. I need to accept my grandfather's terms. Make it right."

"That doesn't make you cursed," I whispered, my heart breaking for him, realizing this was what he had been stewing with for the past week, alone. His sisters might have resolved something, but Oliver was dealing with old wounds only he could heal.

"The press mentions me and the stock in the company drops five points. The team that was going to recruit me—my friend got the spot. His first game he wrecked his knee, never got to play again. My sisters? Constantly berated by the media. The accident blew up every single aspect of my life and the lives of the people around me."

I wanted to suck all his pain into my body. "You went through something incredibly traumatic. No one can fault you. Grief is a personal and painful thing."

"Oh, but they do. *I* do." He tried to pull away, but I refused to let him.

"And what's so great about them?"

"What?"

I reached up, swiping the tears that streaked his face. "What's so remarkable about them? Cousin Carter? Not exactly a competent individual. What about that time your uncle decided to fumigate his house from snakes and ended up burning it down? Or your white and rhythmically challenged cousin struggling to start his rapping career by recording a Tupac tribute album?"

Oliver blinked slowly. "Yeah, that was . . ."

"Racist?"

I pressed my forehead to his, thumb brushing against the apple of his cheek, the roughness of his beard contrasting with his smooth skin. "I'm not trying to make fun of your family. Well, maybe a little. But only because they're the ones who let *you* down."

"You may have to keep reminding me of that." The lift in his voice caught in my chest as I rubbed his shoulders.

Every day. "It's your life. Do you want to live in a boardroom for another thirty years, or is there something else you're passionate about? Something that makes you eager to face the day?"

His nose brushed mine, our breaths mingling. "You enjoy your job that much?"

"It may take a cup of coffee or two in the morning, but yeah, I love it." This project might have wanted to break me, but it had also reminded me of all the things I loved and reaffirmed that I was capable of doing this on my own, without Dad as my safety net.

"I can vouch you are not a morning person."

"Smart-ass." I scratched my fingers along his beard, leaning back, examining his features, making sure he was truly all right, brushing away the tears.

The tips of his lips quirked, contrasting with the sadness that remained in his eyes.

I couldn't relieve his grief, but he didn't have to be alone in it. "My mom left when I was a baby," I confessed.

"I'm so sorry, Petal." His palm ran down the length of my forearm. It was unnerving how comforting that single gesture from him was.

"Thank you. I realize it's not the same thing, but I know what it's like, to have no control over them being gone."

Oliver nodded. "But you miss her?"

"Sometimes. Mostly, I'm just angry she couldn't handle Dad's job and left me behind too." I offered him a soft smile.

He pressed his face against my breastbone, murmuring words I couldn't understand as I held him.

"We don't have to finish today," I mumbled.

"No interest in seeing my childhood bedroom?" he teased, finally a bit of levity in his voice, and I squeezed him tighter.

Of course I was interested. "We could check out what naughty things you have stashed under your bed."

"Okay, we can stop." He snuggled in closer, nose nudging the fabric of my suspender.

"Oh, come on, tell me. Blondes, artistic types—I'm so curious. What did teenage Oliver fantasize about?"

"I will take it to my grave." He mimed sealing his lips.

"Bl8z3 will tell me."

"Sir is a fan of—"

Oliver cut in. "Don't complete that sentence. I will reset you to factory settings so fast." He scowled at the ceiling before burrowing into my breasts as I chuckled.

"Petal, this week, I'm sorry, I—"

I shook my head, not that he could see. "You have absolutely nothing to be sorry about. I'm honored I'm the one you talked to when you were ready."

I swayed us back and forth, running my fingers through his hair, content to stay as long as he desired.

CHAPTER TWENTY

It took us the entire day to clear out the west wing. The only breaks were the two meals Oliver insisted on.

I was an ocean of questions in his bedroom. I demanded an explanation for each trophy on his bookshelf and asked where all the photos on his wall had been taken. He was terrible at bragging about himself, mostly shy and mumbling a lot. It was adorable.

The crew was eager to clock out, as Jeff kept texting to remind me until I confirmed it was okay for them to leave. The next day was our last break before the final push. We'd be working through weekends, late nights . . . it was going to be brutal. But I refused to fail.

"What are you doing?" Oliver's gaze followed me as I set the book from his childhood bedroom, with its bookmark indicating the last page he read, down on the nightstand in our room, next to a picture of his parents.

"Decorating."

"What's the point? We're going to pack it all up soon, anyway." He scrunched up his nose, as I fought the urge to kiss it.

"I'm practicing." I spun away, walking clear across the room.

"Practicing what?"

"Creating a home." *For you.*

I didn't realize he had moved until he was standing behind me, arms wrapping around my middle, chin balanced on top of my head.

"You surprise me at every turn, Petal." His voice, barely a whisper, struck me in the chest.

"A good surprise?" I was so tired of fighting this thing between us. We were alone in the mansion, alone in our room, and all I wanted was him.

His fingers pushed my ponytail out of the way, lips traveling to the back of my neck, a shiver vibrating through my body.

I attempted to twist with one destination in mind, but he denied me. "Is this okay?" His voice throbbed with the desire licking my veins.

"You're not kissing me," I grumbled, spinning to tug his head down to mine.

"Is that what you want?"

I nodded furiously, giving up on his lips and sucking on his collarbone, shifting his T-shirt to lick at those freckles I stared at too often.

"I enjoy making you happy." His thumbs discovered the space between my shirt and shorts, stroking the exposed skin. "*You* make me happy." It sounded for a moment as if that surprised him.

"Tell me what you want." I reached to release his ponytail, running my fingers through the soft strands.

"I can't decide." His teeth grazed against my jaw. Firecrackers exploded in my chest. "Should I taste you again? Or learn how you feel clenched around my dick?"

Fucking anything. "Is all the above on the menu?"

He chuckled as he let me yank his shirt off, the thin fabric almost ripping. The moment he was free, my fingers skimmed along all that smooth skin, unleashing every desire I had lying near him each night. As he kissed me, I felt it again, the press of his cheeks against mine, the lifting of his lips. He only smiled when his lips were touching me, and the realization did something funny to my stomach.

I wanted more of his smiles, more of him. His gruff, impossible vulnerability, the way he made me feel things no one had ever before. We had wasted a lot of time not doing this, and I would not let another moment pass.

My fingers dipped along the edge of his pants before tracing down his erection, my smile hopeless to hide with the groan he made, fingers digging into my hips, sliding up my suspenders.

"As long as you're on the menu, I'm good." He snapped the fabric over my nipple, his thumb immediately smoothing the bite. "I need to fuck you in only these."

"Does that mean you're going to fuck me?" My voice came out a little breathless as he repeated the move on the other side, making my body sing for him.

"For as long and as hard as you want."

I released the button on his pants. "We should get started on that."

I flung off my clothes as quickly as possible, glancing up, expecting to find him naked too. Oliver had removed his shirt and unzipped his pants, but his hands were frozen at the waist as he gnawed on his bottom lip, one palm protectively covering his left thigh, as if he were still deciding whether to push the fabric down.

It hit me that this would be the first time I'd seen him fully nude. He'd never taken off his pants in front of me. He always wore long sweatpants, long pants, never allowing his legs to be exposed, even as the weather grew oppressively warm.

"The scar is still pretty gnarly. I don't want you to . . ."

"Come here." I pressed my lips to his, fingertips tracing every inch of skin available to me, before letting my hands rest against his. "Whatever you are comfortable with."

He nodded, linking our fingers together to rest at the waist of his pants, both of us pushing down, and then his boxers. I searched his face for any hesitation, any sign he wanted to stop, but his flush of pleasure only grew, his erection popping up to greet me. Pulling him toward me, I licked along those freckles as he relaxed into my body, hips pressing into mine, dick resting against the curve of my stomach, purposefully keeping my hands above his waist.

"I'm okay, let's just"—his erection pulsed as heat flooded me—"let's maybe go slow."

"Slow's perfect." I stepped back, my hand gently roving, discovering. Surrounded by a light brushing of black hair, the scar started from the top of his thigh, a divot in the fat, following along past his knee, ending just below.

He sucked in a breath as I traced it, the skin noticeably rougher, but a reminder he was here, whole. My lips pressed together tightly. It was the most beautiful leg I had ever seen, the reminder that he had survived, was here with me now.

His palms wrapped around my biceps, stopping me as I began to kneel down. His mouth was rough against mine, as he removed the flower that was still in my hair, placing it on the nightstand. He sat on the edge of the bed, bringing me to stand between his parted knees, eyes on me like I was the sexiest thing he had ever seen. My skin flushed, my throat was dry, because *right back at ya.*

Before I could kiss him, he connected us chest to chest, skin to skin, my heartbeat somehow racing in time to match his. The hair on his chest lightly brushed against my nipples.

His hand shook as it smoothed over the skin on my back, goose bumps breaking out as the erection between us became impossible to ignore, my hips shifting.

"We don't have to," I whispered, pressing a kiss to his sternum.

"I want to . . . but it's been a while. I don't want it to be bad for you." His voice wavered, fingers digging into my thighs.

My heart gave a flutter. "Outrageous."

"You're . . ."

"A chaotic loudmouth, who annoys the living crap out of you?" I offered, humming as his hand moved to the side of my breast, stroking the skin the way he had stroked other parts of me in what had begun to feel like a fever dream.

"Well, I was going to say smart, gorgeous, and too good for me. But what you said also works."

I pushed him, not that he moved an inch, laughing with his small grunt of exaggerated discomfort. His fingers wrapped around my palm, bringing it to his lips. Everything in me pulsed to that one spot of skin as his tongue dipped out.

"I have absolutely no idea what you see in me."

The raw honesty in his voice made me pause. "That you're incredibly brave, kind, and passably attractive." I couldn't show all of my cards; I wasn't even sure what they were.

"And you don't even care about the inheritance."

"I mean, I could renovate so many more homes."

"You could *buy* so many more homes." His thumb moved to the juncture of my thigh, swiping enticingly there. "You might be the first person who's ever seen me."

I pressed my mouth to his pulse point, wanting the name of every person who had ever hurt him. "It is shocking to me that your personality didn't win them over. Banishing someone is so attractive; it's like playing hard to get."

"Definitely what I was going for there." His thick, long fingers slid against my pussy as I moved to straddle him. He traced my lips before delving deeper, immediately using two fingers. I couldn't hold back my moan as my body rocked, trying to bring him closer. "Petal, you're soaking."

"What are you going to do about it?" I held onto his shoulders, digging in.

Any comeback flew out of my mind as he picked up his pace, kissing along my chest, using his body for my pleasure, every touch of his skin igniting me further.

I wasn't worried about how I looked or which way I moved. There wasn't a single thought except how to keep chasing this. My palm wrapped around his erection as he slowly slid his fingers out. My protest was lost on my lips as he sucked on the digits, eyes closing in bliss. "Better than I remembered."

The fire in my veins became liquid, making me melt into him, which only made it easier for him to delve back, three fingers this time, the stretch achingly good, my hips lifting faster and faster. I did my best to keep up my rhythm on his dick.

I shifted, wanting to taste him too, but his hand on my thigh kept me rooted, expression eager. "Let's not end this before we get going."

His thumb brushing my clit, my body climbed higher and higher. All I could do was clutch him as I went along for the ride.

"You are soaking my fingers—you're going to come for me, aren't you, Petal? I want to feel you come." There was a desperation in his voice, urging me on, confirming I wasn't alone in this feeling that was trapped in my chest.

My traitorous body obeyed as his thumb swirled, his opposite hand delving into the fat of my thigh. I bit down on his shoulder as I called out, shaking as I fell over the cliff and he caught me.

"Condom." I was still coming down from the high, already begging for more, conscious of the dick in my palm, the way he surrounded me. My thighs opened wider to him.

"Don't you dare move."

I ignored him, sitting up slightly as he reached into his nightstand table, pulling a condom off the strip, watching as he checked the expiration date.

"Ambrose, uh, went shopping," he confessed, a blush highlighting the curves of his cheek, and I did my best to not swoon.

"Remind me to thank him."

As if my heart wasn't full enough, he sat up, kissing me, softly, sweetly, with an aching tenderness that promised, *I'm in this.*

I didn't want to be anywhere else but here, with him.

I tore the condom open, unrolling it onto him slowly, taking my pleasure in the throb of his dick, his length, the slight curve, how thick and long he was. Appreciating the first time I got to see all of him in a million ways. My thighs quivered at his size.

"What do you want? What will make it good for you?" I asked, because it was beyond perfect for me already, and I was desperate for it to be even better for him. I wanted him to remember me, remember this moment, this heartbeat.

He wouldn't let me rush, lips brushing my cheek, voice soft in my ear. "It's always perfect with you."

"Liar."

"Do you consistently have to be so disagreeable?"

His laugh, his kiss to my neck, the flutter of my heart. I could hide nothing about the way he was making me feel. "I am a gem. Sunshine may actually come out of my ass."

"It is a good ass." He palmed it for extra emphasis, bringing our bodies closer together again.

But I refused to be distracted by gorgeous eyes and the way his forearms flexed under my fingertips. "Tell me."

"I'm hoping I last more than five seconds." His head ducked, trying to get to my cleavage, but I stayed seated in his lap.

"Oliver."

"Come on, Petal, want to go for a ride?"

I snorted, but lifted as his hands grabbed my hips, sinking slowly onto him, unable to get very far, because all of this man was huge. Three fingers had not been enough to prepare me. My breath caught in my throat as his eyes darkened.

"You're too big."

The way his eyes lit up was predictable, but the gentle way his palms slid down my sides did something soothing to my insides, ribbons twirling in my stomach, reaching up to wrap around my heart. "You can take it." His voice was pure sex.

Every shift of my hips brought me further and further down. His thumb brushed my clit as he murmured in my ear how well I was doing, how soft I felt, how perfect it was.

"You sure you don't want to banish me?"

"Trust me, it's the last thing on my mind."

With a final swirl of my hips, my ass seated against his thighs, and we both exhaled. My body was full of him, his scent, his cock, his eyes promising we were falling into place.

He leaned forward, burying his head in my neck. "Don't move."

My insides clamped at his movement. He was delicious, and my body was ready for the full experience. "You okay?"

"Don't. Move." He spoke through clenched teeth.

And I didn't. Didn't lick him, bite him, like I wanted to. Didn't rub my fingers against his silky beard or kiss him. It was impossible to ignore the way I ached, my pussy begging me to shift, wanting the friction his body promised.

"Should I talk about something else? I mean, something that doesn't include how soft and wet I am." Okay, I was a little mean.

He grunted.

"They finished painting the ceiling in the ballroom. They're handling the library next." Of course the first thing that had popped into my mind that didn't involve sex was work.

"All you like me for are my books." His lips brushed against my pulse point, causing it to jump.

"Are books a euphemism for something else?"

"Yeah . . . books." His breathing was slowing down, less of a sprint and more of a marathon now.

"You are so unpleasant." My body clenched and we both moaned. Part of me was desperate to begin moving; another part, entirely content touching him, being with him.

"Are there naked people on my ceilings?"

"Yes, having fun. Something completely foreign to you."

"Guess you'll have to teach me all about that."

"Kinda busy right now." It was getting harder and harder, pun intended, to stay still.

"Yeah." His palms slid underneath my breasts, cupping them, making me wonder if he could feel my heart racing.

My brain was mush. Anything I would say would be too vulnerable, too open, too much. If I gave him all of me, what would I have when I inevitably left?

He moved, leaning his back against his headboard, trapping my eyes to his. "Petal?"

I was soft in my acknowledgment, my heart doing something funny in my chest.

"I'm glad you came here."

"Me too." And I meant it more than I could ever explain.

"Can I fuck you now?"

"Please." My arms wrapped around his shoulders, using him for leverage, as he maintained his favorite position, thumb swirling my clit, gripping my thigh, fingertips almost hard enough to bruise me.

And I wanted him to. I wanted to remember him there in the morning when I woke up. Remember this feeling, crawling up my back, my stomach, down to my toes.

His face pressed to my neck, beard brushing against my skin, collarbones, my chest as he sucked on my nipples. The beard burn felt good, igniting me further. "Fuck, don't stop," I begged as he used his teeth.

There was nothing else beyond this room, this bed, us. Bodies moving together, sweat dripping, moans that grew louder by the moment as we started the same climb.

"Did you know that first day?" The baritone of his voice caused me to clench around his dick, his eyes dilated to a delicious black. Wicked man. "Did you know it would be this good?"

It was working too. Troubled, I was troubled.

"Maybe for me it was the moment you started obsessing over wallpaper, or—" He grunted. "Window sconces."

"And you think I'm the talkative one?" Sex had never been like this for me, conversation and laughter, and this endlessness.

"You love it."

"Yeah?"

"Your cunt gives my dick a death grip every time I take a breath. I'm never getting it back, am I?"

No. "Do you want it back?" I panted, my forehead pressed to his, our sweat mingling. I had no idea anymore where I ended and he began.

"Keep it. My dick's yours now."

My body shook, fingernails dragging down his back, lips searching for his, as I let go, knees pressed to the mattress as I rode him, sobbing through my climax. I needed to bring every part of him closer, make him my new home.

We bounced for a moment as he laid me flat on the mattress, shifting me on his dick even further, somehow going deeper. He chuckled darkly against my lips as he raised my leg. His movements lost their concentration, everything he was holding back. The press of his teeth to my shoulder, the rough grab of his fingers, reaching his own peak, my name on his lips, somehow tripping me into another orgasm.

I was spent, ruined.

I wasn't the only one. He was halfway on top of me, halfway on my side, fingertips tracing my skin. I wanted to do the same, but I was too blissed out to do more than close my eyes and appreciate it.

The feeling in my chest wasn't new, not since I had entered this house, but it had been building, overwhelming me, distracting me for too long. I liked him. Liked him as more than a friend despite my best intentions. I enjoyed the sex even more because I liked him, because it was *him*.

"You're staying?"

At his question, I wrapped my arms around him, desperate to erase every hurt he'd ever had. Every fear that he'd be alone, that he wasn't enough.

"I'm not going anywhere." I kissed each freckle.

"Need anything?"

"You." I wasn't this person, this soft relationship person. But I couldn't lie either.

"Let me get rid of this condom. Then you can have anything you want—all of me."

I knew he meant more sex, some cuddling and sleep, but my stomach was on a carnival ride.

The wall around my heart had been obliterated, and there was now an Oliver-shaped hole in it. Something casual wasn't in my vocabulary. My feelings were everything but.

As he left the bathroom, I faced the right way on the bed, but he beat me to it. He lifted my body as if I weighed nothing, cradling me to his chest as he pulled back the covers for us to get under.

"Oh, wait."

I bit my lip as he reached into his wardrobe, still naked, allowing me an opportunity to admire his round bubble butt.

"I ordered these. It took a bit. They're supposed to be the best." He held up his prize.

Pillows. The man had bought pillows.

Big, fluffy, firm, fuck-me pillows.

"Does this mean you don't want me to sleep on you?" The words tumbled out, before I did something dumb like ask if this meant something.

"You better," he growled, pretending to yank them away from me.

I was satisfied, but the moment he pulled out pillow protectors and pillowcases, I was hungry to go again.

"And you mentioned a weighted blanket?" He was too concentrated on his task to see me panting.

How was he single? "You can lie on top of me; it gives me the same serotonin fix."

"I'm going to crush you."

"Please do."

He finished placing the pillows on the bed, then slipped under the covers with me. Before I could fully fluff my new pillow, he tugged me into his body, our curves pressed together.

I needed to take a shower, get rid of the sweat and everything that had dried on my skin. But I was tucked into my favorite nook, Oliver's fingers sliding into my hair at the back of my neck. And I wondered, not for the first time, if this was what home felt like.

CHAPTER TWENTY-ONE

40 Days Until the Deadline

Constantly living a life on the move, too many mornings involved waking up, not remembering where exactly I was. Unfamiliar smells, sheets—it was disorienting. There was no restful rousing, just a jarring shock to the system. *Where am I?*

Until I woke up enough to remember. *I'm supposed to be here, for now.*

As I drift to consciousness, there's no panic, no wondering. My body surrounded by Oliver, his scent, the new pillows he bought. For me.

But also holy shit. I had sex with Oliver; all right, I had sex with Oliver *again*. The whole face-sitting thing definitely counted too. But now Oliver and I were naked. We had woken up in the middle of the night and he'd gone down on me. My brain was working entirely in headlines: *WILD. THINGS. ARE. HAPPENING.* News at 11. My body ached in a new, delicious way.

Oliver's lips pressed to the back of my head, his arm wrapped around my torso, palming my breast, hips snug against mine, half hard.

This was perfect, too perfect. My brain was still half asleep, the other half preparing to panic.

"Morning." His thumb brushed my nipple, his voice deep from sleep.

And we have a winner. "Morning." I snuggled further into him.

He shifted, kissing the back of my neck, a small sigh dipping. Contentment, but the fire was smoldering in my stomach, waiting to see if he wanted to go back to sleep or stoke it further.

Worrying about what was happening between us could be reserved for another time. We had this one day. No plans, no to-do lists, no deadlines. Just us.

"I enjoy sleeping next to you." He brushed my messy bed head out of my face.

"Yeah?" The warmth spread up my chest.

"Though you are pretty violent."

"I am not!" I started to struggle against him.

"Feet kicking me, a few elbow jabs. I'm a delicate man."

"A delicate ego, you mean?" My hips shifted, brushing against his erection.

"Mmm." His tongue dipped out, tracing the shell of my ear, my eyes closing automatically.

We were in the perfect pocket of pleasure. I never wanted to move again, wanted to exist here forever, happy and sated.

"Petal?"

I hummed back, letting his teeth, tongue, and lips explore my exposed patches of skin. My palm moved to hold his hand to me as my heart rate continued to climb.

"Are you still sore?" His thighs nudged my legs, delving into the available space. "Good dreams, hmm? You're so wet, you're soaking my thigh. Was last night not enough?"

I squirmed against him, aching all over again. "Wouldn't want you to tire yourself out, old man."

Oliver scoffed. "Old man? I'll show you who's getting tired."

While I expected him to increase his pressure, instead his fingers were painting me delicately. Still in that half-asleep trance, a slow-burning fire.

"I've never done this before." It wasn't until he froze that I realized I had spoken aloud.

"Last night was that forgettable?" he grumbled.

"No, that's not what I meant," I rushed out.

His palm shifted away from my pussy, all of him, except for one specific part, growing stiff. "What do you mean? Don't get quiet on me now. Not about anything," he growled.

I was glad to be facing away from him. The flush on my skin had to be obvious. "This, the uh . . . relationship sex." The moment the words were out, I buried my face in my pillow, groaning. I should not be allowed to speak until caffeinated.

"Relationship sex?"

"You know, the soft, slow, comfortable exploration. The waking up in the middle of the night because you need it, know how good it can be, will be. First thing in the morning because you're pressed together, and your bodies fit perfectly. Everything is so soft, warm, familiar in that perfect way that surprises you because it keeps getting better. That's what I, uh, hear."

Maybe lighting would strike and put me out of my misery.

"I have zero belief that you haven't been in a relationship." He chuckled but hadn't fully relaxed yet.

And I kept digging my hole deeper. "I mean I've dated. But my career doesn't lend itself to relationships or commitment." I had taken over the frozen board position.

"How so?" His thumb stroked my lower stomach.

"No one wants to date a person who's going to leave a few months later, never to return. Not even sure where they're moving to."

"Says who?"

"People." One specific person was flashing across my eyelids.

"They sound like assholes. Tell me their names. I want to have a conversation with them," he growled, as he pressed closer to me somehow.

I laughed, unable to help myself, giving him a real elbow check right to his gut.

His fingers traced along my thigh, the roundness of my ass. "Trust me, you are a forever girl. A "build the dream house, and your entire life around it, to make her dreams come true" type of girl. All I'm hearing are the broken hearts you left behind every time you moved."

I tried to swallow, my mouth suddenly dry. "You sound pretty sure of yourself."

"Well, I *am* the 'sir.'"

"There is nothing you can ever do to get me to call you that."

"Ah, a challenge. Accepted."

I was still sore from riding the Oliver train to pound town. The man should come with a warning label: "Guaranteed to make you walk funny the next day." But I moaned as he sunk two fingers inside of me.

He was fully hard now, erection pressed to my thigh, having returned to his infuriatingly slow pace, designed to get me there, but only when he was good and ready for me, while I squirmed.

When I tried to press my fingers to my clit, he pulled my hand away, bringing it to his mouth, licking each finger individually, as if I was his dessert to savor. "Be good—no cheating."

"Please," I begged.

"Let me grab a condom."

"Don't move." My arm wrapped around his, longing for him to come closer. It was intoxicating, his chest hair scratching against my back, being surrounded by him.

"Anything you want, Petal. Anything."

Then he shocked me. Dragging his fingers through my pussy, he gathered my wetness, smearing it on my thighs before dipping in again. "You going to be good? Nice and wet for me?"

"Oliver, yes, please, yes."

"Good girl." This time, he used it to jack himself. My heart thumped with the movements of his hand.

It wasn't until he shifted my legs closed, surrounding his dick, that I recognized what he had done. Used me as his own personal lubricant. My rock-hard nipples were throbbing, body trembling as he slid at that same achingly slow pace, his dick tunneling through my quivering thighs.

"Is this what you needed? Me to fuck you anywhere, anyway I chose?"

"Please." Another breath. "Baby."

He bit down on my shoulder. "I guess we figured out how to make you agreeable."

"Such an—" I hissed as his hand returned to my clit. "Still not going to say it."

"I'll tell you a secret." His lips pressed against my ear, my gasp coming out louder, pulse pounding, even though his rhythm hadn't changed. "I like it when you call me 'asshole.'"

"Not a secret." I pursed my lips, reaching down, my thumb brushing his slit, swirling along the head of his cock.

"What did I say about cheating?"

"This is too good. I can't remember."

His heavy thigh held my body to his, using me as if he were inside me, and despite the aching emptiness, I liked it. I liked it a lot. All of him aligned against all of me. The infinite ways we could bring each other pleasure.

"You are temptation itself. I'm barely touching you, barely moving, and you love it. Say it." He demanded, lips pressed to my ear. "Say it again."

"Please. *Baby.*"

"Mine, tell me you're mine."

"Just like you're mine, you asshole."

This time it was his orgasm that triggered mine, spurting over my hand, soaking the sheets as I squirmed, biting down hard on the pillow.

It let me hide my face as he whispered in my ear how badly he wanted to keep me.

39 Days Until the Deadline

It was a heady thing, spending a whole day with Oliver. Being the center of his attention. Sharing stories, dozing on each other, we built our own little bubble.

The morning of our first day back to work, there was no pretending this time, no hiding. The condom wrappers alone that we needed to pick up before Ambrose came up here to make the bed (he insisted I never did it right) made it impossible.

I glanced down, double-checking that the beard burn on my thighs was covered by my shorts. Oliver stepped in front of me, insisting he help me with my suspenders, a smirk on his face the entire time, both of us remembering what he had done with the pair that was lying by the bed, ruined.

His hands were in my shorts' pockets, squeezing my ass, and I had to say something. Because the fear had returned—what would happen when we stepped out that door? "We have to remain professional." My nails were scratching up and down his naked chest, so it wasn't exactly clear who that remark was aimed at, me or him.

He quirked an eyebrow at me, and I wanted to feel my lips against his beard again.

"No touching." I pulled away, fingers hungry.

"I'm perfectly capable of—"

I twisted my neck, as one of us still had hands on the other's ass, and it wasn't me.

He changed tactics. "Is there room for this to be negotiated? This place has a lot of closets."

"Nope. The crew should be here any minute. It's time for me to get downstairs, make sure everyone has their to-do lists."

"The world would fall apart without those lists." He still hadn't removed his hands, and I hadn't stepped away. "And it would fall apart if they saw me touch you?" There was that vulnerability in his voice again. I didn't have the answers, didn't have room to explore them—not with everything else waiting for us. How much we both needed this project to succeed.

"Yes," I squeaked.

"Petal, if this is about what you said about not being a forever kind of person—"

"No." I crossed my arms. "This is about them taking me seriously. This is my first contract without my father. I don't want them thinking I got it or that any success will be because I was providing services to the Killington heir on the side." Even with my clothes on, I felt naked before him. "You promised you understood."

Oliver sobered, gently removing his hands, smoothing my hair back. "The only world that exists to me is the one that sees how brilliant you are."

My foot kicked his, chin resting on my chest, trying to disguise my pleasure. "Careful with the compliments there."

"I'll banish you later."

"Good."

I pecked him quickly on the lips, my body desperate not to leave. Anything more and I was liable to get naked again and end up underneath my favorite weighted blanket of a human. Talk, sleep, memorize his skin, see if I could make him smile. Only I knew the shape of his mouth, the way his cheeks rose on the side when our lips were pressed together.

But reality came knocking in the form of Jeff and the crew. Even Cousin Carter stopped by, trying to get Oliver to spill Killington secrets, having heard the same rumors that Sebastian had about the company, that it was diversifying in an attempt to lift the stock price.

Oliver kept to his promise, keeping things professional during the daytime. Even though it was beyond tempting every time I laid eyes on him to yank him into a closet, touch his hand, or seek him out despite the millions of things I had to do. And at night, when we were alone in his room, in his bed, color swatches surrounded me on the sheets until he told me to give myself a break, let him take care of me.

Each moment was better than the last.

But every whispered secret, every kiss, brought us closer to the moment when we'd both have to leave.

CHAPTER TWENTY-TWO

16 Days Until the Deadline

There were many aspects of older homes I found charming. The decorative touches, old-fashioned appliances, the number of completely unnecessary rooms for people to sit uncomfortably on couches. Don't get me started on the magic of a secret passage.

But fireplaces . . . I couldn't say much for those, other than appreciating a cozy fire every once in a while.

Yet here I was. Scrubbing.

"I thought the fireplace guys were coming today?" Oliver was crouched, peering at me as I squatted in one of the too many fireplaces in the estate. The current bane of my existence.

"Tomorrow. Their last job was on the other side of the country." I sounded annoyed because I was, in fact, annoyed. This team was the best, which was why it was so difficult to get on their schedule— that was the only reason I'd agreed to this schedule so close to our deadline. They had fit us in between two jobs. But they still had to finish the first.

"But the furniture arrives tomorrow."

Including the fireplace grates. "Correct." Didn't he have somewhere to be?

"This place will be perfect even if the fireplaces aren't working yet." His tone was soothing, but it was having the opposite effect on me. I knew what he was attempting to accomplish, but obsessing over the mansion and my deadline stopped me from fixating over other things. Like how we had been sharing a bed for a few weeks, and it had been the best time of my life.

His gaze concentrated on me. "I know this is scary. It's scary for me too."

"I'm not scared." I was determined, calm. I'd even give him stubborn. But not scared.

"Talk to me. Take thirty seconds and talk to me."

"I don't have time right now." It was simpler that way, to keep scrubbing until my fingers felt like they were going to bleed, the soot so thick it made my eyes water, my nose stuffed up.

"There's always time if it means you won't have soot-covered lungs." He passed me a water bottle.

"Fine. Thirty seconds." I took a gulp, finishing more than half before passing it back.

"Better?" His tone was full of concern.

"Maybe."

"What's wrong?" The vulnerable wobble in his voice made me pause.

"My dad called. He wanted to discuss next projects." I took another swig of the water, my throat still too dry. Dad's call was normal—usually we'd already have something lined up by now. Give ourselves maybe two weeks before we were on to the next.

"Oh." Oliver let out a shaky chuckle, gripping the back of his neck. "What did you say?"

I shook my head. "Told him I had to think about it." This should be an exciting time—my career was taking off. Instead, I was off-kilter.

"Because of us?" He was getting just as dirty sitting in the chimney with me as I fiddled with the water bottle cap.

"I—" He reached for my hand, and I yanked it away, wincing. "You promised."

"We break that rule all the time."

"No, we don't." I scrubbed harder. Each layer revealed more dirt.

"Yes, we do."

"When?"

"In bed last night." His voice burned through me, calling up memories, forcing me to close my eyes until I could get my erratic heartbeat under control.

Last night, he had intertwined my fingers with his, pushing our hands up against the headboard as he thrust inside of me, his eyes never leaving mine. But that didn't count. Sex hand-holding wasn't real hand-holding. Even if all my blood had rushed to my wrists as his thumb brushed along there.

"Well, we don't during the day." My protest sounded weak even to my ears.

"I thought it was because I was respecting your boundaries."

"Yes, boundaries are good. They make things defined." It was easier to operate in black and white. Nothing blurred. Blurred created this feeling in my stomach. Blurred involved me staring off in a daydream. Blurred made me wonder if something could truly happen between us after the repairs on the estate were finished. What were we going to be once I no longer was staying here, no longer in his bed every night? He hadn't given me any hints as to what he planned to do at the end of the summer, whether he was going to accept his grandfather's demands or explore an unknown future.

"And that's how things are between us? Clear?" He grimaced, displeased with his own word choice.

I had zero experience in being a person with a relationship and a career. I was so close to my goal, I couldn't allow myself to be distracted, or to be a distraction when he had his own life-changing choices to make. "What's with all the questions today?"

He saw right through my bullshit. "We sleep in the same bed every night, we have sex, we talk. I've told you things I've never shared with anyone else. I know you've done the same." He scooted closer. "This means something to me. *You* mean something to me."

I gulped. "You mean something to me too."

"But?"

"But I'm terrified." I confessed, wringing my hands. "I'm overwhelmed that we're not going to finish on time. I'm overwhelmed by my feelings for you. I lo – like you a lot. But we're both leaving."

With a single nudge, he had prodded everything that had been swirling around inside of me to come pouring out. Everything I had battened down and tried to ignore. What use was it to think about it? I needed to push through. There was too much out of my control. But I could clean this fireplace.

He scooted until he was sitting next to me in the filthy chimney, the space tight enough that we were shoved up against each other, not that I minded.

He cupped my face, thumb brushing against my cheek, which had to be covered in soot. "I believe in you. We keep doing this, and when it comes time, we'll figure it out—no pressure, no rush, okay?" My fingers met his.

"Yeah, I can do that."

"Will you tell me why you doubt your ability to be in a relationship?" Of course he had been paying attention and realized there was another layer.

I trusted him; it was my heart I didn't trust. "The project I was working on over a year ago now. His name was Dan, and we . . . well, I thought we . . . connected. He worked on-site too, and—well, you get the idea."

His narrowed eyes conveyed he did, lips softly brushing against my forehead.

"I had assumed it would last, but he made it clear it was a short-term thing for him. He'd never even considered it being something more." I shrugged, my shoulder knocking into his. "My profession, my personality, everything about me screamed to him it was casual. I'm not the forever girl."

He shook his head, snorting, ignoring my soot-stained clothing, and hauling me closer by my suspender. "Thank you for sharing with me."

I leaned my head on his shoulder, his arm wrapping around my back, drawing me into the comfort, the warmth his body offered.

"I dismissed change for a long time. I'm a mess. But you, my Petal, are someone who deserves to have the world set at your feet. Your every dream coming true."

Tears welled in my eyes, my fingers digging into the cotton of his shirt, overwhelmed by his words, by him.

"And if at any point you change your mind or don't want to do this anymore, promise you'll say so."

"Don't you mean both of us?" I brushed my nose against his, liking how I left a mark behind. *Mine, mine, mine.*

"No chance of that."

"So smug."

"Confident, Petal."

"Yeah?"

"Confident in you, too. The woman I met a couple months ago wouldn't have dropped everything to help me pack up my family's section of the house. She definitely wouldn't have taken advantage of a day off to let me explore every inch of her body."

I blushed, unable to contradict him.

"She would have told me to shove it. Clearly, meeting me has made you a better person." The chuckle he released vibrated through me. The man I'd first met wouldn't have laughed to save his life.

"But I would have felt bad after I did it."

He tilted my chin. "You know this is the room where we met?"

I picked my head up, glancing around, realizing he was right. The wainscotting had been fixed, same with the hardwood floor. The room was entirely empty of any furniture, but just like this room, we had come a long way. "You mean the room you first banished me in?"

"I remember it being much more romantic than that." His nose wrinkled in that cute way of his. "We got this, Petal. We're the icing. But it's okay to ask for help."

I gave a brisk nod, wanting to hug him, kiss him, bring him upstairs, lock the door and never leave.

The more comfort he offered, the more my body eased into his. A memory of its own, fitting into all the grooves and nooks that I wanted to call my own. The shoulder I leaned on when we made it through the end of *Lord of the Rings*, and he asked to check out the sequel. The hip that bumped mine when a magazine reached out to interview me as an "Under 30" to watch. The hand I held every chance I got, and he knew it. The lips that kissed away every single one of my tears. Somewhere along the way he'd burrowed himself under my skin.

After a lifetime of having it ingrained in me to always answer no when asked, I tried something new. "I could use some help, yeah."

And the world didn't end. He didn't look at me any differently.

He leaned in, brushing his lips against mine, smiling. "All you have to do is ask."

"That's hard to do," I grumbled, snuggling further against his soft cotton shirt.

"I know." His lips brushed my forehead. "But someone really stubborn taught me it's okay to not be so alone all the time."

"Sounds like someone really smart."

"Brilliant. Devastatingly gorgeous."

I snorted. "We're not having sex in a chimney."

"And you think I'm depraved."

I breathed him in, giving myself this for a minute. "If we're going to knock everything off the lists, we need all hands on deck."

"You figure out what has to be accomplished. I'll worry about the additional hands. My grandfather wants to show off. Even he realizes you're going to slam this one out of the park." There wasn't a hint of doubt in his voice.

It was time to get me out of the hot seat. "How are you doing with your own choice?"

"It's hard, but I'm embarrassed to say it's hard because if I don't take it, I'm not sure what else to do with my life."

"Can you still be involved in the company, but not in a way that puts you in the public eye? I don't enjoy picturing you miserable unless I'm the one making you that way." He had spent too long in his grief, not allowing any joy into his life, believing he didn't deserve it. I could ease things with his grandfather by completing the estate, but I couldn't fix this for him, as much as I wanted to.

"It might be possible for me to offer him something else." He appeared lost in thought for a moment before shaking his head. "Petal, you make me angry, not miserable."

"A significant distinction." I snorted, but I was hopeful he wasn't resigned to his fate.

"A very important distinction. No one gets under my skin like you do." His words burned with something.

"I do like being under you," I murmured, before scanning the room. Our thirty seconds had long passed. Any minute we were likely to be interrupted by someone searching for one of us.

"Careful, Petal, it's not nice to tease a man with what he can't have," he growled, my stomach flipping and tumbling in anticipation.

"Delayed gratification, baby."

He grunted, and my grin only got bigger.

But I couldn't send him away—not yet. "What do you want? What do you picture when you dream at night?"

"Impossible things."

"With that trust fund, I'm positive most things are possible."

He reached for my hand, tracing along the lines of my palm. "It's not something you can buy."

It was silly. There were a million things he could be talking about, and none of them had to be me. "Shoot for the stars."

"Yeah?" Was that hope in his voice?

"Yeah. What do you have to lose?"

He scrubbed his knuckles against his jaw, the sound making my skin hum with memories. After a moment he said, "I should let you get back to work."

I kissed his cheek before shifting out of his lap, reluctant to release him. Every second that drew us closer to the deadline drew us closer to goodbye.

There was no missing the mischievous look in his eyes, his lips making contact with mine too briefly before he stood up, swiping his palms together and mostly producing a mess with all the soot that now covered both of us.

He gave me one final, searing glance. I was still nervous, but the conversation had helped.

I wanted to do what Oliver had asked. Worry about my project first, figure us out after. Easier said than done.

"Tell me you ate today?" Oliver was there, caging my body against the door. We both knew that I hadn't, too distracted by work. It was nine PM and the last few workers, including Jeff, had only just left.

I shifted to my tiptoes, moving closer, until my mouth was a hair's breadth away from his. Oliver's beard scratched my face. I could see every speck in his eyes, the freckles that dotted across his nose from all the sun he had been getting recently. I tugged on the lock of his hair that had fallen out of his ponytail. "Tell me you weren't waiting for me?"

"No, I ate, but we've kept something warm for you." His kiss was too brief before he interlaced our fingers, pulling me to follow him.

"I'm going to inhale whatever it is. I need a shower and sleep badly." My mind was shifting to tomorrow's tasks, things I had to add or remove from the list. I needed to send another update to Dad, consider whether an ottoman a contact had thrifted was worth trying to restore, and rinse away all this soot.

"Well, hold off on that for a bit."

Nick, Rue, and Ambrose were all seated in the newly installed breakfast nook—larger, cozier, and with additional padding. Oliver promised it was a vast improvement, but not comfortable enough for me to sleep on.

The moment we stepped through the swinging door, Rue shot up, grabbed a plate and silverware, and set it down as Oliver ushered me toward the bench.

"Welcome to a meeting of Team Bellamy," Nick announced, shuffling papers in front of her. "The first order of business—"

"Team Bellamy?" I searched the surrounding faces, trying to understand.

Oliver plopped down next to me. "We're at your disposal."

I'd figured he'd go to his grandfather and ask for additional workers, which would help, though this place was already overflowing with hired contractors. But this was better. None of them would need explanations. It was the easiest, most obvious answer, and one I hadn't considered.

Oliver reached for a chip on my plate, and Rue smacked his hand away. My jaw dropped. "When you work as hard as Ms. Price, you can steal her food. Until then, remember your manners."

Nick snickered until Rue glared at her.

"We are at your service." Ambrose bent his head in my direction.

"All of us," confirmed Bl8z3.

"Oh, right, thank you. Are you sure? These next two weeks will be busy for you all as well."

But four eager faces met mine. It was late; it had been a long day, and that they were so willing to help meant too much.

Oliver passed me my iPad, our fingers brushing, as I tried to get my composure back.

Ambrose nudged my plate closer and cemented it for me. I talked them through the broad strokes. I had always struggled to delegate, needing to be everywhere, oversee everything at once. I trusted Jeff, but he was only one person and had a specific role in all of this. Now that we were in the end game, and with the deadline, it was going to be impossible to be in every room to ensure that they were being set up exactly as designed, to answer every question and troubleshoot.

But they cared about the house as much as I did, probably more. Oliver's thigh pressed to mine, Nick already ahead of the game while Rue and Ambrose needled each other over who would be more helpful.

Requesting help, needing someone else, admitting my weakness always gave the impression I wasn't enough—too young, too female. It was also lonely.

But I hadn't accomplished this alone. Finn's amazing mural, all of Dad's advice, everything Oliver, the staff, and my friends, had already done. Maybe I wasn't in this alone.

Nick placed her hand in the middle of the table, waiting until everyone, even Ambrose, did the same, our hands piled in, each one supporting the other. "Go team."

CHAPTER TWENTY-THREE

Day of the Deadline

There was nothing left. I had checked each box on my lists off—and then double-checked. Jeff and his crew passed Mr. Killington in the driveway as they fled before I could remember some other task for them to complete.

Jeff was invited to the party, but he and Dad insisted it was my moment to shine. Neither were the types to attend a society gala anyway. It wasn't exactly my scene, but I knew what was expected of me, and it was a networking opportunity.

Rue had bounced up and down all through the final reveal of the kitchen. "Have you seen this stove? The things I'm going to make. These burners." It was like witnessing a religious experience—all I could do was laugh as they opened every cabinet, searched every drawer, shouting about everything.

Even Ambrose had his moment. "I didn't request a steamer."

My fingers fluttered at his grim tone. "It's supposed to be the best." Top of the line, actually. Oliver had checked the reviews for me.

"I, uh . . ." His face crumpled with emotion.

He squeezed my hand before shooing me out of the room, insisting he still had to work on my outfit for the dinner.

The days blurred in a flurry of light installations, wall sconces, rugs, and every piece of furniture imaginable.

But now there was nothing left to do but survive Mr. Killington's party. A grand reveal for the estate—and for Oliver.

Each person invited had accepted. Dressed in suits and floor-length gowns, no one observed museum etiquette, instead examining everything.

This was it, no hiding now. I had to face the music and whatever the response would be to the new and improved Killington Estate. I stood at the top of the stairwell, soaking it in. The chandelier was lit, each crystal individually cleaned. The light bounced, filling up the entryway, making a statement. I glanced anxiously at all the unfamiliar faces, everyone speaking in faux whispers, as I descended the stairs—until I saw him. Because they weren't just whispering about the dramatic transformation. No, they were openly staring at the returned Killington heir. When his gaze hit mine, I almost tripped over my feet in my rush to reach him.

Oliver was dressed resplendently in a tux, his hair—the glossy black that filled my dreams—brushed back, curling around his ears. He met me at the bottom of the stairs and rested his palm on my lower back.

"Petal," he murmured.

"Oliver." He was handling this better than he had predicted; he was stronger than he allowed himself to believe.

"Wait, are those . . . ?" His fingers clenched mine. "Are these suspenders?"

My Ambrose original was a creamy, buttery yellow, a shade off being a full spark of sunshine. But there was a warmth to it, a softness to the fabric, which he assured me was silk. "Dress" wasn't exactly the right word to describe it, though that was the initial impression it gave. When I took a step, it revealed itself to be pants with a cape that split around my waist. There were a multitude of straps, two of which stretched over my shoulders, connecting to the cape.

I felt like myself, and more than gorgeous, aided a bit by the way Oliver's eyes burned for me.

My cheeks rounded into a smile. "I think they're Ambrose's version of them."

"We should go upstairs and . . ." His voice rumbled in my ear.

"Well, Oliver, are you going to introduce me to your little date here?"

Oliver's fist squeezed for a different reason as we faced the man of the hour, the moment we had both been dreading.

"Grandfather, I'd like to formally introduce you to Bellamy Price of Price Restoration. All the compliments you have been getting tonight are because of her."

Compliments? I couldn't pretend that the opinion of Mr. Killington and his friends wasn't about to decide the course of my career, but this moment wasn't about me. They were in some sort of stare-off I wasn't sure how to interrupt. Oliver hadn't seen his grandfather in the flesh since his parents' funeral. His sisters had had the right idea, doing this in a nonpublic forum, but the Killington patriarch did not have the same sensitivity.

"Ah, Ms. Price. Of course. And now the family is all together." He gestured as his granddaughters joined our circle.

The tension rolled off Oliver as I greeted his sisters. Both murmured compliments about the house.

"Where is that idiot fiancé of yours?" Mr. Killington questioned Grace, voice carrying.

Grace didn't seem disturbed with how her soon-to-be husband was referenced. "He came in the car with us, right?" She glanced at her twin for confirmation.

I laughed, but apparently it wasn't a joke, with the strange looks I received, so I tried to convincingly switch to some sort of cough, because, you know, breathing can be difficult.

"Maybe we lost him." Remy stared at her nails, flicking her middle finger first before closing her fist. Subtle, that one.

Mr. Killington's face lit with a maniacal grin that made me uncomfortable. "I think it's time to move into the dining room, shall we? Make sure that this isn't some sort of facade. Really kick the tires."

He escorted his granddaughters ahead of us, Grace's fiancé forgotten. I thought his name was something like Tim? Jim? Right now, I wasn't confident Grace could tell me his name either.

"Not the metaphor I would have used," I muttered under my breath to Oliver, nudging him away from the throng of guests following their valiant leader. "You okay?"

"Why wouldn't I be fine?" He grunted but allowed the back of our hands to brush against each other before we padded to the dining room, my fingers itching to hold on. Finn's mural shined in the fully furnished room, the rug highlighting his color choices.

As the guests found their spots based on the gold lettered table cards, Mr. Killington remained standing, raising his champagne flute. "Please be seated, friends. I wanted to say a few words in greeting."

Carter was halfway up, almost falling forward onto the dining table, seeming to lose his center of gravity. Total disaster only averted by Grace's fiancé, Jim—Ted? No, that wasn't it—who grabbed at Carter's jacket and hauled him into his seat. Mr. Killington didn't even blink.

Oliver was in the chair of honor to his grandfather's right, his sisters seated across from him. My seat was toward the middle of the long table, on the same side as Oliver's, making it almost impossible to see him without being obvious.

My knee jiggled under the table as Mr. Killington cleared his throat. "Thank you all for coming here today. It's a bit of a trek out to the middle of nowhere. This house—well, to say that if you had visited months ago, you would have seen something that should have been condemned would be putting it nicely." His voice rumbled throughout the room, filling up every space, every inch of attention, as the guests chuckled.

"I had a few suggestions and offers to bulldoze the place, but that seemed cruel, what with my grandson living here."

That earned him even less laughter, more awkward coughs. Carter cackled in full support, as if a flashing audience sign was above him. Gunning hard for the top spot in the will.

"All right, all right, enough with the jokes. This property has been in my family for generations. It was time to bring it back to its original glory, like our name, which has been wrongfully tarnished for years." His gaze roamed to his right, landing on Oliver, as I crumpled the linen napkin in my lap. "When we reached out, there was only one name that was recommended."

A pause.

"And then, when he was unavailable, we went to his daughter."

I was desperate to crawl under the table and die. Here lies Bellamy. She was killed by professional embarrassment for having the audacity to be a girl.

"We had a few hiccups, but luckily my grandson was here to keep things in line." The attention of the table focused on Oliver as he defiantly stared at his grandfather, and I hated that I wasn't sitting next to him. "But I'm glad to say I discovered a diamond in the rough. A jewel in hiding. Sugar, stand up."

I tried not to roll my eyes, tempted to pretend I wasn't aware of who he was referring to because my name was not in fact "Sugar." Or how he'd glossed over how he'd doubted me every step of the way and sought to short us the money.

"This young lady, under the daily observation of my grandson, brought this place back from the brink. I encourage you all to wander around, ask Ms. Price questions—though, please, not about the price tag."

More awkward laughter. I tried to return to my seat, but Mr. Killington narrowed his eyes. I was expected to keep living through this humiliation.

"And if you use her services, don't forget who discovered her."

I wanted to stab that man's hand with a fork as he lifted his glass. Everyone else followed suit.

Except for one. Oliver leaned further back in his chair, eyes catching mine. Filled with fire and pride, he raised his glass toward me. The stupid speech was left behind as I winked at him, reluctant to sit and lose this chance. His hair was falling into his eye and my fingers itched to touch it, push it back.

"So, you are *the* Bellamy Price I've been hearing so much about." The woman seated to my left, with her gray hair in a chin-length bob, gently brushed my arm to snag my attention. It took me a moment to recognize her.

"Oh, Ms. Roth."

The nerves were back and in charge. She didn't merely work at the Bib; she was the head curator. The woman who'd inspired me and made me think there could be a different path from the one my father had forged. "It's an honor. I can't tell you how much I respect you and your work." I took a peek back down the table, ready to share my excitement, but my view to Oliver was blocked.

Her hand batted away my compliment. "I have never had someone come across my desk so highly recommended."

Recommended? By whom? I hadn't sent in an application yet. I was waiting until the estate had been finished, a plan I had assumed Dad was in full agreement with. "Ms. Roth, if my father called you . . ."

"Oh no, though I reached out to him for some more information. I know Maurice well. These are small circles we operate in. But no, I've been sworn to the strictest confidence. What I can tell you is that you have an enormous fan."

My stomach flipped, mind wracking for who it could be.

"They wrote a generous note about how competent you are and shared some before and after pictures. Made you sound like a miracle worker. I spoke with your contractor too and a few of your other contacts, and now I'm quite sure there was no exaggeration. You are the future of our profession."

Was this happening? I was talking to Eileen Roth, and she was complimenting me?

"I assume you have something already lined up, but I would love to have you visit the museum. See if we could interest you in a position? It may not seem as exciting, but there are benefits without all the hassles of travel."

I had to pick my jaw up off the floor. "I would love that, yes."

"Wonderful. My assistant will send you an email, and we can set something up. No doubt you're going to have many offers, but I must express how impressed I am with what you've done here. And from what I've heard, under an impossible deadline." Her eyes quickly glanced at Mr. Killington holding court at the head of the table.

"Oh, well, Mr. Killington—"

"Say no more."

I wasn't sure I had said anything, but I nodded, still floating somewhere around disbelief and shock. And a nagging concern for what this meant. I should be happy. This was everything I had wanted for years. It filled me with pride to be sitting in this room, my vision coming together, all the small touches, down to the color of the candlesticks.

With little prodding, she shared with me the current events at the museum. Plans for upcoming exhibits and long-term changes she was hoping to implement in the next few seasons. She had me walk her through what the process at the estate had been like.

We were all in different phases of dessert when an "Enough!" rang out, silence descending on the room. Even I could admit that was a useful skill. Everyone's attention focused on Mr. Killington, who appeared to be in a standoff with the rest of his family based on the glares and Carter's wide-eyed gaze. Throughout dinner there had been whispers that were becoming harder and harder to ignore—about Oliver, the family, the future of the business.

"Why don't our guests start their tour of the house? Then we can all head to the ballroom," Oliver suggested, the tenor of his voice reminiscent of his grandfather's commands.

The room stood, me with them, when Mr. Killington's eyes caught mine, and he jerked his head, beckoning me over to where the family sat. This time I dropped into the seat next to Oliver's.

It was clear why this man led boardrooms, had subordinates who were rumored to leave his office weeping after being in there for only a few minutes. He was the picture of intimidation.

"Ms. Price, tell me, how has my grandson occupied himself this summer?" Mr. Killington leaned back in his chair, causing the wood to creak.

Oliver's suspicions that I was a spy didn't seem so farfetched now. I sat on my palms, afraid that he would feel this was some sort of confirmation. "Things were quite hectic with the remodel and construction. We didn't spend much time together."

Oliver and I had discussed it the night before: he had begged me to limit his involvement, selflessly standing aside so that he wouldn't be recognized for his contributions.

"Ah, well then." My response seemed to confirm something for Mr. Killington.

"I actually helped extensively with the remodel," Carter cut in. "You mentioned Oliver oversaw the project, but I was here too. I think Bellamy would say I was a vital piece to the puzzle, the puzzle of the remodel of the . . ." Carter got lost in his metaphor, staring down at his hands as if they would reveal the answer.

Oliver's hand wrapped around my wrist underneath the table, and I pulled it onto my lap.

"Well, Oliver, I'm disappointed to have never received a response to my offer. It doesn't appear that you are taking your duties seriously. I have given you enough time to experience your freedom, or whatever is that you've been doing in this dump. But now it's time to buckle down and assume your place."

Oliver's lips were pressed together in a straight line. I'd take his anger, his frustration, growling—anything—but not this defeat. His grandfather was all but confirming Oliver's belief that he had let his family down.

"Your lack of commitment is frustrating your sisters, who both believe they are better matches. I'm not sure I'd go that far, but at least they are doing their duty. And the board is getting anxious.

The stock is a mess. It's time for an answer." Mr. Killington's fist landed on the table, rattling the glassware.

"Are you moving up my deadline?" Oliver's tone was flat as he met his grandfather's eye.

"No, I will honor our agreement. But a preview would be appropriate. It's not just you this decision effects."

"Oh, come on, who wouldn't want to be CEO of a major international conglomerate? Not me, I can tell you that much." Carter searched around the table for someone to agree with him. His family ignored him, probably used to his, well, Carterness. "It's so great how family centered this company is. Always finding room for every member of the family."

"Carter, get me a scotch. Tell them if they haven't opened it yet, it's time for the twenty-year Macallan." Mr. Killington dismissed Carter, and I couldn't deny my relief. Things were tense enough.

"Listen, if someone else is a better fit, I'm happy to end up somewhere else in the company," Oliver announced to the table, the strength returning to his voice. "If the goal is the stock price, what if I can offer an alternative, something better?"

I squeezed his fingers, proud he was speaking up for himself.

"If you believe we haven't explored our options, you are sorely mistaken. Your father expected it of you, I expect it of you, the public and the board expect it of you. You are the heir. It's time to accept your place and stop living in this fantasy."

Grace and Remy glared at their grandfather before exchanging dark glances with each other. I had hoped they would ally with their brother, but the divide Mr. Killington was stoking between the siblings was alive and well.

"You kept out of the media better than your sisters. I will give you that. They seem to think that showing their cooter or getting high off their ass at three AM, sprawled on a bathroom floor, is the making of a CEO." Mr. Killington beat his fist on the table again. "It is time to stop fucking around."

"I—" Remy began just as Grace said "That was taken out of context—"

Tim/Jim was noticeably quiet, staring into his wineglass, searching for something? His guts?

"Enough! I told you both how this was going to go. I am the Killington Empire. This is my decision. You can either sit here silently, or you can leave." Mr. Killington gulped down the rest of his goblet of wine. "And let me make this crystal clear for you . . ."

My thumb brushed against Oliver's palm; his pulse was racing.

"The appearance that you have a choice is a fallacy. There is no decision. There is this one future. On your thirtieth birthday, we will announce you as the next CEO."

The rest of the Killington clan's attention was on the table in front of them, no one willing to speak up as a crease formed between Oliver's eyes. I had no experience with boards or stocks, but I understood family.

So I pushed back from the table, stood on shaking legs, and demanded, "Stop it."

CHAPTER TWENTY-FOUR

Mr. Killington blinked.

I'd had enough. He could discount my work all he wanted. I knew my worth. But I wouldn't stand for him bullying Oliver.

"In your boardroom, you get to torment your employees. But not here, and not him. Oliver is your family. All your grandchildren have been through hell. And here you are pitting them against each other, caring more about your company than their well-being.

"Have you even considered where we are? Their family vacation home. A place filled with memories of their parents that I did my best to preserve. Not for you. For *him*. For what he felt like he lost because you have the emotional capacity of a cabbage."

Oliver coughed.

Right. I attempted to rein in my anger. "He has been working on the house this entire time. He's invested in it, searching for something he enjoys as much as football. And while it's wild, how bad he is at things . . ."

"That's not exactly helpful, Petal," Oliver muttered.

"The point is—" I spoke louder, blushing. I had never done this before, and realized I was rambling. "The point is, he's trying and that should be enough, should be more than enough. You should want him to be happy and healthy. That's all I care about."

I shoved my chair backward, and Oliver stood with me, not hesitating as we walked out of the dining room, neither of us glancing back.

His hand wrapped around mine, hauling me into a side room.

My body trembled. "Crap, that was so dumb. I'm so sorry, but I could not sit there and let him berate you any longer."

"That was . . ." He brought our hands to rest on his chest, where his heart was thumping in time with mine. "That was amazing. No one's ever done something like that for me before. Petal, I—"

The door banged open, and I spun around. His twin sisters had waltzed in, both women effortlessly glamorous.

"Well, that was thrilling." Remy gave me a slow clap.

Grace's expression remained flat. "I'm jealous. Been wanting to tell him off for a while. I'm positive he's about to screw me out of this deal with Japan I've been working on for months." Grace passed me a flute of champagne, offering me a nod. Maybe not of approval, but of respect.

I attempted to take a discreet step away from their brother. In all our discussions, we hadn't brought up what we were going to share with his family, or his sisters at least.

"We could plan a kidnapping." Remy batted her eyes at us, ignoring the horror on our faces. "A small kidnapping. It'll be like white-collar prison. Trap him in a hotel suite somewhere."

"Why would we do that?" Oliver inquired. I pressed the flute to my lips, attempting a passive expression. Everything I'd learned about his family had always seemed exaggerated, but now I wasn't so sure.

"Well, consider how high the ransom could be. He won't listen to reason voluntarily. So, a kidnapping is the obvious answer." Remy shrugged as if to say "duh."

"Listen, the only reason any of us will ever go to jail is for money laundering or insider trading," Grace promised. I had thought Carter was a lot, but this family continued to baffle me.

"I'm just saying kidnapping is becoming very popular again for reasons." Remy tapped her forehead, but it still made no sense to me.

I glanced at Oliver; he offered me an eyebrow raise and a wink.

"Ah, yes, the well-known tripanow method," Oliver said with a straight face.

"Oh, of course, the tripanow method. Works every time." If you can't understand them, join in the foolishness with your own fake kidnapping method.

"Noted in all the best kidnapping blogs." We were going to have to work on his improv.

Remy and Grace stared at us with matching smiles.

"*This* is an interesting development," Grace murmured. "I'm dying to know—"

"Oh well, let her die then." Remy interrupted, her eyes twinkled with mischief.

Grace released an exasperated breath. "Honestly, what is wrong with you?"

"What isn't wrong with me?" Remy offered. "But also, what is your fiancé doing?" Remy pointed through the partially open door to the ballroom where Tim/Jim did some sort of dance that involved waving his arms around, and not in time with the music.

"As I was trying to say, I am dying to know if you are the reason our brother appears almost"—Grace peered at her brother, examining him—"almost . . . happy?" Grace frowned.

I had nothing to say to his sisters about how I was or was not making their brother, uh, happy. I stepped further back, ready for the evening to be over, overwhelmed by the Killingtons and their drama.

"Come on, Ollie. Billions of dollars, power, and the family's legacy? I don't even have to think about it. Cousin Carter was right, who wouldn't want that? There's a reason Grandfather's able to have all three of us battling over it—because we all want it." Grace's shrug said it all. They truly couldn't comprehend why Oliver would refuse their grandfather's proposal.

"I've seen him try to paint trim. Trust me, Oliver is not fighting for it." It was hard not to laugh at the adorable way he had bitten on his lip, concentrating. I had let him do whatever he wanted to me in exchange for giving me back the paintbrush. I had no regrets.

"Are you banging our brother?" Remy tipped her chin at me.

"Maybe we could go back to discussing kidnapping?" I suggested.

"Oliver, are you in love with her?" Grace asked.

"Man locks himself away for almost a decade and still finds love. And all you get is the suck-up. Oh, Grace." Remy snickered, shaking her head. I had to agree with Remy. There was someone for everyone, but I struggled to understand what bold, stubborn Grace saw in Tim/Jim, a man so boring I still couldn't recall his name.

"Doug is—"

Doug. I wasn't even close. Man looked like a Tim/Jim though.

"How did he propose?" Oliver asked instead, and I was so thankful for him offering a distraction, I could kiss him. Except I couldn't. Because we were professionals, and this was a professional event. Tuxes should be outlawed, the way they highlighted all my favorite parts of him.

"He—"

"It is an amazing story." Remy clapped with glee. "Let me tell you. It involves a yacht, the Coast Guard, smugglers, a turtle, and strangest of all"—how could it get stranger—"no drugs were involved."

"We've been telling people he proposed during a family vacation. But thank you, Remy." Grace tossed back her champagne before smoothing her hair.

"I wouldn't worry about it. You wouldn't believe the things I've done with at least half the people in that ballroom. Guaranteed, they were illegal in parts of the world, probably illegal in parts of this country." Remy shrugged.

"I'm sure you must see something special in him," I said. "I hope you two are very happy together." I wasn't sure I believed it, but hey, to each their own.

"She gets off on bossing him around, getting him to do her bidding." Remy sniggered.

"Some people are into that." My mind flashed to Finn and Sebastian. Not that I planned to have a conversation about kink with Oliver's sisters the second time I was meeting them. That was a third meeting topic or, you know, never. Preferably never.

"You actually did a decent job with the house, but I have to say this shindig is pretty boring." Remy made a sound similar to a snore.

I focused on the compliment. "I work in historical home renovations, not party planning, but thank you."

Grace dipped briefly into the ballroom, returning with a champagne bottle to refill us all. "I'm sure Grandfather forced you to plan it. That man is so cheap. Why hire someone else when he could put more work on you?" The tension in her voice conveyed solidarity. "Not that you'd know anything about that, Oliver, since you've hidden yourself away from any family responsibility."

"Remember when we were last here? A few months before they died, some random weekend. I can't even recall why." Remy stared out the window, the lights of the backyard highlighting all the work the gardeners had put in, ignoring her sister's dig at their brother.

Oliver hummed in agreement, closing some of the space between us.

"You had gotten those new riding boots and begged to try them out. They could never say no to you." Grace's eyes glazed over, lost in the memory too. "Youngest siblings." She rolled her eyes toward me as if that explained it all.

"I might remember you begging for a pool and almost convincing Dad." Oliver nudged Grace.

"I forgot how much I loved this place. Grace and I'd complain the entire drive out here, and then kick and scream when it was time to leave. There's a simplicity here, being so removed from everything and everyone, nothing else close by. No friends to visit, no trendy restaurants. We only had each other." Remy's body language was no longer so ramrod, her spine loosening.

Their appreciation meant so much to me. These were the people whose heights were carved into the doorframes. They were the ones who knew all the secrets: the squeaky step on the stairs that needed to be fixed, which cabinet in the kitchen was a false door and hid the good liquor. Oliver knew every nook and cranny of this place. Which parts were the ones worth preserving, worth keeping, and which ones just required a new piece of plywood.

The approval I had most wanted was his, and he had given it to me in how he had helped me bring his home back to its glory and gave me his ideas and his favorite memories. In how he listened to me and never got tired or sick of it.

Remy finished the rest of her glass in a single swallow, winking at me. "Well, time to lighten this place up. Coming, sister?"

"Can't we be off for one night?" Grace groaned.

"If you say no, I'm going to grab Doug and Cousin Carter and really do some damage. We know someone snuck a phone in despite Grandfather's rules."

I was quickly warming to their tactics.

With that, Remy pranced into the ballroom, high heels clicking on the marble, nodding her head at a few guests, shaking her hips in a sultry manner. She headed straight for the stage where the band was set up and whispered something in the singer's ear. His eyes were concentrated on her exposed cleavage, but whatever she said, it worked, and he stepped aside.

"What is she doing?" I asked Grace.

"Being Remy." She rolled her eyes and tossed back the contents of her flute, passing it to a waiter on her way to the stage.

"Killington Estate, how is everyone doing tonight?" Remy shouted into the microphone as Grace stepped onto the platform, their Grandfather holding court in the back of the room.

No one said a word, but they were clearly fascinated by what the two paparazzi darlings were about to do.

Oliver was behind me as we stood at the edge of the ballroom. I was torn between wanting to support him and thinking this was an excellent moment to make an Irish exit.

"What are my sisters doing?" He bent his head down, fingers brushing against the small of my back.

"Your guess is as good as mine," I whispered back, fingers clutched together to stop myself from doing something silly, like holding his hand.

"You all know this one!" Remy didn't seem to understand how a microphone worked, that the yelling was unnecessary, especially with how few people there were in the large space.

Barely Even Friends

The band strummed her selection while Grace grumbled at her sister.

With the rush to complete things for the party, I hadn't had time to admire my work. The refreshed fresco on the ceiling, scratch-free marble pillars that gleamed, not a single fingerprint on the glass wall. Everything sparkled from the chandelier. It wasn't the ball I had pictured in my mind, but it was the beginning of something.

The dresses, tuxes, jumpsuits. A guest with a buzz cut in a breathtaking ballgown. So many people pushing the fashion envelope.

The chords to "Love Story" rang out, familiar and comforting. Crap, I had some sort of compulsion when I heard a Taylor Swift song. I had to sing along.

Remy was goading her sister into joining the chaos. Grace didn't exactly scream karaoke royalty to me, but people could surprise you.

I laughed because what else was there to do? This was less boring than watching everyone chitchat in their evening wear while elevator music strummed in the background. The stressful part of the evening was over. Now I could relax, or at least observe the festivities.

Oliver spun my body toward his, propelling us to the group of couples swaying along to—well, not the off-key singing, but to the chords the band was playing. "I want to dance with you."

He relocated my hand to his shoulder before intertwining our fingers together, like this was some sort of old-fashioned waltz.

"This isn't breaking the rules," he whispered in my ear as I tensed, unable to stop myself from checking to see what attention we were gathering. But his sisters were receiving the brunt of it, Remy incapable of keeping a tune while Grace glared on, not joining in yet. But a few were staring—not at me, but at Oliver.

My flush was from the champagne I had drunk, trying to keep up with his sisters. It had nothing to do with the way our bodies were pressed together, the lightheaded way I felt when he was around, his concentration entirely focused on me.

Then he decided to wreck me. Oliver began to murmur the lyrics softly in my ear. The song I had listened to countless times, of a love that on the surface made little sense but somehow persevered. The type of love I'd dreamed about as a little girl.

Grace finally joined in when Cousin Carter offered to be Remy's duet partner. Oliver's thumb brushed against my waist, and there was deep emotion in his voice. He was sure of the lyrics, but shaking.

I closed my eyes, leaning my head against his chest, ignoring everything else in the room but the feel of him under my cheek. I couldn't pretend the fact that he knew the words wasn't a serious turn-on.

"Since when do you listen to Taylor Swift?" I laughed as his sisters mostly screamed the lyrics of the bridge, even Grace falling into the thrall that was a Taylor Swift song.

"You like her music." Oliver's fingers squeezed mine, as if it were that simple. As if it was nothing, learning the lyrics to my favorite artist's songs. The artist I listened to for comfort, for joy, and for every emotion in between. "Besides, I liked that book you recommended. I figured I'd give her a try."

What was this man doing to me? To my heart? "What book?"

"There was only one bed . . ." His thumb brushed along my spine.

"That's in a lot of romance books," I teased. But the book I had been reading when I first got here had that trope, and I had a sneaking suspicion it was the book he was talking about. The duke's estate had run out of rooms. Whoops.

"I'm a big fan."

"I bet you are." I was too, funny enough.

He made it too easy to forget we were in a room full of people, his hand holding mine, engulfing it.

I wanted to question him about how he was feeling. Wanted to share about Ms. Roth, ask him what he thought I should do.

My problem wasn't that I had trouble expressing myself to Oliver. My problem was I felt inclined to say too much. To share every little nagging thing, the little annoying parts of my day and the big victories. He was the person I craved to lean on.

For the first time in my life, I wasn't sure how to say goodbye.

CHAPTER TWENTY-FIVE

I shut the door to the west wing behind me, leaned back against the stained wood, and closed my eyes. For a small party, it had lasted late into the evening, especially after Remy and Grace became the entertainment. There had been dancing, a lot more drinking, and discussions about more money than I could ever imagine seeing in my life.

Oliver had escaped, escorting his sisters and Tim/Jim (I kept forgetting his real name) to their waiting limousine. Despite the family's offer of lodging, all the guests had arranged for rides home after the festivities were over. I was one of the last stragglers, compelled to speak to everyone as they raved about the restoration.

And I was reluctant to go upstairs. Because it was over. The dinner had been the culmination of my work; all that was left was a final meeting at the Killington office in the city in a few days, and the contract would be complete. Which meant it was time for me to say goodbye to Oliver—and that was the last thing I wanted.

We were alone in the west wing. Oliver had chosen to take over the primary bedroom, asking for my advice on the linen, the pillows, the furniture, even the paint color. He was already in the room, attention on the far wall.

It gave me a moment to admire him, still wearing the shirt from his tux, sleeves rolled up, exposing his delicious forearms, back straight, muscles flexing from whatever he was doing. His shirt was loose, covering that bubble butt, his pants molded to those thighs. I was going to have to thank Ambrose for his expert tailoring skills.

Palms fluttering to my chest, I was taken entirely aback when I realized what he had been doing while I was still downstairs. All my idea boards that had hung in our previous room, I'd had removed. But here he was, putting them back up on the walls, in the exact positions they had been in before.

In the past, the closer I got to the end of a project, the more compartmentalized my life became. Things slowly and steadily returned to my suitcase until there was nothing left to do but walk out the door. All that remained were the changes I'd brought to the home.

"Oliver." My hand pressed to my mouth, unable to say anything beyond his name. My stomach was flipping over and over in a mess of nerves and butterfly wings fluttering around, tapping against my heart and taking my breath away with them.

His shoulders hunched as he finished placing the board before stepping back to examine it and then meeting my gaze. "I wanted to finish before you got here."

This man was hanging up my things as if this was my space too. And the more I examined the room, the more my heart banged around in my chest. Loudly enough that I wondered if he could hear it. My T-shirt stuck inside his sweatshirt over the couch from when I'd worn it the other night, and he'd pulled it off me in one fell swoop. His book sitting on top of mine because of the way he had put it away, leaning over me, kissing me goodnight.

The bathroom counter, I knew without glancing in, contained a smattering of both of our things. Our towels hung side by side. Somehow, I had gone from room-mating with him to living with him, and I hadn't even realized it.

He shrugged at me, lost, not able to put into words what this was, but understanding, nonetheless. Because it was more. More than friends, more than a hookup.

"How did it go downstairs?" Oliver stood before me, hair loose, having tossed his bow tie, his shirt unbuttoned almost all the way, his tux jacket tossed haphazardly over the desk chair as if he had been in a hurry to get going on his project. As if it had been important to him.

I wiped my hands on the silk of my pants before I realized what I was doing. "A lot of questions, but no offers."

"I doubt they'll be able to wait beyond tomorrow morning. Everyone can see how brilliant you are." His eyes were smiling at me.

My plan was to be brave and discuss everything with him—how he was feeling, how I was—but it all fled my mind. Unable to stop myself from reaching for him, I removed a piece of tape stuck to his shirt.

"Thanks." His lips pressed to my forehead, and I felt his smile.

"No problem. Didn't realize you were getting into arts and crafts."

"The walls were missing something."

"Ouch, don't tell that to your interior decorator."

He sat on the side of the bed, waiting for me to take my place next to him, which I of course did.

"I missed seeing them on the walls." His hands, pressed to his thighs, seemed to fascinate him.

I scoffed. "You missed seeing paint colors that you refused even last week to a admit were not all the same shade, or close-up shots of different wood finishes?" My head was shaking in disbelief as I leaned back on my palms.

He shrugged. "You like it, and I enjoy having your stuff here."

"It won't be for much longer," I mumbled as the pounding in my chest grew louder. The reason I had delayed thinking about any of this was now over. No more excuses, no more reasons to delay.

"You're not dying."

I kicked him hard, not that he even gave me a grunt. "Not what I meant, asshole."

"Am not," he grumbled, nose wrinkling.

He had me grinning again as I sat up, nudging his shoulder. "Don't forget 'stubborn' and 'grumpy.'"

"Anything else?" He curled a piece of hair behind my ear, fingers drifting to play with the straps of my outfit, my body swaying into his. My life had always had a natural progression. Request for a project, the planning phase, execution, and then on to the next, rinse and repeat. I'd never considered staying before, or examined what that would look like. And here he was, making the impossible happen.

"Well, you could smile more." It was easier to shove everything back down than to release it, still too scared to have him reject me.

"I smile." His jaw ground in genuine outrage. Was he being serious?

"In one very specific situation." He had to realize it after all this time.

"Oh, really?"

"Yes, really." The laughter bubbled out of me.

"You know me that well. The one specific situation I smile in?"

"I appreciate that's your concern, not the complete-lack-of-smiling aspect." Another day, another flirting session that mostly involved my word vomit.

"Prove it then."

A dare I was more than happy to fulfill. He lifted his palms as I straddled him, our bodies moving in sync as I settled myself.

I caressed the curves of his cheek with my thumbs before pressing up. "We should start exercising these muscles. They seem to have forgotten how to work." The world deserved his smiles, though I selfishly enjoyed keeping them to myself.

"Adorable." His voice was dry as he let me have my way with him.

"I am."

He didn't dispute my statement. "All right, then what's this one situation when I smile, Miss Know-It-All?"

I leaned in slowly, waiting to see if he would catch on, but he merely closed his eyes, tongue dipping out to moisten his lip, still not connecting the dots.

I went cross-eyed as I watched it happen, the slight curvature of his lips, the pull of his muscles, pushing his cheeks out further as our lips brushed together. I shifted away, hoping to capture it in action, but he chased after me, nipping at my lower lip, bringing me into the circle of his arms. My bottom landed firmly on his thighs. Safe. I was safe with him.

We were both breathless, his lips red and swollen as we separated.

"You ever going to tell me?" He was terrible at faking his frustration.

"Really, still?" I laughed, almost giddy. My heart did a little pirouette at the realization it was automatic for him. He didn't consider what he was doing, didn't even think about it. Being with me made him smile.

"Tell me, now I need to know." His fingers traced along the features of my face. I had to wonder if my smile was different for him.

I brushed my lips against his for a moment. "It's when you kiss me," I breathed against the mouth I fantasized about when it wasn't touching me. Pillowy soft, the bottom lip thicker than the top. These lips were dangerous, and when I felt him smile, my only impulse was to kiss him more. Make him smile more.

"I do not." There was more disbelief in his voice than anything, his eyes wide as he considered me.

It was a challenge I was happy to accept as my tongue dipped out, tracing his lips, my fingertips pressed to the rise of his cheeks. "Oh yes, you very much do." He was too stubborn, even as I stroked his beard.

When I sat back, arms wrapped around his neck, his eyebrows were pulled together.

"What's wrong? I like that you do it, as if it's our secret." Like the secret way we held hands when no one was looking.

"Nothing's wrong," he defended, before his eyes clashed with mine. "You make me happy."

"You make me happy too," I whispered back.

"I do?"

"Promise."

"Even with my messed-up family?"

I rolled my eyes. He still had to meet my onesie pajama-loving father. "It's not like they're the mob. Your sisters are great."

He nodded, letting his hands rest on my hips.

"Hey, blood makes you related, loyalty makes you family." The words slipped out. There was a movie quote for every moment.

The groove between his eyebrows dug deeper into his skin. "What?"

"Hm, maybe I don't have friends. I have family." This was too much fun. The endless list of movies and TV shows I craved to show him and hear his opinion on.

"Are you quoting a movie at me again?" He couldn't even feign surprise at my expense.

I had lost my mystery; how disappointing. "I live my life a quarter mile at a time."

"What does it say about me that I find this attractive? You quoting movies to me I've never seen."

"You should be thankful I'm not kicking you to the curb for not seeing the epic action series *The Fast and the Furious*. Honestly, there are so many quotable gems. This must be rectified."

"Guess that means we have to keep chipping away at that list you put together."

"Well, it's criminal for you to live your life having not seen the rest of the *Lord of the Rings* trilogy, or *The Fast and the Furious*. Tell me you've at least watched *The Mummy*." Maybe it would be simpler to give him a list of my favorite movies and see which ones he would check off, though I had a not-so-sneaking suspicion it would be none except for the few I had shown him during my time here.

"Tom Cruise is in that one, right?"

My gasp was legitimate. "You're lucky you're hot." We did not talk about that version of *The Mummy*. "Have you seen *Speed*?"

His brow furrowed, and I reached out to touch it. "About some sort of bus crash or something?"

There was hope for him yet. "It is a high-speed romantic adventure film where Sandra Bullock and Keanu Reeves barely look at each other yet somehow fall in love as they save a busload of people and the city of Los Angeles from a psychopath. Gah, the sexual tension is just . . . I'm seeing the plot in a whole new light right now."

He smirked, his palms pushing the cape away, landing on the fabric of my pants.

"I'm ashamed of myself for being swayed so easily by a nice beard. Our differences are too great for this to go on any longer." I probably would've been more convincing had I not been squirming on his lap.

"You like my beard, huh?"

"A real shock, I'm sure."

"What else do you like about me?" His voice was all confidence, but his gaze bore into mine, fingers tightening.

"Hmm, it's hard to get over the whole *The Fast and the Furious* thing. I deserve someone who's going to appreciate my genius."

He lifted my hair from my neck. It was a marvel it was still mostly in its original curled status. "Well, I like this brain." He pressed a kiss to my forehead, his words thick. "I l-like how it catches the small things people can miss. You gave Ambrose the room of his dreams. Built Rue a five-star dining establishment. Somehow got me willing to walk into this wing, let alone have my room back in here."

"You did that," I exhaled.

"No, *you*. And don't interrupt." He kissed my nose, soft, tender. "I like your eyes, how they miss nothing, including apparently how I smile." A flush spread across my body as his lips pressed to my closed eyelids. "Your button nose is perfect." I couldn't help but giggle. "These cheeks. Because you have no problem smiling, I get worried when I don't see it. Means that the roof may literally come down around us."

"Hey, we stopped that from happening." It was still too soon to laugh about the restoration hiccups.

"And these lips."

"These lips that don't stop chatting?" I pursed them at him.

"These lips that speak with my favorite voice, that are the first thing I think of when I wake up and the last thing before I dream about you." He proved it by sucking on my bottom lip enough I felt it to my toes. "Kissing you, talking to you, how much you care . . . all somehow got me to care again when I had stopped for a very, very long time. You cared enough to invest in helping me figure out my future."

His lips pressed to the V of the top I was wearing, his hand giving a slight tug on the zipper in the back. "Can I take this off?"

"Please." My voice cracked.

He was achingly slow as he sat tall, watching my every reaction as he slid the zipper down, bracket by bracket, the sound popping in my ear. When he was done, he didn't slide the straps off my shoulders. Instead, he fiddled with the suspenders. "Ambrose deserves a raise."

"I thought they were a nice touch."

"It's perfect. You are perfect." His touch felt reverent, smooth fingertips against my skin as he slid back and forth again, eyes on my heaving chest, leaving me topless on his lap.

He palmed my breasts, thumbs brushing against my nipples. "I think it goes without saying how I feel about these."

"A fan, are you?"

"Understatement." He cupped my breast, bringing his mouth down, eyes on me as his teeth gently bit my nipple. I gasped, my fingers diving into his hair as his tongue swirled. "I could do this all day."

"You would—you're mean like that."

"Trust me, it wouldn't be mean." His exploration led him to my ass, squeezing for a moment, then lifting me. I gave a slight squeal

in surprise as he set me gently on the bed and switched our positions, one knee between my legs as he gave each breast another kiss,
then my lips, my nose, before stepping back.

Oliver's palms skimmed my sides, touching every dip and curve
of my waist, slow, tracing and teasing along the fabric of my outfit,
catching my underwear as he pulled it all down, leaving me naked
on his bed.

Before I could make a smart comment, bring this back and
away from the way my heart was beating in my chest—the words
caught in my throat, the feeling in my fingers, my veins, my body
calling his to mine—he unbuttoned his shirt. Slowly.

"Tease."

That earned me a laugh. He knew exactly what he was doing to
my squirming body, and he was taking his time. He popped the
button of his pants and dragged his zipper down. But he had forgotten about his shoes, and he almost tripped over his feet. He
chucked them across the room in his eagerness to get naked, then
returned to the bed that had me on it.

"What do you want to do with me?" My voice was hoarse, deep,
as he crawled toward me, caging my body in with the frame of his.

"Petal."

"Tell me what it means," I begged, desperate to learn why he'd
given me this nickname. But here I was, my heart flipping over
every time his lips formed a "p" sound.

"Not yet."

"Still feeling mean, I see."

"Still trying to keep you interested," he confessed.

"You think you have to try to hold my interest?" My hands ran
up and down the soft skin of his back, reveling that I somehow got
free access to touch him. He leaned on his forearms, stomach
pressed to mine, legs on either side.

"I worry about it, yeah."

"You're a secret softie, aren't you?" I lifted my head to kiss him.

"Maybe," he begrudgingly admitted as he offered me another smile. "About very few things."

"About me."

"Maybe."

I searched for a single ticklish spot, but no luck. My leg curved around his hip, a moan erupting the moment his erection brushed against my center. "You can do anything you want to me."

"Anything, huh?" He shifted so he could trace my right arm with his finger. "I can hold your hand?"

"What?" In the haze of horniness, it took me a moment to grasp his words, what he was asking for.

"Bellamy," he asked, holding my gaze. "Can we have that for tonight?"

CHAPTER TWENTY-SIX

I swear I almost caught his smile as he leaned forward to kiss me, sucking my tongue into his mouth, letting me pull his body against mine. And it hit me with the weight of his delicious body. He was my favorite person. The person who, every time something good happened, I sprinted to share it with.

His fingertips traced my callouses before looping us together. A single heartbeat, a single breath. He had painted the walls of my heart with gray, the colors of his eyes bleeding blue in the center.

My heart was knocking on my brain, and I wanted to shut both down, revel in this moment.

My fingernails dug into the sheets as he kissed every inch of my soul, chasing each press of his lips with his tongue, my back arching off the bed each time he used his teeth. It was more than owning my body, my pleasure; it was giving a name to the feeling stuck in my throat, choking me with the emotion of it.

Love.

We were making love. My heart was swelling and breaking all in the same moment.

He licked a path up my slit before burying his face in my pussy. His beard scratched against my inner lips as he smiled, tasted, and touched every single piece of me, moaning against me as he sucked on my clit, enjoying it just as much as I was.

I was coming apart under him until I was one pulsating emotion. My hips lifted, calling out for him, as I dug my fingers into his hair, scratching at his scalp the way he liked.

My heart was shouting, *Tell him you love him, you moron!*

And I was. Every time I brushed his hair out of his eyes, saw those dumb freckles, felt him sigh because this was frenetic and different, and we both wanted more. The recognition of what this was, it was all I could think about, all I could hold back from crying out as he brought me down from my orgasm, whispering against my skin how good I was, wondering if I could feel his smile.

My legs immediately wrapped around his hips as he settled against me, his beard still wet from how thoroughly he had gone down on me, his erection rocking against my hip. "There's another rule we could break." Could he feel my heart beating out of my chest? How badly I wanted him as close as possible, nothing between us?

"Yeah? Tell me Petal."

"Condoms."

His finger tracing patterns against my shoulder stopped moving.

"Oh, I mean, not if you don't want to."

His hips pushed into mine, our smiles aligning.

"I've been tested and I'm on birth control, but if you, uh, don't want, we, uh . . . Of course, I mean, let me grab a—" Eloquent as ever, the fluttering of my heart taking over, as I traced the scar on his left thigh.

I reached for his bedside table, but his palm curled around mine until our fingers intertwined. This was more than every other time we had held hands during sex. This was entirely intentional, this was feelings. My heartbeat bursting out of my grip on his, speaking the same language.

I love you, you fucking asshole. I wish I could keep you. I want to keep you. See? I could be romantic.

"I've been tested too." His voice was hesitant, but his fingers were firm as he grasped my hand.

"I've never done this before." My confession tumbled out, betraying my nerves. I traced the line of the scar on his thigh as I waited.

"Me neither."

"I want to with you. I want to *everything* with you."

It was too easy to lean in and capture his lips. To pour out every emotion I had tried to lock away.

A slight grunt as he aligned our bodies together, the head of his dick pressing up against my clit, my breath rushing out, skin flushed. Our gazes met as he teased us both before he put us out of our misery.

"Oh." My fingers curled around his biceps, sliding to his shoulders, his ass. "Baby," I hummed. It was like being plugged in, knocked to the next level, the feel of his dick with nothing between us.

He opened his mouth, as if he was going to say something, eyes concentrating on me, before nipping my skin. "Tell me you want this."

"Don't stop," I begged. "Please, never stop."

His head buried into my neck, teeth lightly snapping at the juncture of my shoulder, in time with his hips. "Fuck, it's too good."

"Yeah?" I grabbed at the back of his scalp, all thought fleeing my mind except how to make this last longer.

"I'm going to die here, freaking happy." His laugh vibrated against my cheek, shaking both of us, lighting my body with every ounce of his pleasure.

"Not yet." I bit at his earlobe, and he made another delicious moan as I clenched around him, the wet sounds my body was making almost obscene. "It keeps getting better."

And it did. He smiled, his beard brushing against my skin, a kiss to my pulse point, and he kept fucking smiling. Because here we were, doing this. Breaking the rules, allowing ourselves this moment.

It was overwhelming, his heartbeat against my chest, the way he begged me not to come, not yet, how he filled me up, nothing in between us, no barriers, not even the pretend ones. This was us, and it was fucking perfect. His thumb pressed to my clit, brushing against where we were joined. My lips pressed to his freckles, touching every inch of skin I could.

And I wanted it.

I wanted to argue about all the movies he hadn't seen and laugh at the ridiculous quotes he had no reference for. Let him show me a football game when he was ready.

Because it wasn't a home I needed—just him.

I could picture it as the tears built behind my eyes, my throat clogging, fingers gripping him tight to me to hold on to this moment, to hold on to him as if he was mine to keep. I couldn't pretend anymore—I didn't want to leave. He'd left me bare, unable to hide even from myself. This was everything I had been too scared to ever want, and now it was mine to take.

"Petal," he breathed out, pushing up slightly on his forearms, pressing his lips to mine, dragging his cock out, then thrusting back in, both of us gasping at the heat and throb of it.

It was slow and rough and messy. We were all limbs and teeth, with barely a breath between us. All of him was driving me into the mattress as it built, swirling around my stomach, my fingers tight with it.

With his smile pressed to my skin, my body shuddered and clenched around his, my heart bursting.

Two more strokes and he followed behind me, lacking all form, hips thrusting into mine. My body would be permanently outlined on his bed.

"You okay?" He pressed a kiss to my cheek; another landed on the corner of my eye.

"Mm-hmm." I couldn't vocalize what was churning inside of me, the aching pleasure of it. He hadn't pulled out yet, merely drew me down to lie on top of him. His hands never stopped moving. My hips, my thighs, my back, reaching my cheek, cupped it, thumb caressing.

His words were quiet, pressed to my forehead. "I can't imagine a world where you don't walk through my front door." He toyed with my hair, both of us sticky with sweat.

"Me neither," I whispered back, holding him tighter.

My body with a road map of him. Of beard burn, red marks from his mouth where he'd sucked and played my body as if it were his favorite instrument as he traced where my suspenders were supposed to be.

Because no matter where we went from here, I'd broken the biggest rule of all.

I'd fallen in love.

For the first time since I had moved into Oliver's bedroom, I woke up alone, the alarm blaring in my ear. It wasn't just the sex, though I was still aching—Oliver and I had learned we were big fans of the no-condom rule, but I was rested because I had let my heart decide.

If this had been any other job, I'd be finishing packing, tossing my iPad into my backpack, erasing the final pieces of me from the house. But this time I would be coming back. I'd need to take my miniscule wardrobe for while I was back at Dad's for my meetings, but after that, the drawers that lay empty in Oliver's dresser were going to be filled.

As I tied my hair off into a ponytail, my breath caught in my throat. Sitting on Oliver's bedside table, among all the frames of his family, was the one of me with Sebastian and Finn. But that wasn't what clogged my chest with emotion. I reached down to pick up the photo of Dad and me, the one that had been damaged months ago. Somehow Oliver had gotten another copy of the picture and put it in a frame that matched the others. My stuff fit in seamlessly with his, our families together.

I practically sprinted down the stairs, humming. Rue was already in the kitchen, preparing breakfast. With the full kitchen available to them, they had been cooking up a storm, trying out all their new appliances.

"Just on time." Rue gently pushed me toward the breakfast nook, to sit next to Nick while my gaze searched.

"Ms. Price, perfect. I was thinking of tailoring some more of your outfits, or maybe you wouldn't mind allowing me to build you a few more pieces or even a full wardrobe. Your clothing choices leave a lot to be desired." Ambrose was in motion, pulling out the place settings for all of us, but it was difficult to concentrate on anything. I was practically bouncing.

"Not until I teach her how to ride a horse." Nick glared at Ambrose. "I think you'll enjoy it now that you have some free time." She slid a USB stick toward me. "Thought you might like your own version to take with you, for when you get homesick."

Nerves rattled my veins. "Thank you."

"You don't even know what it is." She rolled her eyes in that perfect way teenagers have as they suffer through dealing with adults. Oh, to be so perfectly jaded and untouched by the world. "It's Bl8z3. Not the advanced version I've been tinkering with, but the Bl8z3 you're familiar with."

It was embarrassing that it still took another moment for it all to click into place. "It was you."

Nick tilted her head, a smile faint on her lips. "Who else would it be?"

"Bl8z3 never told me." I felt ridiculous for having never figured it out, that I'd given Oliver all the credit for Nick's brilliance.

Oliver hadn't merely given them a home; he was giving them the opportunities he had never taken for himself. He'd gifted Nick stables, a place to work on her skills, the opportunity to beta test her genius invention.

"I'm working on Bl8z3, version 2.0. Thinking about entering some contests, maybe get a scholarship or two." She was humble, as if she would not take over the world one day. Emotion exploded in my chest. I threw my arms around her, barely having to duck down. I felt like I was truly seeing her for the first time.

Nick laughed, shoving me away as Rue set our plates down.

"I have to head back to the city today, to give my final presentation to Mr. Killington to fulfill the contract." Nick had been helping me with the slides for my PowerPoint. It was on the tip of my tongue to assure them that it was only a visit, I would be coming back, but Oliver was the first person I needed to tell that news to. "Actually, do you know where Oliver is?"

All three exchanged looks before Ambrose spoke, scooting out of the nook so I could slide out. "I think what you've been searching for is in the gardens past the library." As I stood, he puffed his chest out, twisting his mustache until he released a frustrated sigh and pulled me into a hug, albeit a stiff one. "Don't break his heart."

Shock froze my reaction as I wrapped my arms around him tightly. "Never," I promised.

My heartbeat only increased as I almost sprinted through the house. I had my own memories here now. The wallpaper Oliver had helped me restore, the bookcase he'd clutched as he'd kissed me for the first time, the doorway where he always squeezed my fingers, just briefly, before anyone else could see. Somehow I had found my place here, even as I'd taken it apart and put it back together.

Standing outside with pruning shears I had never seen before, bending over a bush of roses, was the person who'd changed me most of all. The sun spilled out behind him, almost acting as a spotlight, catching on every hue of his hair, the pale blue of his T-shirt.

Oliver spun toward me, a rose in his hand. He brushed a kiss across my forehead before tucking the flower around my suspenders. So many of my questions were being answered today.

A giggle had both of us searching for the source. Rue, Ambrose, and Nick were all leaning past the glass door, not even hiding their eagerness to watch. Their buddy comedy routine required some work.

"This is the best part," Nick said before glancing up at Rue, rolling her eyes, and running into the house.

Rue used an oven mitt to hit Ambrose on top of his head, disheveling his hair, which of course caused him to flee, shouting about being undignified or something.

With a final order of "Don't fuck this up," Rue closed the door, at least giving us some semblance of privacy.

I shook out my arms. This was it. I could do this. I loved him and needed to tell him. The words were almost exploding out of me, my heart already his whether he knew it or not. *I love you.*

"I'm sorry I was gone when you woke up this morning, Petal." He tweaked my suspenders before smoothing the material, his fingertips stroking.

"I wanted to talk to you." I gripped his hands, enjoying how they dwarfed mine, kept me secure, safe, wrapped up in him.

"Finally." He was slightly shaking. "I've been waiting for you to tell me how things with Eileen Roth went. Did she offer you the job on the spot?" He bit his lip.

Wait, what? "Ms. Roth?" *He* was the one who'd recommended me to her?

"I reached out because I knew how badly you wanted the job, but she was already aware of you and your work. So I put in a good word, made sure she knew what she'd be missing out on if she didn't hire you."

A record scratched, fingernails scraped down a chalkboard.

My heart was melting on the ground around us. Everything that had been on the tip of my tongue to confess—to admit and see if he felt the same way—dried up. He'd known I wanted to do this myself, not earn it because of who I was sleeping with. I wanted a recommendation from *Adrian* Killington, not his grandson who hadn't even been the one to hire me. It felt transactional: I'd saved Oliver's home, he'd gotten me my dream job, and now we could wipe our hands of each other. But that wasn't what it was between us.

Why had he done the one thing that would assure I would leave? Unless . . . that was what he wanted? It made this easier for him.

His eyes searched mine, brimming with happiness, with hope. My heart warred with the anger that he had interceded, not trusting me to accomplish this myself. I blew out a breath to try to see through the emotion clouding everything.

"I couldn't stop myself. If I could help make your dreams come true, I had to."

He'd reached out to Ms. Roth. The job, the Bib—they were in the city. Six long hours away from him and the estate. But I shoved the rising panic back down—he hadn't known I was thinking of staying. This didn't mean he was pushing me out the door, right? That all of this was temporary to him.

No, I refused to believe that last night, as we'd fallen asleep, would be the last time he ever kissed me, the last time we ever made love. All the things that scared me, the relationship things, they were all I wanted with him now. To wake up in the middle of the night and confess my fears and my dreams to him. To hold his hand through family events, let him know I was always on his side, in public, any time we wanted. I wanted to experience my life with him, to know that no matter where my career took me, I always had a home with him.

I opened my mouth, ready to risk it all.

But then he said, "My sister called: that's why I got up early. I guess my grandfather is screwing her on this project she's been working on for months." Oliver released my hands, leaving me cold and alone. "She was asking me for help, and she needs me, Bell." His voice sounded like one huge apology.

"You're taking the job? You're saying yes," I finished for him.

"It's my family. I owe them, especially my sisters, what with how long I've been gone. I can't . . ." His gray eyes searched mine, maybe for absolution or to make this easier for him. I could do this, bear it for a bit longer. While my heart shattered like a pane of glass.

I nodded. "You're getting everything you wanted. Your family is back, and your grandfather will give you the deed to this place." I waved vaguely at the estate. "We're both getting everything we wanted." I strained to keep the bitterness out of my voice.

Back in March, if you had told me this would be the end result, I'd have been thrilled—for both of us. Our dreams were coming true, and I was genuinely happy that his sisters were trying, welcoming him back. But as I stood there on a warm day in August, it all felt empty, like it wasn't enough. I'd known that the paths of our lives were going to diverge, and here it was.

"Everything, yeah . . ." Oliver shoved his fists back into his pockets, shoulders raised.

We stood in the heartbeat, the final breath. This was the end. I knew this feeling well—my happiness came in spurts of time, never this long, continuous thing. I'd been part of this phase of his life, and now he was moving on to bigger and better.

"We said we'd figure this out once the mansion was finished, and I guess this is us figuring it out." It was impossible to swallow the lump in my throat. "Your sisters are lucky to have you."

He was taking the job, the one he hadn't wanted. *Self-sacrificing asshole.* But I couldn't stop him, not when he had so much to gain. Not when he was standing here telling me that this was what he wanted.

We were both being cowards: me, unable to tell him how I felt, and him not having the guts to tell me that it was over. It was all there, shining in his eyes: pride, affection, and the cloudiness of his belief that somehow, I wasn't a fit for him.

What would be the point in pouring out my heart when he had already decided?

"I should get going." I had tears to weep. His nose wrinkled, arm stretching as if he was going to hold my hand. But I stepped away, not allowing him to see me break.

We stood there, surrounded by beauty, as our final moment crumbled around us. The sun rose over Oliver's head, forcing me to shield my eyes, no longer able to see him clearly.

Maybe I never had.

CHAPTER TWENTY-SEVEN

Two Months Later

Change was something I knew how to adapt to, even if my chest had a gaping hole in it that wouldn't allow me to pick up a romance novel. I had purged my life of Oliver, blocking any mention of him, instructing Bl8z3 to do the same. The gaping hole in my chest would fill, with time. That's what I kept telling myself, even as it seemed to grow bigger by the day.

I'd wake up in bed, still searching for his warmth; come home ready to tell him about my day; pick up my phone to text him, but never hit "Send." I refused to get in the way of his relationship with his sisters. This was what he had wanted.

I was fine.

Work was fine. Ms. Roth had offered me a position at the Bib on the spot. My opinion was valued, as I witnessed how much creativity and research went into each decision. It was everything I had dreamed about and more.

Barely Even Friends

Things with Sebastian and Finn were fine. We hung out on the regular, as I third-wheeled, refusing any suggestion for a double date.

I'd finally moved out of Dad's place and had an apartment of my own, though I was too busy to decorate beyond a couch and bed. Nothing adorned the walls; my photos were still at the estate, and I just couldn't do it. It felt wrong to make another home after his.

I was fine, things were fine. Fine, fine, fine.

It was silly, the thing that broke me. It had been accidental—I hadn't listened to Taylor Swift in two months, but there was *Lord of the Rings* ready to be streamed. My finger stumbled on the trackpad of my laptop, the movie resuming right when Gandalf shouted that the monster shall not pass.

I crumpled into my couch.

"Bl8z3?" I cleared my throat.

"Yes, Ms. Price?" The response was instantaneous.

"Is there, uh, any news about Oliver or his family?"

It gave off a technical chirp, almost a laugh. "I'll send it to your email now."

There were articles upon articles. Oliver reuniting with his family, speculation he would be named his grandfather's successor. Traveling with his sisters. Grace had gotten the recognition she had earned for the Japan deal.

And then came the announcement that he'd been named vice president of Philanthropic Endeavors, a position created entirely for him. His first initiative was starting a fund to restore historic homes, preserving history for generations. The stock continued to decline, but it was rebounding at the news of new technology being acquired. AI created by an unknown tech designer.

"He turned down his grandfather." My chest filled with pride—and concern about what that meant for him and the estate.

"Keep going," instructed Bl8z3.

I clicked on another article: a picture of Oliver filled the entire first page. He was standing at the estate, back to the camera, facing the garden, the glass doors of the library open. It hurt in a good way to see him, but I was desperate for his face. Was he happy? Was he still sporting his beard?

The article detailed how Oliver was ushering in change to the Killington Empire. He had spent the past eight years as a ghost investor in a nonprofit that taught coding to kids. With the announcement, he was also starting up a college scholarship fund—the first of which was being awarded to Nick Rue, who'd been chosen by an anonymous panel that didn't involve Oliver.

My face dipped lower beneath my T-shirt, as if to contain the feelings that wanted to erupt from my chest. Because after that was photo and photo of Oliver being hounded by the paparazzi, him with his sisters, him alone shielding his face. The rest were from outside the estate's gates, where presumably Oliver was inside. Was he shutting away the world again? Did he even have a home to go to since he'd reneged on his grandfather's deal?

Time had done nothing to dull how I felt about him. I hadn't stolen nearly enough of his clothes to sleep in to satisfy myself.

But it wasn't my business; he'd made sure it wasn't.

A pounding fist slammed on my front door. "Bellamy, I swear if you don't open this door, I will kick it down."

"How are you so confident that I'm even in here?" I shouted to my best friend as I picked myself off the couch.

"Finn and I finally remembered the Find Your Friend app we turned on in college to make sure one of us wasn't killed by a random in the night."

The moment I opened the door, Sebastian, with Finn in tow, pushed in, carrying a stack of poster boards.

"They could have killed us in the day too," I muttered under my breath.

"Okay, it is time for your intervention," Sebastian declared, pointing me toward my couch.

"A love intervention," Finn corrected, straightening the poster boards to line up along my bare white wall.

"Why on Earth would I need an intervention?"

This was strange even for them.

"If this is about you not being a 'forever girl' again, I am calling extreme world-ending bullshit on that." Sebastian gave me his don't-mess-with-me face. "You are a forever person. You are one of my forever people."

I glared at him as I flopped back down on the couch.

"Temporary is the nature of your work. It's not a characteristic of your personality. You are loyal to a fault. Your dad, Finn, me. Even that strange AI you brought back with you." He started to pace in front of me. "Vulnerability is hard. Trusting someone with your heart, having feelings that aren't entirely in your control. That stuff can't go on a to-do list."

Wow, was I really that predictable?

"If I recall, Bell, you gave me a similar talk when I complained to you about dating an artist who lived his life from one painting to the next." Sebastian offered heart eyes to Finn before resuming his glare at me. "Falling in love is scary. It's freefalling into a void where you have no idea where you'll end up or if you'll ever make it back out. And with the best ones, the forever ones, you don't. You keep falling and trust in the fact that they are right next to you, holding your hand."

I needed new friends.

"He got me my job—he *sent me away*." But as I glanced back at my laptop, my conviction was failing.

"Oh my gosh." Sebastian clutched at his chest. "He helped you pursue your dreams. Wanted you to be happy. Why didn't you say he despises you?" His dramatics were not appreciated.

I closed my laptop. "It played itself out."

"Keep saying the words. Some of them may even be true at some point." I threw up my hands, but he ignored me. "I don't think the guy who called me when you were upset about the pipes bursting, so he could ask about a photo he needed a copy of, was trying to send you away. Feel free to get me a medal as the world's best friend." He plopped down on the couch next to me.

"That's nice, but—"

"You don't jump into bed with just anyone, Bell, let alone share a room."

"Why can't you support me in whatever I do, and never criticize me?" What happened to unequivocal loyalty in all things?

"You're thinking of a regular friendship, Bells." He patted my hand, as if explaining this to a child. "You have the best friend package here. No holds barred, even when I know it's something tough to hear."

"It also comes with illustrations," Finn announced now that he had finished laying out whatever this was.

"Did you make a presentation?" I asked. Horrifying was what this was.

"Yes, when your boyfriend is a hot artist, you ask him for help." Sebastian beamed toward Finn, which would have been cute if they weren't about to offer me some sort of lecture. Was it too early to start drinking?

Finn flipped the first poster board over. "They're storyboards. If I had more notice, they would have been fully animated. I've been dabbling with—"

Sebastian coughed, getting Finn back on track as I absorbed the illustration. Finn had drawn out my time at the Killington Estate, featuring me and Oliver.

"I lived it. I don't need a reminder." I yanked down the blanket covering the back of the couch, wrapping it around my body, something else to hold onto as my fingers itched to open my laptop back up.

Sebastian had note cards too. "Okay, as you can see, your relationship built naturally. Aided by the only-one-bed situation you contrived."

"Contrived?" I almost shouted.

"You had an unlimited budget. I'm sure you could have ordered a mattress to be delivered. We both know it was a convenient lie. You told yourself you had to sleep in his bed."

"He slept on the couch," I muttered.

Sebastian puffed out his cheeks. "The entire time?" He didn't even wait for my response. "Reason two is . . ."

They had walked in at the worst possible moment. I was vulnerable, heart aching, because I did miss Oliver—every piece of me missed him. Was he at the estate, thinking about me? "What is the point of all of this?"

"That you are in love with him," Finn and Sebastian pronounced together, hinting that they had rehearsed this a few times.

I stood, keeping the blanket wrapped around me. "That isn't breaking news. I *know* I'm in love with him. I'm fully aware I screwed up too. I don't need you to kick me when I'm down."

"Ah." Sebastian's eyebrows drew together, talking to Finn as if I weren't in the room. "We have a martyr-type situation going on here. Time for plan B."

"What about all my ideas for double dates?" Finn walked farther down the wall. "Fine," he grumbled. "But I'm going to remember this later, Cheeks."

Finn's next board merely read *The Article.*

I crossed my arms over my chest. I had zero interest in reading what new gossip was being printed about Oliver.

"You won't be making that face once you read it." Sebastian handed me the physical magazine, already flipped to the correct page, with a few lines highlighted in yellow.

This page held what I was hungering for: a photo of Oliver. I drank in those heavy eyebrows and how he tugged at his beard, the camera angle making his hand seem even larger. My body shivered in memory, heat spreading as if he were a room away.

But he wasn't.

Oliver had sat down for an interview, the first he had ever granted.

"Grief is a heady thing. There is no right or wrong way to experience it, but it's a tough thing to go through alone. It took me letting someone in to realize that it didn't need to be that way. The world didn't have to be something I was scared was going to hurt me again."

"Sounds like a special person."

"Very special. Too special for me to hold on to."

My eyes were heavy with tears, my lashes wet as I allowed my fingers to trace along his features.

"He even sent it to me." Sebastian shrugged. "People don't take an interest in historical homes unless it will get them laid."

My breath shuddered, the magazine pressed to my chest as if it was an adequate way of expressing what was springing back to life and had really never left, no matter how much I had attempted to tamp it down.

Fuck, I missed him.

"For such a private person, this was a declaration of love. Of *'I fucked up, I should have never let you go. Come back to me please,*

please—'" Sebastian waved his hand in the air. "What was his nickname for you?"

"Petal." There was no stopping the tears now. I knew what I had to do.

"Please, Petal, come back so I can lick chocolate off your body."

A laugh escaped me. "Why did you have to make it weird?"

I had made up my mind the moment I had seen that photo of Oliver, but I needed the shove only a best friend could provide. Oliver wasn't better off without me—the paparazzi, his grandfather, they were all circling him, and I left him alone in that, abandoned him. Out of what—fear?

"You love him. All lovey-dovey heart eyes, palm sweating, butterflies in your stomach that make you want to throw up." Finn was too giddy.

There was another knock at my door. "I'm not too late, am I?"

"You invited my dad?" I exclaimed as I let him in.

"We've already done it, Mr. Price, but we're not sure we've convinced her yet." Sebastian huffed.

"My darling—"

"Referring to your car again?" I interrupted, catching the keys as Dad tossed them at me.

"No, my darling, I am referring to you. Go, talk to him. I can't stand seeing you here with a broken heart." Dad clutched my hand holding the keys to his car.

They weren't playing fair; a lump formed in my throat at the love in the room. At the love maybe waiting for me if I only could reach out for it and grab it.

"You don't even have a TV." Sebastian waved his arms in front of my empty wall. "If there was ever a cry for help, that's a big one."

"An alarm I've set up at the estate is going off," Bl8z3 interrupted.

"What?" I glanced at Sebastian, panicked.

"It appears something is happening with the piping. There may be some flooding. I am running some reports."

"Fuck."

After everything, I refused to let his home be ruined.

CHAPTER TWENTY-EIGHT

The clouds in the sky blocked out the sun, making the trip back eerily similar to the one I had made more than seven months ago. But I wasn't the same girl who had driven this road.

This Bellamy wasn't a coward.

The six hours crept slowly, my slippery palms sliding against the leather of the steering wheel, but finally I was pulling up to the familiar gates. Repaired, yet somehow still creepy. The driveway was littered with cars, paparazzi pressed to the wrought iron, immediately snapping pictures of Philippe.

Before I could even think about rolling my window down to reach out to the call box, the gate opened just enough, immediately closing the moment the Mustang cleared.

I hadn't packed a single thing, only had taken a shower and rushed to get on the road. My heart was beginning to race again.

Ambrose opened the door as I approached. "Ms. Price, what are you doing here?"

"I heard about the flooding. Did the pipes burst or something?" I glanced around as thunder boomed, but nothing looked amiss, or even slightly damp.

"What flooding?" His eyebrows drew in confusion.

"My sensors might have malfunctioned," Bl8z3 interrupted, voice carrying through the foyer.

"Excuse me?" I glanced at the ceiling, wishing Bl8z3 was corporeal so I could shake it. But it didn't matter, that wasn't the real reason I was here. I had decided to come even before the fake flooding alert. "How is he?"

Ambrose didn't pretend to misunderstand whom I was talking about. "How do you think he's doing?"

"Can I see him?" I didn't need to ask permission, but I remembered how Ambrose had asked me not to break Oliver's heart. It was time I recognized that by walking out the door, I had let fear win— we *both* had—rather than staying and fighting for what we had built together.

"He's in the tent."

The tent we'd put up to build and stain the furniture under? "I thought that was getting torn down."

"He told them to leave it up." Ambrose wasn't snippy, but it wasn't the warmest of welcomes either.

"Oh." I wasn't sure what else to say.

"Go." Ambrose gave me a soft push, and it was all I needed to run through the mansion.

Oliver was in the tent, hammering something together. Sweat glistened on his face, his hair tied messily back as he bent over in concentration. I allowed myself a moment to soak him in, some of the ache in my chest easing at the confirmation that he was okay, that his grandfather hadn't taken the estate away from him. My heart pounded, and my stomach swirled with the storm in the air. Every word I had practiced saying on the drive fled my brain.

But then he kicked at one of the wood pieces, swearing before chucking the bent nail.

"Hey," I choked out, barely able to hear myself over the sound of my pounding heart.

Oliver's back stiffened, and he slowly turned to face me. Bearded, broad-shouldered, in a white T-shirt that clung with the sweat, forearms exposed. Here. He was *here*.

"Hi." He shoved his fists into his pockets.

"I, uh . . ." I could lie, say that the article, the potential flooding, a million other things had brought me here. Or I could tell him the truth. "I needed to see you."

"Are you okay?" He stepped forward, almost reaching for me.

"Sorry, yeah—I mean physically, yes, I'm fine." I tugged on my suspenders, relief flooding me at the familiar way his gaze traced them.

And then we stood in black cloud–covered silence, the wind rustling the leaves of the trees, crinkling with anticipation.

Lightning lit up the sky before a crack of thunder rumbled the ground, and we remembered we were outside in a tent made of metal poles.

"Run," Oliver demanded, grabbing my hand as we raced toward the library. But halfway there the downpour began, freezing rain immediately drenching us to the bone, and I yanked away because I couldn't hold it in anymore.

"No, I need to say this. I've been mad at you, so incredibly mad at you." He opened his mouth, but I shook my head, water flying as we stood in the eye of the storm. "I don't want to be your friend—I mean *just* your friend, only your friend." I was screwing this up so badly. "Being with you—you made it okay for the first time for me to be me. I wanted to stay, but then you sent me away—"

"Bell—" His voice barely carried over the pounding of the rain.

"No, don't call me that. I let my fears that this was temporary win out, and allowed your fears to push me away. Because this is hard and scary."

He turned toward the house, and I wrapped my arms around my torso, fearing he was going to leave me out here. But he spun around. "You frighten the hell out of me. I had my life and therapy, and tried to ignore the rest of the world. And then *you* had to come barging in, with your ideas that I was worth something. And I started to think that maybe there was more to my life than hiding away."

Another strike of lightning as the hairs on my arm rose.

"We can't do this here." He grabbed my hand again, not letting go this time. "I don't want you getting hurt."

We didn't have to go far to enter the library, both of us dripping water everywhere, and I was panting, still not sure what he was trying to say.

But he didn't keep me waiting. "I did make you leave—I know that—because even as I held you, touched you, breathed you in, I still didn't trust it was something I deserved. You deserve the world, and I—"

I couldn't let him believe that for another instant. "Are my absolute favorite person," I interjected. "You gave Nick, Rue, and Ambrose a home without even trying. You are a good man, the best man. I saw what you did for Nick." I couldn't stop staring at him. The smirk, the beard dripping water, those eyes that expressed everything he was feeling.

"You did?" He took a step forward, eyebrows raising. "The article?"

"Not exactly subtle, sending it to Sebastian. Are you happy, working for the company?" I was desperate for every thought he'd had while we had been apart.

"It seemed to be the perfect compromise. I'm still part of the company, like they wanted." Oliver's nose crinkled in that allergic-to-emotions way I adored.

"But the estate?"

"My sisters intervened and threatened to go to the press with it. Tied his hands." He shrugged, as if it was nothing, and my heart surged, thankful he'd gotten his family back.

"But if things are okay, why are you here?" The question rushed out.

"The attention from the paparazzi was too much. I needed to regroup." Now that we were covered from the storm, emotion swirled around us. "Because I was an idiot and let the smartest, most brilliant woman I have ever met walk away, and I've been trying to think of how I can show her how sorry I am for hurting her—for letting her believe for one moment that I didn't want a future with her."

I gulped, the water dripping from our clothes onto the wooden floors the only sound in the room. "I let my fear win out too, and I'm sorry. I never wanted to stay in one place before, but with you, I did. I *do*."

He took a step forward. "Every time I wanted to touch you, I had to stop myself." As he shoved his hands deeper into his pockets, I finally recognized the restraint he carried himself with. The same restraint that governed my life. The fear. The unwillingness to fight for what I wanted outside of my professional life, no matter how badly I desired it. "I'd be in hotels and stare at wallpaper, hear your voice as you talked about color schemes and lighting."

My entire body was grinning. "I want you to hold my hand. I've always wanted you to hold my hand. All of that was to protect me, protect my heart." I unwrapped my arms that had been hugging my middle.

"I hate the word *friend.*" He winced.

"It is abhorrent." Everything in me wobbled as he took another step. "It should never be spoken again."

I bit my lip, the hope spreading across my chest. "What word should we use, then?" I breathed out as his fingertips trailed down my arm, the small hairs there rising until he reached my palm. We twined our fingers together in a way that felt solid, permanent.

"Whatever you want, Petal. Boyfriend, partner, lover." Promise burned as he spoke each word.

It was so tempting to jump on him—to kiss him—but I had to finish. "I'm sorry I left like that."

"I'm sorry I didn't beg you to stay. I was so worried about losing you that I pushed you away." His other hand came around, completing the circle, as if we were one unit. One heart thrummed through my veins into his. "I wanted to call you, but I needed to be the man who deserved you."

"I'm never leaving again. You won't be able to get rid of me." Because, unlike the last time he held my hand, this was the start of something, not the end.

"What about the Bib?"

"I got the job."

"Of course you did." Pride was beaming from every inch of his body.

"The moment I got the offer, all I wanted to do was call you and tell you. I—" Personal growth sucked. Vulnerability was not something that would ever come easily to me.

He pulled me closer into the circle of his body, our wet clothes squelching, as he raised my arms, kissing each pulse point before wrapping them around his neck. "Tell me now."

"I missed you," I whispered against his chest, throat clogged.

"This place was empty without you. It's not my home unless you're in it." My fingers played with the hair plastered to his neck. "I love you, Petal."

I pulled back to stare at him. "I wanted to say it first." I laughed in a failed attempt to keep the tears I was fighting at bay.

His lips pressed to my forehead. "You're too difficult."

"You broke it, you bought it."

"Say it," he urged, and the desire to make this man happy overwhelmed any other.

"I love you. I love you. I love you." I pressed my face into his chest, embarrassed, but mostly giddy. Because he loved me too. Wanted me. My mess wasn't too much for him. Our edges blurred together, melding, fitting into the puzzle. We made no sense and every sense. I squeezed him tighter. "All I need is you."

"Good, because I can't make a bookcase to save my life."

I glanced around his shoulder, recognizing what the pieces of wood hammered together were. He had made multiple attempts. The shelves were uneven, the stain patchy in some parts. None could hold any books.

"You're building bookcases." I would have swooned if he hadn't been holding me up.

"I *attempted* to build *you* bookcases." He growled.

My skin felt tight. It couldn't hold all the emotions rushing through me. "That is the most romantic thing anyone has ever done for me."

The smirk was back. "More romantic than the pillows?"

"I love you." I could feel every breath he took, his fingers trembling as they wrapped around the back of my suspenders. "Tell me what it means," I begged. "My nickname."

"Petal." He drew out the pronunciation, and I savored it. "Because you bloom in the sun, and I was scared my darkness would consume you."

"You didn't," I assured him.

"No, you dragged me, kicking and screaming, into the sunshine with you, but I'm not afraid anymore." He brushed the wet hair out of my face. "You reminded me I could feel again."

I sniffled, the guilt creating an ache in my chest. "And then I left you."

"No, you didn't leave me." His voice was firm. "I needed to figure things out for myself. You couldn't force me, and I couldn't do it for you. It had to be for me."

I wiped at the drop running down his cheek. "You don't have to be strong or brave for me. You can be sad. You can miss them. I want it all—the good, the messy, the hurt."

Oliver's eyes were glassy as they met mine. "Can I kiss you now?"

"How have you not done it already?"

"I'm failing at this, Petal."

I stood up on my tiptoes, unable to mask my eagerness. "No, you are absolutely perfect because you're mine."

His lips brushed against my ear. "Forever might not be long enough."

His hand squeezed my hip, cupping my face again, tilting my chin. I refused to close my eyes, wanting to see it as he leaned in closer, his palms grasping my hips as he walked me backward.

"Why are we not kissing?" I grumbled as my back pressed against the hardwood of a bookcase, and my head tilted up. "Such a romantic."

He crowded me against the wood, leaning over me, my body arching to meet his. I was desperate for his skin to be on mine.

Finally, our lips crashed, my fingers pressing into his back, moving to his ass, begging him to give me everything.

I could kiss him forever. Feel his smile against my skin, the tickle of his beard. How had I been so blind to pretend that this was anything else other than love?

His palm touched the sliver of my stomach our position had exposed, lightly tracing, drawing a pattern as his tongue slipped into my mouth. A combination of a sigh and a moan escaped my lips as everything we had said, everything we still needed to say, would say, would do, poured out as we met in the middle.

"Say it again." His growl would have been more effective if I couldn't feel his smile, lips pressed to every piece of skin he could access.

"I love you."

"Again." He kissed my cheek, my ear, making a path down my neck, licking up every trace of water, setting his own stream of lightning into my veins.

"Baby." I shivered at the feel of his palm, the way it felt like his heart was crashing into mine.

I shrieked as he picked me up by my thighs, which I instantly wrapped around his hips.

"I'm going to build you all the bookcases you want."

"I want it all."

"You're going to have it." The confident way he growled drove down to my toes before settling in my center.

"Big words."

"As long as I get to be the guy next to you, holding your hand." That was all he had ever asked of me, to hold my hand, be there with me, and it was all I wanted now. No matter where life was going to take us.

"Heck of a consolation prize." I was trying to yank off his shirt, but it was plastered to his skin.

"You could never be a consolation prize."

The brush of our lips was gentle as I pulled him closer, chest heaving, my breasts heavy, nipples pressed against his chest.

"Forever, Petal."

"I love you." My words were muffled as he pulled my shirt off my body, somehow still balancing me against the bookcase.

With a laugh that was a little bit his and a lot mine, the wind howling, storm erupting outside, it was perfect.

Perfect because it was us.

EPILOGUE

Three Months Later

"You're welcome!" I yelled across the field, offering another wave.

The sunshine was not doing much to keep away the chill from the winter day. We spent most weekends here at the estate, and during the week we'd stay at my apartment—him at work with his family, his sisters mostly, and me at the Bib, Oliver bringing me lunch half the time to ensure I didn't forget to eat.

"Where is he?" I asked the moment I stepped back into the mansion.

"Bedroom," Bl8z3 responded.

I sprinted up the stairs, heading into the west wing, drawn in by the calming baritone of his voice.

"Gotta go, guys." Oliver waved at his phone before slumping in his chair. "I forgot how exhausting those two are."

"How was FaceTiming your sisters?" My lips brushed his as he chased after our too-brief kiss.

"Fine."

I knew it was more than fine. He anticipated their weekly catch-ups more than he would ever admit. "How's Grace?"

She was trying hard to get their grandfather to name her as his successor since Oliver had stepped aside, but she hadn't gotten very far with it yet.

"Still engaged to that idiot."

"Probably want to call Ti—*Doug* something else if he's going to be your brother-in-law." I moved to the bed, straightening everything before reaching for the television remote.

"I will when you stop thinking his name is Tim/Jim."

I spun around. "He looks like a Tim/Jim." He was right; it didn't seem like Grace's fiancé was going anywhere, even though she could do better.

Oliver snorted, grabbing the bowl of candy from me and setting it down on the comforter.

I plopped on the mattress, sliding my feet under the weighted blanket we kept at the foot of the bed. "You sure you still want to do this?"

He gave a stiff nod. "Can't have you explaining to everyone that a snap involves both teams in a snapping competition."

"Okay, but that would make it even more interesting."

He grunted as he slid next to me, offering me a Twizzler. "What did they think?" Oliver asked, clearly wanting a distraction. His body screamed "walking to the executioner."

"They loved it."

"Of course they did."

The moment I returned to the Killington Estate, I had a few things left to complete.

With Nick's help, we planned a new stable, demolishing the old. Which needed to be christened. Sex in every room was a real endeavor when it involved an estate. One Oliver and I were more than happy to fulfill.

And today I had been giddy with revealing my latest project. Rue, Nick, and Ambrose had all lived in a small, aged cabin at the edge of the property, rather than in the mansion, at their own choosing. But not anymore.

It was the most modern build I had ever worked on, but they were the clients this time. Still on the edge of the property, Rue had another magnificent kitchen, Ambrose the closet and sewing machine he had requested. And Nick's massive room took up the third floor, giving her privacy and plenty of space to figure out Bl8z3's update.

"Ambrose fought back tears as he walked through." I squeezed Oliver's hand, a grin taking over my face at the memory, pleased to have won over the butler.

He grunted. Mr. Emotionally Constipated had declined to be there for the actual reveal, despite having paid for the build with the funds from the trust he now had access to. I had refused a commission because it was also a thank-you for safeguarding Oliver from being alone during his self-imposed exile.

I watched as he rubbed the spot where his scar lay underneath his sweatpants.

"We could watch something else. I hear they have these things on all the time."

He twisted my body, placing my feet in his lap. "No, I want to. I want to do this with you."

I relaxed into him as I flipped on the TV. I had zero interest in what teams were playing. But this was the first time that Oliver had watched more than a random highlight of football since his accident.

"Okay, but I had a rumor that if the team is losing by a certain amount, the cheerleading team takes over." I bit my lip, hard.

He groaned as some of the tension in his body eased. His fingers slid up my legs while he patiently explained the rules to me again.

The game started as we passed the bowl of candy back and forth. He was mostly feeding me, which I appreciated. Candy tasted better from his fingers.

I swirled my tongue around his thumb to get the last bit of chocolate.

"Petal," he growled.

"It's a commercial. Wait, do these matter for the points too?"

"How do you come up with this stuff?" He shook his head before kissing the tip of my nose.

"I'm brilliant."

"That you are." He rolled us so he was hovering over me, running his fingers down my ribs, my hip, until he pulled my leg to wrap around him, causing my thighs to spread further.

"How do you feel?"

"That watching football is better with you. Everything is better with you."

I pressed against his left thigh, reminding myself for the millionth time he was still here. "I am pretty great."

He pressed a trail of kisses across my shoulders, inducing a shudder. "I might go for a blitz."

Why was it so hot when he spoke football terms to me? "I don't know. This might be a fumble." My breath was rushing out as my heart raced at the familiar but exciting feeling of having his hands on me.

I patted him to shift over. The game was back on, and I refused to let him distract either of us, my attention half on the game and half on him.

He answered all my questions, some of them real, some just because I liked to hear him laugh. I enjoyed his smile as he kissed my cheek.

"What are you thinking?" His breath warm against my ear.

"Well, you still need to watch *The Fast and the Furious* movies. I may offer you an incentive." Since our reunion, when we were alone together, we had spent little of it watching screens. We had spent part of Christmas with my dad, who had insisted on matching pajamas, a request that Oliver had humored.

"You haven't seemed to complain about how we've been spending our nights." But he sat up, my legs thrown back over his thigh, my body tilting more into the pillows with his movements. Seeming to debate something as he glanced down at me. "Do you still like my beard?"

My fingers moved lightly across his jaw. "I love your beard. Why, are you thinking of getting rid of it?"

He nipped at my finger. "Do you still love me?"

My stomach sank as I searched his eyes. "Babe, what's wrong?"

"I promise everything is perfect, Petal." His fingers traced patterns on my stomach before drawing a circle around my nipple. No one had explained to me the wonderful freedom of loving someone, the infinite ways you could touch them, knowing they were just as eager for it. "Do you still love me?"

"Most days." I grinned wildly at him as he brushed against my nipple before snapping my suspender.

His eyes were soft, hand trembling, everything about him tender. "You still want forever with me?"

"Always." I was breathless. "You have it. You had it when I walked into this estate. You could have trapped me here." I had meant it when I had promised him I wasn't leaving.

"Tempting, but I'm talking about a certain type of forever. One that involves a question."

Oh. "You don't have to ask me a question to get forever with me." I reached for his shaking hand.

"It's too traditional, but I want it, can picture it. You in a white dress, me . . ."

"Not smiling." I traced his lips.

"I'll be smiling at the best part—when it's over, and I'm your husband."

I was going to melt into this bed. "So, what's your question?"

"If I asked one day soon, would you?" He stared at our clasped hands.

"Well, you'd have to speak to my father. And probably Sebastian." Both of whom might love Oliver at this point more than they loved me.

"And we both know they'll ask me what you want."

"Of course." Those cornballs. Then Finn would go off and start planning our wedding without us.

"So, what do *you* want?"

"You." Loving him had become as integral as breathing for me. "You, always."

"And marriage? Babies?"

"Not too many babies. Bl8z3 is not a nanny."

Oliver lowered to his forearms, surrounding all of me. "I thought my life was nothing but misery until I met you."

"That's because you didn't watch TV."

It was the biggest smile yet. Brushed against my lips, covering my face. "I lived in too much silence. I needed you filling up every available space with your words, your laughter."

I let out a sigh, feet sliding on the covers. "What do *you* want?"

His fingers pushed up my top, exposing my stomach to his hungry gaze, eyes fixated on the small section of my bra he revealed. "I want this—you forever."

"I like you best."

"And I think I should get you naked."

"The game's not over." My protest was halfhearted as I let him pull my shirt off, my suspenders slipping off my shoulders.

"Have to explain more football terms to you. I plan on going long."

My brain was mush. "Better get started on that then."

We had all the time in the world to watch movies and football games, read every book in the bookcases he had built me. He had restored every part of me, making me shiny and new.

My home was built inside his heart.

Forever.

ACKNOWLEDGMENTS

It is unbelievable for me to be typing the acknowledgments to my first published book. I did not get here alone, and there's no music to play me off.

I'm incredibly lucky to have such a cheerleader in Cole Lanahan, who never doubted that this book would sell (even when I did). Jess Verdi, from that first call where we fangirled over BatB, I knew this book was in the right hands. Your edits only made this book stronger, and I'm so thankful for you and the team at Alcove, including Rebecca Nelson, Thai Fantauzzi Perez, Dulce Botello, Stephanie Manova, and Mikaela Bender, for making my dream come true. To Mallory Heyer for the incredible cover, and to Jill Pellarin for "dragging" me through copy edits.

My sister was the first person I confessed this dream to, and I wouldn't be here if it weren't for her telling me to *finish the darn book already.* I'm incredibly thankful to have my family cheering me on. To my parents, siblings, and siblings-in-law—I don't have words for how much your support has meant, so I won't try to come up with them, but love you. And a big shout-out to my nephews and niece, who I hope will always dream big—and never read this or any of my books because I will never make enough money to pay for that therapy.

I am incredibly lucky to have met so many friends through writing. If you've ever read my words and encouraged me, just thank you. Amanda Wilson, my first writing friend, you are an absolute gem; our wine nights are sacred to me. To my #bteam: Christina Arellano (Blue—who enthusiastically demanded to read every iteration of this book), Kate Robb (who named Bl8z3), Aurora Palit (my fellow 2024 debut), Jessica Joyce, and Rebecca Osberg—with every gif and word of encouragement you have kept me going, and I'm so thankful to have you in my life.

Chloe Liese, you have been an amazing mentor and friend to me with every Zoom session as you help me figure out what I'm trying to say with my mess of words while I fangirl. I appreciate you so much.

Elizabeth Everett, you held my hand through so much of this, making me laugh with your blunt honesty. I cannot wait until we can exchange signed copies of our books.

Alicia Thompson, Elle, Sarah Brenton, Dani Frank, Ambriel McIntyre, Naina Kumar, Jannat Noor, Ruby Barrett, Beck Erixson, and Ali Hazelwood—I am incredibly humbled to be able to call you friends, for your insights and just for everything. My fellow 2022 KissPitches—I could not have asked for a more amazing group of friends, and I can't wait to add each and every single one of your books to my shelves. Nick Resendes—thanks for my incredible author photo.

To the romance books that come before and after me, romance has brought me so much joy my entire life, especially the books featuring fat/curvy main characters. It means so much to be able to

Acknowledgments

have a book on the shelves with so many greats. There are too many to mention, but to every author, every book, every main character (and side character) that has helped me feel seen, thank you.

A massive shoutout to Bookstagram. All my friends, too many to list, everyone who cheered me on (if you think I'm talking about you, yes, I am)—you are incredible.

His Highness King Louis Reginald III (yes, I'm thanking my cat), you are of course sleeping while I type this, but thanks for always listening (?) as I talk out a plot issue and never complaining (much), and for all of the cuddles when I need them.

Taylor Swift's music is the soundtrack to my life and my writing playlist, and has gotten me through some of the most difficult periods of my life. While she'll never read this, I have to thank her because I don't think I could have written *Barely Even Friends* without her (or the *Reputation* album).

And to save the very best for last—thank *you*, dear reader, for taking a chance on my debut. I wouldn't be here without you.